THE WAKEFIELD DYNASTY

2

GILBERT MORRIS

The
WINDS
of
GOD

TYNDALE HOUSE PUBLISHERS, INC.
Wheaton, Illinois

Textile design courtesy of Kravet Fabrics, © Weave Corporation

Cover illustration copyright © 1994 by Morgan Weistling

Scripture quotations are taken from The New King James Version. Copyright © 1979, 1980, 1982, Thomas Nelson Inc., Publishers.

Library of Congress Cataloging-in-Publication Data

Morris, Gilbert.
      The winds of God / Gilbert Morris.
          p.   cm. — (The Wakefield dynasty ; 2)
      ISBN 0-8423-7953-3
        1. Great Britain—History—Elizabeth, 1558-1603—Fiction.
2. Great Britain—History—Mary I, 1553-1558—Fiction.
3. Protestants—England—History—16th century—Fiction.   4. Family—England—Fiction.
5. Armada. 1588—Fiction.   I. Title. II. Series: Morris, Gilbert. Wakefield dynasty ; 2.
PS3563.08742W54   1994
813′.54—dc20   94-28712

Printed in the United States of America

99
6   5

To Jill Van der Lee, a niece to be proud of!

CONTENTS

PART FOUR: ARMADA!—1586–1588

GENEALOGY OF THE WAKEFIELD DYNASTY

Margred Morgan
(1492–1522) ——————┐
Sir Robert Wakefield ├— Myles
(1470–) │ (1507–)
married 1506 │ married 1532 ——
Jane Harwich │ Hannah Kemp
(1475–) │ (1508)

┌William
│(1533–)
│married 1555 ——┐
— Blanche Holly ├ Robin
│(1532–) │ (1558–)
├Thomas
│(1543–)
└Alice
(1548–)

Bloody

1 5 5 3   **Part** / **ONE**   1 5 5 8

Mary

DARK CLOUDS

Y ou are not a witch, I trust, Mistress Holly?"
Miss Blanche Holly blinked with astonishment, her fine
eyes growing stormy as she shot an instant retort at her
dancing partner. "A witch, Mr. Wakefield? How *dare* you suggest
such a thing!"

The tall young woman whose hands were locked in those of
William Wakefield tried to free herself, but could not. "Let me
go!" she whispered furiously, looking around to see if they were
being watched. She made an appealing picture, her dark eyes
flashing and her full lips pressing together. When she saw that they
were being observed by their host and two of his sons, she at once
forced herself to smile and continue with the dance.

William Wakefield was no taller than this young woman, so he
could look directly into her eyes. "I only ask such a question,
Mistress Holly, because I cannot otherwise explain my behavior."
Wakefield was a slender young man of twenty, and his black suit
served as a perfect foil for his red hair. He had blue-gray eyes, a
clean-cut jaw, and was in all a handsome young fellow.

"I can't guess at your meaning, sir!"

"Why, I simply mean," young Wakefield said, a smile lurking
on his lips, "that no man would throw himself at a woman on first
meeting her unless he were either demented . . . or bewitched."

The young woman's stern lips lost some of their tension, curving upward imperceptibly at the corners. She *had* noticed that since she had met Mr. William Wakefield less than two hours ago, he'd not allowed her to get out of his sight! Truthfully, she'd rather enjoyed his obvious interest, but she couldn't let him know that. He was impudent enough as it was!

She lifted her chin slightly and said as sternly as she could manage, "Then, sir, I suggest that you betake yourself to Bedlam, for since I am no witch, you must by your own admission be quite mad."

"Aye, Mistress Holly, I do fear it. The moon is full, and 'tis well known that young men often turn lunatic with its beams." He drew her closer as they moved in the dance, squeezing her hand. When she tried to hold back, he shook his head. "No, don't pull away. If I am indeed driven to lunacy by the moon, who knows what terrible thing I might do if you resist me."

Blanche Holly was amused by Wakefield's antics. He was, she understood, the son of Sir Myles Wakefield, one of the most respected peers in England. *He's rich, handsome—and eligible,* she thought suddenly. *What more could a young woman want in a suitor?*

Seeing the fair object of his pursuit hesitate, Will Wakefield pressed his advantage. Holding Blanche even more firmly, he said, "I think this lunacy is getting more severe. I fear the only thing that will cure me is a carriage ride." Laughter lurked in his direct blue eyes, and he nodded as if assuring himself. "Yes, I think that will restore my sanity. The fine old silver moon, and a beautiful lady beside—"

"I fear you are being annoyed, Mistress Holly!"

Wakefield turned quickly to find a tall man of some twenty-five years regarding him with a pair of cold gray eyes. Before the young woman could speak, Wakefield said curtly, "Sir, we're doing very well without your help. Be on your way." Then he turned his back contemptuously on the intruder, saying, "Now, Mistress—"

But he never finished, for he was cut off abruptly when a strong hand grasped his shoulder and shoved him rudely to one side. Catching his balance, Wakefield stared into the insolent eyes of his attacker.

The man merely smiled at him with a nonchalant air and said, "I think it might be best if you left my house. You do not fit well in the company of gentlemen."

"Please—!" Blanche spoke quickly, glancing about at the couples who were beginning to note what was happening. "Let us not have a scene!"

Wakefield stared at the tall young man facing him as anger threaded its way along his nerves. But he, too, was aware that many in the room were now watching them intently, and he forced his tone to be level and calm. "Your house, sir? I understood this to be the home of the duke of Northumberland."

"And I am his eldest son, as Mistress Blanche can tell you." A sneer twisted the man's lips. "I need not ask your name, for you will not be staying."

"Jack Dudley, this *is* unseemly!" Blanche spoke intently. She lifted her head high, and a flush of embarrassment colored her fair cheeks. "I assure you Mr. Wakefield was *not* being offensive."

Dudley's eyebrows raised slightly, as though he doubted her sincerity. "Your effort at kindness is appreciated, Mistress Holly. However, he does offend me." He turned back to Will, his expression condescending. "Who invited you to this company, may I ask?" Running his eyes over Wakefield's plain black suit, he asked, "And what are you, fellow? Some kind of parson?"

Before Will could respond, a deep voice came from behind him. "Jack, what's the trouble here?" He looked and saw that a slight man of not more than average height had moved across the floor, halting not three feet away from them. He had a pair of fine eyes, brown and glossy—but rather blank, like chestnuts. "I trust you're not insulting our guest?"

Taken aback at the man's words, Jack sputtered in response. "Why—!"

The slender man cut him off with a wave of his hand and directed his gaze at Will. "Mr. Wakefield, I believe?"

"Yes, I'm William Wakefield." At once Will realized this man was his host, Duke John of Northumberland, who was perhaps the second most powerful man in England. He knew some even went so far as to say the duke was the *most* powerful, for he had more influence with the young King Edward than any other man.

The duke smiled. "I thought so. I am so glad your father accepted my invitation to bring you to our home tonight." He cast his son a withering glance, saying curtly, "I trust that answers your concerns, Jack. Now, you have my leave to retire."

Jack Dudley was not accustomed to rebuffs; few would dare such a thing with the eldest son of the duke of Northumberland. Anger swept over him and his face reddened, but he did not answer. He did, however, cast a look of hatred at Will before wheeling and stalking across the floor, his back stiff and his head held high.

"You must excuse my son," Northumberland said with a smile. "He's insanely jealous of any man that Mistress Blanche looks on with favor." He cast a smile at Blanche, who colored prettily. "I pray you will not hold Jack's actions against him, my dear."

"Indeed, no, my lord," she conceded.

"Good, good. Nor, I trust, will you, Mr. Wakefield. We must forgive passion when it is attached to such a lovely object, must we not?"

Will met Blanche's eyes and smiled. "Yes sir, of course."

"Well now, and is your father here?"

"No sir, but he asked me to meet him here, so I'm sure he'll arrive presently."

"Ah, that's splendid! When he gets here, please ask him to come to me—and be so kind as to accompany him, if I may ask it. Now then, you may continue to pay your attentions to this lady."

A moment of silence held the pair as they watched the duke walk away, then Blanche said in a subdued tone, "We had better go on with our dance, sir."

"Yes," Will said, nodding. "We've furnished quite enough entertainment for the other guests." They moved in the patterns of the dance, each a little shaken by the encounter. Will tried to enjoy himself and concentrate on his graceful partner, but the pleasure of the evening had been blunted by the scene with the duke's son. Blanche remained silent, and finally Will asked stiffly, "The duke's son is your admirer, I take it?"

She gave him a level glance. "He 'admires' a great many young ladies, sir."

The answer seemed sharp, and Will's response was quick. "I apologize for my behavior, Mistress." His smooth forehead suddenly wrinkled, and he shook his head with a slight bewilderment. "I . . . do not usually make such a fool of myself over a lady."

"Don't trouble yourself, Mr. Wakefield. Jack is spoiled to the bone. He offends everyone sooner or later."

"I'm glad to hear that. But still, I hasten to assure you that this is the first time in my life I've ever attempted to monopolize a young woman."

"You *are* a parson then—too holy for such frivolous creatures as young women?" Her eyes were filled with humor, and he saw that she had put the unpleasant incident out of her mind. She had been, he realized, calmer than he himself, and he both admired and envied her composure. "I plead guilty to one charge, and innocent to another."

"Let me guess! You are not a parson, but you do find young ladies frivolous."

"Totally incorrect," he said, sweeping her around in a graceful turn to the music. "I *am* a parson—of sorts, anyway—and I do not find young ladies in the least frivolous."

"You dance too well to be a parson." Blanche smiled at him. "I do not think a dancing foot and a praying knee can grow on the same leg."

He laughed, delighted by the mirth in her voice and eyes. "My teachers at Cambridge would say amen to that! But I tell you true, my lady, I am, indeed, a parson." He saw her incredulous look and went on to entertain her by relating several of his escapades at Cambridge, that noble seat of learning, that almost got him expelled.

Blanche listened with amusement. Wakefield was a good storyteller and at least capable of some sort of humility, for he always made himself the butt of his stories.

They were moving around a massive room, the walls of which were covered with vivid paintings depicting the kings and rulers of Christendom, all dressed in appropriate costumes and set in the proper historical and geographical surroundings. Well-padded furniture covered with rich cloth lined the walls. Tables and cabinets of rare woods, elaborately worked and carved and decorated, glowed under the many lamps and candles that illuminated the room. Several of the largest tables were piled high with food, and rich silver and gold plating seemed to glow with warmth.

Will took in their surroundings with an appreciative glance. "A gorgeous room, isn't it? Enough gold and silver to build another Cambridge." Looking toward the duke he added, "But the duke's tastes do not run in that direction, do they?"

"How mean you, Mr. Wakefield?"

"The common talk is that he spends fortunes on his own private army."

"I've seen some of his troops," Blanche said, nodding. "They are better trained than the king's own, or so I'm told." She glanced around the room and shook her head. "Truly, the duke has come a long way from his beginnings. Do you know his history?"

"Only a little." Actually Will knew much more than this, but he wanted to get Blanche off the dance floor. "Why don't we look at the house while we talk? My parson's gait isn't right for the dance."

"You dance very well, for a parson." She dimpled at him, then inclined her head slightly, and the two of them moved from the floor. As they wandered through the house, Wakefield was amazed that the opulence of the ballroom seemed to be reflected in every room. There were five inner courtyards with fountains playing water dances. Passing one of these, Will and Blanche walked through a labyrinth of rooms and suites and formal chambers, noting the rich tapestries, velvet curtains, and the hanging pictures and portraits. Will paused once to touch a curtain gently. "This is delicate enough to serve for a veil for a queen!"

"Yes, it is." He looked at Blanche with interest, for she seemed unimpressed. Then he reminded her to speak of the rise of John Dudley, and she did so as they walked. "He came from poor beginnings," she said, "so that he's the first Englishman to become a duke who hasn't a drop of royal blood. . . ." She spoke of how Dudley had caught the king's eye because of his horsemanship and how he had won command in the field by his brilliant qualities as a soldier. "Then, when Henry VIII died, he out-maneuvered the uncles of the boy-king, Edward, to become the king's adviser."

"Does he truly have as much influence with the young king as everyone says?"

"Yes, it would seem so. And he made himself duke of Northumberland."

They had come to stand beside a tall cabinet with drawers open for the viewing of coins and jewels and curiosities made of gold and silver and decorated by every kind and form of jewel. Looking at the priceless treasures, Will suddenly said, "They glitter, but there's no warmth in them, is there? Look at those diamonds; they're like ice!"

Blanche glanced at him as though his remark intrigued her. "Yes, they are cold," she replied with a nod. "But men will kill for them."

"And women, too," he returned, but he was thinking how her fine dark eyes and smooth cheeks had more beauty than all the jewels that glinted in their cases. He was about to say so, but something held his tongue. He could not explain why he felt this way, but he was almost certain that here was a young woman who was not moved by such speeches. He studied her face for a moment. "You don't care much for compliments, do you, Mistress?"

"Too many of them are empty," she answered quietly, though he thought there was in her eyes a look of surprise that he'd discovered that much about her so quickly. "I care not a pin for these love games that are so popular today. They are clever enough, I suppose, but beneath all the flowery phrases, they reek of lust."

"Why—!"

"Do I shock you, Mister Wakefield?"

He nodded slowly. "In truth, you do. I must admit I'm always a little shocked by honesty. It's a rare jewel in this world of ours." He waved toward the sparkling rubies and emeralds. "Much more rare, I dare say, than those trinkets." He studied her more carefully. *I've been so besotted with admiration for her beauty that I've failed to see the noble woman beneath.* Aloud he said, "I will pay you a compliment, though, despite the fact that you don't like such things. You are, Mistress, a young woman of uncommon sense and discernment."

A smile bloomed on her face, and he felt slightly dazzled by its radiance as she responded, "Thank you, Mr. Wakefield. *That's* the sort of compliment I do appreciate."

They moved away from the cabinet and returned to the large room where the dancers were moving across the floor. Glancing around, Will noted a newcomer to the gathering. "There's my father. I want him to meet you." The two made their way through the crowd until Will touched an older man on the arm and said, "Sir, this is Mistress Blanche Holly. Mistress, my father, Sir Myles Wakefield."

The gentleman turned to Blanche, and she found herself gazing into a pair of piercing blue-gray eyes. Sir Myles smiled gallantly. "I'm happy to meet you, Mistress Holly."

As Blanche murmured a brief response, she noted that the father was even more handsome than the son. Sir Myles Wakefield was over six feet tall and, for all his forty-six years, was still trim and athletic. He had auburn hair with a widow's peak and bold eyes set in a square face. He had a short nose, long mobile lips—and a pugnacious chin. *He looks like a very kind sort of man,* the young woman thought, then recalled herself and said aloud, "Oh! I had almost forgotten. The duke wishes to see you, Sir Myles. And Will."

"Yes, that's so, Father."

"Well, come along, Will," Myles answered. "It's never wise to keep a duke waiting. Especially this one."

Will nodded then turned reluctantly to Blanche. "Only the duke could take me from your side, Mistress Holly. But I will be sure to see you again."

Myles watched with surprise as his son gently took the young woman's hand, raised it to his lips, and kissed it. He noted with interest the slight pink that tinged her cheeks at this action, and when she turned and left, he raised one eyebrow in inquiry. "So, Will, have your lessons at Cambridge included classes in charming females?" Will's face flamed, and Myles laughed and slapped him on the shoulder. "Never mind, boy! She seems to be a nice young woman."

"I like her a great deal, sir." Will saw his father's eyebrow go up a fraction of an inch, but lifted his chin stubbornly. "I mean to see more of her."

"Oh?" Myles considered his eldest son more carefully, for this was the first sign he had seen that the young man had any interest in pursuing young women. Apparently he had finally found one that he wanted to impress. "Well, by all means, see more of her if that's what you want. After, of course, we find our host and see what he requires of us."

As the two walked across the room searching for the duke, Will asked, "Why did the duke invite us here, Father? I wasn't aware you knew him."

"I don't, really." Myles shrugged. He paused and murmured to one of the servants, who led them out of the hall. As they followed the man, Myles continued, speaking in low tones so that the man could not hear. "I've met the duke twice, I think. But up until now I've been beneath his attention."

"What could he want with you?"

They reached a massive door just as Will asked the question. The servant knocked, waited with his ear cocked, then opened the door and turned to them. "You may go in, sir."

Myles and Will passed through the entryway and found themselves in a room perhaps twenty feet square. Two of the walls were lined with books and charts. The duke had been sitting at a massive desk but rose at once and came to put out his hand. "Ah, Sir Myles—good to see you! I've already met your son." Smiling at Will, he shook his head sadly. "A firebrand—almost came to blows with my boy Jack over a pretty woman."

Myles cast an interested glance at his son. "Oh? I didn't hear about that."

The duke laughed and waved his white hand in the air. "Ah, now, we fathers mustn't be too hard on the young men. We probably did much the same when we were twenty—at least *I* did!" He moved to a table where bottles of liquor caught the reflections of the heavy candelabra overhead. The duke talked to them over his shoulder as he began pouring drinks. "Sit down and we'll have a quiet drink. Get to know one another."

For the next half hour the two Wakefields were dazzled with the wit and intelligence of the duke of Northumberland. He had been in the heart of the High Councils of England for a long time and tossed the great names around as if they had been only mere mortals.

Will sat there almost stunned at the man's quickness of mind. *No wonder he's risen so high! I didn't realize a man could know so much!*

Myles listened carefully, nursing his drink along in small sips. He had heard the duke speak before, though not in such intimate circumstances. He had known the man to be brilliant, but that only made sense. After all, one didn't rise to a position of such authority by being stupid. But that only made Myles more certain that the duke had wanted to see them for a purpose.

Finally the duke got around to that very thing. "I'm sorry to inform you that the king is ill—very ill, indeed!"

Myles shook his head sadly. "He was never very strong, was he, sir?"

"No, not even as an infant." Dudley swirled the amber liquid in his glass slowly, staring at it as if it held some great truth. His face was delicate, almost effeminate, but there was strength evident in the set of his firm lips and the deep gaze that he now put on the pair before him. "King Edward has never had his father's physical strength. You know what Henry VIII was like—a bull of a man!"

"Elizabeth is the only one of his children to whom he passed that vitality." Wakefield spoke quietly, his eyes searching the duke's face—and he thought he detected a break in the man's composure.

"Would to God that Edward had received it, not that offspring of a witch!"

Will was shocked to hear Elizabeth so named. He had heard it said that Anne Boleyn, Princess Elizabeth's mother, was a witch—but that did not prepare him for the hatred that flared out of the duke. Young Wakefield glanced at his father, noting that he also had caught the emotion that had practically exploded from the duke at the mention of Elizabeth.

With a deep breath, the duke regained his calm demeanor. "Ah, well, can't be helped." He shrugged, then leaned back in his chair and began to speak of the affairs of England, ticking off the problems that beset the nation. After ten minutes he sounded tired.

"Well, the future is obscure," he said, then he directed his strange eyes to Myles, all but ignoring Will. "The most critical time in the history of England may be only hours away, Sir Myles," he said softly. "Between the time one monarch dies and another is crowned, there is danger for the state. Danger," he almost whispered, "for all of us."

"'Tis true, we live in troubled times, my lord," Myles Wakefield agreed. Then he met the duke's intense gaze and added, "God will be with us if we will be faithful to his truth."

The duke of Northumberland seemed to be transfixed by the statement. "'God will be with us,'" he repeated, "'if we will be faithful to his truth.'" His lips scarcely moved as he spoke, and then in a sibilant whisper he asked, "But what *is* truth? That's the question Pilate posed to Jesus Christ, isn't it?" He lifted his head, and there was a cruelty in his expression as he continued. "But Pilate received no answer, did he? Not even from the Christ. Indeed, 'twould seem truth is a hard fish to catch, don't you agree, Sir Myles?"

"Any virtue is hard to catch, my lord, but if we make our nets fine enough, we will succeed."

"Ah, very good! Very good indeed!" The duke rose, and the other two men, sensing they were dismissed, rose with him. "You are known to be a practical man—and an honorable one," he said suddenly to Myles. "In the days to come, I will have need of such men." He paused, as though weighing his words. "Tell me, sir, can I count on you?"

Myles felt the power emanating from the man and knew there was more to the question than was evident. Undaunted, he put his shoulders back and again met the duke's gaze. "I trust that the Wakefields will always stand ready to fight for the truth."

"Ah! That's what I want to hear!" The duke put his hand out, gave Myles a hearty grip, then turned to Will. "Come here often, young man. Make friends with my sons—oh, Jack can be a terrible bore, I know, but he's a good fellow. This country of ours will need young fellows like Jack, and like you."

So saying, he led them out of the room and closed the door firmly behind them. Will grabbed his father's arm and pulled him around to face him. "What was *that* all about?" he demanded. "He didn't say what he wanted at all."

Myles shook his head. "He said it, Will."

"Well, *I* didn't hear it!"

The elder Wakefield's face was suddenly tense. "He said that we're either going to have to be with him or against him."

"In what?" Will shook his head in bewilderment. "What's going to happen?"

"King Edward is going to die," Myles said slowly. "And when he does, there's going to be a battle."

"As to who will rule England?"

"Yes, Will. As to who will rule England."

Will thought hard. "Who will the duke be for, sir? Surely

15

Elizabeth! He'd never be for Mary. He hates Catholics, I've heard."

"Yes, he does, and it seems a simple assumption that the duke will be behind Elizabeth, but—" Myles broke off and shook his head. "Let's get away from this place, Will. I don't believe I like it."

As they left, Will sought for a glimpse of Blanche, but didn't see her. When they were in the carriage, he said dejectedly, "I don't even know where to find her!"

"Who?"

"Why, Blanche Holly, of course!" He glanced at his father with surprise, then said, "You know, I've always been one of the first to mock the poor fools who fell in love with some woman at first sight." He laughed sheepishly. "And now I've done it myself!"

Myles relaxed and leaned his head back. He closed his eyes and seemed to drift off to sleep—but after a few moments he murmured, "Son, don't be thinking of marriage."

"Why not? You and mother are always after me to look over some nice eligible girl and to give you grandsons."

This had been a long-standing joke, but there was no humor in Myles Wakefield now. Looking at Will steadily, he said, "There's a time for marrying and a time to refrain from marrying. In this England of ours, a man will need all the strength he has to survive the coming days. Wait for a time, Will. Then you can marry."

The carriage rumbled on, and Will sat silently, going over the events of the evening. He thought of the silky sheen of Blanche Holly's cheeks and the luster of her dark eyes. She drew him as no woman ever had, and he knew he'd have to see her again. Then he glanced at his father, who seemed suddenly old and almost drained of strength.

He's just tired. He'll be all right tomorrow. Will was so accustomed to his father's steady strength that he could not imagine a world without it. But as the carriage bounced over the cobblestones, he had a sudden dark thought—one that dealt with the passing of time and the loss of all things. Being young, he shook it off easily, then leaned back to think again of how wonderfully Blanche's smooth, round neck set off the simple pearl necklace she'd worn.

Two

A TIMELY WARNING

The largest of the goldfish rose majestically through the green water. He was almost eighteen inches long and, as the afternoon sun touched his tattered fins, he seemed to exude an incandescent glow. Suspended lazily near the surface, he made O's with his mouth, seeming to meditate on the nature of his watery world. The lesser denizens of the cosmos formed by the large pool clustered on the bottom, vague shadowy forms that floated, ghostlike, in the murky depths.

"I wish I had no more worries than you!"

The speaker was a young woman of twenty who sat on the rocks that made up the fishpond. The same sun that brought color to the carp touched her hair, transforming it into a sparkling red crown, fine as blown silk. Her face was thin and pointed, almost like that of a fox. Her eyes were pale blue-green, and those who knew her well said that when they were blue, all was well—but beware of Princess Elizabeth when her eyes glowed with a pale green fire!

The sound of her own voice seemed to startle the young woman, for she cast a sudden glance at the large iron doors set in the wall that surrounded the house and grounds. For one moment she remained absolutely still, her only motion the tossing of her fine red hair. There was a deerlike caution in her attitude, much like a doe who pauses to listen hard for the sound of an enemy creeping closer to her hiding place.

They might come today—and I have no place to hide; not here . . . not even at the king's palace . . . nowhere in all of England!

Her high forehead, smooth as alabaster, was disturbed by three fine wrinkles, but she blinked and, with characteristic swiftness of motion, bent and picked up a stick. Grasping it, she suddenly plunged it into the pond, laughing when the sudden prod startled the carp into a frantic somersault. "Got you that time!" she cried. "Let that be a lesson to you!"

Leaning over, she peered into the depths of the pond, straining to see the fish, but he cowered behind some of the larger stones at the bottom. Something about his efforts to hide drove her laughter away. Tossing the stick to the side with an angry gesture, she spoke to the fish again, "Why are you hiding, you coward? You're the biggest fish in the whole pond! For shame! If *I* were the biggest fish in *my* world, I wouldn't be such a coward!"

Elizabeth was a creature of sudden mood changes, and her laughter exploded abruptly—a hearty sound that reminded many of her father, King Henry VIII. Henry had passed his powerful voice to his daughter Mary, his laugh and stamina to Elizabeth, and almost nothing to his son, Edward. None of the three had been born with their father's big strong body. Elizabeth had received the slender but curved figure of her mother, Anne Boleyn—the same figure that had driven Henry to divorce his wife Catherine so that he could have her.

For some five minutes Elizabeth sat staring down into the depths of the pond, her mind overflowing with thoughts, her body still. The huge carp forgot his fear, emerged from the rocks, and floated again to the top of the water. His pop eyes considered the form of the young woman, but since she didn't move, he felt no fishy fear. He allowed the movement of the water to ripple his tattered fins—signs of old age, Elizabeth supposed.

Softly she whispered, "Father Fish, you are very old, are you not?" It was a habit she had, choosing something to talk to—a horse, a dog, perhaps. Anything that would not use her words against her. Growing up under the shadow of danger had taught her to hold her tongue. By nature a voluble young woman, she longed to speak whenever she felt the inclination, but in certain circumstances to do so could mean death. And so she spent much time alone, walking or riding, sharing thoughts that she could not speak to any human being with the horse and the dogs that followed.

She studied the fish thoughtfully. "When my mother was alive and beautiful, you were doing just what you're doing now—floating and eating bread crumbs." She broke off a morsel from the chunk of hard bread she'd brought out to feed the fish, tossed it into the water, and watched as the circles spread over the surface, nodding as the fish moved to take it. "So safe in your world! The day my mother died at the block—that was like any other day to you, wasn't it?"

She had long ago wheedled the details of Anne Boleyn's death from those who had witnessed it. Knowing only that her mother had died, but not knowing how or why, had been a source of nightmares. She had felt sure that knowing the details would drive the horror out of it, for then her imagination could not concoct scenes and build on their vagueness and violence. Sir Myles Wakefield, her friend, had finally understood this and so had given her the details.

"When she was told that she must die," Sir Myles had said, *"she declared that if the king would allow it, she would like to be beheaded like the French nobility, with a sword, and not, like the English nobility, with an ax."* Elizabeth, peering into the murky water, could almost hear Sir Myles's voice as it had been that time years ago when he'd finally given in to her plea. *"There was no such executioner in England, so it was necessary to postpone the execution until*

21

one could be brought from France. They said she slept little on Thursday night. She could hear the distant hammering as they built the scaffold.

"The next morning the headsman was waiting when the Constable of the Tower appeared, followed by your mother. She was dressed in a beautiful night robe of heavy gray damask trimmed with fur, showing a crimson kirtle beneath. She had chosen this to leave her neck bare. A large sum had been given her to distribute in alms among the crowd. 'I am not here,' she said simply, 'to preach to you, but to die. Pray for the king, for he is a good man and has treated me as well as could be.' Then she took off her pearl-covered headdress, revealing that her hair had been carefully bound up to avoid impeding the executioner.

"'Pray for me,' she said, then knelt down while one of the ladies-in-waiting bandaged her eyes. Before there was time to say a Paternoster she bowed her head, murmuring in a low voice, 'God have pity on my soul.' The executioner stepped forward and took his aim—and with a single stroke his work was done."

For one moment, Elizabeth seemed to hear the hissing of that sword—and she rose quickly and walked around the pool, her eyes filled with torment. After a moment she took a deep breath, then sat down on the rocks and forced herself to address the fish in even tones.

"As soon as he had executed my mother," she whispered, "my father appeared in yellow with a feather in his cap, and ten days later he was married to Jane Seymour." Picking up a stone, she weighted it, looked at the fish, then shrugged and tossed the stone to the ground again. "She was the wife he loved best—always submissive. But she died eighteen months later, old fish." She cocked her head, leaned over, and inquired, "What did you do the day my mother died? Nothing but swim and eat bread, I suppose."

The sound of a horseman riding at a fast trot came to her sharp ears, and once again she seemed to freeze, all but scenting the air for danger. When she heard the horse stop, she whispered, "Now

Edward VI, the child Jane Seymour died to give birth to, is dying—and what will you do, Elizabeth Tudor?"

As the door in the walls was swung open, she stood up and spoke again, as though addressing her own spirit: "What will *I* do—?"

Still mounted, the horseman passed through the gate. Seeing who it was, a wave of relief washed over the young woman. A single gasp passed through her lips, and for one instant she felt a weakness that caused her to sway. Always impatient with weakness, whether in others or in herself, she jerked her head forward and called out, "Sir Myles—over here!"

Myles Wakefield turned at once toward the sound of the voice, and seeing Elizabeth, he smiled and dismounted with a smooth, easy motion. Surrendering the reins to a groom, he murmured, "Feed him, will you? He's had a hard ride." Then he turned and walked across the courtyard, a tall, strong man with an unusual grace in his stride. Taking Elizabeth's hand, he kissed it, then smiled. "For once I find you not at your books. Have you given up on them?"

Elizabeth's narrow face showed the pleasure she felt at Wakefield's unexpected visit. She smiled, and her eyes gleamed as she spoke. "I would rather read men than books! Now, sir, sit beside me, and let me read your face."

Sitting beside her, Myles allowed himself to be teased. He was well aware of the heavy pressures that had hung over this young woman for years. He was a busy man, but it had been his duty—and his pleasure—to try his best to bring some lightheartedness into her life. Now as she spoke quickly, her mind darting like a bee, he thought, *I don't think there's another woman like this in all of England! She has the intellect and will of Henry, and the beauty of her mother.*

Elizabeth saw something flit across Wakefield's face and demanded, "Now, what thought just came to you? You have too honest a face, Sir Myles! You must learn to hide your thoughts, for this England of ours is no place for an honest man."

"I would not like to think that, Elizabeth."

"Only in a world where all are honest can the individual be so," Elizabeth declared. "God's truth, Myles, I can count the honest men and women I've known on the fingers of this hand!" She held up her slender, well-shaped hand and there was anger in her face. "Honor and truth are good for taking us to the block—or worse. Isn't that where it took your good friend William Tyndale?"

"Yes, but he would have it no other way." Myles thought of the days he'd spent with Tyndale, the great scholar, and a smile touched his lips. "He swore he'd have every plowboy in England reading the Bible in his own language—and he accomplished that."

"And at what cost? He's dead, burned at the stake!"

"We must all die, Elizabeth," Wakefield admonished her mildly. "It's the cause for which we die that is important."

Elizabeth stared at Wakefield, her eyes half shut in thought. "You really believe that, don't you?"

"Yes, I do."

"And somehow you believe that in the end wrong will be defeated and right will be victorious?"

"Yes, I believe that as well."

"Why?"

"Because, I suppose, that is what God's Word promises us. And any other conclusion would be intolerable."

The two were facing each other, and for a few moments a silence held them. Myles was remembering conversations such as this with Elizabeth from years back. Along with her sister Mary she had been declared illegitimate by her father, and for both young women, life had been hard. Mary had never complained, but Elizabeth, Myles remembered as he faced her, had been demanding even as a child. *She always wanted to know things—and most of the things she demanded to know could not be explained.*

Elizabeth sighed explosively, then in a rare demonstration of affection, reached out and took Myles's hand, squeezing it. "You are good for me, Sir Myles Wakefield!" she exclaimed with a strange intensity. "Ever since I was a child, I've been surrounded by people who want to use me—and by those who want to destroy me. But you have always been there to—to love me." She gave him a forlorn look, adding, "I can hardly say the word *love*. I've known so little of it!"

Myles had never heard her speak so plainly of herself. "Whatever devotion and loyalty I have, Princess," he said quietly, "you have it, as did your mother."

Tears came to Elizabeth's eyes, and she withdrew her hand from his quickly. She hated to cry and had not wept before any man for years. "I weep like a foolish woman!"

"No, indeed not. You weep for your mother, as I have done myself."

"Tell me about her, Myles. I hear such stories about her— about her terrible ways with men."

"Lies! All lies! Believe none of them!"

"Are you being honest, or just trying to take away my grief?"

"No, never that!" Myles struggled to find the words to comfort this strange young woman. "Queen Anne was loving in her ways—and some misunderstood this, taking it for something else." He spoke earnestly, telling of the time when he'd been a young man and of his admiration for Anne Boleyn. Finally he shook his head sadly. "She was kind to me, Elizabeth, and I was nobody then. She had a temper—a trait she has passed on to you—but she rarely showed it to me." He hesitated, then added, "It was your father who was untrue. He had to have an excuse for divorcing your mother, and his underlings created it. Your mother, as I have said, was sometimes too open, too bold in her expressions and manners, and they used this. They manufactured evidence to convict Anne for adultery—I know it! Your mother loved your father!"

For a long time they sat there, Wakefield's words washing over Elizabeth like a soothing rain. She trusted his honesty as she trusted that of no other man in England. He had been loyal to her mother as very few in the court had, and he had been faithful through the years of Elizabeth's childhood to stay as close to her as the circumstances permitted. His home was far from the court and he was a busy man, but he had come often and written more often. As the girl had grown into a woman, the certainty that she could trust this man had grown stronger and stronger.

Finally Elizabeth spoke in a quiet voice. "I'm glad you've come, old friend. I . . . needed some comfort." Then, as if ashamed of revealing such a thing, she rose. He stood with her, and she said, "Now, you must stay the night. Let's see what sort of dinner Mr. Parry can find for you."

The dinner was very good indeed, but Myles was aware that Elizabeth ate only a few bites. An almost tangible air of tension seemed to permeate the house, and later, after Elizabeth retired, Myles noticed that Mr. Thomas Parry, the steward of the household, was keeping very close. Myles had gone to the library and was reading the Bible, but when the steward entered for the third time, he put the big book down. "Did you wish to speak to me, Mr. Parry?"

Thomas Parry was a timid man, always expecting the worst in any situation, but his great virtue was that he was devoted to Elizabeth. Now he said nervously, "I don't want to be a bother, Sir Myles—but I'm dreadfully worried." He blinked like an owl in the sunlight, ran his hand through his thinning gray hair, and finally said, "Is there trouble, sir?"

"Yes, I'm afraid there may be, Thomas."

Parry bit his lower lip, his brow furrowing. "I don't understand these things, Sir Myles. Is it because of the king's illness? But how could that bring trouble to Mistress Elizabeth?"

Myles had long known Parry to be the simplest of men; he would have to make the matter very plain indeed. "Sit down, Parry, and have a little wine while I try to explain it."

Parry protested over the wine and felt uncomfortable being seated in the presence of Sir Myles, but finally he settled down and listened as the other man spoke.

"The trouble lies in the question of who will rule England when Edward dies. When King Henry died, Edward was only a boy, and a sickly one at that."

"Aye, sir, I pray for the king every day!"

"Good for you, Parry. So do I. But Edward has been sinking fast, and if God takes him, there will be trouble over who is to rule the country."

"Why, since Mary is the oldest—"

"Yes, she's thirty-seven and Elizabeth is twenty—but there's a problem. Mary is a Catholic, Parry. Her mother, Catherine, was strong in that faith, and she passed her passion for the Catholic Church along to her daughter."

Parry gave him a frightened glance. "I've heard of the Spanish Inquisition, sir. 'Tis said the Catholics torture those who won't join their church—and burn them at the stake. Would Lady Mary bring that to England?"

"Well, that is the problem," Myles agreed with a nod. "Many fear Mary would do *exactly* that. Henry himself broke away from the Catholic Church, and we now have our own faith, the Church of England. Should there be an effort to bring England back to the old ways, well, there would be terrible trouble."

"And Mistress Elizabeth?"

"She is not Catholic, therefore some want her on the throne when her brother dies."

Parry pondered the complexities, then shook his head. "You

mean, Sir Myles, no matter whether it's Mary or Elizabeth who becomes queen, there'll be trouble?"

Myles hesitated, not certain if he should complicate the matter. *The old fellow needs to be prepared—all of us do. He cares for Elizabeth and I must try to get him ready for whatever comes.*

"Actually, Parry, it's even more difficult than that. King Edward is strongly influenced by the duke of Northumberland. Some of us are afraid that Northumberland will get his own daughter-in-law, Lady Jane Grey, named queen when Edward dies."

"But—she's not a daughter of King Henry!"

"No, but one of her ancestors was Henry VII, the father of Henry VIII." He let that information sink in, then took pity on the old man. "Well, we'll hope that all goes well."

"God won't let anything bad happen to Mistress Elizabeth!" Parry said vehemently, then added, "Thank you for explaining it to me, sir. I'll be praying about it."

"So will I, Parry—so will I!"

❦

"Mistress Elizabeth, please wake up!"

The voice shocked Elizabeth's mind like a burning coal. She sat up instantly, her eyes wide and her hand at her throat. "What is it?" she demanded, throwing her legs over the side of the bed and rushing toward the door. Sliding the bolt, she saw the pale face of Thomas Parry, his eyes wide and staring.

"It's someone from the palace—," he began, but Elizabeth cut him off.

"I'll be right down. See that Sir Myles is awakened, and tell him I must see him!"

Slamming the door, she leaned against it, her mind racing. *It could be nothing but a message saying that Edward is improving.* She rejected the thought, for the physicians had given up on her brother a week earlier. Moving to the window, she peered out, keeping herself hidden. The early light of dawn reflected off the stone and brick of the courtyard, and the waiting horses stamped and champed their bits, tossing their heads. The action sent the swarms of clustering flies into angry clouds that rose then settled again.

Eight armed men—too many to bring a simple message! Fear bit at her throat, but she had learned to deal with fear long ago. Calmly she moved away from the window and slipped into a rose-colored robe, then sat down and waited. Five minutes later, a tap sounded at her door. "Come in, Myles."

Sir Myles had not paused to comb his hair, and the auburn locks fell over his brow. He wasted no time, demanding at once, "What is it?"

"I don't know," Elizabeth answered. "Go down and speak to the leader, then bring me word."

"Yes, Princess." Myles wheeled and left the room. As soon as he was gone, Elizabeth rose and began to pace the floor, her fertile imagination concocting scene after scene. This ability to create such scenes was both a blessing and a curse, for though it enabled her to imagine almost any difficulty, it also was often tinged with forebodings of doom.

Time seemed to crawl by, but finally Wakefield returned—and this time he entered without knocking. He had a paper in his hand and offered it to her instantly. Opening it, she scanned the brief message, then looked up at Myles. "It's from Edward," she said evenly. "He says that he's dying and he wants to see me before he goes."

Myles stood silently before her; he knew she wanted to hear his thoughts. His mind ran quickly over the possibilities, and finally he asked, "Are you certain it's from Edward? Is it in his hand?"

"The king is too weak to write," Elizabeth answered slowly. "So they tell me." She glanced at the note, studied it, then said,

29

"He calls me by a pet name: 'To my sweet sister Temperance.' Only Edward ever called me that."

"Did others know of the name?"

"Oh yes, everyone in the household." Elizabeth watched his face carefully. She had lived precariously for so long, relying on her own wits, that she was unaccustomed to seeking counsel. Once when she was but fifteen she'd been brought before a court on charges of immorality and had held her own before a panel of sharp judges. But this time . . . this time she needed another's perspective.

"Should I go?"

Seldom had Myles Wakefield been so surprised—for he had never known the woman to ask for advice. As a child, she had been more gentle and trusting, but she had come through a harsh school. Carefully he answered, "It could be innocent—or it could be death, Elizabeth."

"I know that, Myles!" Her face was pale, and her eyes were sharp as green diamonds. "Tell me what you think."

Myles shook his head. "I looked out my window at the escort, but knew none of them. And I have never seen the leader before. Perhaps you should meet him. Do you recognize any of the escort?"

"No, not a one." Her lips compressed into a tight line. "You fear a trap? From whom?"

"From the same man you fear. The duke of Northumberland."

The princess's lips relaxed slightly, then lifted into a bitter smile. "You could go to the Tower for saying so."

"I've been there before, as was my father."

"Yes, I'd forgotten. Well, we think alike, Sir Myles." She ran over the thing in her mind, then said, "Northumberland has married his son Guildford to Lady Jane Grey. She is not a direct descendent, but still she comes from the Tudor line. Only three people stand between her and the throne: King Edward, myself, and Mary."

"Only two, I think." Myles received the shocked look that Elizabeth gave him calmly. "I believe that Edward is dead."

"But we would have heard—!"

"Who is in charge of all the arrangements? Who is in your brother's room at all times?"

Elizabeth blinked, then nodded. "Yes, it's possible, Myles." She glanced downward where the messenger waited, then shivered. "If what you are saying is true, I would be going to my death."

"And Mary is in the same danger. Someone must warn her."

Elizabeth made up her mind. "Go tell the messenger I am ill—and have Parry send for the physician."

Myles nodded, his eyes warm. "I think that is wise." Then a thought came to him. "I'll put on my sword just in case the messenger wants to argue the point."

He turned and walked to his room, then having armed himself, he went downstairs. The man who'd given him the note was named Jennings. He was a tall middle-aged man with hard eyes and an arrogant manner. "Well, sir, I trust that Lady Elizabeth is ready."

The glance that Sir Myles Wakefield directed at Jennings was cold as polar ice. "Mistress Elizabeth is ill, sir. You may so inform your master, and add that as soon as she is able to travel, I myself will escort her to the king."

Jennings blinked, and then a flush lit his lean cheeks. For one moment he seemed ready to contest what he had heard, but he swallowed, muttered, "Very well!" then whirled and stomped out of the room.

From her window Elizabeth watched the man mount his horse and ride off, followed by his men. She turned as Myles entered, her eyes wary. "The gentleman seems angry. I think a trip with him would have been most—unpleasant."

They both understood that the thing was not over, and Myles said, "You must go to bed. I will bring the doctor myself."

"So you can be my witness if I am brought to trial over this?" Elizabeth shook her head, a wry smile tipping her lips. "For an honest man, Sir Myles Wakefield, you think almost like a lawyer and a scoundrel!" Then she sobered and added, "It is very good . . . to have a trusted friend."

He came to her, took her hand, and kissed it. "God will bring you through this, Elizabeth."

She smiled suddenly, saying, "You always say that. You always did, even when I was a child and had the measles. Must it always be God who saves us?"

"Yes, indeed! Vain is the help of man."

"No, not all of them. Sometimes God sends one of his own to help."

"Angels, you mean?"

"Sometimes, perhaps . . ." Elizabeth put her steady eyes on the tall man and whispered fondly, "Sometimes he sends Sir Myles Wakefield!"

QUEEN JANE

Quiet as a stone, she sat, trying to make herself smaller
. . . Lady Jane Grey, already so tiny she could have been
mistaken for a child when seen from behind. The table
made an island, surrounded by the powerful duke of Northumberland and his followers, all much larger and stronger than
the small young woman who had become the most important
woman in England.

As the loud talk of Mary echoed in the air of the magnificent
dining room, Jane looked down at her hands, trying to shut out
the sight of the gleaming jewels of those gathered around her, and
the flashings of cruel daggers and encrusted sword hilts. She
herself wore wide velvet cuffs, and her hair was tucked away out
of sight under a big white kerchief. A small nosegay of jasmine
and heliotrope was tucked into the front of her bodice where it
opened into the fluted white embroidered collar, and she quickly
bent her straight little nose down to sniff at it.

Suddenly a white moth came fluttering in from the night. Jane
watched as it moved drunkenly around the room—and then flew
into a tall flame from one of the candles, where it was shriveled
instantly. *Dead,* she thought, and her face twisted with pain. *And
now they say that Mary has to die.* They had been planning it—and
her heart cried out that it could not be right! Her father had said

that Mary was a papist, so that settled it. But Jane did not like to think of Mary dying. Mary had been kind to her; she had given her a pearl necklace and a gown of cloth of gold. *I wish they'd let Mary be queen! I don't want to be!*

Northumberland was saying, "We will find her, I tell you! She cannot escape!" His glance fell on Jane, and he said abruptly to the others, "Can you not see that the queen is not feeling well?" His voice cut into her as though it had been a sharp knife. "You are not well, Your Majesty. No doubt it is past your bedtime."

Instantly Jane was pulled to her feet by a tall, strapping maid-servant, but she cried out, "I won't be queen—I won't!"

The duke merely ignored her, and when the small figure had been pulled from the room, he snapped, "Don't listen to the whining of a crying child!" His eyes fell like a blow on Jane's father, the newly appointed duke of Suffolk. "You raised her ill, sir, but we will educate her to be a queen! Now, be on your way. All you have to do is round up Mary and her few retainers, clap them in the Tower, and the thing is done. Your daughter will be queen of England, and my son, as her husband, will be king!"

"Of course, my lord." Suffolk nodded nervously. "But you are the best soldier in the kingdom, and you should command the army. I have never been a soldier at all. The Council—all of us agree that this is the best course."

Northumberland cursed him roundly, but in the end he had little choice.

"The old man is a fool," he snapped later to his son, Guildford. "It will be no trouble, for Mary is alone—but I can't risk the chance that she might escape."

Guildford nodded. "It's best, I think. Shall I go with you, sir?"

"No, stay here and see that the Council does nothing." A smile touched Northumberland's lips. "Have you gotten through her resistance yet?"

The handsome face of Guildford Dudley flushed. It was a sore point with him that Lady Jane, who had been forced to marry him, kept herself aloof, refusing to have anything to do with him, keeping their marriage a marriage in name only. "When I am king, sir," he grated, "we shall see who will keep the key to the royal bedchambers!"

"Good! I'm glad to see you have *some* spirit!"

At that moment the new queen was in her bedroom with a man—but it was only her tutor, Sir John Cheke. Cheke, who had been the tutor of Edward VI, stood before the small young woman. She asked him abruptly, as was her manner with him, "Do you believe I should be queen?"

Cheke, tall, handsome, and austere, nodded. "What other choice is there? Only through you can the Church of England continue. Remember, this was planned long ago by King Henry VIII himself, when he disinherited his daughters."

"But he restored their rights," she said, feeling desperate.

"Only some of them, and only with the provision that if they and King Edward died childless the crown should go to the issue of his sisters, of whom the younger, Mary Rose, was your grandmother."

Jane listened, her eyes wide and staring. "But what of Mary? Must she die?"

Cheke answered carefully. "King Edward has declared you, his cousin, to be his rightful heir. It was his will that you preserve the new religion, undefiled by papacy and the superstition of the Mass." As he spoke, Cheke watched the play of emotions on her childlike face.

What a shame this burden should be thrust upon this child! She has no longing for power—but will be used as a pawn. And if those who use her ever fail, she will pay for the sins of others with her life! This last thought was almost too much. He opened his mouth to warn her of the dangers that lay ahead of her, but she spoke first.

"Write a letter to be published, Sir John. Let it say, 'We are entered into our rightful possession of this Kingdom, by the last will of our dearest cousin King Edward, as rightful Queen of this realm. . . .'"

⸺⸺⸺

Myles had always had trouble keeping secrets from his wife, Hannah. Their marriage had been the sort that many doubted could be real, for it was too perfect. One distant cousin had remarked, "They *can't* get along as well as they seem to. No one can be that close to a husband or wife. It's only an act they keep up in public!"

Myles had heard of the remark and had smiled. "A good marriage can only exist between good friends." When pressed to explain, he'd said, "One can't let his best friend down, and Hannah is my best friend—as I am hers. Friends may argue and quarrel, but in the end, they cling together." Such a view of marriage was so foreign to the minds of most men and women of the time that most people agreed with the cousin: Sir Myles and Lady Wakefield were merely better actors than most.

But they were wrong. It was not acting that bound the Wakefields. It was the truest form of love. This time, however, when Myles came home, his clothing stained with travel and his face lined with fatigue, he wished that for once he *could* hide something from Hannah. But one look at him and she demanded, "What is it, Myles?"

He'd entered the bedroom just as night was falling, and the pale yellow candlelight gave his eyes the appearance of being sunken into their deep sockets. He did not speak, but put his arms out, and she came to him at once. For a long moment they clung together, then he drew back. "How have you been? How are the children?"

Hannah stared at him, giving him the time he needed to tell

her what was on his mind. "We're very well," she answered evenly. "Shall I get something for you to eat?"

"No, I ate at Blakely's Inn." He removed his coat, threw it on the floor, then sat down heavily with a gusty sigh. "By heaven, I'm tired!" He pulled off one boot, then the other, dropping them—and then looked up into her face abruptly. "Never could hide anything from you, could I?"

"What is it?"

"William." The single word seemed to exhaust Myles, and he leaned back in the chair and closed his eyes. With an effort he said, "I tried to talk to him, but it was no use."

"He's joined Northumberland?"

"Yes."

"Oh, Myles, can't he *see* how dangerous that is?"

"I think he sees, but doesn't care." Myles opened his eyes and sat up straighter in the chair. Running his hands through his hair, he shook his head hopelessly. "All he can think of is what would happen if Mary were on the throne. Only Lady Jane can save us from the papacy."

Hannah looked at him and after a moment spoke evenly. "He may be right, Myles."

"I know, but Lady Jane will never be queen."

"Maybe she will." Hannah moved over and began massaging the back of Myles's neck. Her face was still, but her eyes were alert as she thought rapidly of all the possibilities that faced their house. "It's like a chess game, Myles," she observed quietly. "It seems simple, but it is truly complex. If we make a wrong move, we'll be taken and removed from the board."

Myles had closed his eyes, but grunted in agreement. "An apt analogy. Right now, Hannah, the duke seems to have the most powerful princes—and all Mary has is a few pawns, like us."

"What would you like to see? Mary as queen?"

Myles suddenly sat up, then rose to his feet. Dissatisfaction lurked in his blue-gray eyes, and he said shortly, "I'd rather have Edward VI, but he's dead. If Lady Jane Grey becomes queen of this England, we'll see a tyrant that will make Henry VIII look like a mild-mannered country parson!"

"You mean Northumberland?"

"Yes. Jane would be a mere figurehead. Northumberland's married her to his son, so he'll control this realm totally." He put his hands on her shoulders, looked down into her fine eyes. "She's lost, Hannah. She can't win."

"And what of Will?"

"We must pray that he stays in the background. Mary will win, but she can't execute everyone who's supported Lady Jane."

"Let's pray now," Hannah said instantly, and the two of them knelt, joined hands, and began to pray. This total and instant willingness to call on God for their needs was something that Hannah had brought to their marriage. On their wedding night, she'd asked a favor of Myles: *"Let's not let things go, Myles. Let's pray about every problem as soon as it comes. Let's be restfully available—and instantly obedient!"*

It was a request that had stood them in good stead for many years now. So it came naturally for them to kneel and pray as simply as two children, asking God to keep their son safe. When they arose, Myles said, "It's going to be a hard time—but God will never fail us."

"No, he never will!"

⁕

William Wakefield rode not at the front of the line of steel-clad knights but at the rear. He had joined Northumberland's forces, fired with a desire to play a part in the great battle—but there had been no battle at all. They had ridden north and east through flat fields and fens, passing through villages from time to time. The heat burned the riders, and the few gray stone castles they passed looked like shadows through the mist that smudged the horizon.

Occasionally they heard the sound of bells pealing, and once William asked the lieutenant in charge of his unit, "Are those bells pealing for Queen Mary or Queen Jane?"

The officer gave him a sour look, replying, "God knows, but we don't!" He was a short, stocky man named Brighton, and as the force moved wearily in pursuit of Mary, he grew a little more friendly with William. When they got to Newmarket, he looked around and said with disgust, "No reinforcements! The cowards have gone to earth!"

"We'll pick up more strength soon," William said confidently.

"What strength?" Brighton demanded. "We should have taken Mary long ago. As long as she's on the loose, the noblemen won't have the stomach to join us."

"But the navy is for Northumberland!"

"Is it?" Brighton asked, doubt dripping from his voice. "We'll see, Wakefield. We'll see!"

Northumberland had four thousand troops, a quarter of them horsemen, and positioned them strategically so as to cut off the forces that had declared for Mary and were marching to join her. The weather broke, and a strong easterly gale drove scuds of rain and torn leaves across the road. On the third day of the journey, Lieutenant Brighton's company was called to the head of the line. It was exciting to young William Wakefield to be close enough to the duke and the high-ranking officers to hear them call out orders.

At dusk a rider came thundering down the road, raising a cloud of dust. He pulled his lathered horse to a halt, and the duke called out, "What news, Jack?"

The rider, William saw, was Jack Dudley, the duke's eldest son. His face was twisted with anger. "Sir—it's the navy—!"

At once Northumberland cried out with alarm, "The navy? The ships aren't sunk in a gale?"

"No, they're safe in harbor at Yarmouth, but they've gone over to Mary!"

The duke stared at his son, then began to swear. "No! They wouldn't do such a thing!"

"It was Sir Henry Jerningham, sir," Jack Dudley said bitterly. "He went to Yarmouth and led the entire fleet to mutiny against us!"

Brighton was close enough to whisper to William, "That tears it!"

"We can win without the navy!"

Brighton stared at the young man with disgust. "Using what to do the fighting?"

"Why, the people will rise up," Will said confidently. "They won't have a Catholic ruler on the throne."

But the people didn't rise up. As the hours and days passed, it was evident that the common people were for Mary. Dudley frantically threw himself into capturing the small woman, but she was now perched on top of one of the towers of Framlingham Castle.

Now Will began to hear a few of the "common" people muttering, "It ain't right, to do the Lady Mary out of her rights!"

Once Will tried to reason with a blacksmith who'd stood outside his shop. "Would you have the Inquisition here in England as it is in Spain?"

"Don't know about that," the man said stubbornly. "But it's Mary who's the daughter of Henry VIII!"

Will stared at the man, then turned away. He saw that Lieutenant Brighton had been listening. "Are these the common people who're going to fight to put Jane on the throne?" he demanded harshly.

"We'll win!"

Brighton stared at Will as if he'd said something particularly stupid. Shaking his head, he stepped to his horse, mounted, and then leaned down. "Better come with me, boy."

Will stared at him. "Come with you where?"

"To France—or Holland, maybe."

"You're deserting?" Will could not believe his ears. "It isn't over! We can still win!"

Brighton gave him a sad look. "Mary's won, Wakefield. And every man who supported Jane Grey had better look to it, for his head won't stay on long when Mary is crowned. She'll put every man jack of us to the block!"

⋯⋯

Indeed, miraculously, Mary had won.

This prim old maid had slipped away in disguise, with a tiny company of six gentlemen. All tried to convince her to flee to France, but she refused. She was alone with no money, no arms, and with no one to advise her. She rode on to Framlingham, one of the strongest fortresses in the kingdom, and reached it safely.

And that was when the miracle began to happen. Men flocked to her side. First Sir Henry Bedingfeld, then Sir Henry Jerningham, then many others—until within a few days her army had swelled to thirteen thousand—all volunteers. Many of the farmers came, some armed with longbows, others with hayforks. They knew little of Mary, but they believed she was being done out of her rights, and they gathered around her.

They found a little woman with a big voice, much like that of her famous father. They heard her laugh and did not see her cry. She reviewed her troops, and, though startled by their cheering, she bustled among the ranks, showing pride in them.

Finally the day came when she received the news that Northumberland was a prisoner and his sons arrested with him. Mary had been proclaimed queen in every city in England, and the "reign" of Jane was over!

Mary at once gathered her forces and made for London. Her chaplain was with her as she rode through cities and a countryside alive and ringing, singing, mad with joy in her triumph. Turning to her chaplain, she said, "God has chosen me, stupid and weak as I am, to be his servant."

"Amen!" The chaplain, Bishop Clapton, was a tall, broad-shouldered man. "Now the true church will be planted forever in this England!"

"I will be harsh to no one, Bishop," Mary said thoughtfully. "My father sent many to death, but I would be known as 'Good Queen Mary.'"

Bishop Clapton stared at her, then said diplomatically, "We will certainly pray to that end, for charity is the premier virtue. However, some will not welcome Your Majesty. Your father deserted the Catholic Church, and your brother, King Edward, established Protestantism in the land."

"The truth will be received when we teach the people," Mary said adamantly. "Our people *must* renounce the heresy my father and my brother created!"

At that moment a large company suddenly appeared riding toward them. Many ladies and gentlemen in glittering dress and harness came, and then hundreds of horsemen in white and green, their satin and taffeta coats shining like the waves of the sea. And at their head rode a tall woman, whose hair blazed like the ripe corn.

"Your sister, Lady Elizabeth, has come to escort you to London," the bishop observed.

At the sight of Elizabeth, Mary's face grew tense, and she said so quietly that the bishop could barely hear, "And *she* will have to find the true religion as well as others!"

"Greetings to Your Majesty!" Elizabeth pulled up her horse, her face beaming. "We have come to escort you to your capital."

"You recovered from your sickness rather quickly," Mary said, an edge in her voice.

"When I heard of Your Majesty's victory, I could do no other than recover!"

Mary had heard the history of Elizabeth's escape from the clutches of Northumberland and now demanded, "Who warned you that the king's summons was a lie to lure you into the duke's hands?"

"Why, I guessed, madam."

"You are very wise."

"No wiser than Your Majesty," Elizabeth protested.

"I had a message to warn me," Mary said bitterly. To herself she said, *She is more clever than I. I would never have guessed it was a trap.*

Elizabeth said quickly, "I was thinking more of how Your Majesty has triumphed over the enemy. No general could have done it more effectively. To be brought to the throne by the will of the people!"

"It was the will of God!" Mary said sharply.

Suddenly Elizabeth knew that this was the real difference between herself and Mary. Elizabeth's creed was to trust the people; Mary cared little for them. Mary was convinced, Elizabeth saw, that her rise to power was the result of Divine Providence. She felt a stab of fear, for the mild eyes of her half sister seemed angry. "Yes, the will of God," she agreed quickly.

Mary stared at Elizabeth, then looked at the gentlemen ranged behind her. One of them caught her eye, and she lifted her voice, saying, "Sir Myles Wakefield—!"

Myles moved his horse closer and bowed in the saddle. "Your Majesty, I rejoice to see you."

Mary's eyes narrowed. "I do not see your son, Wakefield." She saw Elizabeth start and knew the truth. "I have heard that your son joined himself to the traitor Dudley. Is it so?"

Myles lifted his head and answered clearly, "I fear it is, Your Majesty. I ask pardon for his youth and inexperience."

Wakefield's frank manner stirred the new queen's admiration. *This will be my first act of mercy,* she thought, and said aloud, "My father would have had him drawn and quartered—but we will show mercy."

"I thank Your Majesty," Myles said fervently. "It is good to have a monarch who understands the power of forgiveness."

Mary nodded and passed on, and Elizabeth turned her horse so that she rode bridle to bridle with Myles. "She is changed," she murmured.

"Power does that," Myles answered. "But she may be changed for the better. She was telling the truth about my son. Your father had many executed for far less."

Elizabeth was watching Mary carefully. She was aware that people were staring at her instead of Mary, and her ears caught their words:

"There's the red lass!"

"King Henry's daughter, no doubt about that!"

"Look at that hair! A real Tudor!"

One of the women threw a flower, a red rose, and Elizabeth caught it and waved it at the crowd, who applauded and cried out with pleasure.

At that moment, however, Mary turned in the saddle and stared at Elizabeth. Myles started, for he could not miss the keen anger in the queen's face. When she turned away from them again, he murmured, "Don't be *too* popular with the people, Lady Elizabeth."

"No, it would be dangerous to one's health." Elizabeth gave him an odd look, then said, "Tell your son to stay away from heretics, Myles. Mary will be watching him—and you."

The cavalcade moved on, entering the City of London. The sun was setting, and the streets were a sea of dim white faces. The people were yelling loudly, and to the new queen of England it seemed that fully as many of her subjects were cheering her red-haired sister as were lauding her, the rightful monarch.

They love her as they have never loved me, she thought dismally. Stealing a look at Elizabeth, she nodded slightly and resolved, *They may love Elizabeth, but they will obey me!*

At that moment, Mary was possessed with one thought: to bring the Catholic Church back into power in England. And if blood must be shed, so be it! A sense of power surged through her small body, and she sat straight on the charger thinking of the glorious day when all her subjects would walk in truth—and not in the Protestant heresy!

Four

A HUSBAND FOR MARY

L ike an actor who had performed his part blatantly but
rather poorly, the year of 1553 slunk away, making room
for a new cast. The old was rung out by the churches of
England, and the bells celebrated the coming to the throne of
Queen Mary, and already her once-sickly brother, Edward, was
fading into a pale memory.

Those who loved the Protestant cause wept for the boy-king,
who had, in obedience to his father's wishes, done all that he
could to promote "the new religion" and to eradicate Catholicism. On the other hand, now that Mary was on the throne,
Catholics throughout England were watching her carefully, hope-
ful that once again the old religion would be brought back.

It was the fifth of January when Elizabeth entered the room
where the new monarch was waiting. The two women looked at
each other carefully. Mary, being nearsighted, waited for one
moment to say, "Good morning, Sister. You slept well, I trust?"

"Very well, Your Majesty, and I trust you did the same?"
Elizabeth was wearing a rather plain dress, not at all in accordance
with her usual, rather flamboyant style. She had thought it wise,
perhaps, to mute her tastes, at least until she saw how it would go
between her and this older sister of hers. The two women talked
for a moment and then Mary said, "No doubt you'd like to see

the jewels I have inherited. Yes, even those robbed from the tomb of that blessed martyr, Saint Thomas à Becket. His tomb was the glory of Christendom, rifled to make thumb rings and necklaces for the king and queen of England. Look!" She held up a great red ruby that gleamed with red fire as it caught the morning sunlight—a gleam that Elizabeth saw reflected in the eyes of Queen Mary as she said sharply, "Your mother wore it. Would you like to wear it, Sister, on those delicate fingers that you're so anxious that all the world will notice?"

Elizabeth flushed with embarrassment. She was always embarrassed at references to her mother, especially by Mary. Mary, of course, had to remember that it was for Anne Boleyn that Henry had cast aside her own mother, Catherine.

Elizabeth shook her head. "I care nothing for such things. When have you seen me wear jewels or even do my hair as the more fashionable women do?" She touched her hair, hoping to change the subject. "Do you like my style of hairdressing now?"

"No," Mary said, "The Scriptures tell us that a woman's hair is her crowning glory. I see no point in stuffing it all under a net or a cap as you do." And then she snapped off bitterly, "Except when, by some strange accident, it flies out into a flaming aureole, as on our entrance into London."

Elizabeth had known that Mary resented the people's attention to her, but could think of nothing to say.

"Oh, do as you will," Mary said dismissively. "But I sent for you on a more important matter than caps and gowns and hairstyles." She rose from her seat, took three paces toward the window, then stared out for a moment, watching as a flight of blackbirds sailed by giving their raucous cries. They seemed to fascinate her, and she watched them so long that Elizabeth wondered if her sister had forgotten she was there. Then Mary turned and walked back to face Elizabeth. "I've sent for you because you have said you need instruction before entering the true church. You ask for books as though religion were intellectual exercise, but what of your conscience and what of your soul?"

"I'm sorry that I displease you in this matter. It's just that I was not brought up as you were, and it's more difficult for me."

"But why did you not attend Mass last Monday?"

"I was ill," Elizabeth said simply, "I'm not well, you know." Mary stared at her, not at all satisfied with the explanation, but she knew Elizabeth was never a simple woman. She changed the subject by saying, "My first act of Parliament will be, of course, to reinstate my mother as the lawfully wedded wife of King Henry, and myself, therefore, as his only surviving legitimate child. Is that plain to you, Elizabeth?"

"Your Majesty could not be plainer."

"Do you object? You look as though you are not happy."

"What objection could I make? I had a mother, as Your Majesty has had. I don't have the good fortune to remember her, as you do your sainted mother. I can have no public reason to object, but at least give me leave to regret in private the slurs cast upon my mother's memory."

Mary stared at Elizabeth, her small eyes half shut. Throughout the years she had experienced such mixed feelings about this young girl, and now—queen or not—she felt old and unable to handle her. She made an uncomfortable motion with her shoulders, then reached up and touched her hair nervously. "You know I'm being urged by my counselors to marry."

"So I've heard."

"Well, women older than I have married and borne children. I'm not yet thirty-eight, though that must indeed seem withered to one not yet twenty."

Elizabeth now looked somewhat nervous herself. For years she had considered Mary a confirmed old maid. "Madam, forgive me for not thinking of your marriage, but it's because I have never thought of it for myself."

"No?" asked Mary.

"No, madam, I've had small reason to think of marriage during my years gone by."

Mary suddenly felt ashamed of baiting this sister of hers and said, "Well, I can assure you, Elizabeth, I have not thought of it, either, but now they all seem determined that I ought to marry. The trouble is that they all offer me young men, about half my age. Their favorite is Edward Courtenay, who is twenty-four years old." And then she shot a question, "And what do you think of him, Sister?"

Elizabeth answered, "He's fine-looking, of course, a handsome young man, but scarcely suitable."

"Perhaps not for me, but he's only five years older than you." She smiled unexpectedly—a smile with a malicious twist to it—and said, "I've heard him say that if you were not a court lady, you would make a charming courtesan."

"Well, he hardly sounds like a prospective husband," said Elizabeth calmly.

The two women spoke for a few moments longer, Elizabeth casually remarking that perhaps the emperor of Spain would welcome a match for his son, and then she said, "Wasn't there a plan, when I was a small child, to marry you to the emperor and me to Prince Philip?"

Mary shook her head. "It came to nothing, as usual. I wonder why?"

Elizabeth's reply was adamant. "Because we had both been declared illegitimate, and when the emperor demanded our reinstatement, our father would not unsay what he had said."

Mary's mouth went tense in the peculiar way it did when a statement came hard for her—as if she had bitten into something sour. Scarcely allowing sound to pass her lips, she said, "I have thought of Philip," the admission seemed to embarrass her, and she shook her head, saying, "Oh well, the counselors will talk, and that's all there is to it." Then she raised her voice more stridently, and a fit of anger seemed to take her as she said, "And be at Mass next Sunday morning, and every Sunday. Do you hear me, Elizabeth?"

"Yes, of course, Your Majesty. You must give me time. I am but a learner." Then she added, "If I may go back to my study, I think I will be able to learn more about the old religion."

"Go then."

As soon as Elizabeth was out the door, Mary went over to the window and stared out again, not speaking, deep in thought. As she looked out, she finally broke the silence of the room. "Philip . . . what if it were God's will for me to marry Philip?"

But Mary, for all her hopes, was not to be happy. It had already broken her heart when the gentry had confessed their error against the pope, but had refused, point-blank, to give up one scrap of the church property they had amassed. Then there was the changed attitude of the common people at her coronation, where it became necessary to take all sorts of precautions to guard her safely from those very crowds that had roared themselves hoarse with joy at her entry into London.

She made her first attempts to restore Catholicism and had the Mass said in public, even while it was illegal by the existing law of the land. Some were glad to hear it again and drank in the sound of the Latin that they had missed. They wanted to hear again the chime of the chapel bell, comforting in the black silences of the night; to see lights again in the windows of the monastery guest houses that had long been dark, giving no welcome to tired travelers.

But this was the older generation. The younger people were anxious for change. They believed the world had come out of its darkness, and now they were not going back into it—to be scolded and frightened like children with old tales of hell and purgatory. Rome was the monster, the secret invader, and the prying fingers of the distant lands seeking to take money out of the country all the while putting foreigners into it.

England, in truth, was in the flush of a new national pride. King Henry had not given them military conquests or victories, but he had engendered a sense of oneness. He had done this by severing them from the Catholic Church—and to the younger generation it seemed that England had leapt ahead with one vast stride.

To England's queen, however, this was blindness. In Mary's mind, England had gone back into the darkness. It was her mission to recall it to "my mother's way." She would bring back the Mass and the old allegiance to Rome. She intended an even worse thing, at least so the rumors said, and that was to bring the Spanish Inquisition itself.

But Mary's biggest problem, for the moment, was what to do with Princess Elizabeth. She knew Elizabeth's popularity—and she feared it. Finally, she made one gesture that settled the matter.

Queen Mary held a banquet at which all the nobles, all of the court, were present, watching carefully. Elizabeth swept a deep curtsy as the queen passed, and she rose to follow as was her place—then froze to the spot. For Mary had held out her hand, not to her sister, to take precedence of the court, but to her cousin, the duchess of Suffolk, the mother of Jane Grey.

Elizabeth turned pale, for by this one act the queen declared publicly that she regarded the mother of a convicted rebel—for Jane Grey had been convicted of treason and thrown into the Tower of London—as the first lady in the land, next to herself—rather than her own sister! There could have been no clearer sign than that Mary refused to acknowledge Elizabeth as the heir to the throne of England.

Almost instantly Elizabeth reeled, broke away, and ran to her own apartments. She knew that this was more than just an insult. Falling from favor could be a matter of formality—or it could mean the Tower. Elizabeth went into one of her blind rages, stalking up and down in a tornado of rustling silk, swearing with shocking and surprising proficiency, striking out at anything in her way. She looked, in fact, very much like her father, Henry VIII, in one of his towering rages. At least so thought her secretary, Mr. Parry, who sat at his writing desk, trying to look invisible. Finally, however, she turned to him.

"Write to my sister that I will leave the court." When Parry hesitated, she said, "You idiot, do what I tell you! Why does your hand shake? What do you mutter? She will give her permission. She will!"

***

Mary Tudor was a well-meaning woman of rigid moral principles—a simple, painfully honest woman who was narrow in outlook and limited in experience. She was hopelessly out of her depth in the complicated, unprincipled world of high politics and possessed none of the toughness of mind essential for a successful working monarch—such as one saw in Elizabeth. Everyone took it for granted that Mary needed a husband to relieve her of the burden of government, but to the disappointment and dismay of the country, Queen Mary made it clear that she would not choose an English husband. When she announced that she intended to marry the emperor's son, Philip of Spain, she stirred up anger in England such as had not been seen for some time.

Opposition to the Spanish alliance grew rapidly, but Mary clung to her purpose. "I know this is God's will for me, to marry Philip," she insisted, and she was immovable. She paid no attention to those friends and counselors who tried to warn her of the storm that would occur if she carried out her plans. The result of this, in February 1554, was the most serious revolt in recorded history against the authority of the Crown of England. Sir Thomas Wyatt and his Kentishmen came very close, indeed, to gaining control of the capital. That they failed was due, in a large part, to Mary's own courage—and her stubborn refusal to be intimidated by violence. Ignoring advice that she should seek her own safety, she went down to the city and made a fighting speech in the crowded Guildhall—a speech that not even Elizabeth could have bettered. There, in the midst of the battle, she stood fast, a gallant little figure watching from the gallery over the gatehouse, sending word that she would be unmoved, and rallying her people, her soldiers, to the task of putting down the rebellion.

Mary's forces triumphed, but the queen could now no longer afford the luxury of showing mercy to her enemies. As her counselors told her, "It is time for heads to roll."

Soon Queen Mary, who had come to the throne determined to be known as "Good Queen Mary," took the first step down the path that would earn her the title "Bloody Mary."

Lady Jane Grey and her husband, Guildford Dudley, were beheaded on Tower Green on the twelfth of February. On the last night of her life, Lady Jane wrote letters, giving all of herself that she could in the last moments. It was growing dark as her women brought out candles for her and shut out the oncoming night. She asked to be left alone again, and they spoke to her gently through their tears. Finally, when she was alone, she took out her lute and sang a song and then said an evening prayer. But finally the lute slid from her grasp, tears came hot into her smarting eyes, and she almost cried herself to sleep. But she thought, *What need have I of sleep, who will soon sleep, never to wake again?*

But sleep she did, and she dreamed of her childhood, of how secure she had felt in her grandfather's big house. She remembered the red, warm walls, the imposing orchards, and the gardens full of scented flowers. She dreamed of the trout stream that went tossing, tumbling over the smooth boulders, and she remembered the wishing well where she had sat with her tutors—where she had made a wish that she and Mary and Elizabeth should continue in their friendship.

She was awake when the two ladies came for her and then walked with her to the place of execution. They wept, but she herself was calm. In a brief speech upon the scaffold, she admitted she had done wrong in accepting the crown. She asked those present to bear witness as she died a good Christian woman, who looked to be saved "by none other mean, but only by the mercy of God and the merits of the blood of his only Son, Jesus Christ. And now, good people," she ended, "while I am alive, I pray you to assist me with your prayers." At the last dreadful moment, this young girl, though frail as a reed, had the strength to remain true to the Protestant faith and reject the age-old comfort of prayers for the dead.

A blindfold was tied over her eyes, and then she was alone, groping in the darkness. Someone came forward to guide her, and she laid her head upon the block, stretched forth her body, and said, "Lord, unto thy hands I commend my spirit." And then the executioner struck the blow. Later that day, the butchered remains of Henry the VIII's eldest great niece were thrust, unceremoniously, to lie in a tomb between his two headless queens, Anne Boleyn and Catherine Howard.

Elizabeth stepped into the litter that was waiting to drive her into the smoky, dark smudge of the city. She went by the queen's command and, of course, by armed troops. It had been of no use to plead illness, for the command was stringent.

She tried to pray for Jane's soul, little Jane whom she loved. Jane would not have treated her so, as her last words on the scaffold rang in Elizabeth's memory, "Good people, pray for me, as long as I am alive."

Elizabeth could not think of Jane and herself other than as two little girls. She remembered at a Christmas party, Mary, the kind, elder sister and cousin, had given her five yards of yellow satin to make a skirt and had fastened a gold pearl necklace around Jane's thin little neck. Today Mary's executioner had cut through that slender neck.

All her life, Elizabeth had thought of her sister as poor old Mary, an old maid who was always in bad health, with no force or motion. But now Mary had acted as swiftly and boldly as ever Henry VIII himself had acted. That had meant death for Jane. Elizabeth wondered what it was to mean for her.

They entered Whitehall Palace through the garden, and she was taken into the great hall. She braced herself, waiting to look Mary in the face, to search for signs of death. She need not have troubled; the queen refused to see her.

For three weeks she waited in her room at Whitehall, guards close about, to learn what Mary would do with her. She knew, of course, that the queen was being urged to take this opportunity to cut off her sister's head, but Mary did not seem anxious to do so. Instead, the queen went to Oxford to open her Parliament and ask her lords to keep Elizabeth safe, and during this time Elizabeth knew her first easy breath.

All around her England waited, too, stirring uneasily, as one tradesman said in the streets, "That lady, Elizabeth, she was the real cause of Wyatt's rising." Witnesses had sworn that Elizabeth was a party to Thomas Wyatt's efforts to overthrow the Crown, but she had been judged innocent.

Elizabeth knew that persecution had begun, through Mary. Little Lady Jane now lay in her grave, and the woodsmen at her home rose up and took their axes and cut off the top of the oaks to show their grief and anger at her death. Old Goody Carickle had been burned to death a few months ago for approaching the cross on her knees; young Tom of Ramsun had been flogged for refusing to kneel to the same cross. Parson Smith had been heavily fined for refusing to allow his village girls to pray before the image of the Virgin, and Parson Manley was put in the stocks for throwing her image in the dung hill. All over England, images were being thrown down and put up again. Elizabeth feared that Mary had unloosed some sort of force that only civil war would settle.

Finally, a deputation of nine members of the queen's counsel came and questioned Elizabeth for hours. They told her that Wyatt had accused her of being the instigator of the rebellion. "Confess," they said. "They've told all. Confess, and you shall be forgiven."

But she gave nothing away. She stood before them, proclaiming her innocence, looking in their faces openly. Finally, Bishop Gardner, the chancellor, said, "Tomorrow you must go to the Tower."

The faces of the counsel made a blur around Elizabeth. She looked for a kind face and saw one: a tall, burly, elderly fellow with a rubicon face, now slightly purplish, who stood with his thumbs in his belt, quite unaware that he was watching her with some compassion.

Elizabeth suddenly thought of his name. "My Lord of Sussex, surely Her Majesty will not send me to that place?"

But there was nothing, evidently, that Sussex could do. When the royal daylight came, the earl of Sussex accompanied Lord Rochester and the guards to tell her that the barge was ready to take her to the Tower.

Cold rain cut into her face as Sussex took her arm and helped her into the waiting barge, the floor of which was already waterlogged. Elizabeth knew as she stepped aboard that there was no chance for her—and the rough, gray, relentless river bore her fast away. Finally, carried by a raging current brought on by heavy rains, she arrived at that supreme and dreadful moment at Traitor's Gate. With sudden clarity, she thought of the moment in May eighteen years ago when all the birds were singing and she and her mother, a young and lovely woman, had landed in this place.

Suddenly Elizabeth felt that she was part of a large scheme, larger than she had known, and she looked up to the heavens and cried out to God. Then she gazed at the dark gates sprouting at the head of the water stairs and saw the wardens and servants of the Tower drawn up to receive her.

"I won't land there. I'm no traitor."

"Your Grace has no choice," said Rochester gruffly and threw his cloak over her against the heavy rain. In a fury she dashed it from her and stepped out into the swirling water and up the stairs where a grim future awaited her.

But then a strange thing happened among some of the servants of the Tower—some fell on their knees, and one cried out, "May God preserve Your Grace." Some of the soldiers did the same, and their captain tried to check them and threatened them with punishment. Then Elizabeth nodded and said, "God knows my condition. He will not abandon me."

With that, she was taken inside, the Tower closing in, her prison narrowing until it should take the shape of a grave.

❦

Bishop Hugh Latimer looked carefully at the young man who walked nervously back and forth in front of him. *He looks almost like a caged animal,* Latimer thought, *and little wonder. He's much like the rest of us, afraid of what's going to happen.*

Aloud he said, "Sit down, Will. I must talk to you."

Will Wakefield turned abruptly, moved over to take the seat across from Latimer. His eyes were deeply sunk in his head, and lines of strain marked his mouth. "I'm sorry to bother you, Bishop," he said, "but I don't know who else to come to."

"You did right, my boy, but I must tell you the truth—this is no time for evasions. You know, of course, that Mary has agreed to marry Philip of Spain."

"What else has kept me awake all these weeks since she made that public?" Will said bitterly. He looked up, and anger was in his eyes. "There'll be a revolution. England will never stand for it."

"The time may come," Latimer said, "but for the meanwhile, you and I, and others of our persuasion, must be very wise. The country is dry as tinder and one spark will set it afire. Queen Mary has successfully withstood two revolts. People will not rush to join a third, I think."

Young Wakefield stared gloomily at him, and silence fell over the room. When he spoke, his tone was somber. "I've been thinking of marriage, Bishop."

At once Latimer shook his head. "You know what the apostle Paul says on that subject. He counseled men and women to remain single. It was a dangerous time for Christians in those days—as it is today."

"Yes, but people can't stop living because it's dangerous. Living is always dangerous."

"Of course you're right," Latimer said wearily. *How impossible to counsel young blood,* he thought with a sigh. *I am old and dry and this young man is filled with youth and love. He did not come here to hear me tell him to stay away from the young woman.* Still, he tried: "I'm sure your father has told you, William, how dangerous things may be, especially for you."

Will gave him a puzzled look. "Why especially for me? Isn't the danger the same for all?"

"Oh no, some men and women are very quiet in their beliefs. You are not. You," he said with a wry smile, "will proclaim what you believe at the top of your lungs in the palace. Just exactly the sort who will go to the block—or to the fires first."

Will looked at the bishop somewhat indignantly. "But we are commanded, sir, to proclaim what we know from the housetops."

"We are also commanded to be wise as serpents——" here Latimer shook his head—"although, I've always thought that was a strange conceit. I could never see why serpents seemed to be the symbol for wisdom. Nevertheless, the meaning is clear: 'A wise man,'" he quoted, "'looks well to his going.' And that's what I'm going to have to counsel you to do, my boy. Look well to your going."

Will shifted uneasily and nodded. "Exactly what my father says, and what I shall do, of course."

The two talked for some time, and finally they rose and Latimer came over to touch the young man's shoulder. "Be very careful, William, very careful. For we are going through the fires, and if we are not faithful, God will judge us. But we must also remember, as I have said, that this is a time to be wise. I will pray for you, and for the young woman, and for your entire family."

"And I for you, Bishop."

The two men looked at each other fondly, then said their farewells. Will left the church and went at once to Blanche, who had been waiting to find out the results of his meeting. She met him at the door, a question in her dark eyes. Eagerly, she drew him inside. "What did the bishop say?"

For one moment Will thought to dissemble, but he could not. He took her hands in his, his expression sober. "He says what we already knew—that with Mary on the throne, hard times are coming for those who believe in the true gospel."

"What did he say about us?" she said hesitantly.

Will shook his head, but a grin touched his lips. "He said it would be better if we didn't marry."

"Oh, he said that did he?"

Will looked at her, and love came to him as it often did when he glanced at her. She was gentle and pretty, but there was more than that to her. There was an inner strength that he had long admired, and now he put his arms around her and held her close.

"We will not obey the bishop's counsel." Then he pressed his lips to hers, and for one moment they clung together, he enjoying her warmth and softness, she pressing against him, holding to him tightly.

Blanche felt she had loved him from the first and they had waited faithfully, but now she wanted to be a wife and a mother. She pulled away from him, determination in her eyes. "Will, I want to marry you, and I want us to have children."

Will's eyes, for all their soberness, suddenly twinkled. "Aye, that's the proper order all right. First we'll see about this marriage, though." Then his lips grew tight and he shook his head. "It's not fair to you, Blanche, not fair at all—but I must have you. Come, we'll go tell Father and Mother, then we can tell your parents."

⁂

Philip of Spain put on silver and gold embroidery and white hose for his first meeting with his future bride. He had had a miserable time since coming to England, although he had done all that his father had advised him to make himself pleasant. And he could still remember his grandmother whispering, "Those slant-eyed Tudors, they're not strong, but they make themselves so by guile. Watch them as you would watch the smiling, beguiling sea—the cruel, traitorous sea. Be careful of the seas around England—they are strong allies. But most of all, beware of love, which is fiercer than the winds." Now as Philip marched through the thick darkness into the bishop's garden, he thought of his grand-mother—everyone had said she was a witch. With an impatient sigh, he pushed her from his mind.

He followed the butler into the queen's private apartment, which actually was a long gallery, where several people were standing, watching as one small figure paced restlessly up and down, jewels glittering at every turn.

Mary came quickly, hardly giving the time to the two torchbearers who had to proceed her. She kissed her hand, in the old English fashion, before she held it out to Philip, and he, remembering his instructions, kissed her on the lips. Hers were dry and rather hard, and they met his uncertainly, yet eagerly. There were no men of England of sufficient rank for her to give even a formal kiss. She was shy and timid as a young girl—in her heart, perhaps, that was what she was—but on the surface he saw a middle-aged woman whose intent gaze was appealing to him, not only as a political ally and partner, but as her sovereign and lover.

Mary recovered from her embarrassment, became gracious, cordial, even lighthearted. He noticed that her skin was fair and very clear. Her rather thin hair had lights in it like a sandy kitten's where it had not gone gray. *She must have been very pretty as a young woman,* he thought. But her little round face and pointed chin, which had for so long kept her youthful shape in solitary refinement, were drawn into hollows, and the struggle she had had with her ungrateful country had made her look old.

The men around, especially Lord Admiral Howard, a blunt high sailor, made jokes that Philip could not understand. Old Bishop Gardener, the chancellor of England, stood close to Mary, almost protectively. Finally Philip asked, "Why is your sister Elizabeth not here?"

An awkward silence fell on the group until Howard said, "Lady Elizabeth was involved in the Wyatt Rebellion. We have had her in the Tower for some time, did you know that?"

"No. I trust not for long?"

Mary, hearing this, said spiritedly, "Until we decide whether she is our faithful servant or not."

Philip's eyes narrowed. "And have you decided, Your Majesty?"

Mary hesitated, then shook her head. "She is ambitious. And she has not yet returned to the true faith." Almost carefully she touched the arm of her future husband and whispered, "You must help me with this. I need your wisdom!"

It was a long night for Philip, but finally it ended and he returned to his apartment. For the next several days he acted as a prospective bridegroom should. "The one purpose," he said to his retainer, "is to have this woman bear a son. That would set heaven's final seal of approval on the match. Then Spain will rule England!"

At last the marriage came, and Mary put her dry little hand, like a withered leaf, in Philip's. Her thin lips moved in silent prayer, her nearsighted eyes, blank and blind with rapture, were fixed alternately upon the crucifix and on the plain gold ring that he put on her finger.

To her the marriage was the meaning for her existence. The old times would come again, the right and the ancient ways of serving God through his one true church and his viceroy, the pope. All just as it had been in her father's day when he'd gone to Mass with her mother and herself as a little girl, holding their hands.

This was in Mary's heart, but many hearts in England were filled with sadness as Mary Tudor was wed to Philip of Spain—for they feared the country was entering a dark and perilous hour.

And they were right.

Five

TILL DEATH DO
US PART

"The doctors are certain now that Queen Mary is with child."

Hannah glanced up from her embroidery, concern in her eyes. She saw that Will, who was writing a letter at the long table, had stopped abruptly as his father spoke.

Myles put his Bible down, studied the long shelves of books that lined the wall. His squarish face was strong in repose, but lines had appeared lately around the corners of his blue-gray eyes. Since Queen Mary had married Philip, Myles had grown more silent, more thoughtful, as he pondered the perils that lay ahead for those called by the name of "Lutheran" or "Protestant."

"The doctors can't be certain of the result," he said quietly, "especially at her age and with her delicate health. She may die in childbirth."

"But if the child lives, England might have another rebellion," William said gloomily.

"Yes, Will. What the queen cannot understand," Myles said, shaking his head faintly, "is that the country will never return to Catholicism."

"She is blind to not see it!" Will snapped, throwing his quill down and making a blotch on the table. He shook his head fiercely. "How can she miss that practically the entire country is furious with her for marrying Philip? Why can't her counselors convince her of her mistake?"

"It's too late, I'm afraid," Myles answered. "You must remember, Son, that Mary grew up under a devout Catholic mother. She would never divorce or abandon her husband. Queen Catherine wasn't able to hang on to King Henry VIII, but when she lost him to Anne Boleyn, she determined that her daughter would always be true to her faith."

Hannah listened quietly as the two spoke of the conditions of the times. She knew as well as her husband and son that they were on the razor edge of a terrible upheaval, and the thought of it brought grief to her heart. Finally she said quietly, "God will be with us, no matter what happens in politics."

Both men glanced up in surprise, then exchanged smiles. Will rose and went to kiss his mother on the cheek. Straightening up, he murmured, "I believe you, Mother. I learned that from you and Father a long time ago." He turned and walked quickly out of the room.

"He's like you, Hannah," Myles said as he too rose and came to sit beside her. He gently took her hand and smiled at her. "'He who finds a wife finds a good thing.'"

Hannah pulled his head down and kissed him, then held him tightly. "She who finds a husband finds a good thing, too."

"Is that in Tyndale's Bible?" Myles teased.

"No—but it's written on my heart!"

On the very morning they were speaking, Mary and Philip were walking along the river that flanked Hampton Court. She had come to the palace in April to have her baby. Hampton Court had been filched by her father from Cardinal Wolsey and had always been Mary's favorite home. The morning was clear as she walked beside the river, and she looked back to admire the red-brick palace, which rose like a cloud from the riverbed valley. She turned to Philip, who was holding a sprig of rosemary to his nose as they walked along the brick path. "Isn't it beautiful, Philip?"

"Very beautiful," he said, nodding. He spoke for a time of the castles in Spain, then smiled. "We will take our son there to see them some day."

Mary's face flushed and she reached for his hand. Philip took it, thinking as he did so how dry and old it seemed. He had been under no illusions about Mary's appearance, but it had been difficult for him to play the role of an attentive new husband. He had been happily married before to a woman he adored. After his wife died, he had taken a beautiful young woman for his mistress. To come from these young, passionate women to a woman dried with age had been difficult. Still, he had played his part well.

As a result, he usually got his own way, and now he said casually, "I think it would be wise to invite Lady Elizabeth for a visit." He did not miss the jealous glance that Mary gave him and was careful to show only a mild interest. "Since you have refused to put her to death, it would behoove us to come to terms with her."

"Terms! You don't know her! She wants to be queen of England!"

"I daresay she does." Philip smiled benignly. He reached out to stroke her hair, which still held traces of its youthful beauty. "But she will never be that. When our son is born, England will have a male heir to the throne." As he had known they would, his words calmed Mary, and she gave him a grateful smile.

What have I to fear from my sister? I have a husband—and she has none! For Mary to think of Elizabeth with charity had become impossible. When they were growing up, Mary had been much older. Both she and Elizabeth had been declared illegitimate by their father, and this had been a common bond. Now Mary had been declared legitimate, but that did not seem to sway the common people, who still appeared to prefer Elizabeth to their queen. *Elizabeth even looks like Father!* she thought angrily, then snapped, "She is a hypocrite—and worse! Oh, she is pretending to be a Catholic, but that is all false."

"Perhaps not—"

"And she charms every man she sees, though I don't know how!" Mary shot a suspicious glance at Philip. "I am afraid for her to meet you."

"How foolish!" Philip laughed. "You are my bride, and nothing can change that." He saw the anxiety in her eyes and said soothingly, "Invite her here. That will show that you are fair and just. And as for her charming me, my dear, if she does that, you can send her back to the Tower."

He spoke in jest and was slightly shocked when Mary's lips tightened and she nodded. "Yes! I can do that!"

The days passed, and the eyes of England were fixed on Mary, the queen—looking for the heir to the throne.

But the child did not come. The cradle, gorgeously decorated, sat in her room all ready for the day. Baby clothes and swaddling bands were piled high, some of the embroidery worked by herself. Even toys were all ready, a rattle with silver bells, a coral mounted in gold to cut his first tooth on, a jack-in-the-box, and even a painted hobbyhorse for him to ride.

But no child was born.

The doctors said soothingly, "Any day now, Your Majesty—!" But it was rumored they were saying such things only to comfort the distraught woman. And the people continued to wonder: Was the queen with child or wasn't she?

Elizabeth came to Hampton for a visit, and from the first day Mary looked for a sign of her charms working on Philip. And if one looks hard enough, it becomes possible to see almost anything. When she saw Philip riding with Elizabeth, she grew ill; and when he was brought to her, she cried out, "I might have died while you were out riding with—*her!*"

"No, my dear, you are well."

"She is a witch!" Mary insisted. "She is the daughter of a witch. Anne Boleyn had the beginning of a sixth finger on one hand—a sure sign of a witch!"

It was the first of many arguments, and time after time Mary had Elizabeth brought in. The young woman had to stand before the torrents of rage that flowed out of the queen, and at times Elizabeth was certain she was on her way back to the Tower.

And after each fit of rage, Mary would weep for hours, her hand on the decorated cradle, knowing that her only hope was to see it occupied by a new prince.

⁕⁕⁕

"I think there's nothing like an English morning in May." Hannah and Myles were walking through their garden, admiring the tiny explosions of color that were so bright they almost hurt the eyes. Leaning over, Hannah picked a fragile, sky-blue sweet william and brushed it against her cheek.

Myles had arrived only an hour earlier, and the two had breakfasted, then come out to enjoy the cool morning. He reached out and touched her cheek, saying, "You're more beautiful than any flower, Hannah."

"Oh, don't be foolish!"

He smiled and shook his head, but she saw something in his face that belied his seeming ease. "Is something wrong, Myles?"

"The queen has had her baby. A boy, I hear."

Hannah dropped the flower and turned to him. "How did you hear?"

"A ship from Antwerp arrived. They say the great bell has pealed, announcing the news of the birth of the child. A new prince of England."

They stood in the midst of the garden thinking of the past months. The baby was long overdue. The queen had been lying-in at Hampton Court, and finally the doctors had admitted they had

69

made a mistake in their date—that the child might not be born for a few weeks.

But Myles had heard it whispered that if a prince were produced, it would be no son of Philip and Mary, but hatched from a cuckoo's egg laid in the royal nest. "Did you hear about Mrs. Malt?"

"Why, no."

"She lives in Aldersgate. I have it on good report that she was asked by certain lords in disguise to give up her newborn son. But she said she would not—not for all the gold in the Tower."

"That cannot be true!"

"I agree, but I cannot help but wonder. In truth, it's been too long!"

That was exactly what many thought, and what some said. The time ran on, the doctors kept extending the date of the proposed birth—and *still* there was no child. Soon it was obvious to all that there would be no child. At long last the doctors released the news that the queen had suffered from a tumor, that there never had been a child.

Philip saw that his plan to join Spain and England by becoming king was spoiled. "I will never be accepted," he told his chief lieutenant, "except as a queen's consort. We must return to Spain."

And so it was in late August he bid Mary farewell, promising to return. He had spent a whole hateful year in England and nothing had been accomplished.

Mary insisted on accompanying him to Greenwich. As they drove through the streets, countrymen and cockneys yelled themselves hoarse, thronging round the litter of the sick woman. They yelled in defiance, showing her how they hated her husband and her church.

After Philip was gone and she was back in her palace, Mary walked slowly along the ornate halls. Her face was pale with sickness and twisted with anger. A deep rage boiled up in her that she could no more control than the winds or the sea.

She was alone. When she spoke her voice crackled with bitterness. "They are evil, these demons who fight against the true church! I have tried to be kind, but now we shall see! They may call me Bloody Mary before I am through, but I will have the heretics rooted out of my kingdom!"

Elizabeth was sent to Woodstock in the charge of faithful Sir Henry Bedingfeld. Never had her life been more in danger, and one day she used a diamond to scratch a bleak message on a pane of glass:

> Much suspected—of me,
> Nothing proved can be,
> Quoth Elizabeth, prisoner.

News of Queen Mary's continued bad health swept the country, but her health did not stop her from ordering a purge of those who stood fast against the Catholic Church. Over three hundred men and women were burned at the stake for heresy—including Bishop Cranmer, who had served Mary's father. Smithfield, where the executions took place, was mantled with the smoke like a black pall.

Just after dawn on October 16, 1555, William Wakefield entered the cell where Hugh Latimer and Nicholas Ridley were awaiting their execution. Latimer rose at once and came to embrace his pupil. He was pale and emaciated from his imprisonment, but his expression was no different from what it had always been: serene and kind.

"Will, my boy, I'm glad to see you."

The warmth of the greeting brought tears to Will's eyes. He

blinked them away and held on to the older man for a moment. He could feel the fragile body, and the thought of what would happen to it in three hours brought grief and anger.

"Mr. Latimer, is there *nothing* to be done?"

"Nothing, Will." As calmly as if he were in his study, the bishop turned to the table and picked up a bottle. "Sit down, have a glass of this sherry. It's very good—a gift from the sheriff."

Will sat down in the chair, his limbs trembling. He had not slept for two nights, and it had been a wild impulse that had brought him to Smithfield. His parents and Blanche had tried to dissuade him, but he had insisted doggedly, "I must go!"

Now that he was in the presence of the two men, he had no words. He stared mutely into the wineglass and shook his head. Finally it was Latimer who had to speak. "I'm glad you came, Will. I wanted to say good-bye to you."

"It's . . . it's *hard,* sir! I can't . . . tell you how I grieve! Though I'm sure it's harder on you, of course."

Latimer replaced the bottle and glanced over at his companion. Ridley was staring blankly at the wall and seemed not to be aware they had a visitor. The hand of death was on him and he had none of the cheerfulness of the other man.

"Why no, it's much harder on you, my boy," Latimer remarked. He sat down and studied the young man. "You see, I really believe in what the Bible says. Don't you?"

"Certainly, Mr. Latimer!"

"Then you will recall the words of Paul as he faced his exit from the world. Let me see . . ." He picked up a worn Bible from the table, thumbed through it, then said, "Ah, here it is." His voice was pleasant, and his mouth relaxed as he read, "'For I am hard pressed between the two, having a desire to depart and be with Christ, which is far better. Nevertheless, to remain in the flesh is more needful for you.'"

William Wakefield listened to the familiar words, and when

Latimer looked up at him, he said, "I think it *is* needful for you to remain here, sir! You are the shepherd of the flock."

"God will raise up other men, Will. But now is the time of my departure at hand, and I rejoice in it!"

"But—what of the pain and the humiliation!"

"Only a moment's pain, my lad, and then I will see him whom I have served so many years." He rose and moved to stand beside his fellow prisoner, putting his hand on the man's thin shoulder. "Is that not so, Mister Ridley?"

Ridley seemed to be recalled, and he answered numbly, "Yes, it is glorious to die for faith in Jesus."

Latimer kept his hand on Ridley's shoulder as he continued to speak. "Now, Will, you must take up the burdens of which I shall soon be free. Your faith is strong, and it has been my joy to see Christ formed in you. Others may be weak, and it will be your task to set them an example. Fight the good fight, my boy, and you will receive the reward of the good servant!"

Will remained in the cell for half an hour, and then another visitor came. As Will prepared to leave, Latimer rose and embraced him. "My son, you have been a joy to my heart. Be faithful to the Lord Jesus!"

After he left the cell, Will almost left Smithfield, but something kept him there. It was not the morbid curiosity that drew the mob, rather it was a need to see the faith of a man of God. He set his jaw and waited, praying and walking outside, and then when the shouts of the crowd grew louder, he moved inside and found a place to stand.

Latimer and Ridley had already been tied to the stakes. The crowd was noisy as the executioner piled the dry wood around their feet. Then there was a silence, and in that moment Will could hear Ridley weeping. His head was slumped down, and the sound of his crying was a pitiful thing.

Hugh Latimer turned his head and looked at his friend. His

voice was like a clear trumpet as he cried out, "Be of good comfort, Mister Ridley, and play the man. We shall this day light such a candle, by God's grace, in England, as I trust shall never be put out!"

His words sent a thrill along William Wakefield's nerves, and he knew that as long as he lived, the echoes of that cry would sound in his spirit. He watched as one of the men set fire to the faggots. Then came the sigh of the crowd, like wind trapped in a chimney on a winter's night.

The tongues of flame began to lick upward along the dry wood. It made a merry crackling sound—the same sound Will had always enjoyed when building a cozy fire to warm his room. The flames grew longer and more fierce, igniting the garments of the two men. Will's eyes were fixed in horror on his friend's face as the sparks flew upward and settled in his hair. His lips were moving in prayer and his eyes were turned upward.

Suddenly Will could bear no more. He turned and blindly made his way out of the arena, followed incessantly by the noise of the crowd. As he blinked back tears, he heard again the words of Hugh Latimer, bold and courageous, and knew that his friend was not afraid.

Like you, dear friend, I will not be afraid either, he vowed, lifting his head up. *By the grace of God, I will not be afraid!*

He made the long ride toward the country, seeing nothing of what passed before his eyes. He was an introspective young man by nature, and the scene that he had witnessed drove him to ponder the future. By the time he had reached Blanche Holly's home, he had made plans. Slipping from his horse, he gave the reins to a servant. Blanche came out to meet him as he approached the house.

"Will, come inside," she said quickly. She knew him well, and the strain on his face was plain.

He allowed her to lead him into the library and was grateful that her mother merely greeted him, then left. "We've been worried about you," Blanche said. "Was it—terrible?"

Even with the tension that had not left him, Will admired Blanche as she stood before him. She was tall and fine, with a supple figure. Her black eyes and dark brown hair were attractive, and there was a pleasing air of comfortable elegance. He drank in her presence, feeling it refresh his saddened and parched spirit.

"Yes, it was," he said wearily. She put out her hands, and he took them. They were warm and strong, and suddenly he drew her close.

Blanche felt the tension in Will, and she held him tightly, her lips broad and maternal. *If he would only weep!* she thought, but knew he likely would never do that. There was little that a woman could do in such a case, but she knew by the way he clung to her that she was a comfort.

Finally he drew back and his eyes were clearer. "I don't want to talk about it, not the details, anyway. But I must tell you of Mr. Latimer's last words."

Blanche listened as he repeated the bishop's remarks, and when he was through, she whispered, "He was a fearsome man, Hugh Latimer!"

"He was that! I didn't know a man could go to that kind of death with such—such joy!"

Blanche looked at her beloved with compassion. "You will miss him."

"Yes, I will."

"What will happen now?"

Will understood what she meant. "You fear for my safety. Well, I can't give you comfort." He turned from her and went to stare out the window. She moved to stand beside him, and he was intensely aware of her presence. It had always been like that. All she had to do was enter a room where he was, and all his senses seemed to grow sharper. Not knowing what to say, he watched as a fat young coney hopped across the yard, stopped in the center of a flowerbed, and began to nibble the stalks. Suddenly there was a roar of a hound, and the small animal exploded into a dead run. Will watched as the black hound closed the distance; and then, just as the coney was five feet from shelter, the dog seized the smaller animal and killed him with one shake of his head.

Abruptly Will turned to face the woman standing close to him. "Blanche, you and I must not see each other any longer." He saw his words strike against her, and he added hurriedly, "It would be dangerous for you."

She met his eyes. "Do you love me, Will?"

"Why—of course!"

"Do you believe I love you?"

"Yes, but that's—"

She lifted her hand and placed it over his lips. A smile tilted her lips, and her eyes were soft and fierce all at once. "I love you, William Wakefield, and we must never be parted. God made us for each other. Isn't that what we've always said?"

Will nodded, then whispered huskily, "You are a fearsome woman, Blanche Holly!"

"I am a woman in love," she said simply and drew his head down. When she pulled away, she said, "We must go and be married."

"Now?"

"If we wait, our parents will object. I'll get my things. You go harness the buggy. We can get married today."

Will had never seen such determination in Blanche. He tried to protest, but found that she was not to be dissuaded. Finally he said in desperation, "We don't know how long we'll have together."

"We'll have what God gives us, Will," Blanche said calmly. "Now—go harness the team."

They were married that day, and when they were in their room in the inn that night, he held her tightly. She stirred in his arms and lifted her lips for his kiss. They clung to each other, and finally Blanche said, "We have each other, Will. That's enough! So many men and women never have love like ours." She saw the doubt creep into his eyes and whispered, "For as long as God gives us—fifty years or fifty days—we'll have each other!"

Six

"I WILL LIVE IN OUR SON!"

I t was a cool English February morning in 1558 when Myles Wakefield rode up to his son's home. Dismounting, he walked slowly up the stairs to the door and knocked. The door opened and Blanche stood there, looking at him intently. Myles could not form words, but he did not need to do so. As soon as Blanche saw her father-in-law's face, she knew all.

"It's Will, isn't it?"

Myles moved to stand in the center of the room, his face pale. He had never dreaded anything more than what he now was forced to do. Slowly he nodded, and the bitter words were wrung from him. "He was arrested after the meeting on charges of heresy."

A sword seemed to pierce Blanche's heart, and she suddenly swayed. At once Myles leaped forward and, taking her arm, led her to a velvet-covered lounge. "Here, sit down, my dear," he said, then sat beside her. As he watched her struggle against the faintness, a bitter thought tolled through his brain: *Just over two years—two short years! That's all they had!* Then he said as heartily as he could, "We mustn't give up. It surely will mean prison, but we can hope."

Blanche took a deep breath, and some color came back into her cheeks. She examined Myles's face, then shook her head. "For some that would be the penalty, but not for Will." She met his eyes, and her expression stilled his objection. "We both know that, Myles. Will has been a marked man. Mary's agents have been after him for weeks."

Myles wanted to argue, to explain—but he knew she was right. Still he said strongly, "There's always hope, my dear. We must have faith in God."

Blanche sat quietly for a time, aware of Myles's forced effort to be optimistic. Finally she said, "I must go to him, Myles—at once."

"I don't know that they will let you see him."

"I will stay until they do."

Myles shrugged. He knew his daughter-in-law was a young woman of iron will. "Get some clothes. I'll rent you a room in London so you can visit Will as often as possible."

Blanche put her hand on his strong arm. "You and Hannah . . . are suffering terribly." He could not reply, and she moved away and went to her room to pack. When she returned, they walked from the house together. He had brought his carriage, and he handed her in, then said to the driver, "London. And quickly, Ned."

As the guards brought Will to the place that so many feared, he looked up at the four spires that marked the Tower of London. He had to pass through several gates, and he found himself amazed by the heart of the fortress, the White Tower. He had expected a palace, not a citadel, and so was unprepared for the city-within-a-city, which covered some thirteen acres—all of it swarming with soldiers and guards.

Four hundred years old, this Tower—a place of ghosts, of history, and of legend at its most flamboyant. It contained, Will's father had told him, not only a council chamber, chapel, and banqueting house, but barracks, dungeons, and the torture chamber as well. An involuntary shiver swept him as he thought of the latter, and he steeled himself, determined not to show fear.

Finally he was brought to a cell that lay buried in a labyrinth of passageways. The guard nodded at the door, grunted, "Get in," and waited only long enough for Will to enter before he slammed the door. The harsh metallic clanging of the bolt made Will flinch—but he was alone now, and no one could see his reaction.

The cell was no more than ten feet square with a barred window high up in the wall. At once he moved the wooden bunk under it, and by stretching up on his toes, managed to see the outside—which consisted of a strip of pavement and some sort of exercise area flanked by an ancient stone wall. Getting down, he peered around, the dim light barely illuminating the cell. There was no ventilation, save for the window, and no candle. The only furnishings consisted of a pallet bed, a stool, and a bucket in one corner.

Slowly Will sat down on the bed and leaned back against the stone wall. He had dreaded this moment for months, for he was a man who loved the outdoors. Being kept inside by even a few day's sickness had been a torture for him all his life—and now he was here!

Time crawled on, and the light faded until the room was in total darkness, save a thin sliver of light that outlined the bottom of his cell door. Lying back on his bed, he dozed fitfully, awakening nervously as muted sounds from the corridor reached him. Lying there, he found it impossible to fall asleep except after what seemed like hours. Sleep would have been a blessing—anything to escape the sense of being buried alive!

When he was awake, William's active mind tortured him by playing through the scenes that he knew would come. This cell would not be the worst of it, of that much he was certain. He thought of Latimer and Ridley and of many others among his acquaintances who had died in the fires of Smithfield—and it was a struggle for him to keep from beating his fists against the wall and screaming to be released.

It would have been useless, anyway. There would be no release. As this truth permeated his being, one word cried out in his mind: *Blanche!* A deep pain shot through him and he leaned his head back, clenching his eyes closed.

What will happen to her? he thought time after time during the night as his mind turned again and again toward the moment when he would be tied to a stake. His keen imagination took him through the steps with minute detail—and he could almost smell the smoke and hear the crackling of the faggots.

Finally morning arrived, and a guard came with food. Will tried to elicit a word from him, but the man merely cursed, harshly slamming the door behind him. Again the click of the lock was like a death knell.

The day passed, and the night came. Will had not yet been able to eat the food the guard had left, but in the darkness he groped until he found it. It was cold and greasy, but he ate it, then drank thirstily from the jug of lukewarm water.

Afterward he paced the floor for hours to keep warm. Anything was better than curling up beneath the thin, evil-smelling blanket they had given him. Another morning came, the guard came with more food, emptied the bucket, then left the prisoner alone. The day moved slowly, and many times Will stood on the bunk, peering out the window. Twice he saw guards hurrying by, but it was evidently a little-used section of the Tower. He studied the bars, picking at the mortar with his thumbnail—thinking of escape.

That's foolish! No one escapes from this place! He paced the floor and thought, *My grandfather was kept in the Tower once. I wonder if it was in this cell?* The thought crossed his mind that his grandfather had been released from the Tower and had lived many years—but he dismissed it. *He didn't live in the days of Bloody Mary!*

Noon came and passed and then afternoon began to wane. He was sitting on his bunk staring at the wall when the sound of the bolt in his door sliding open brought him to his feet. The door swung in, and the guard said, "Only ten minutes!" He leaned over, placed a candle on the floor, then left, slamming the door shut.

Unaccustomed to the light that filled the doorway, Will could see only a dim form. Then he felt arms around him, and Blanche's voice whispered, "Oh, Husband!"

"Blanche!"

The two clung to each other, and in the fetid cell he caught the sweet scent of violets that always surrounded her. He breathed deeply, remembering their wondrous times together, and felt a calm come over him. "How did you get in?" he whispered.

"Your father bribed the jailer, I think!" She drew back and peered at his face. "Are you all right, Will?"

"Yes, they haven't harmed me." Now that she was here, he could think of nothing to say. Staring at her, she seemed more like a dream than reality. As if to assure himself of her presence, he stroked her smooth cheek with a hand that trembled. "I'm sorry you have to come to such a place as this."

Blanche shook her head violently, whispering, "Will, it's all right."

"No, it's not," he muttered grimly, then held her again. He kissed her hair, then her cheek. "It's going to be bad, Blanche."

"Will—"

"I should never have married you," he said bitterly.

"Don't say that!" Blanche put her hand up and covered his mouth, then hesitated. Finally she whispered, "We're going to have a child, Will."

Wakefield stood still, his heart seeming to pound. He swallowed, then whispered, "Blanche, are you certain?"

"Yes!"

Her voice was quiet and there was pride in it. But Will groaned and turned from her. "Blanche . . . this is . . . the hardest of all!"

She took his arm, pulling him around to face her. "You must not be sorry, Will. You must not!"

"How can I help it? What will you do?"

"I will do as God tells me, just as you and I have done together."

"The child will have no father!"

"You don't know that," she insisted. "But if you are taken, God is the father of the fatherless. He will be with us, my dear, no matter what happens."

She stood there, holding him, and all too soon the door opened, and the guard spoke harshly. Blanche reached up to touch Will's face with gentle fingers, and her face filled with a tender love. "I must go, beloved. But we will talk again. I had to see you, to tell you about the child—and to give you this." She passed him a small package, then kissed him while he held her tightly.

They spoke for what seemed like only a few seconds, and then the guard spoke up again. "Come now, it's time!"

The door closed with a terrible bang, and Will was alone again. The candle flickered, the yellow flame standing straight in the airless cell. He looked down at the object she had given him and saw that it was a small Bible—one of Tyndale's.

He sat down and tried to read, but her words echoed in his mind. He had not once considered such a thing—to leave a widow *and* a child. The desire to live rose in him, and he had to clamp his lips together to stop the moan that rose in his chest. *"Play the man, Mister Ridley."* Hugh Latimer's last words rang in his mind, almost as clearly as if they were being spoken in that dark cell. With unsteady hands, Will opened the small book and began to read.

Elizabeth stared at the tall man who stood before her, then said, "Myles, you know not what you ask!"

Myles Wakefield bowed his head slightly, but said adamantly, "Aye, Princess Elizabeth, I know it full well."

The princess's pale eyes narrowed, and she shook her head in disbelief. "You want me to go to my sister and ask a pardon for your son?"

"Yes, Princess." Myles straightened and his mouth grew tight. "I have always hated to ask favors, and I would not do so for myself. But this is my firstborn son, and I would do anything to save him."

A hot reply leaped to her lips. Many came to Elizabeth Tudor for favors, but no one would dare ask for something like this! She studied the honest face of the man in front of her, and she remembered his many kindnesses—his unfailing loyalty when it had not been popular to show favor to an illegitimate princess. Her lips softened, and she said gently, "Myles, you could not have picked a worse advocate! My sister despises me. If anything, it would make matters worse for your son if I begged her to release him."

"Nothing can make the matter worse," Myles said simply. He drew himself up with an effort and bowed his head. "But I was wrong to trouble you. Those slender shoulders of yours have borne too many burdens. Forgive me."

Elizabeth waited until he had reached the threshold, then cried out, "Myles! I—I will try."

He came back at once and knelt before her. Moved by his action, she touched his shoulder. He rose and said huskily, "Thank you, Princess. With all my heart!"

And then he was gone, leaving the tall woman with confusion. She had made an impulsive promise—something she rarely did.

But she knew that time was racing and so sent at once, asking for an audience with her sister. To her great surprise, she received a note the next morning commanding her to come to the palace.

Soon she was ushered into Mary's private quarters. The queen did not rise, but gave her a direct look. "Well, what is it?" she demanded.

"I hardly know how to put my request, Your Majesty." Elizabeth hesitated. "It will not please you."

"Tell me what you want," Mary snapped. "I shall decide if it pleases me." Mary was looking ill. She had lost weight since Philip's departure, and her eyes looked hollow.

"Sir Myles Wakefield came to see me yesterday," Elizabeth said carefully. She was aware that she was treading on dangerous ground, and for a moment her courage failed and she could not speak.

Mary glanced at her sharply, then said with outrage, "And he asked you to beg for the life of his son, the heretic?"

"Yes, Your Majesty."

Mary's face, pale as it was, suddenly flushed with rage. She raised her great voice, always shocking in so small a woman, and began to scream. "You *dare* to come into my presence with such a request? You know the man is a heretic! You know it because you yourself are exactly the same!"

"No, Your Majesty—!" Elizabeth protested, but she saw at once that her sister was gripped by one of her uncontrollable rages. Silently she stood there, bearing the brunt of the woman's fury, until finally Mary was gasping for breath. She had known Mary to have men *and* women sent to their deaths when in such rages, and she fully expected to be sent to the Tower.

But Mary seemed to have expended her rage. She sat there, her bosom heaving, and finally said, "Get out before I have you sent to join that heretic."

"Yes, Your Majesty," Elizabeth whispered and left the room at once. Her heart was beating fast, and when she had calmed

herself, she wrote a simple, sad note: "Myles, it was hopeless—
though I tried." Sealing it, she gave it to a servant she trusted,
along with a coin. "Be certain to deliver this into the hands of Sir
Myles Wakefield."

Later, when she was alone, she let the grief wash over her. Myles
was one of her most loyal and cherished friends, and she hated
that he must endure the pain he now faced. But she knew that
Mary was implacable.

***

Will stood up and his parents embraced him. His mother was
weeping, but she whispered, "Oh, my boy, I'm proud of you!" She
kissed him, then, her shoulders shaking, turned and moved to the
door, where the guard was waiting.

Myles kept his voice even with an effort as he took his son's
hand. He said simply, "Will, you are God's man. We will—meet
again."

At once Will nodded, then not trusting himself, he said, "Yes,
Father, Christians always meet again. God bless you. I know you'll
be a father to Blanche. And to the child."

"Yes! You have my word, Son!"

Then Myles left the room, his arm around Hannah. As they left,
Blanche entered. She came to him at once and slipped her arms
around him, whispering, "Will, my darling!"

"Blanche, we have only a moment." Will drew back, his eyes
calm, his voice steady and clear. "Sit down. I want to tell you
something."

When they were seated, he began to tell her how God had
strengthened him. "At first I was terribly afraid, but in these last
days God has given me a peace I never dreamed of."

"I know what you mean." Blanche nodded. "He's given me his
peace as well."

"I'll miss so many things. I'll miss you most, of course. And I'll miss the land and the rivers of England."

"You'll have a far better land!"

He smiled and kissed her hand. "Yes, you are right. That is what God has showed me. I'll miss the child—my son, as you insist he will be."

"God has told me it will be a boy," Blanche said quietly.

"I believe you." Will spoke quietly of some things that had been on his heart concerning the child to come, then said, "Know this, my dear, that you will have a friend in my father. And God will help you."

"Is—is there anything else . . . about our son?"

Will said slowly, "I am leaving this world for a better one. But in one way, I will still be here. I will live in our son, Blanche." His eyes grew bright, and his voice had a triumphant note. "That's what God has shown me in my cell—that when I am gone, the son I leave will be doing some of the things that I will never be permitted to do. I've written him a letter." He drew it out of his pocket. "Give it to him when he's able to understand."

They talked until the door opened, and then they rose. Will put his arms around her, whispering, "God will be with you and the boy. His name will be Robin."

"Yes, my love." Blanche held him fiercely, then released him slowly. "You have been my life," she said simply, then turned and left the room.

Standing alone, Will nodded and whispered, "And you have been mine, sweetheart!"

Myles and Hannah embraced Blanche, and they left the prison in silence. When Will was first arrested, Myles had told Blanche that Wakefield was her home. Now he helped his wife and his daughter-in-law into the carriage, and they left London as rapidly as possible.

They were still within hearing distance of the bells of the city when the bells tolled twelve, the hour set for Will's execution. Blanche uttered one cry and fell into Hannah's arms. None of the three spoke, and it seemed to Myles as though the earth and all of time had stopped. He closed his eyes, fighting the tears of grief, and whispered brokenly, "Father, I give thee my son. Welcome him home."

Myles Wakefield had assigned the task of bringing his son's body home to his faithful steward, Hal Bedlow—a task that Bedlow performed with great care and sadness. Two days later, the funeral was held in the open air. The pastor of the local church had volunteered to have it in the parish church, but Myles knew that this might get the good man thrown out of his position, if not into the Tower.

A large crowd was gathered around the open grave—the family, the servants, and many neighbors who had loved Will. They listened as Myles himself spoke the final words. He told them simply what a fine son Will had been, then spoke of his son's love for God. He said nothing about the state, but ended by reading from the Bible that Will had been reading in his cell. "'This mortal must put on immortality . . . death is swallowed up in victory. O death, where is your sting? O Hades, where is your victory? But thanks be to God, who gives us the victory through our Lord, Jesus Christ.'"

Then he closed the Bible and said, "William was faithful unto death. Jesus Christ was his Savior. Though Will cannot come to us, we can go to him. And one day we *will* meet again."

Blanche stood beside Hannah, her face covered with a veil. She had said nothing during the service, but now she whispered in echo to Myles's words: "Yes, I will come to you, Will!"

A FRAIL CRY

The thin light of a dim September sun filtered through a high window, illuminating the woman who sat on a large chair. Tiny motes danced in the golden beams, and the amber light formed a sort of halo over the head of the child at her feet.

Suddenly Blanche Wakefield was grasped with a spasm of pain so vicious that a slight moan escaped her lips. She clenched her fists as nausea seized her, then slumped back in her chair, her lips pressed close together.

"Aunt Blanche—are you sick?"

Alice Wakefield scrambled to her feet at once, her large blue eyes filled with worry. She had been sitting at Blanche's feet listening to her read. The only daughter of Myles and Hannah Wakefield, she was still very shy even at the age of ten. Not quick to make friends, the girl had not accepted her sister-in-law at first. Blanche's kindness, however, had soon won her over. Both she and her brother, Thomas, had learned that their new "aunt" knew many games and was almost always available to play them. Tom, at the age of fifteen, pretended to be above some of them, but Alice noticed that he was usually there when playtime arrived.

"Oh no, Alice," Blanche said, summoning up a smile. "I'm just a little dizzy." She reached out and touched the golden hair of the girl who was looking up at her with a worried expression. "When a woman is going to have a baby, sometimes she gets a little dizzy."

"When will the baby come?"

Blanche laughed, ignoring the pain that gripped her stomach. "Oh, by November." She reached out her arms, and Alice came to her at once. Hugging the child, Blanche whispered, "Won't that be something to thank the good Lord for? A brand-new baby who'll grow up to be just like your brother Will?"

"But—how do you know it will be a boy, Aunt Blanche?"

"The Lord told me."

Alice stared at Blanche, her oval face still as she pondered that fact. "What did God sound like? Did he have a big voice like Rev. Holland?"

Blanche shook her head, waiting for the pain to fade, then found a smile. "God doesn't usually speak out loud." As she explained how God moved in the heart, she thought of how precious Alice and Tom had become to her. She had never had a niece or nephew, and these two had helped to keep her mind off the loss of Will.

Thank God for Myles and Hannah, Blanche thought, as she had done many times in the past few months. Her own mother had died when she was ten, and her father had married a woman who was sickly. If not for Will's parents, Blanche would have had no place to go, but they welcomed her with open arms. She had been with them now for seven months—since February—and the time had been precious to her.

I can scarcely believe it is already September, she thought, glancing at the calendar she had placed on the wall. *Only two more months and I'll have my baby.*

Alice asked suddenly, "Aunt Blanche, may I take care of him?"

"Of course you may, dear!"

The door opened and Hannah entered, fresh linens piled high

in her arms. "Alice, Aunt Blanche has read to you enough," she said firmly. "She needs to lie down and rest."

"But, Mother, she was reading the new book to me."

"She can read it later." Placing the linens on a table, Hannah nodded. "Off with you now, but you may have one of the tarts I left out to cool." As Alice darted out, Hannah called after her, "Only *one,* mind you!"

The door slammed, and both women blinked at the sound. Blanche said, "She's so much company for me, Hannah." She started to get up. "Now, let me put the linens in the chest."

"You'll do no such thing! What you will do is lie down on that bed after I've changed the sheets," Hannah announced. She moved to the table and began storing the linens, speaking cheerfully of little things. As she stripped the bed and put the new sheets in place, she glanced at the young woman who sat so quietly. Concern creased Hannah's forehead. *She's not well—we'll have to ask the doctor to come back and take a look at her.*

Blanche looked up and caught the expression on Hannah's face. "Don't worry about me. I'm fine."

Hannah blinked with surprise, but she had learned that her daughter-in-law was adept in reading people. Giving the sheet a final smoothing, she moved to take a seat across from Blanche. "It won't hurt to have Doctor Gilley come by."

"No, it won't hurt." Blanche's agreement was belied by her tone, which clearly said: *It won't do any good, either.* But the younger woman knew both Hannah and Myles were worried about her. She'd had a difficult pregnancy. Not just the usual morning sickness, but terrible nausea and pains that went through her groin and stomach like a white-hot sword. It had been impossible to hide the pain, though Blanche had tried not to complain.

"I'll be glad when the baby comes," Hannah murmured. "It's been such a hard time for you."

"A hard time for you and Myles, too."

"We've been blessed to have you, my dear. You've been such a good friend to Alice. And to Tom."

They sat there talking quietly until they heard the outside door slam. "That will be Myles." Hannah nodded. "He's never closed a door quietly in his life!" She smiled then, adding, "Alice and Tom both have learned that's the only way to close a door."

Voices came faintly, then the door opened and Myles entered with Alice on his back and Tom clinging to his hand. It was a picture that stayed with Blanche—the way the children clung to Myles and the loving care he took with them. *I wish all fathers were as gentle with their children.*

"When's supper?" Myles demanded.

Hannah glared at him. "Just *one* time, Myles Wakefield, I wish you'd say something when you come home besides 'When's supper?'"

Myles winked at Tom, but kept a straight face as he answered, "Well, when a man has to beg for his supper, things have come to a pretty pass!" He suddenly plucked Alice from his back and tossed her into the air, making her squeal with delight, then set her on her feet. Turning to Tom he demanded, "I don't suppose you'd care to go hunting early in the morning, would you, boy?"

"Yes, sir!"

"All right, go to the shed and get the gear ready. And no arguments when I pull you out of bed before dawn tomorrow!"

Tom grinned and dashed out of the room, followed by Alice, who was never discouraged by her brother's remarks about how troublesome younger sisters were. Alice slammed the door, and Hannah looked up with a hopeless gesture. Myles came to his wife, bent over and kissed her cheek—then did the same with Blanche. "God is good to me, letting me live with the two best-looking women in all England!"

"Never mind all that!" Hannah said briskly. "Did you bring the cloth I ordered from town?"

"Cloth?"

Hannah shook her head in disgust. "I *knew* you'd get to talking and forget!"

Myles grinned at her, looking very young in the fading sunlight. "Well, I'll have you to understand I *did* get the cloth—and some ribbons to go with it. Now, you can start apologizing for treating the best husband anywhere in such a shameful manner!"

Blanche sat there, saying little but enjoying the banter between the two. Her own observation of married couples had been limited, and before her own marriage she had reached the conclusion that marriage seemed to be a rather dreary affair. A pang of regret struck her, strong and intense. *Will and I were like these two—always having fun and joking. I can see now he learned it from his parents. And we could have taught the same to our children.* . . . The grief over her loss was never totally gone, and now she struggled to subdue her thoughts. It served no good to dwell on the fact that she would never have such a joyful, content home with Will.

Drawing a breath, she looked intently at her father-in-law. "Is there any news, Myles?"

He hesitated, then nodded glumly. "Giles Stafford has been arrested."

"Oh, no!" Hannah exclaimed. "On what charge?"

"The usual. Heresy."

His words seemed to hang in the air, and Hannah quickly rose and busied herself with lighting the candles. "I grieve to hear it. He's a good man."

"There are others," Myles said. He had lost his lightheartedness, and the planes of his face sharpened. The candles cast a glow on his face, showing the strain in his expression. Clearly, the past three months had been hard beyond belief for him. The agents of the state had been convinced that as the father of a heretic, he had been the source of his son's determined stand against the Catholic Church. The Wakefields had been spied upon, and their home had even been infiltrated by spies. Myles had been called three times to London to testify before the Council, and both Hannah and Blanche knew that he had come close to being arrested.

Now he added quickly, "There is one ray of hope."

"What is that?" Hannah asked.

"The queen is very ill. And though I hate to find hope in the misfortune of another, this could be the thing that God will use to save us."

A silence fell over the room, and Myles shrugged. "The truth is that as long as Mary is on the throne, no Protestant in England is safe. She's determined to root out and destroy those who don't hold Catholic views."

"She's always been sickly, hasn't she?" Blanche asked. "And yet she survives."

"Yes, but I have it on good report that this is different." Myles grimaced, then added, "As I say, I don't wish Her Majesty any ill fortune, but—"

"It's difficult not to hate her, isn't it?" Blanche murmured. "But we must not!"

"No, you are right, Daughter." Myles nodded. "I've struggled much with this, but Scripture is clear."

"When Robin grows up," Blanche said quietly, "he must one day hear how his father died at the hand of Queen Mary and the Catholic Church. It would be easy for him to learn to hate those who killed his father, but that must not be."

"No, we will see that he doesn't fall into that trap."

Blanche's delicate features glowed under the amber light of the candles, and her soft lips grew firm. She reached out her hands, and when they were taken by the two near her, she said, "We will pray that Robin will be a man of love, not hate."

"Yes, my dear," Hannah agreed at once. "Those who allow bitterness and hatred to rule their hearts only destroy themselves."

The three bowed their heads and prayed for the child who was to come. A holy quietness filled the room, and Blanche knew that God had heard—and that he would be faithful to keep her son from the perils of bitterness.

━━━⟡━━━

The year of 1558 was a full year for deaths. Emperor Charles V, after a life of ruling an empire, laid aside his crown, his robe, his power—and entered the kingdom of death as do all other human beings: naked and alone. Cardinal Pole, the man Mary had brought from Rome to impose Catholicism on England, died the same year, totally conscious that he had failed in his task.

Queen Mary of England died before dawn on the morning of November 17, 1558. The last three years of her life had been nothing but increasing bad health, unhappiness, and disillusionment. It had been a time of economic depression and political unrest, all made worse by the religious persecution which, she came to realize, would forever darken the memory of her reign.

Indeed, at the queen's death, there was little pretense of mourning. The church bells pealed and bonfires illuminated the streets, but the entire nation ate, drank, and rejoiced that Bloody Mary's time was ended—and that the reign of the new monarch, Queen Elizabeth, was about to begin.

Sir Robert Dudley, the earl and son of the same John Dudley who had led the revolt against Queen Mary, rode through fields that were burning with gold and red. He had escaped the catastrophe that his father had brought upon his family and had long been a favorite of Elizabeth's. The two of them had formed a firm relationship in the Tower, and if he had not been married, she would have considered him for a husband.

On this day, he found Elizabeth sitting under an oak tree, and he gave her a loud salutation. She rose to greet him, her eyes alive with anticipation—as they always seemed to be when he appeared.

"The old queen is dead," he cried when he had dismounted and came to bow before her. "You are queen, Elizabeth!" The young woman laughed for joy, and he took her hands to cry out, "All England will be laughing now!"

He spoke truly, for the crowds that lined the roads as Elizabeth went to London to be crowned laughed with joy when they saw her. She wore sparkling white, and her red hair glowed with a pale fire. She knew that the bookmakers of Europe gave her six months to rule on her shaky throne, but the gloomy predictions did not dim the joy that rose in her—and that was reflected in most of her subjects.

Her first test came later at Somerset House, when all her lords and ladies and foreign envoys thronged before her. She spoke to them in Latin, French, Italian, and most often in English. The words flowed from her curved red lips, sounding with the same direct ring as similar words had done from her father's straight-cut mouth.

Then the grandee of Spain, with the diamond Order of the Golden Fleece, approached her. The room fell silent, for all knew that this man was among the greatest of Spanish noblemen—and that he had come to determine what the queen's policy toward the Roman Church would be. Very carefully, he asked, "How may I serve Your Majesty?"

In effect, the grandee was asking if she would proclaim herself Protestant or Papist. Elizabeth well understood the danger. If she defied Rome, she would almost certainly lose the crown in a war with Spain or France. On the other hand, if she proclaimed herself Roman Catholic, she would abandon all those who had supported her during Mary's bloody reign.

In all that vast assemblage, she stood alone, but her eyes never faltered. She let the silence run on, then said gravely, "My intent is to serve God with all my heart and soul."

Well, there was nothing the pope's emissary could say to that! Her reply delighted her court, and a murmur of laughter spread around the room.

Safe for the moment! she thought, exhilarated. *But there will be other tests.* She did not know how she would fare, but of one thing she was certain: she was going to rule England. And that was enough.

She kept her delicate balance between the two forces until her coronation day arrived on January 15, 1559. Dressed all in cloth of gold with jewels on her red-gold head, she was escorted to the ceremony in a chariot, followed by a procession of a thousand glittering horsemen. On the way, the crowds broke through again and again—and she did what Mary could never have done. She received them with joy, gathering into her arms simple winter nosegays that poor women and ragged boys threw into her chariot.

"Look at that!" The speaker was a Catholic priest who was sullen and morose as the chariot passed. "She pretends, yet she cares nothing for them, the common people! She is making a new religion for them, I tell you. A Protestant religion! She will be burning *us* as her sister burned the heretics!"

The ceremony went on, despite the fact that it was difficult to find Catholic bishops to serve. But Elizabeth smiled as the sacerdotal robe of gold was placed upon her, in the same ritual that consecrates a bishop. Her spirit soared as she thought of the years to come. She ended the ceremony, the orb and scepter in her hands glittering in the wintry light of day, and on her head the great ruby of the Black Prince which Henry V had won at Agincourt. Then a cry went up from all that seemed to shake the earth.

On the very day that Mary died and Elizabeth became queen of England, November 17, 1558, Blanche Wakefield stretched herself in agony on the bed. After over twenty hours of labor, she was near death, but her spirit rose and she would not surrender.

Outside the room where the doctor and the midwife were cloistered with Blanche, Myles stood rigidly, his teeth set and his fists clenched. "How much longer can she bear this?" he demanded, his voice hoarse.

Hannah's face was drawn as she came to stand beside him. She had no answer. She could only shake her head in silence and put her arm around him. They stood there mutely, having long since said all that could be said. The labor had come quickly, but it would not end. The doctor could give them no encouragement.

"She is not doing well," he muttered. "There is some problem, as you know. Something beyond my skill."

As the hours dragged on with no relief, Myles turned to Hannah, his face drawn and pale. "I didn't know it could be like this for a woman!"

"Our children came easy," Hannah said. "We were fortunate." She was tense with apprehension, for she was wiser in these things than Myles. Now she wanted to give him some encouragement, but feared to raise false hopes. "Could you eat something?"

"No!"

She knew he didn't intend to be sharp, that it came from his concern for Blanche—and she went to him again, wrapping her arms around him in comfort. Clinging together, they waited. Finally, the door opened and Doctor Gilley stepped out. At once Myles moved to stand in front of him. "Is she well?" he demanded.

Dr. Gilley was a middle-aged man, more skilled at his profession than many others. He had a high forehead, dark blue eyes, and a firm mouth. Drawing his lips together he shook his head glumly. "I do not like to tell you, Sir Myles, but your daughter-in-law cannot—" He broke off and glanced at Hannah, then amended what he had planned to say. "She is in serious condition—very serious!"

Hannah lifted her eyes to his and held his gaze. "You were going to say she cannot live."

Gilley lowered his eyes and stared at the floor. "I do fear she cannot. I am sorry." Frustration brought a grunt from him, and his lips twisted. "I cannot understand it! She is outwardly a healthy young woman—she should have had no trouble. But she is dying, and I can do nothing for her!"

"What about the child, Doctor?" Myles asked, his lips drawn into a bitter line.

"A fine boy, healthy in every way."

"May we go in?"

"Yes, there is no harm in visitors."

Myles moved to the door, then hesitated. Turning to Hannah he whispered hoarsely, "Why has this happened? *Why?*"

"God knows, my dear. And we can only trust him. Come, Blanche needs us."

As they entered the room, Myles saw the midwife cleaning the child. He moved to one side of the bed, Hannah to the other. As he looked down at Blanche, his heart seemed to miss a beat, for he thought she was dead.

But Hannah leaned over, gently took the limp hand, and whispered, "Blanche?" The dying woman's eyelids flickered, then slowly lifted. "Blanche, you have a fine baby. A boy, as you have said for all this time. Robin . . . and he is healthy and strong."

Blanche's face was swollen and drawn, and her cheeks were pale, almost colorless. But when she looked at them, she whispered, "God is faithful." Then she turned her head and said in a stronger tone, "Let me have him. Please."

Hannah stepped beside the midwife, took the small bundle, and moved back to the bed. She placed the child beside Blanche, pulling back the blanket to expose the tiny face. "He's like his father, Blanche."

Carefully the new mother examined her child, and her lips curved in a tired smile as she traced the soft red cheek with her forefinger. "Oh yes, he is like Will."

"Like you, too, Daughter," Myles said, struggling to keep his voice steady. "I can see both of you in him. He is a fine boy!"

Hannah and Myles stood there for as long as they dared, watching while Blanche spoke in ever-weakening whispers, crooning over the baby. Then she grew quiet.

"Shall I move him?" Hannah asked.

"In a little while." Blanche didn't turn her head. She was too weary for even that now. Her eyes clung to her child's face, and for a long time her lips moved silently.

Then she turned to face the two who had shown her so much love and support, and when she spoke, her breathing was so faint that she could barely speak. "Don't . . . let him . . . hate," she whispered, then strained to say something else, but could not frame the words.

And then, even as life left her, a moment's strength came. She opened her eyes, and there was peace there as she said clearly, "Teach our son . . . to love!" Suddenly she arched her back, drawing in a deep breath—and a radiant smile touched her weary lips. "Will—?" she whispered, then, sighing softly, she closed her eyes and was still.

For a moment, silence reigned in the room. Then Myles whispered, "She's gone!"

"Yes," Hannah said, tears filling her eyes, "but she left something of herself. And something of Will."

"Yes, something of both of them."

Myles picked up the baby, and Hannah arranged Blanche's still hands, then brushed her hair back. Finally she moved to stand beside her husband, and both of them looked down at the small bit of humanity who suddenly began to cry. It was a frail cry, as if the babe knew he'd lost something—or so Myles fancied.

"Don't cry, Son," he said gently, reaching down to lift the infant in his arms. "You're not alone. You have those that love you."

Hannah's eyes were suddenly blinded, and she dashed the tears away. But she said almost fiercely, "Yes, and you will learn to love, Robin Wakefield! I swear it!"

"Amen!" Myles echoed, pulling Hannah into the circle of his arm. They clung together, each thinking of the years ahead. The memory of their son was very strong within both of them, and as they turned away to leave the room, each was praying for Robin Wakefield to be a man whose life would honor his parents.

END OF PART ONE

Young

1 5 6 8   Part
         TWO   1 5 7 7

Queen Bess

THE TENTH YEAR

Robin had risen before dawn and slipped outside the palisades. His heart beat faster as he made for the river. *If I don't get back by ten o'clock, Grandfather will cane me for sure!* He had wrung permission from his grandfather to run his lines in the river the night before and had received the warning: *Well, go then—but if you're late for your own birthday celebration, I'll have the hide off you!* Robin well knew that his grandfather was as faithful to punish disobedience as to reward good behavior—and besides, one didn't have a tenth birthday but once! He shivered as a wintry blast struck him, then pulled his coat closer. "I'll be back before they wake," he announced to Pilot, the huge mastiff at his side. Pilot lifted his massive head, said *woof* in a throaty voice, then started for the river in a lope that pressed the boy to keep up with his giant strides.

Winter had stripped the trees of their foliage so that they seemed to reach up with skinny arms toward the sky. Both riverbanks, except for those spots where houses and the village stood, were covered with thick dark woods, cut through in places with deep cart tracks. Squirrels, badgers, foxes, and hares abounded, even in winter. Something about the woods was deliciously ominous—and Robin ventured here often, his heart sometimes pounding with fear. When his grandmother Hannah had warned him about the dangers of the place, he could only say, "But Grandmother, it's *fun* to be scared!"

Perhaps he had soaked up some of the tales told by the tenants of the manor, who insisted that witches lived there. But he had never seen such a creature. He *had* seen Kate Moody, who lived in a shanty on the west side of the river. Now, *she* might be a witch! Robin had crept close to her house more than once, holding his breath and tingling with apprehension—but he'd never had the fortune of seeing her turn anyone into a crawling reptile as she was reported to do. He would rather have liked to see this, as long as *he* was not the victim!

The sound of Pilot's heavy breathing drew him back to the present, and he leaped over several dry creeks. During the rainy season, these beds filled up with glimmering oily water. Now, however, they had sunk to silent yellow mud, and the only sounds around the boy were the cry and flutter of birds that sounded like lost children crying.

Robin reached the river, which made a serpentine shape through the valley. At once he ran to the spot where he kept his lines out and shoved Pilot aside as he drew one in. Empty! What was worse, the bait was stripped. And the next two lines were equally barren.

Barely daring to hope, he picked up the last line—and gasped when he felt a heavy weight on it. Pilot crowded close, barking excitedly as Robin hauled the line in. "It's a big one!" he cried, for the weight on the line was heavier than any he'd felt before.

But he was puzzled at the lack of action. "It's like pulling in a log!" he told the huge dog. "Maybe I've snagged a chunk—" but he broke off when, heaving mightily, he almost fell backwards as he pulled a dark shape from the murky water.

Robin frowned fiercely. "Blasted old turtle!" He had not pulled in a fish at all—still, turtle was good to eat. He hauled the huge, moss-covered beast onto the bank, and Pilot circled it, snarling and barking mightily—all the while staying safely away from the terrible beaked jaws. The monster's head was enormous, and Robin cautiously pulled his sheath knife. The seemingly malevolent eyes of the turtle were fixed on him.

"You could bite right through my arm, couldn't you?" the boy said. He was afraid, but there was a streak of stubbornness in him that wouldn't let him back down. He grasped a nearby stick, extending it toward the turtle's jaws—then drew back quickly when the stick was promptly snapped in two.

He thought hard, then his eyes brightened. "I'll get you!" he muttered. Glancing overhead, he noted a thick branch and threw the line over it. Then he hauled the turtle three feet into the air. Securing the line to a sapling, he watched as the weight of the turtle stretched his neck out. Carefully he jabbed at the neck with the sharp knife, and though the snapper gyrated wildly, finally the boy managed to sever the head, and the armored carcass fell to the ground. Robin danced around with excitement, then noticed that the jaws of the beast were still opening and closing. That fascinated him, and after he had tied a loop around one of the feet, he stared at the head.

"I'll get one of the men to mount it for me," he announced.

Carefully he wrapped the huge head in his handkerchief, tied it to his belt, then looked up at the sky. He looped a piece of the string around one of the turtle's horny hind legs, tied the other end to the back of his leather belt, then headed back toward Wakefield, Pilot loping along beside him. The weight of his catch forced him to lean forward, and more than once he almost abandoned his task. However, he knew his grandmother loved turtle soup, and so he persevered.

He decided not to follow the faint trail in the woods, for the awkward carcass would catch in the roots and saplings. Instead he set out on the worn path that followed the course of the river.

Pilot didn't seem to mind the change in direction. He followed along, sniffing the air with casual interest.

The woods were thick along the path, and when Robin came to a well-worn path that ran east, he hesitated, then loosed the string from his belt and turned. A hundred yards down the path, he paused and moved behind a gnarled yew tree, surveying the small dwelling that occupied the center of a cleared space. Warily he approached, moving from tree to tree, pretending that he was Robin Hood stalking the sheriff of Nottingham.

He was within twenty feet of the house, proud of the silence of his approach, when a voice broke the stillness of the glade.

"Who are you? Come forward if you have business!"

Robin whirled to see Kate Moody standing there. She had been sitting beside her cabin, almost hidden by a small hedge. He resisted the impulse to whirl and run away—his pride wouldn't let him do such a thing. He spoke up as strongly as he could. "I'm Robin Wakefield."

Mistress Moody was sitting on a three-legged stool watching the boy with a pair of sharp, deep-brown eyes. Her whole face was sharp, but she was not old, no more than twenty-five or so, Robin guessed. She wore worn dark clothing and was tall and lean. "Wakefield, eh? Come closer boy!" When Robin hesitated, she laughed, and he was surprised that it was a cheerful enough sound. "Do you think I'm about to turn you into a frog, boy?"

Robin *had* been considering some such possibility, but now he straightened his back and marched up to where she stood. A black dog was lying beside her. He lifted his head and snarled at Pilot, who had followed Robin but now was keeping well back and doing his own snarling. A raven, perched on one of the beams that made up the roof, uttered a solemn, hoarse, cawing sound that ran along Robin's nerves.

"Wakefield, is it? You'll be Myles's grandson."

The raven suddenly dropped from his perch and lit on her

shoulder—which made her look *very much* like a witch to Robin. Still, her features were not cruel, as he had always supposed. Her hair was dark, but her skin was smooth, and her lips were red and held a trace of a smile.

"I—didn't mean to spy," Robin said abruptly, ashamed of what he had done. A sudden burst of inspiration came to him, and he said quickly, "One of our servants, Meg, is sick with ague or something. She's coughing terrible. I—I thought you'd have some medicine for her." He congratulated himself for his quick thinking. And it wasn't a total tale: Meg, one of the servant girls, was ailing, and Robin had heard that many came to Kate Moody for her herbs and medicines.

"You're not the first to spy on Kate," the woman said, smiling as though she could see right through his ruse. She nodded, then cocked her head, observing him. Her eyes, Robin saw, were as bright as those of the raven that perched on her shoulder. "Aye, I can cure the girl. Comfey and licorice, that's what'll do it."

Robin blinked in surprise. Now what? "I—don't have any money."

"What's that on your belt, Robin Wakefield?"

"Why, it's a turtle head."

"Let me see."

Robin untied the handkerchief, and when the head fell to the ground, it shocked him to see that the huge jaws suddenly opened and then snapped shut.

"Ah, that's a fine big one." Kate nodded, then looked at him. "Where's the rest of him?"

"Down by the river. I was taking him home."

"Go get him and bring him here. I'll have the medicine for you."

"All right." Robin was tired of hauling the heavy weight anyway, and besides, he was fond of Meg. Turning at once, he retraced his steps to the river and hauled the carcass back to the cabin. Kate Moody gave one approving look, then handed him a small packet and a clay vase that was sealed with wax. "Cook them leaves in boiling water and have the woman drink it. The licorice will take away the cough."

Robin took the medicines, stared at them, then asked, "How do you know about cures?" Shaking his head, he said, "It must be good to cure people."

Kate Moody blinked with surprise; few people had ever paid her compliments. Most who came to her were so afraid of her they could barely speak. "A good thing? Aye, if you don't get burned as a witch for it!" Then something in the boy's face caught her interest. "You be interested in herbs?"

"Well, I don't know much—just what my grandmother taught me. I'd like to know more, especially about what cures animals. Then I could help with the cattle and the dogs."

The woman stared at him, then waved at the stool. "Sit down, boy," she commanded, and when he gingerly seated himself, she began to talk. "Saffron for measles, saxifrage for the stone, neat's foot for chilblains . . ." Kate Moody had few listeners, and none as fascinated with her as the lad whose steady blue-gray eyes were fixed on her. Time ran on, and her voice rose above the silence of the still glade. For nearly an hour she spoke, pausing from time to time to rise and get a sample of her wares to show the boy.

Finally the raven croaked hoarsely from his perch on a nearby tree, and Kate Moody gave the boy a sharp look. "Suppose we make a pact, Robin Wakefield. You bring me a bit of game—rabbit or squirrel—from time to time, and I'll teach you about herbs."

Robin stared at the dark face, wondering if it were a trick to make a witch out of him, but what he saw satisfied him. This woman was no witch. He was sure of it. And he would never be afraid of Kate Moody again. "All right. I'll come when I can."

"Don't tell people," she warned, looking pleased with his quick response.

"I'll tell my grandfather. I tell him everything."

Again, his answer seemed to please her, and she nodded. "Right! Now off with you. I'm having turtle soup for my dinner!"

Robin scurried away, whistling for Pilot. He noted that the pale winter sun had climbed alarmingly high, and he broke into a trot, thinking over all Kate had told him—for he remembered almost every word—and wondering when he could come back to learn more.

Arriving at the gate that served as the main entrance to the manor, he passed by the stables, then hailed several of the field servants who were lounging in front of the windmill. He dashed across the open courtyard, took a right, and made his way to the manor house that enclosed a quadrangle on three sides. The fourth side faced a wide depression that once had been a branch of the river, but now that side was open except for a castellated tower with low walls flanking it and a big gate under the tower. At the north of the house was another tall tower pierced with loopholes for bows or muskets. From this spot, one could see any and all who approached. On all sides the house was protected by stockades and earthworks, a sign that the house had been built long ago when at any moment enemies might come to destroy it.

Slipping into the house through a side door, Robin scurried to his room, slipped out of his muddy clothes, and washed in the basin on the table by the wall. Quickly he slipped into the new clothes his grandmother had made for his birthday—dark green breeches, a finely embroidered white shirt, and a new pair of supple leather boots, black and gleaming. Finally he combed his shock of auburn hair as well as he could, and as he finished he heard his grandfather approach. "Robin—?"

The door opened and his grandparents entered, smiles on their faces as they took in his new apparel. "Now look at that!" Myles grunted approvingly. "Not a baby anymore, Hannah!" Even at sixty-one, Sir Myles had a youthful appearance. His neck was thick, and lines touched the corners of his eyes, and silver gleamed in his thick hair—but in an age when the average life span was thirty-five years, Myles Wakefield was something of a marvel. He still rode a horse better than any of his fellows, and he was agile enough to teach his grandson the use of the lance, the broadsword, and the rapier.

"Happy birthday, Robin. You look splendid!" Hannah was one year older than Myles, but she too had been blessed with good health. By some miracle, both she and her husband had been blessed with fine teeth. Many people suffered with cavities, and even wealthy folk revealed yellowed and rotting teeth when they smiled. Hannah's teeth, however, were even and white as she smiled. "Turn around," she commanded. "Let's have a look at your finery."

The couple surveyed the boy, and each of them suddenly thought of Will as he had been at that age. Hannah almost said, *He's very like Will, isn't he?* Instead she glanced at Myles, who nodded slightly. Myles admired the boy's lean, strong, athletic figure, the steadiness of the blue-gray eyes (so much like his own!), and the way the boy planted his feet firmly. Hannah studied the fine, chiseled features—the short nose, the firm broad mouth, the shock of auburn hair with the widow's peak, and the deep-set, well-shaped eyes. *A handsome boy!* she thought, then said, "Well, you'll do, I suppose. Now, you'll be expecting presents?" She laughed at his expression, then took a small package out of her pocket.

Robin took the package, opened it, and looked up with a pleased expression. "Grandmother, it's so pretty!" He stared at the heavy gold ring with the bright red ruby. "It's your father's ring!"

"It was, but now it's yours." Hannah smiled. "I had the

goldsmith cut it down to fit for now. As you grow to be a man, he'll have to make it larger."

While Robin was thanking her and admiring the ring, Myles stepped outside, then returned bearing a sword in his hand. "You'll have to grow into this, my boy! But it won't take you long."

Robin stared at the foil, grabbed it with excitement, and pulled it from the sheath. It seemed to fit into his hand, the finely worked handle settling into his palm, the guard closing over his fist. He lunged with it toward the wall, then cut through the air making a highly satisfactory *swishing* sound.

"Careful!" Myles laughed. "You'll have your poor grand-mother backed in a corner!"

"Oh, Grandfather! It's—it's the best sword I ever saw!"

"Well, we'll see at practice how well you can use it—but not now. Come along, it's time to go to the celebration!"

The three of them left Wakefield Manor and drove to the village of Wakefield. The air was cold, but as they entered the small town, nobody they saw seemed troubled about that. Color was everywhere—the villagers wearing their best to celebrate the tenth anniversary of the reign of Queen Elizabeth. Every year there was a celebration, but the end of the decade was special. Streamers made of crimson, green, and yellow strips of cloth fluttered from every house and shop, and the streets were filled with music and the sound of laughter.

"A fine celebration, isn't it, Robin?" Myles asked.

"Yes, indeed it is." Robin hesitated, then added, "When I was little, I thought the celebration was just for my birthday."

Hannah laughed and patted his knee. "Did you now? Well, being born on the same day Elizabeth became queen is handy. You can count on wonderful celebrations and everyone being in a grand mood."

"And it makes it easy to remember your birthday, doesn't it

now?" Myles chuckled. Then he frowned as a thought came to him. "I wish Alice and Tom were here." Alice had married a fine young man named Matthew Blacken six years earlier. Blacken had moved to the north of England, and it was a long trip. Myles and Hannah got to see Alice's two children only on rare occasions.

The mention of Tom interested Robin. "When is my uncle coming home, Grandfather?"

"No saying about that, boy. He's on a long voyage with Sir John Hawkins and Francis Drake." Gloom suddenly marred Myles's features and he added, "It'll be a year or more, I fear, before they return."

"Why do they go so far?" Robin asked.

"Well, the Spanish say they come as pirates to steal their gold. Queen Elizabeth calls them her Sea Hawks, or sometimes her 'adventurer businessmen.'"

Hannah laughed aloud. "Elizabeth is so greedy, she'd call them *tea cakes* if they brought back gold and silver and jewels from the Spanish Main."

Myles was displeased with this. "She came to the throne and found out that England was bankrupt," he insisted. "I know she's been faulted by the Council for being miserly, but in her short reign she's restored confidence in the currency and made the country prosperous."

"Still, it's the Sea Hawks she looks to for cash," Hannah insisted. Then she added, "But you're right. She's a vain woman, but England has prospered under her. I just wish she'd marry, don't you?"

"I doubt she ever will. We need an heir to the throne, but what if she married a Catholic? We'd be right back in the days of Mary." He hesitated then shrugged wearily. "It'll be Robert Dudley, I fear. She shows him more favor than any other man."

Elizabeth had made Dudley master of the House and had

showered him with attention. This tall handsome athlete, whose dark skin led his enemy Lord Sussex to call him "The Gypsy," was never far from the queen. He had married Amy Robard at seventeen but had tired of her almost at once. When she had been found dead of a broken neck, the entire country ran rife with rumors. Elizabeth had ignored them, and scandalous stories about the relationship between the queen and Dudley were widely circulated. Elizabeth was a woman who thrived on admiration and was all too ready to flirt with the handsome young men she had collected around her—but Dudley was her favorite. Lord Burghley, Elizabeth's chief counselor, had told Myles privately, "I live in fear that she will marry Dudley. He would be a tyrant such as England has never seen!"

Suddenly Robin broke into the conversation. "I'm ten today, how old is the queen?"

"Thirty-five."

"Why, that's *old!*" Robin remarked.

Hannah shot an amused glance at Myles, saying, "If thirty-five is old, you must think we're *ancient,* Robin."

Robin looked at her, then at Myles. "No, you're not old," he announced. "You won't die for a long time."

"I'm relieved to hear it," Myles said dryly. "Now—let's celebrate the queen's tenth year on the throne—and your tenth year on earth."

Robin missed nothing that day—not the jugglers, the acrobats, nor the bear-baiting. But the latter displeased him. It consisted of chaining a large black bear to a stump and letting the hunting dogs attack it until the beast died. "Elizabeth likes this sort of thing," Myles said with distaste. "I think it's cruel. Come along, Robin."

The three of them had reached one end of the street, which was lined with vendors selling trinkets and sweets, when Hannah said, "Look—there's Martha Spenser. And that must be their little girl. We haven't seen her since she was born."

"Aye, so it is." They crossed the busy street and Hannah said, "And how is the youngest Spenser?"

Martha Spenser was short and overweight, and she still had not lost the weight she'd gained during her pregnancy. She was no more than thirty and still retained traces of a youthful beauty. The Spensers were Catholics and for this reason were stiff with the Wakefields, though Myles and John Spenser got on well enough. "She's as busy as any a four-year-old," she said.

"Let me hold her, Martha," Hannah begged, and received the warmly dressed child. Peering under the child's hood she said with delight, "What a beauty! Look, Robin."

Robin peered at the child and saw nothing beautiful. She had fine blondish hair and dark violet eyes. "What's her name?" he asked.

"We called her Allison, an old family name." Martha Spenser was pleased with Lady Wakefield's admiration. She herself had come from a family that had some noble blood, though not enough for an earl or a duke to marry her. She had married John Spenser in a moment of youthful and romantic fervor—and regretted it almost instantly. Sir John Spenser was a good man, but despite his title, he was basically a farmer. Martha, who had been accustomed to a much more luxurious life, had grown bitter, making their marriage unhappy. She envied Hannah Wakefield, but saw the wisdom of staying on good terms with her.

Hannah held the little girl for so long that Robin began to fidget. She glanced at him tolerantly. "Go amuse yourself, boy!"

Grateful to be dismissed, Robin darted off, found some boys his own age, and spent his pocket money for sweets. He passed them around, and as they ate them greedily one of the boys, Giles Horton, remarked, "I'd think you wouldn't want to be friends with them Catholics."

"Why not?" Robin asked casually. He was aware of the tension that existed between Catholics and Protestants, but had accepted it with no resentment.

Horton was the son of a schoolmaster and knew his history— as well as the history of the Wakefields. "Well, now, if somebody killed *my* father, I'd not have anything to do with them!"

Robin stood stock still staring at the boy. "What do you mean by that, Giles?"

Horton shrugged. "You must know that it was Bloody Mary who had your father burned at the stake. Her and the Catholics. And one day Philip will come with the Spanish army, and we'll have to fight them. I'm going to be a soldier and kill all the papists I can!"

Robin turned pale and said no more about the matter. On the way home he was very quiet, but Hannah attributed it to his being tired. Then, just as they reached the house, he asked abruptly, "Did the Catholics kill my father?"

Both Myles and Hannah had always known and dreaded that this moment would come. They had avoided telling the details of Will's death, saying merely that he had died and that his mother had died when Robin was born. Now, they both saw the pale, tense face of the boy, and Myles knew that he had to speak.

"You must remember, Robin," he said carefully, "that there has been war all over the world for a long time. Those who are Catholic and those who aren't have been fighting in England for many years. And many have been killed on both sides, Catholic and Protestant."

"But did Mary kill my father?"

Myles gave Hannah an agonized glance, then proceeded to tell the truth—as much as he thought the boy could bear. But no matter how he put it, he saw that the shock had gone deep into the boy. He finished by saying, "It was a very sad thing, Robin, but it was a long time ago. Now we have a queen who wouldn't permit such things."

"But she's not a Catholic, is she?"

"Well, no, but—"

"And are the Catholics still killing people?"

Myles didn't answer—he could not, for he knew the Inquisition was torturing and killing people all over the world. Robin looked at his grandfather and saw the truth.

"I *hate* them for killing my father!"

They arrived at home, and Robin ran away as soon as the carriage stopped. As he disappeared, dashing out of the gate, Myles said, "God help us, Hannah."

She took his hand, and the two of them sat quietly. Finally Hannah said, "He's got good blood, Myles. And he has us. We'll teach him to love—just as Will and Blanche would have wanted!"

Nine

ANOTHER
"QUEEN MARY"

The peregrine is yours, Robin. A Christmas present!"
Myles and his grandson had left the manor very early
with the birds hooded and now had arrived at open
country. Myles had allowed the boy to bring the peregrine, while
he chose its smaller mate—the tiercel. The birds sat hooded and
silent on their wrists. The two men had dismounted, and Robin
had been completely engrossed in holding Mars, as the tiercel was
named, on the gauntlet that adorned his left arm. Now his face
lifted and his eyes were filled with astonishment. "Really, Grandfather?" he exclaimed. "But it's not Christmas yet." Hastily he
nodded, adding, "But thank you, sir." He stroked the hood that
covered the fierce head almost reverently.

Myles examined the boy, admiring the sight of him as he held
the bird. He could tell from the healthy flush on the boy's face
that he was enjoying the clear morning air as much as Myles
himself. The day was one of those December oddities—grim and
yet alive in some way. Unseasonable heat had come to break up
the ice, and one could hear the water flowing in streams and
brooks, trickling out of woodland snowbanks, oozing into horses'
hoofprints. The spring was almost palpable, though it lay months
away. Wool-puff clouds against the sky seemed rinsed clear and
purified.

"A fine day for hawking," Myles remarked, looking up at the sky. "I think these days with you out in the fields are some of my very favorites."

"Mine too, sir," Robin said quickly. He looked up fondly at his grandfather, the memories of many mornings flickering through him. Out of the past he seemed to hear the calm even voice again, teaching him about the noble sport of flying falcons:

"These leather thongs attached to the talons are jesses. When the bird comes to your gauntlet, tie his talons to your arm with them.

"When a falcon lights on an object too thin—such as a clothesline, he will turn upside down and hang there helpless. A fine hawk will never light on the ground. That's how we're able to teach them to come to the gauntlet.

"Never overfeed your hawk!"

Robin's memories were interrupted as his grandfather's voice broke in: "Actually, boy, we're breaking the law by flying a peregrine." Myles was amused at the shocked look that flew across Robin's face. "Oh, it's an old law—one that nobody heeds any longer. But it says that only an earl may fly peregrines."

"Springwind is the prettiest peregrine we have," Robin said, admiring the smaller bird on Myles's wrist.

"I had a difficult time training her to lure. But she's strong. She even takes large hares—not a bit afraid of them." He made sweet clucking noises to her.

Robin held the tiercel high, admiring the powerful chest and enjoying the sensation in his wrist as Mars flexed his talons, almost penetrating the leather glove he wore. "I love it when Mars goes rook-hawking." He saw a flight of rooks nearby and asked eagerly, "Can I fly him now?"

"Yes."

Robin slipped the hood from the bird's head, then raised his arm. The peregrine beat the air with strong pinions, and the two watched as he climbed rapidly. Soon he was high over the rooks, and then he dived, his wings driving him down at a tremendous speed. When he hit one of the rooks a devastating blow, the black feathers seemed to explode at the impact. The rook was killed instantly and tumbled to the ground, Mars following.

"I love to see them kill," Robin confessed as they walked toward the bird, who was tearing into the carcass of the rook. "Is that wrong, Grandfather?"

Glancing down at the boy, Myles shook his head. "I don't know, boy. We never eat the kills the birds make. It's not like hunting for food." Despite the pleasure of the hunt, Robin's face was somehow tense, and Myles felt certain he was thinking about how his father died.

I wish I could help him—but he's closed Hannah and me out somehow. And he's become preoccupied with death. Quickly he tried to take the boy's mind away from the dark thoughts. "I've got a surprise for you."

"Yes, sir?"

"I'm going to London day after tomorrow—to the court. The queen has sent for me. I thought you might like to go with me—just the two of us."

Instantly Robin's face was illuminated, his eyes alive with excitement. "Oh yes, sir!" he burst out. He'd only been to London twice, and never to the court. "Will I see the queen?"

Happy that the boy's mood had swung, Myles nodded. "I wouldn't count on it, but we'll see. Now, let's see if we can get these birds to bring down something a little more impressive than a rook."

***

Myles never forgot the trip to London with his grandson. Robin, too, held the memory of that journey in his mind as long as he lived. The trip itself was exciting, for the two of them rode together, mounted on fine horses and staying at inns where there was a fascinating variety of travelers. Some of them were seamen, and at the eager boy's urging, his grandfather would entice one of them into accepting a meal in exchange for stories of the sea.

After one particularly wild tale, Myles allowed the fierce-looking sailor to leave, then grinned. "I wouldn't believe quite all of that yarn, Robin."

"Was he lying?"

"Some of the time." A look of disappointment marred the pleasure in the youthful face, and Myles added, "A sailor's life is hard—the most difficult of all, I think. But in one way it's like all other professions. Long, hard, boring hours with a few moments of action and glory. The sailors tend to forget the boring months and remember the sound and the fury of battle. It's natural enough."

"I hope I can be a sailor like Uncle Thomas!"

"I'd wish for an easier life for you, but we shall see."

The next day Myles pointed ahead to a cloud of smoke before them. "That's London," he announced. "But the queen and her court are at Theobalds—William Cecil's house. It's finer than the palace." As a look of disappointment crossed Robin's face, he added, "Cecil spent an incredible amount of money building the place, just so he could have a fitting place to entertain his queen."

When they crested a small rise and looked down on the house, Robin gasped. The place was enormous! As the two rode down an ornamented gateway, which entered into the forecourt of the house, he said, "It's *big,* isn't it, Grandfather?"

The stone, brickwork, and glass of the three-story facade loomed over them. Four square towers stood there, all evenly spaced and balanced—each with four turrets upon which gold lion weather vanes glittered to mark the turnings of whimsical breezes. In addition, there were twenty-four towerlets. And at the center of all, the entrance and a broad sweep of stairs. Beside the building was an enormous turret, made to resemble the shape of a lantern, hung with twelve bells—each of a different size, pitch, and tone—which, by a cunning mechanical contrivance, tolled the hours of the day.

The two Wakefields dismounted and entered the mansion, admitted by a servant. Inside, they were greeted with the sight of dozens of people, all attired in a blaze of colors. Robin's eyes widened at the women, all dressed in the richest and most fragile of silks, satins, taffetas, velvets, and laces. The men wore doublets and hose, loose-slung decorative cloaks, or delicate jerkins worthy of an Oriental potentate.

"Quite a party, eh, boy?" Myles grinned. "Not much like our poor Wakefield, is it?"

"I like Wakefield better," Robin answered stoutly, then added, "Do they dress like this all the time?"

"Yes, and it gets to be tiresome. After a time a man wants to put on old clothes and get out with his dogs and his hawks." He would have said more, but a small man with a pair of sharp brown eyes had approached. Inclining his head, Myles said, "My lord, it's good to see you. This is my grandson, Robin. And this is Sir William Cecil."

The man who stood before them was in some respects the most powerful man in England. He had been the first person Elizabeth had chosen for her Council, naming him chief secretary of state. He was a quiet, austere man—and Myles had encountered him enough over the years to agree with Lord Sussex, who said of the man that "of all men of genius he was the most a drudge; of all men of business, the most a genius." But Robin had been given a clearer picture of the secretary on their journey. "He's the exact *opposite* of the queen," Myles had told him. "She is a most dramatic woman, while Cecil always tries to stay invisible. But he's the kind of man she needs—someone to caution her against the wild schemes she dreams up!"

Now Cecil greeted Robin courteously, but at once turned to

the man. "Sir Myles, the queen wishes to speak to you as soon as possible."

"May I know on what business?"

Cecil glanced down at Robin, weighed the face of the boy, then seemed to feel free to say, "It concerns the Scottish queen, I believe. But she will tell you herself. If you'll come with me, I'll arrange a meeting."

Myles and Robin followed the secretary to a large ornate room dominated by a huge table surrounded by oak chairs. "I'll see if the queen is free, but it might be a long wait. I'll have some refreshments brought in." A fretful expression crossed Cecil's face. "You know how she is, Sir Myles—never on time."

"I know. It's all right, Sir William." The diminutive man eased himself out and closed the door, and Myles laughed. "Well, we might be in for a long wait. Would you like to go look around?"

"Yes, sir."

"Don't get lost," Myles admonished him. "When you come back, knock on that door. But don't enter until I say so."

"Yes, sir."

Robin scooted out the door and for the next half hour moved around the huge mansion, eyes wide with wonder. He was intrigued by the fountain that tossed its jet almost to the ceiling. The base was made of precious stones of every color and hue, and the water changed color from time to time, fed by some system that delivered dye into the fountain. The water was caught, as it came back down, by two carvings of young women formed from white marble—completely naked! Robin tried to avoid staring at them, but his eyes seem to return of their own volition.

"Well, look at this. A young courtier!"

Robin twisted his head to see a woman dressed in a low-cut dress made of gold—or so it seemed. She was laughing at him, and he flushed, ducking his head. The tall man beside her was wearing a doublet of deep red wine and a hat with a white feather.

"Be careful of beautiful women with stone-cold hearts, sir," he said, then laughed. "I could tell you a thing or two about that!"

The young woman laughed loudly and reached out to caress Robin's cheek. "And who are you, my fine young man?"

Robin suddenly felt ashamed—it bothered him to have been caught looking at the statues. He muttered, "I'm Robin," then whirled and darted away. For some time he examined the house, then felt lonely in such surroundings. Abruptly he turned and made his way to the room where he'd left his grandfather.

<hr/>

Upon Robin's departure, Myles sat down, wondering what the queen could possibly want with him. The door opened, but it was only a servant bearing a silver platter loaded with beef, chicken, and pork, and a golden flagon of wine. As Myles ate, his thoughts turned again to the queen. The secretary had mentioned Mary Queen of Scots. That woman's story was known to practically everyone. *But what can I have to do with that crafty woman?* Myles wondered.

Slumping in his chair, he carefully rehearsed the history of Mary of Scotland. The most significant thing about her was that if Elizabeth died, Mary would be queen of England. Already she'd done all she could to gain the throne of England by means fair or foul. Everyone knew of her disastrous marriage with Lord Darnley in 1565 and she was widely believed to have been implicated in his murder in 1567 at Kirk o' Fields. After this, she had married Lord Bothwell in doubtful circumstances and had been deprived of her throne. Barely escaping with her life, she had fled to England and thrown herself on Elizabeth's mercy.

Myles's ruminations were suddenly interrupted when the door swung open and Elizabeth entered. Leaping to his feet, Myles took the hand she held out and kissed it, bowing deeply. "Your Majesty," he said, but before he could say more Elizabeth spoke.

"Don't tell me I look more lovely than I did the last time we met!" Elizabeth suddenly laughed at the expression on his face. "But you weren't going to tell me that, were you, Myles?"

"Why—I don't think I was, Your Majesty."

Elizabeth stared at him, and a smile touched her lips. "They all do, you know. All except you and Cecil. I could be ugly as a crow and scarred with the pox. They'd say the same thing."

"Actually, you *are* looking well, my queen. Pardon my familiarity, but your waist—it seems no larger than when I came to visit you when you were sixteen. And you've been getting a great deal of exercise, I see. Your skin is glowing." He had deliberately chosen Elizabeth's two best features and was relieved to see her accept his praise.

"Sit down, Myles, and tell me about your family." Elizabeth was wearing a magnificent dress made of white and crimson satin sewn all over with pearls the size of bird's eggs and adorned with a ruff in which tiny diamonds glittered like dewdrops. She listened intently as he spoke briefly of himself, and when he added that his grandson was with him, she nodded. "We'll see him before you leave. But I'm sure you're wondering why I sent for you."

"Well—"

"It certainly wasn't so you could pay me compliments. I have plenty in this place who can do *that!*" She put her hands flat on the table, and he saw that they were as lovely as ever—and knew that she displayed them deliberately. He remembered suddenly that her sister Mary had envied her beautiful hands, so that Elizabeth used to wear gloves to hide them when meeting with her.

"I hope to serve Your Majesty in any honorable way I can."

His words caught at the queen, and she repeated them. "Indeed? 'In any *honorable* way'?" Her eyes narrowed and she demanded, "What if I ask you to do something that you deem dishonorable?"

Myles held Elizabeth's gaze for a moment, and the silence seemed thick. "I cannot imagine Queen Elizabeth asking such a thing."

"But if I *did?*"

"Then I would have to disappoint Your Majesty." Myles spoke quietly, not knowing how Elizabeth would react. She was as volatile as gunpowder, and he knew of cases where she had gone into a violent rage at men who had said less inflammatory things than he had just said.

But Elizabeth smiled, her face relaxed, and she said almost plaintively, "And so you would, Myles. So you would!" She gripped her hands together and seemed deep in thought. Finally she said, "I need your help . . . with the queen from Scotland."

Myles said carefully, "Technically, Your Majesty, she is *not* the queen. The Scots deposed her and would have executed her if she had not escaped to England."

"It is *God* who set her as queen!" Elizabeth was a devout believer in the Divine Right of kings—the concept that all rulers were ordained by God. She exclaimed vehemently, "I cannot allow my sister queen to be executed. She has come to me for sanctuary, and I must give it to her!"

"What does Sir Cecil say?" inquired Myles.

"The same as many others, that she will be a threat to my throne."

"He is a very wise man, Your Majesty. This woman has already tried to take your crown. If you allow her to remain in England, she will be a danger to you. Every plotter and schemer will support her. Not to mention Rome." Myles hesitated, then added, "And she has a child, Your Majesty. A son."

"And I have none!"

"Mary's son, James, is still a boy. Yet he is king of Scotland. And if you leave no heir, many will insist on crowning him king of England as well."

Elizabeth stared at him. "Think you *I* don't know that? But I will *not* hand Mary over to the Scots to be butchered!"

Myles knew better than to argue. "What can I do to help you?"

Elizabeth leaned forward. "I have housed the queen at Tutbury Castle. I want you to meet her, Myles."

"*I,* Your Majesty?" Seldom had Myles been so shocked. "For what purpose?"

"To read her, Myles. To get to know her. Mayhap even to gain her trust."

Myles stared at the queen. "You mean, become a spy?"

Elizabeth shook her head. "No, that is not it. I have those who will do that sort of work. You are different." She stared at him, and there was a softening of her expression. "You are honest, and you are my friend. You would be surprised at—at how *few* true friends I have." She seemed ashamed of having made such a remark and hurried on. "I need your judgment on what Mary is thinking. She may deceive others, but you are astute. It would be a great help if you would do this for me."

Myles dropped his eyes, for this statement from such a proud woman amounted to a cry for help. "I will do as you ask," he said finally. "Tutbury is close to Wakefield, so I can easily visit the place. But I cannot promise that she will see me—certainly not that she will trust me."

"She will *not* trust you, but she will use you, Myles. She has her own spy system set up. She will know you are an old favorite of mine, so you will be welcome to her. She will do all she can to pluck the thoughts from your mind."

"I will do my best for you, my queen."

"As you always have," Elizabeth said, then smiled. She sobered then, adding, "Now, you must talk with Walsingham about this."

Sir Francis Walsingham was Elizabeth's secretary of state for foreign affairs. He was an ardent Protestant and the only man in Elizabeth's cabinet who dared to stand up to her. Flatly declining to indulge the queen's delight in compliments, he spoke to her bluntly as other ministers dared not do.

"Sir Francis, Your Grace?"

"Yes. He has set up what he calls his 'Secret Service.' Which means a network of spies and agents in the courts of Europe— over seventy of them, I understand." Her long face grew moody and she cursed suddenly, a habit Myles deplored. "If he can have seventy agents in Europe, I suppose I can have *one* here. There's more danger in Mary Queen of Scots for me, Myles, than in all the armies of France and Spain!"

She extended her hand, and when he kissed it, she sighed with relief, "Now—where is this grandson of yours? Let's have a look at him! Are you as foolish about him as other grandfathers?"

"More so, I'm afraid—" As he spoke of Robin, a timid knock sounded on the door. "Robin—?" he called out. The door opened and Robin entered—then stood stock still at the sight of the queen, who suddenly rose and came to stand over him.

"Why, Myles—he's *you* all over again!" Stretching out her hand, she ran it over the thick auburn locks and laughed as Robin blushed. "What a devil you'll be with the ladies when you're older, won't you, Robin?"

"Oh, no—!" Robin cried aloud, then remembered what his grandfather had said about meeting the queen. He bowed awkwardly and managed to say the words he had memorized.

Elizabeth turned to Myles, a smile in her eyes. "He's a fine boy, Sir Myles Wakefield. You must bring him often to court. When he's older, I may keep him here and make a courtier of him."

"Please—Your Majesty—I'd rather be a sailor!"

Elizabeth found this very funny, and her laughter almost rocked the walls. "Some men are both—come and we'll see."

Then she was gone, and moving to follow her, Myles said, "Not many lads your age get asked to become a part of the court of Queen Elizabeth."

Robin shook his head stubbornly. "I'd rather be a sailor!"

⌘

When the earl of Shrewsbury announced to Mary that Sir Myles Wakefield asked audience, she demanded at once, "Who is he?"

"Why, a very fine man," the earl, her official guardian, informed her, giving the details of the visitor's standing. She seemed little interested at first. However, when he told her Myles had "been a favorite of the queen for many years," her dark eyes glowed with interest.

"We will receive him, sir."

Mary waited, her fertile mind turning over possibilities. When the tall man entered accompanied by a boy, she said graciously, "Sir Myles, we are glad to receive you. And you, too, young sir."

"My grandson, Robin," Myles said. "We were on a journey, and I had no place to leave him—"

"He is very welcome. Let me order refreshments."

The two visitors were both taken by the attractive woman—especially Robin. Myles admired the woman's dark beauty, but was sharply aware that that very thing was one of her most effective weapons. When they had eaten some cakes with tea, Myles said, "Your Majesty, I live only a few miles from this place. The secretary, Sir William Cecil, asked me to call. I am happy to do so and to offer you my services."

"I was not aware that Sir William was so concerned about my well-being," Mary said rather coldly. She well knew that the secretary was opposed to her remaining in England.

"The queen also mentioned that it would please her if I visited you."

"Ah? Then you are doubly welcome, Sir Myles, and you, too,

Robin." Mary instantly seized the opportunity that presented itself. "I cannot visit you, of course——" she gestured about her with a wry smile—"but it would please me greatly for you to come. And perhaps bring your wife?"

"Yes, indeed," Myles said, nodding. "She will be glad to come."

For the next half hour Mary chose to make herself charming— a particular gift of hers when she chose to exercise it. When Myles indicated that the two of them must be on their way, she rose, saying, "It has been very pleasant, I assure you. I am not accustomed to surroundings like these," she said, glancing at the rather grim walls, "so you would bring me great pleasure if you were to brighten my little prison with your presence. Please, come as often as you can." She placed her soft hand on Robin's head. "I have a son, you know. I miss him greatly . . . and I may well never see him again." Unshed tears glistened in her eyes as she met Myles's gaze. "If you would come and see me, both of you, it would be a comfort to me."

Myles agreed, and when the two were on their way, Robin said, "Is she really a queen, Grandfather?"

He thought of the sordid tales of Mary's time in Scotland and answered, "She was once, my boy." He leaned down and patted the neck of his horse, then whispered, "And she would very much like to be so again!"

Ten

HOME FROM THE SEA

fine mist blanketed the low-lying valleys that wound beneath the rounded hills. As Robin made his way across a freshly plowed field, he inhaled sharply, savoring the smell of a new spring. The winter had been harsh, burdening the earth with snow and paralyzing the streams with thick sheets of ice. Then the warm breath of April had come to free the land from the fell hand of winter. Robin had enjoyed the frozen whiteness of the winter, but now he rejoiced at the musical gurgle of water bubbling over stones.

As he reached the edge of the field, a covey of birds exploded, their wings sounding like miniature thunder as they sought the sky. Robin started, then laughed. "You just wait! I'll have you roasting on a spit soon enough!"

He filed the location in his head, making a vow to come back and lay snares for the birds later. Making mental maps was a habit the boy had—and a gift. The location of every valley and hill—in fact, every tree and blade of grass, his grandfather said—lay in his mind like a map pinned to a wall. He could remember every deer sign, every stream and where best to fish them, every field owned by the Wakefields.

By the time the mists had been burned off the fields, Robin had reached the Spenser house. It was a large half-timbered house with a thatched roof badly in need of repair. Two tall chimneys stood starkly against the pale blue sky. Robin paused to speak to a man patching the plaster of the wall.

"Is your master at home, Clem?"

"Aw, no he ain't, Master Robin. He went into the village to buy a horse."

Robin bit his lip, disappointed. "Well, I'll try to find him, but if I should miss him, tell him my grandfather said to let the wheat field over against the meadow lie fallow. Can you remember that?"

"Aye, sir, I'll tell him." Clem was a thick-bodied man of twenty-seven with beetling brows and a catfish mouth. "Master Robin, I seen some of them weeds you was asking about—the tall ones with the blue flower?"

"Saffron?" Robin asked eagerly. "Where did you see them?"

"You know the brook that cuts around the oat field? Them three big yew trees at the crook? Well, the ground's fairly covered with 'em there." Clem scratched his woolly head briskly. "Don't know what you want with weeds, Master Robin."

"Betty's children have the measles," Robin replied. "Saffron's good for that."

Light touched the burly servant's eyes. "Kate Moody told you that, I reckon?"

"Why, yes she did."

Clem lowered his eyes and shifted his feet. He had gone to Kate Moody himself on occasion, but always secretly. He, along with many others, was afraid of the dark-haired woman—though he had no solid reasons on which to pin his fear. Now his eyes narrowed and he said in a low voice, "Why, Master Robin, I tell you right out—she's a witch!"

"Don't be foolish, Clem!" he retorted.

"Everybody knows she's made a bargain with the devil. She can turn a man into a snake!"

"I've been spending time with her for six years now. She's taught me about herbs and what can be done with them, and that's all. I've never seen her turn anybody into anything." Robin had heard all this before and paid no heed. "Now, be certain you tell your master about the wheat field."

He turned to go and did not hear the servant mutter, "Aye, you'll think different when her and her master, old slewfoot, drag you off to the pit!"

Robin walked past the house headed for the oat field when a young voice hailed him. He turned to see Allison Spenser come sailing out the door, the April sunshine turning her ash-blonde hair to gold. She halted and looked up at him eagerly. "You came to see us!"

"Well, I left a message with Clem for your father." Glancing down at the young girl, he admired as always her dark eyes. Most people he knew had blue eyes, but hers were a deep violet. They made a startling contrast with her fair skin and blonde hair. "I've got to get on, Allison."

"Oh, don't go yet!"

"Got to go get some herbs. I'll come back another time—" At that instant Martha Spenser stepped out of the door, and Robin said hastily, "Good day, Mrs. Spenser." His tone was civil, but no more. "My grandfather sent me with a word to your husband." As he repeated the message, he was aware of the hard expression on Martha Spenser's face. He was not surprised, for he had long known that she was suspicious of him. And he knew that it was his own fault, for he had made no secret of his hatred of the Catholic religion.

"I'll tell him when he comes home." Mrs. Spenser turned to go, but stopped when Allison cried out, "Mother, can I go with Robin to find herbs?"

"He doesn't want to be bothered with you."

Actually Robin *didn't* want to take the girl, but the stiffness of the woman irritated him. Perversely he said, "Why, I'm just going down to the oat field. She can go if she likes."

Mrs. Spenser shook her head, but when Allison pleaded, "Oh, Mother, *please* let me go with Robin!" she shrugged and went back into the house. Allison jumped to the young man's side and grabbed his hand. "Now, you see? We can both go to the field!"

"Do you always get your own way, girl?"

"Oh no. Mostly I don't."

"You always do with me, it seems."

"Yes, but you're not around much. Come on, I want to show you the muskrat's den!"

Robin allowed himself to be towed along the path that led to the fields. As the girl chattered he watched her animated face. *She's ten now—and a pretty child—I never saw such violet eyes!* Aloud he said, "Do you know the first time I ever saw you?"

"No, when was it?"

"On my tenth birthday. It was in the square, and you were all pudgy and walked funny!"

"I was not!"

"Yes, all little ones are like that." He saw that his words had hurt her and added quickly, "But look how nice you've turned out—pretty as a picture!" As he had known they would, his words brought pleasure to the child. *I wish everyone were as easy to please as this one!*

Allison talked nonstop, pointing out this flower and that bird, and Robin was amazed, as always, at her intelligence. It saddened him that such a bright child received so little attention or affection. What with two older sisters and two younger brothers she seldom received notice, unless it was for some wrongdoing. Robin had seen her father, John Spenser, often enough to know he was a harried man, always in debt. And he'd heard Mrs. Spenser many times nagging her husband about bringing in more cash.

Robin had visited their home several times with his grandfather, and it was always filled with tension.

What he did not realize was that much of the strain was due to his own outspoken criticism of Catholics and their religion. Despite his grandfather's frequent admonishments about this, he persisted with a stubbornness typical of a sixteen-year-old young man who was certain he was right.

Allison was the one exception to his disdain of Catholics. With her, Robin felt quite easy. Perhaps it was her obvious admiration of him that had caused him to separate her in his mind from the rest of the family. He was aware, of course, that she went to Mass and was a Catholic—but somehow he was able to isolate her in his mind from her family. What would a pretty ten-year-old child know about burning people at the stake?

For the next hour the two rambled over the fields, dabbled in the brook, and investigated a hole that Allison insisted housed a family of muskrats. Robin assured her solemnly that, far from a muskrat, it was a troll with long sharp teeth who lived in the hole.

"Oh, that's silly!" Allison scoffed. "I don't believe in trolls!"

"You don't?" Suddenly Robin scooped her up and held her over the cavity. "Well, I'll just put you inside it, and you can see him for yourself!"

Allison squealed and held to Robin tightly. "No, please don't!" She was so frightened she began to cry, and at once Robin was chagrined.

"Now, don't cry," he said hastily, stepping back from the side of the brook. "I was only teasing. There's no such things as trolls." He was tall and very strong for his age, and he was aware of the fragile substance of the young girl. She was light as air, it seemed, and now tremors shook her as she clung to him. Carefully he sat down with his back against one of the yew trees.

You are a clod, Wakefield! he chided himself. *You've managed to frighten the poor child out of her wits!*

He crooned soothing words to her until she calmed, then smiled at her reassuringly. "Let's just sit here awhile, and I'll tell you about the palace and all the beautiful dresses the ladies wear." He plumped her down beside him, but she kept a tight hold on his arm as he related tales of the court—mostly invented for her amusement. Soon she was laughing, and, noting her merry eyes and infectious giggle, he thought again what an amiable child she was.

"Now, I'll take you home," he said, surprised that he regretted the end of their time had come. "I've got to be on my way."

For most of the way back, Allison begged him to stay, and when that did not succeed, she made him promise to come back. "Tell you what," he said, an indulgent smile tipping his lips. "My father and our servants will be over next Wednesday to help with the new fields. Maybe you and I can sneak off and go hunt bird's nests."

"Oh yes, Robin!" Her blonde hair bobbed as she nodded violently, and she clung to his hand as they walked along the path. They were approaching the clearing that held the house when she asked abruptly, "Why don't you like my mother?"

He looked at her, stunned. "Why, I never had any trouble with your mother!"

"You don't like her though. I can tell." Robin struggled to answer the child, disturbed by the troubled look on her face. But before he could come up with an acceptable explanation, she met his eyes and asked, "Is it because we're Catholic?"

Robin Wakefield had seldom felt more awkward. Something in the simplicity of the child's question and the vulnerable expression in her dark eyes silenced him. Vainly he sought for some way to explain his feelings—but as he examined his reasons, he well knew that none of them would serve in this case. Finally he said haltingly, "Well . . . when people have different ideas about things, Allison, they don't . . . they sometimes don't get along too well."

"Don't you like me?" she whispered, her lips trembling. "I'm a Catholic, too."

If Robin had been hard put to find an answer for her before, now he was completely stymied. "Yes," he said instantly, though somewhat lamely. "Of course I like you. We're friends, aren't we?" Looking at her, he saw tears brimming in those wonderful eyes, and he felt terrible. Dropping to one knee, he put his arms around her and said quickly, "Oh Allison, please don't cry."

But two large tears overflowed the girl's eyes and ran down her cheeks. "I—I can't help it!" she moaned. Throwing her arms around his neck, she pressed her face against his chest. "Please don't hate me, Robin!"

"I'll never do that!" he promised. "We'll always be friends, Allison. I promise. And I don't make promises I won't keep."

She looked into his eyes, and he had the strangest feeling that she was searching his heart. After a few moments, she nodded. "We'll always be friends?" she asked quietly.

"Always," Robin asserted. "Now, I must be off. And you need to go inside." Looking at her face, he frowned slightly. "If you can, try not to let your mother know you've been crying. She'd think hard of me."

She nodded solemnly, and he turned and left as she watched him go.

Making his way toward Wakefield, he was beset by troubled thoughts. Ever since his tenth birthday, he'd felt hatred for those responsible for his father's death. However, since there were few Catholics in the area, his animosity seldom took concrete form. The Catholics he did know seemed harmless enough, but the *system*—the structure of the Catholic Church itself—had become a fixation with him.

He didn't think his views were all that unusual. He'd heard

many English, both men and women, tell of their vivid memories of the persecution under Bloody Mary. Some had lost relatives under her command; many more had suffered milder persecutions such as having their property seized by the Crown.

Many of the people Robin knew were not unlike Giles Horton, the boy who had first revealed to Robin how his father had died. Giles had grown into a rabid Catholic-hater. "You just wait, Robin!" he often insisted. "When King Philip of Spain married Mary it wasn't because she was a beauty. He thinks he's the true king of England, and sooner or later he'll come to claim it."

Several of their friends had protested that would never happen, but Giles had only nodded fiercely. "Just wait! When Philip comes, the first thing he'll do is have the Inquisition right here! When the torturer is racking you or stripping your flesh from your bones, you'll see I was right!"

Now as Robin plunged into the woods taking a shortcut back to Wakefield, his thoughts swarmed. He could not reconcile the horrors of the Inquisition with the innocent face of Allison Spenser. Finally he said aloud, "I'll fight the Spaniards when they come, but Allison Spenser has nothing to do with that!"

Making a detour through the forest, he reached the river and followed it until he came to Kate Moody's shack. He found her standing in front of her door as though she had been waiting for him. "Well, Master Robin, what's that you've brought?"

"Saffron," he said, handing her the awkward bundle. "I'm taking some of it home for Betty's young ones, but you can have the rest."

"Aye, it's a handy weed." Taking the herbs, she deposited them on a shelf attached to the wall of her house, then she sat down and began to talk as he took his place beside her on a three-legged stool.

"Have you ever seen a glowworm in the daytime?" she asked abruptly.

"Why, I don't think I have." Robin was accustomed to Kate's odd manner, though her abrupt questions used to startle him. Now he loved to listen to her, loved to be quizzed by her, for no one seemed to know as much as she about her world—the animals, the insects, the reptiles, and every bush, weed, and flower. Apparently she found it needful to impart her knowledge to him, and his head was filled with things she had put there.

"The female has more light than the male. When she's bearing her eggs, she's lit up by them from within, like little embers in the fire."

"How do you know they're her eggs?"

"How do I know? Why, I cut them open to see!" Kate stared at him as if he'd asked something stupid. Then she pushed her long black hair back from her forehead. A white streak was a blaze that ran through it, and her eyes were dark as night itself. Leaning forward she whispered, "I've cut open more than glowworms, boy!"

Despite himself, Robin felt a shiver of alarm. He had spent much time with this strange woman, despite warnings from almost everyone. Now as he saw the intense glitter in her eyes, he suddenly wondered if there was some foundation for the rumors that followed Kate Moody!

"What good does it do to know that about glowworms?" he asked quickly.

"You must know your world, Robin Wakefield!" Kate's voice was very low for a woman, and she studied him as she might one of the frogs or snakes she sometimes kept. "And *this* world," she swept her long arm toward the forest abruptly, "is a better world than the one with people."

"Oh, Kate, that's not so!" Robin protested. "Why, think of

how—how *bloody* the forest is! Remember how the weasel we saw danced before he killed?"

"Animals kill for food. Men sometimes kill for worse reasons— some just because they *like* it!"

As she said this, Robin suddenly thought of his father's death. He nodded. "Yes, they do."

She realized at once what had brought the heavy expression to the boy's features. "Aye, you know something about things like that, young though you be," she said with a nod. "But don't let it sour you, boy. There's nothing worse than a sour man." She grinned. "Unless it's a sour woman! And if you don't mind yourself, you'll be worse than them that killed your father."

"Nobody's worse than them!" The angry words were out before he realized it. Their violence seemed to break the quietness that surrounded the cabin, and the large raven that was never far from the house was startled. He spread his wings and cawed hoarsely in protest.

Kate merely stared at the boy, her eyes fixed on his youthful features. Finally she shrugged.

"Do you know you can read by the light of three or four glowworms?"

***

As Robin strolled through the gates of Wakefield Manor, he was greeted by Pilot, who charged at him and uttered a series of deep-throated barks.

"Get down, Pilot!" he admonished. But the huge dog reared up and put his paws on Robin's chest, his weight almost upsetting the disgusted young man. "Won't you ever learn?" He stepped lightly on the hind paw of the animal, who uttered a short outraged yelp as he dropped to all fours. "You don't have a bit of dignity. And not much sense, either!"

Pilot gave his master a reproachful look, said *woof,* then trotted beside him as far as the door.

When Robin entered the house he was met at once by a tall man who came forward with a broad smile. "Uncle Thomas!" he exclaimed and grabbed the hand that was thrust toward him. "When did you come?"

"Just an hour ago." Tom Wakefield slapped his nephew on the shoulder. "Why, you've grown a foot since last year!"

"Not quite, Uncle. I'm not as tall as you yet."

The older man measured the younger with a careful eye. "You'll be taller than I am in a year," he said. "But I can still put you on your back, my lad!" He was, at the age of thirty-one, the image of his father at that age. Like Myles, he was tall and broad shouldered and had the same auburn hair and blue gray eyes. And he was very fond of his nephew Robin.

For years he had tried to be as much of a companion to the boy as possible. His choice of the sea as a vocation meant that he was gone for long periods, but Robin had been in Thomas's home in Southhampton many times. And to Robin, there was no man on earth finer than his uncle—always excepting his grandfather, of course.

Myles and Hannah had come into the hallway, and it was Hannah who said, "Come now, the food's getting cold. You two can visit later."

Robin fired questions at his uncle as they moved down the hall, and when they were seated, Tom held up his hand. "Hold on, boy! I can't eat and talk at the same time!"

"Yes you can." Robin grinned. "You never had very good manners, Uncle, and I want to know about Drake and the Spaniards."

For the next two hours Tom held his listeners spellbound. He was a fine storyteller and kept them enthralled with the tales of the voyages he had made. Robin leaned forward on his elbows, food forgotten, and his grandfather winked at Hannah at the sight of the boy's rapt attention.

"Did you get any treasure? What's Drake like? When will you—"

Tom held up his hand to forestall the flow of questions. "No, not much treasure. And Francis Drake is the best seaman in the world."

Myles asked with a wry grin, "What happened to all the gold and silver you were supposed to bring back? The queen is expecting a reward for making pirates out of all you sailors."

Tom looked up, a flash of irritation in his eyes. "Not pirates, Father. We're adventurers, sailing under the queen's charter."

"I'm afraid Philip looks on your raiding his ships in a different light, Tom. As a matter of fact, he's making some very harsh comments."

"Oh, he'll make threats, of course. But he's too busy with other things to start a war with England."

"I'd not be too sure about that," Hannah said. "It's no secret that he wants to add England to his territory. He's taken almost everything else."

"No, Mother, he'll never conquer England," Tom insisted. "Not as long as we're surrounded by the sea. It's true, he's got a formidable army, but how would he get them here?"

"In ships, I suppose." Myles shrugged. "The Spaniards have been building many new galleons. What would Philip want a navy for? I think he'll come one day."

Tom sat back and studied his father. *He looks fine for a man of sixty-seven—better than any man I know of that age.* "Have you picked up some information from Mary?"

Myles gave his son a quick glance. "She's been a prisoner for six years now, Tom. And she's tried everything she can to get Elizabeth off the throne so she can be the queen."

"Why doesn't Elizabeth have her head chopped off?"

"She'll never do that," Myles said. "Not so long as she believes in the divine right of kings. In her mind, going against Mary is going against God."

"But Mary's not a queen of anything," Tom protested. "The Scots threw her out!"

"Elizabeth will never touch her." Myles's voice was firm, and he added, "The queen knows that Mary has plotted her death. Sir Francis Walsingham has offered her concrete evidence that Mary has been involved in plots to assassinate her and take the throne. But she will not listen."

"Has Mary been in contact with Spain?"

"Of course she has! Remember, Tom, she's a Catholic, and Philip is the most powerful Catholic sovereign in the world. There was talk of her marrying him, and she'd do it, too. She'd do anything to get her way."

"What's she like, Father?"

Myles smiled suddenly. "Ask Robin. He's been with me several times when I visited there."

Robin was aware of his uncle's interest. "Mary is very polite—and beautiful, too. But it's a strange sort of beauty." He thought hard, then said, "You know how a viper can be very impressive? You can't help admiring them and all, but you know to keep your distance."

"An apt comparison, Robin!" Myles nodded. "She's deadly. And some men are too dazzled by her beauty to see it."

"The duke of Norfolk is one of those," Hannah observed sharply. "He's taken in completely by that woman!"

"Yes, and he'll pay for it someday," Myles agreed, tiring of the subject. He had grown to know Mary Queen of Scots rather well since his first visit, and he disliked anyone who was not loyal to Elizabeth. But he was all too aware of Robin's hatred for Catholics and felt it wise not to pursue the subject. "Well, Thomas," he said briskly, "what is your plan? Back to sea with Drake?"

"No, sir, I have a different idea, but it can't be done without your help."

Myles glanced at Hannah, then turned his eyes back on the tall young man who was so much like himself. "You've been a fine son, Tom," he said simply. "Since we lost William, you've been our hope. And you've never failed us."

"What is it you want to do, Tom?" Hannah asked. She smiled suddenly, the clarity of her skin and beauty of her features belying her sixty-eight years. "It wouldn't be that you want to buy a ship, would it?"

Tom Wakefield stared at her nonplussed, then broke out into a laugh. "I could never hide anything from you, could I?"

"I'm not at all surprised," Myles said, a smile on his lips. "Hannah told me a long time ago we might as well get ready to buy a ship for you."

"What kind of a ship, Uncle?" Robin demanded.

"A fighting ship, Robin. One I can use to sail right up to Philip's front door!" Tom leaned forward, his eyes gleaming. "Philip finances his empire with treasure from the New World. He has to get it to Spain by ship, and those ships can be taken by men of stout will—men like Hawkins and Drake!"

"So," Myles murmured softly, "you'll be a pirate after all." He shook his head before Tom could protest, adding, "I'm not opposed to your plan, Tom. You shall have your ship."

"We'll find one of Philip's treasure ships, Father, and I'll bring back a chest full of gold!"

"That's not why I'm going to buy the ship." Myles looked across the table and paused, his eyes thoughtful. "One day the Spaniards will come. And they'll do so the only way they can—by sea. When that happens, we must have fighting ships and men to sail them, else England will be lost. I'd like to see my son aboard one of the galleons as a captain fighting for Queen Elizabeth."

The four of them sat there for a long time talking about the venture. Tom informed them that a ship must be built, not purchased, and he drew sketches on paper showing them his ideas.

Finally Robin spoke up. "Uncle, take me with you!"

Tom hesitated, giving his parents a quick glance. "You'll have to have Father's permission for that."

Robin turned to his grandfather. "Please, sir, may I go?"

Myles studied the boy for a long moment. "The queen wants you to come to her court. It's a fine opportunity for a young man."

Robin shook his head stubbornly, then gave his grandfather the same words he'd given to the queen: "I'd rather be a sailor!"

A Fighting Ship

A shipbuilder in the year 1575 was no less an artist than the painter who captured images on canvas. One factor separated the two, however, for if a painting was bad, no one died. But if the master shipbuilder failed in his design, men half a world away could become food for the sharks in the depths of a cruel sea.

No two of these wooden ships were ever exactly alike. A ship of the line required ten thousand oak trees, and no two of these trees were exactly the same. The sweeping curves of the ship demanded that men search for trees growing in natural shapes and forms that followed these curves, and then the oak had to be steamed and shaped by heavy presses.

A blueprint could be drawn with exact measurements for every rib and spar, and though two ships could be ordered to fit that design, the vessels would *not* be the same. There was always a slight difference in the materials, and the craftsmen who built each ship never failed to make alterations.

All of this was explained to Robin by his uncle one clear May morning as they stood beside a half-finished ship in Portsmouth. The designer and builder, a stubby Scotsman named James McDougal, had a fiery temper to match his reddish hair. He drove his workers hard, but Thomas had assured Robin, "He may be a hard man to work with, but he builds the finest fighting ships in the world!"

Robin stared at the sweeping curves that made up the skeleton of the ship, his eyes widening. "How do the men know how to make the ribs, Mr. McDougal? None of them are the same, are they?"

"No, boy, each one must have its own shape—" McDougal broke off to bellow, "You there! Johnson! Watch what you're doin'!" He glared at a young man who had displeased him, then turned back to Robin. "Och, come along, laddie. I'll show ye how 'tis done!" He turned and scurried into the shabby building that bordered the waterfront.

Following him, Robin stared around at the clutter of tools, spars, rope, tar, hemp, metal fittings, and a thousand other items. *I don't see how he ever finds anything!* he thought.

"This is a half model, lad," McDougal remarked, holding out a beautifully executed model—or half of one, for it was the left side of a ship split right down the middle. It was made of a very dark wood and was smooth as glass.

Robin reached out to hold it carefully. "Why is it only half made, sir?"

"Because the rib on the other side must match these," McDougal replied. "I need a model to see how the ship will cut the water. But then I make a drawing of each rib. See here?" He dug into a pile of drawings that overflowed a small table, found one, and pointed out to Robin, "A ship will be nae guid unless the men follow these lines." Tossing the sheet on top of the pile, he snapped, "Now, come and ye'll see how it gets off that little paper into a real piece o' wood."

He darted out the door, then stopped beside a bare-chested man with a bald head. He pointed at a large oak beam. "There— ye see it?" Robin saw that the small drawing had been re-created on the beam. The bald man was carefully cutting away excess material, and the finished shape of the curving rib was clearly evident.

McDougal was proud of his work and spoke excitedly of the ship. "She'll be seventy-one feet from stem to sternpost, lad. Not as big as some, but no doot she'll hold her own. She'll have good masts, tackle, and double sails." His small blue eyes glowed as he nodded. "Aye, she'll be a guid sailor." Scurrying along like a terrier, he pointed out, "She's got seven armed portholes on each side, and inside she carries eighteen pieces of artillery—thirteen of bronze and the rest of cast iron."

"She'll have a forge for making nails, spikes, and bolts, too," Thomas added from behind them. He had come from outside to see what was happening, and he ran his hand over one of the ribs lovingly. "And she'll have every kind of weapon we can get— harquebuses, calivers, pistols, pikes, firebombs, fire pikes, bows and arrows, gunpowder, and different kinds of shot. Why, we'll have a floating arsenal!"

Robin was fascinated. He'd come to Portsmouth for a brief visit with his uncle, and every day he was at the shipyard when McDougal and the workmen arrived. He stayed until the master sent him home at dusk, and McDougal once said, "You've got the love of ships in you, lad. If you'd come to me as an apprentice, you'd be a fine shipbuilder."

"Thank you, Mr. McDougal," Robin had said, nodding. "But I'd rather be a sailor."

"Better think on it, lad," the shipbuilder had warned. "You'll not get your head taken off by a round shot here with me."

But Robin knew that he would never be satisfied tied to the land. "I've got to go with you, Uncle," he said time and again. "You've got to get permission for me from Grandfather!"

"I think he'll let you go." Thomas nodded, then grinned. "Father and Mother both know you'll drive them crazy if you don't make the voyage."

"I wish we were leaving today!"

"Well, we're not—and you're going home Tuesday. It'll take months for the *Falcon* to be built, and you'd better put on your best behavior so Father and Mother will let you go." He laughed aloud and reached out to ruffle the boy's thick mop of auburn hair. "Or maybe you'd do better to show your worst side so they'll ship you off just to get rid of you."

"Oh, Uncle Thomas—!"

Tom's eyes glimmered with humor, but that was replaced quickly by a serious expression. "You're going to get a shock, Robin. All boys want to go to sea—I did myself. But it's not going to be what you think. Hard work, bad food, and worse water. There's little but monotony, no privacy, and rough treatment. You'll get no special consideration because you're the captain's nephew."

"I don't care," Robin answered instantly. "I've got to go, Uncle!"

Wakefield nodded, his eyes filled with memories of his own youth. The youthful features of his nephew's face and determination reminded him of himself at that age. "I know, lad. I know how it is. But first, you've got to go home and wait until the *Falcon* sets her sails. Then you'll get your taste of the Spanish Main!"

<hr />

Mary nodded graciously as Myles bent over her hand and kissed it. "It's good to see you, old friend," she said. Her smile was warm, and once again Myles was impressed with the force that emanated from her. "You've been away too long," she added, then turned to Robin and her eyes widened. "And you, young Robin—why, you've become a man!"

Robin disliked Mary—when he was out of her presence, at any rate. But when he was with her, there was something that leaped out of her eyes and made him feel . . . *important*. He had noted that most people were not really paying full attention when they spoke with others. They were thinking of what they would say when it was their turn to talk, or what they would be having for dinner, or how bored they were. But Mary never did this. He had long ago noticed that, when she listened to him, she fixed her wonderful dark eyes on his face and seemed immersed in what he was saying and thinking.

He felt this now, and despite the contempt he had for her religion, he could not help the flush of pleasure that filled his face at her words. He made a bow. "You're looking lovely, Lady Mary, but you always do."

Mary's eyes widened and her lips parted in a sudden giggle. "Why, Robin, you've been taking lessons in how to make pretty speeches!" When she saw this embarrassed him, she at once stepped close to him and put out her hand.

It felt warm and strong in his, and he saw that her skin was as clear and beautiful as that of a young girl. "I shouldn't have said that," she whispered. "You're like your grandfather." She glanced at Myles who was smiling at the two. "Sir Myles is one of the few truly honest men I know. Neither of you would say what you don't mean."

"The boy speaks the truth," Myles said at once. "You are looking very well, indeed."

"Thank you, Sir Myles. And you, too, Robin. Now, how long can you stay? A long visit, I trust?"

"I'm afraid not," Myles said. "We're on our way to London. My son Thomas is building a ship and I'm having to find the money for it. The usurers will have me in their grasp, I fear."

"A ship? What sort of a ship?"

"Robin, you might tell Lady Mary about that. You've talked of nothing else for a week!"

Robin found himself in a chair with Mary, former Queen of Scots, directly across from him. He had known her since he was ten years old, but she seemed no older than the first day he met her in this very room. Her skin was translucent and owed none of its rosy color to paint—not that he could see. She was wearing an upper gown of light blue over an undergown of deep midnight blue. The material was cut away at the neck, and she wore a large solitary diamond on a golden chain. She was a beautiful woman and Robin felt awkward at first, but soon was describing the *Falcon* with enthusiasm.

"She's got all fourteen guns—and most of them are demiculverins, and—"

"A demi *what?*" Mary interrupted.

"Why, a demiculverin, ma'am." Robin nodded. "That's a long-range gun. You see, the old cannons aren't very accurate. A ship has to be pulled right alongside the enemy to be sure of a hit. But when you do that, why the enemy can give *you* a broadside."

Mary was fascinated by the explanation. "And these new guns, they're better?"

"Oh yes, my lady! Much better! With demiculverins our ship will be able to stand off and hit the enemy. They won't be able to reach us with the older guns. . . ."

As the boy spoke Mary listened carefully. As always Robin felt the impact of her full attention, and finally she asked, "And are these new guns used only by the English? If other ships had them, they'd be harder to sink, I take it?"

"Oh, my uncle says that we're not likely to meet any Spanish ships with demiculverins. The dons use the old kind of guns."

Myles felt a tiny alarm go off in his brain and said, "Well, my boy, you mustn't bore Lady Mary with your new hobbyhorse." Turning to Mary he said, "You know how it is with boys—get a new idea in their head and there it is. It's been ships for breakfast and supper ever since Robin came home."

"I wasn't bored, Sir Myles," Mary said quietly. "I'd like to hear more about this wonderful ship." She looked out the high window and seemed to grow very still. "I don't get out in the world, you know. It's a great pleasure when guests come and tell me about what is going on in the large world—outside of my tiny cage."

"We'll stop for a longer visit on our way back from London."

"You'll see the queen?"

"Why yes, I suppose we will."

"Give her my regards. Tell her I grow lonely here." A wistful look touched Mary's eyes and she seemed very vulnerable as a beam of pale yellow sunlight fell across her face. "It would be lovely to visit at court—to see a little color and hear fine music. . . ."

Myles rose and bowed, saying, "I will convey your message to the queen. Now—come along, Robin. We must be going."

When they were mounted and on their way down the dusty road, Robin said, "I feel sorry for her, Grandfather."

"So do I, Robin."

"Why doesn't the queen let her come to court?"

"Well, it's a complicated business, Robin. All sorts of politics are involved. The queen's advisors would never agree to it. As a matter of fact, the Council has urged for a long time for Elizabeth to put Mary to death."

"Why do they want that?"

"Because this country, my boy, is torn between two faiths." Myles turned to the boy, studying him thoughtfully. Finally he seemed to make a decision. "You've been a fine grandson, Robin, in every way but one."

"Sir?"

"Your grandmother and I have been very concerned with your hatred for Catholics."

"They killed my father!"

"The Catholic Church was wrong—terribly wrong! But

Catholics have been put to death by Protestant rulers—who are also wrong. Now listen to me, my boy, you *must* not let this hatred ruin your life. The Lord Jesus commanded us to pray for our enemies, not to kill them. That's the way of the world—hatred and violence. But the kingdom of God is the way of forgiveness and peace. All those who follow Jesus must obey his Word in this matter."

"Then I can't be a Christian!" Robin said bitterly. "How can I love those who killed my own father?"

"Do you hate Meg Tyler? She's a Catholic, but she's been a good friend of the Wakefields for years. And what about Allison Spenser? You don't hate that child, do you?"

"N-no sir, but—!"

"Fight for your country, Robin. A man must do that! But to hate those who differ from you on matters of faith is not right. Can't you see where this bitterness is leading you? It will destroy you." Myles hesitated, then said quietly, "I can tell you this, your hatred would have grieved your father and mother greatly."

Robin said nothing, for he felt the force of his grandfather's words. But there was a dark passion in him that would not be subdued. "I'm sorry—I'll try to do better."

"Good boy!"

Later that night as they got ready for bed in their room, Myles said, "Mary was very interested in the *Falcon.*"

"Yes!" Robin agreed. "She was, wasn't she? Most women don't care for such things."

"Do you know why she was interested?"

"Why, I suppose she just liked such things."

"No, that's not it, boy." Myles pulled off one boot, flexed his toes, and stared at the hole in his stocking. "I don't know why a man can't have a pair of stockings without his toes poking out."

Robin watched as his grandfather pulled off the other boot then lay back with a groan before asking, "Grandfather, why was she interested in the *Falcon?*"

"She's interested in anything that would bring her to the throne, Robin. That's what she lives for." He turned his head and fixed his eyes on the young man. "That's why I feel sorry for her. *You* feel sorry for her because she's a prisoner. But she has a staff of forty servants to wait on her and every sort of food and clothing she desires. And if it were not for Queen Elizabeth she'd have been given back to the Scots, who would have beheaded her in an instant!"

"But—she's a prisoner!"

"Yes, and she put herself in that prison," Myles said grimly. "If she had been wiser, she would still be ruling Scotland. But she threw that away and now spends all her time and energy plotting against the queen—the very person who saved her when she came to England!"

"But what about the *Falcon?*"

"Can't you guess, Robin?"

"Well, I've heard you say that the Spaniards will come over the sea to fight us—" Robin halted abruptly, understanding coming to him. "You mean, she wants to find out all she can that will help the Spanish?"

"Exactly, and you gave her some valuable information."

"But I didn't mean—"

"I know, Robin, I know. She's an attractive woman and she knows how to get what she wants from men. She's been the ruin of several men who were drawn into her web. Now, don't hate her," Myles said quickly. "Pray for her—but don't ever forget that she will do anything to gain the throne of England!"

"Why do we go to see her if she's a traitor?"

"The queen has asked me to do so. She's apprehensive about Mary and wants someone she trusts to watch her. Not a spy," he added hastily. "There are plenty of those! Mary has a network of her own—and Sir Francis Walsingham has many working for the Crown. Her Majesty wants someone to watch Mary on a more personal level."

"Is that why you report to the queen, sir?"

"Yes. And so far for all these years I've had nothing good to report." Myles was so weary he could hardly keep his eyes open, but he said almost fiercely, "Robin, you must be careful! Mary would use you—and she's not the only one. Keep your own counsel. Say nothing to anyone of Mary—and say nothing to her that could be used against England."

Robin said, "I'll be very careful, Grandfather." He lay down beside Myles and for a long time lay awake. He tried to pray but was too weary to do even that, and sleep struck him like a blow. . . .

Somehow the months passed, each seeming to stretch out into a year for Robin. He did his work better than ever, and finally the day came when he climbed into a coach for the journey from Wakefield to Portsmouth. He slept hardly at all at the inn halfway to the coast, and by the time he arrived he was tired and sleepy. It was dark by the time he had disembarked and made his way to the dock—too dark for him to see the ship. He hired a small dory to take him aboard the *Falcon,* and as he stepped on board, he was greeted by Thomas Wakefield, who gave him a slap on the shoulder.

"Well, Robin—here it is, eh? Off to sea, by Jove!"

"Yes sir!"

"Well, it's too dark for you to see the ship, but come to my cabin and I'll show you the charts."

Robin followed the captain below and was delighted with the snug cabin. "A little small, but large enough," Thomas said.

"You'll have your own like this one of these days—but for now you'll sleep with the crew. Good-bye to that nice little room of yours, Robin!"

"I don't care, Uncle," Robin said smiling. "I'm here—and that's what counts."

"Right! Now, let me show you where we're going. . . ."

The new captain was full of his new ship and the venture that lay ahead of them. He had also slept well the previous night and kept his nephew up late. He had some food brought in from the galley at half past twelve, and Robin ate hungrily.

After the sailor took the dishes away, Thomas continued to speak, pointing at the map. The swinging lamp cast sliding shadows to and fro across the paper. The spidery outlines of land and the network of lines seemed to Robin to be constantly shifting. His uncle's voice melted into a constant drone merged with the sighing of the ocean outside the *Falcon's* walls.

Finally the captain took him to the forecastle, where sleeping men covered the deck almost shoulder to shoulder. "Find yourself a place, Robin," Thomas said. "We take the early tide. And from now on, I'm your captain—not your uncle, right?"

"Aye, Captain!"

Robin waited until his uncle left, then stepped over several still forms until he found a spot next to a bulkhead. Tossing his bag down, he fell to the deck and was asleep at once.

He came out of sleep as abruptly as he'd entered it.

"Come on, you lubber! Get your carcass off the deck!"

Robin's eyes flew open instantly, and from where he was sprawled he could see a surly man with a shock of black hair standing over him. He struggled to his feet, but not fast enough, for strong fingers took a fistful of his hair and yanked him upright. Robin blinked with pain but said nothing.

The sailor thrust his face close to Robin's and snarled, "You come for a bloomin' pleasure cruise, lubber?"

"No, I just—"

"You're on this ship to work, you peach-faced lubber! And work is what you'll do, no mistake!" The fingers tightened in his hair, but Robin managed to keep his face from revealing the pain.

"Work is what keeps lubbers out of mischief, and you can thank the good Lord for sending you a shipmaster who'll work you until you drop! Now is that clear?"

The fingers in his hair tightened, and Robin said loudly, "Yes, sir!"

The fingers dug in even more fiercely. "Captain's nephew, are you?"

"Well—yes sir."

"Not no more, you ain't! Yer the lowest piece of life on this here ship! Let me catch you not working and I'll have the hide off you, won't I?"

"Yes sir—!"

"We'll have a gentleman's agreement, you and me, lubber. You work 'til you drop and I don't flog you at the grate, agreed?"

The last speech was accompanied by such yanks and jerks on Robin's locks that he half expected to see his hair come loose in the master's hands.

"Now—get to the galley and help the cook!"

Robin stumbled to the main deck and looked about. Dawn was already tinting the sky, and the *Falcon* was moving crisply before a freshening breeze. The shoreline was no more than a thin gray line on the horizon. *At last—I'm at sea!*

But he had only that one instant to enjoy his new life, for the master's voice bellowed in his ear: "I said help the cook, lubber!"

A boot in his backside sent Robin flying across the deck. He barked his shin against a corner of the main hatch, stumbled, and almost fell right into the firebox, where the cook was stirring the contents of a steaming pot. He jumped to his feet and saw that the cook was laughing at him. "New boy, are you?" He was an

162

undersized individual with not a single tooth in his head. He wore the most filthy apron Robin had ever seen, and his hands were worse.

"You heard about the dog whose bark was wuss than his bite?"

"Yes, I have."

"Well, the master's got a bad bark—but just you wait! Ye'll find out his bite is *much* wuss than his bark!"

For the next week Robin worked so hard he scarcely had time to look at the sea. He was at the beck and call of the captain, the master, the bo's'n, and all the senior mariners. "Fetch that." "Tell the master gunner this." "Clean out here."

He gobbled his food between chores and at night fell asleep as if he'd been drugged. Each morning the master came to awaken him personally. "All right Captain's nephew, get up—!" And Robin would pull himself up and begin a long day of backbreaking work.

Once he paused to look up at the sails that bellied out under a strong wind. *And I always thought the sailors set the sails and the wind did all the work! Never thought about all the other work that has to be done!*

The captain never spoke a friendly word, but kept his commands terse, his eyes hard. He gave no man cause for saying he showed favoritism—quite the contrary!

Late one afternoon, however, he stopped to stand over Robin, who was on his hands and knees wearily scrubbing the deck. "Ships boy!" he said briskly. "Come with me!"

Robin rose with alacrity and followed as the captain moved to the bow of the *Falcon*. When they were at the very point of the ship, the captain turned and smiled. "Had a hard time of it, Robin?"

"No sir!"

Thomas studied the boy, noting the roughness of the hands and the hollowed eyes. "That's the way to talk!" He smiled. "You've done well. The master says you're the best ship's boy he's ever had."

Robin flushed with pleasure. "I—I like it, Uncle—I mean *Captain!*"

"Good! Now that you've proved yourself, I want you to learn more about a ship than washing dirty dishes and mopping decks. Tonight I'll teach you a little about navigation. But for now, let me show you the *Falcon*. . . . "

Robin Wakefield followed his captain, who moved along the ship, pointing out the fine features, and he thought, *This is what I want to be! Someday I'll be a Sea Hawk, like Drake and Hawkins!*

Somehow the dream that had been with him so long no longer seemed impossible. He felt the ship surging beneath his feet like a living creature and looked up to see the full-bellied sails driving the *Falcon* through the green water. Taking a deep breath, he savored the salty tang of the ocean and knew that as long as he lived, he would have to have the sea!

Twelve

NEW MEMBER
OF THE COURT

Queen Elizabeth was not fond of the morning time, as she herself admitted. Sometimes she rose by eight, but usually she stayed in bed while the household staff went about their duties. This suited the maids of the court very well, for the queen thought nothing of keeping them up until after midnight.

Dorcas Freeman, the latest to join the ranks of the queen's maids, saw an opportunity in this situation to win the queen's favor. She made sure she was the first to rise and was always available when Elizabeth sent for an attendant.

Dorcas was the daughter of an impoverished nobleman so devoted to gambling that he had little left of the family fortune. This Sir Matthew Freeman had only one asset: his beautiful daughter. He had pulled the necessary strings and paid the necessary bribes to get Dorcas accepted as one of Elizabeth's maids in the court, then sat back to wait for the harvest. That being, of course, a wealthy husband who could support a father-in-law in fine style.

The court of Elizabeth was the place for such things. The Virgin Queen would not tolerate amours among her attendants. She expected all of them to be as chaste as she. Furthermore, she expected all the young men to give their first loyalty to her, not to romancing. Of course, Elizabeth realized what the coy looks and ecstatic gasps in darkened doorways signified. The rumors of amorous pairings among her retinue did not escape her. She knew as well as anyone what "sickness" it really was that sometimes took one of the maids suddenly from court and kept her in the country for several months. Officially, however, she was ignorant of all this, and whenever a scandal came into the open her rage was explosive.

But Dorcas Freeman did not mind the queen's stand. Indeed, she understood that illicit behavior would bring only short-term pleasure. Marriage with a lord would be far more convenient! Thus she set herself to win the queen's favor.

Jane Barclay, the chaperone of the maids, appeared before the young woman one morning at seven. She had seen many maids come and many leave, so she well understood this new maid's maneuverings. But it was a thing that pleased her, for it meant more faithfulness on the girl's part. "Her Majesty wants you, Dorcas," she told the girl.

Dorcas at once went into the queen's bedroom, where she found Elizabeth in her nightdress, looking out of her bedchamber window.

"Dorcas, I am ready."

"Yes, Your Majesty."

While all of the maids had learned to assist the queen with her cosmetics, Dorcas had realized instantly the importance that Elizabeth placed on personal beauty. So she had become an expert in that area. She knew that the queen preserved her pure white skin with a lotion made of egg white, powdered eggshell, alum, borax, and white poppyseeds. The maid became skilled in beating the milky fluid until a froth three fingers deep stood on it. She washed Elizabeth's hair with a lye mixed with a compound of wood ash and water. Elizabeth swore by this milder form of shampoo, as opposed to the more caustic solutions other women chose to use.

Dorcas knew Elizabeth had little need to use those violent forms of cosmetics used by some to keep her skin fair. Nothing, it seemed, bespoke beauty more than clear, fair skin. To achieve this whiteness, some ladies used preparations with exotic ingredients such as beeswax, asses' milk, and the ground jawbones of hogs. Others used more dangerous substances: sulfur, ground brimstone, turpentine, and mercuric sulfide. But Elizabeth needed no such measures. Her skin, according to Sir Thomas Wyatt, was by nature "white as Albion rocks."

Now, as Dorcas worked on the queen with care, she listened as the older woman spoke from time to time of the court. Mostly she mentioned her favorites, and Dorcas was quick to speak with admiration of Sir Robert Dudley, for he was in the queen's favor—for the moment.

When the cosmetics were complete, she watched as Elizabeth cleaned her teeth with tooth cloths using a mixture of white wine and vinegar boiled with honey. Elizabeth's sense of smell was legendary—she had ordered some people from court for offending with their odor! Often she wore rose water imported from Antwerp, but on this morning she said, "Let me have the marjoram." It was well known that this scent was her favorite—so much so that people had taken to calling it "Queen Elizabeth's Perfume."

The cosmetics done, Dorcas helped the queen don the brilliant yellow dress that she had chosen for the day. The maids of honor wore black and white—perhaps deliberately chosen to set off the striking colors and bright embroidery of Elizabeth's wardrobe. Finally, the queen put on a glittering necklace of diamonds and adorned her fingers with rings of rubies and emeralds.

"Now, then," Elizabeth said with satisfaction, "I am ready for the world." She turned from the mirror and smiled, revealing bad teeth. "You are always here in the morning, Dorcas, no matter how late I keep you up."

"Yes, Your Majesty," Dorcas answered. "That is my duty."

"Others are not so sensitive." Elizabeth moved to stand before the young woman, cupping her chin. "You are lovely," she mused. "And young men have told you so?"

"One or two, my queen."

Elizabeth turned and walked to the window. Staring out at the courtyard below, she seemed to forget her maid. But then she wheeled and asked, "How old are you?"

"Nineteen, Your Majesty."

"And your father wants you to marry well." At the girl's widened eyes, she smiled. "Oh, I know all about how he got you into my court, and it matters not. You are here and you have served me well." Elizabeth studied the girl, trying to read beneath the outer appearance—an appearance that was impressive, for Dorcas had long blonde hair and bright blue eyes. All her features were well shaped, and her figure was slender yet fully curved. "And you, my dear," the queen finally said, "do you want to marry?"

"Why, one day I will, Your Majesty."

Elizabeth nodded briskly. She liked the girl and well understood how things stood. "Most men of wealth and position are old. You would not like such a marriage." Seeing the confusion in the girl's eyes, she said, "Never mind, child. We will find you a husband who is rich, young, and handsome!"

Dorcas knew that the queen was sincere, for Elizabeth loved making matches. "That would be very pleasing, Your Majesty. But the supply of such men is bound to be scarce."

"No doubt, but we will see. Let us look at the possibilities at the entertainment tonight. Perhaps we shall see someone that will do."

Dorcas smiled, a dimple appearing in her left cheek. "You make getting a husband sound like buying a new dress, Your Majesty!"

Elizabeth found this delightful and her laughter was loud and boisterous. As it echoed in the halls, it reminded some of her father, Henry VIII. "I believe your comparison is apt, Dorcas. In fact, many—both men and women—choose their clothes with more care than they choose their mates!"

"I will be guided by your wisdom, Your Majesty. Everyone knows that in matters of love Queen Elizabeth has no peer." Dorcas had learned very quickly that the queen was so saturated with lush compliments from the lords and ladies of her court, that no compliment was too far-fetched.

Elizabeth said thoughtfully, "Something has come to me. A possible suitor for you." Her smallish eyes beamed, and she said, "Wear something colorful tonight—and wear some of my jewels."

Since the queen paid her no special attention during the first hour of the banquet, Dorcas assumed that she had forgotten their conversation. *But she's listening to the music—and when there's music, she pays little heed to anything.*

After the music ceased and the musicians were applauded, Elizabeth suddenly looked up at two men who had entered the room. Then she turned and beckoned to Dorcas, who went to her at once. Sir Robert Dudley was seated beside the queen and listened closely as she said, "Dorcas, go ask those two men to come to me. One is a fine lord and the other, his grandson, a brave sailor returned from sea. Bring them to me yourself." As she spoke she smiled and there was a gleam in her eyes. "We may have a prospect here."

Dorcas understood her meaning at once. Turning, she made her way to the two men and said courteously, "Her Majesty asks that you come to her." The older of the two men nodded his thanks, and they rose and followed her.

"You are late, Sir Myles," Elizabeth said. "But you have brought our young friend with you."

"As you command, my queen."

"Robin, are you content to stay in my court for a time?"

Myles had warned Robin that this request was coming, so he had had time to work through his intense disappointment at not being free to return to the sea. Now he nodded. "Yes, Your Majesty."

Elizabeth said, "You must meet the lords and ladies. I will let my most faithful maid of honor introduce you." She waved her hand saying, "This is Dorcas Freeman, who will be your guide. Dorcas, this is Sir Myles Wakefield. And his grandson, Robin."

Robin and Myles both bowed, and Dorcas said, "If you will come with me, sir, I will make you acquainted with some of the guests."

Sir Robert Dudley laughed aloud. "Keep him away from the temptations of the court, Dorcas. Mister Wakefield is a simple country squire unaccustomed to such dangers."

When the pair had left, Elizabeth looked at Dudley. "It will be confusing, having two men named Robin." This was her nickname for Dudley. "But I shall have no trouble keeping the two of you separate. How old is the young man, Myles?"

"His birthday will be easy for you to remember, Your Majesty," Myles said with a slight smile. "He came into the world the day you became queen of England. When he was a child he always thought the grand celebrations in the village were for his birthday rather than for your coronation."

The queen was delighted with that, and Dudley said, "He is a handsome lad, Sir Myles." Then he added, "Earlier I spoke in jest to the fair maid leading him about. But in truth, are you not afraid that the young fellow will be corrupted by the more venal members of our court?"

Myles considered Dudley, thinking that *he* was one of the *most* venal men in England. But he had ever been a man to tell the truth, so he said, "I think, Sir Robert, that the court of Queen Elizabeth is rather like one of those fascinating carved ivory globes that come from the Orient. You've seen them, I'm sure. They are made of a succession of hollow balls, each inside the other. From the outside, one can glimpse the innermost sphere, but to observe its pattern in detail would be difficult if not impossible!"

Elizabeth had a keen analytical mind and was a poet as well. She nodded vigorously saying, "An excellent figure, Myles! Very apt, indeed. My court *is* complex, but I trust you are confident enough to leave your grandson with us?"

"He is an obedient lad, Your Highness. He will go where he is bid. But his heart is linked to the sea."

"I need good seamen," Elizabeth murmured. "But we shall not spoil him here. I promise you that, old friend."

"I did not suppose any differently, Your Majesty."

When Myles left to return to his table, Dudley asked, "What are you about, my lady? Dorcas is wearing your jewels. Are you matchmaking again?"

"Of course!" she said, smiling broadly. She looked to where the couple stood across the room. "Don't they make a fine-looking couple?"

Dorcas had introduced Robin to Timothy Hatten, one of the favorites of the queen. The two immediately struck up a conversation, and Dorcas was content to stand silent, studying the young man as they spoke. She liked what she saw: Robin Wakefield was tall, handsome, young, and richly dressed. He wore an Italian-style doublet set with red stones, and the jornet about his shoulders was of the same deep red wine color. His well-formed, muscular legs were encased in close-fitting hose, and on his feet were soft felt shoes. He wore a gold chain around his neck, and a rich ruby set in gold flashed from his finger.

He was very tall, quite lean, and his thick auburn hair glinted under the candles and lamps. Suddenly his blue-gray eyes turned to meet hers, and she asked, "Mister Wakefield, would you care to eat something?"

Robin had been dazzled by the court. He felt uncomfortable in the fine clothes his grandfather had bought for him earlier, but he was entranced by the beauty of the girl who was his guide. "Why, I think I might, if you would join me."

"Of course." They found places to sit, and soon Robin was sampling the ornate menu that the court of Elizabeth featured. Course after course came in a profusion of strange foods. Beef after the broth, the rabbit and the capon after the carp, the swan after the stork.

"What is *this?*" he asked, staring at a new dish set in front of them by a servant.

"I believe that's bear." Dorcas smiled. "Do you like bear meat?"

"Never tasted one of the beasts." Gingerly, Robin took a bite, chewed it thoughtfully, then said, "Tastes like what I think a hawk might taste like!"

Dorcas laughed with delight, her dimple appearing. She was wearing an emerald-green dress that exposed her creamy shoulders, and a necklace of jade and emeralds glittered as she moved. "Don't mention it to the queen—the hawk, I mean. She'd have one served at once!"

Robin shook his head. "Do you eat like this every night?"

"Oh, no. Only at banquets. And the queen eats almost nothing—and drinks even less."

The two of them ate some of the custards and jellies that followed, but finally Robin said, "I am stuffed! And I could almost drift off to sleep, it's so warm in here."

"I agree. Shall we go outside for a breath of fresh air?" Dorcas rose and led him through one of the outer doors to a small garden surrounded by a hedge and life-sized statues. "This is nice, isn't it, Mister Wakefield?" Dorcas smiled and turned to him.

"Yes, but please call me Robin."

"Then you must call me Dorcas."

Robin had rarely felt so uncomfortable. He had had few experiences with girls. He was completely inexperienced, except for a few stolen kisses from the young servant girls at Wakefield. As for this exquisitely dressed and beautiful young woman who stood looking up at him in the moonlight—he had no more idea how to speak to her than he would to a Persian princess. "Tell me, Dorcas, exactly what does a maid of the court do?"

Dorcas smiled, the dimple appearing. "Why, we help the queen dress in the morning and get undressed at night. We wait on her at mealtimes, attend her at official functions. We go to chapel with her, see to her linen and her jewels and trinkets . . ."

As the young woman went on, Robin was acutely aware of the scent of her perfume. It made him slightly dizzy, as did the sight of her bare arms and shoulders and the curves of her body. He struggled to concentrate on what she was saying, keeping his eyes fixed on her face. Finally when she ended her recitation, he said, "Do you like it? Being a maid of the court?"

"Yes, I do. All the great men and women of our country surround the queen, and I get to meet some of them." The dimple appeared again. "Young courtiers such as Master Robin Wakefield."

Robin blinked in surprise. "Why, I'm scarcely that!"

"I think you must be, for the queen said so." Dorcas looked toward a bench beside the hedge. "Sit down and tell me about yourself, Robin. If we're going to be friends, we have to know all about each other." She seated herself so close that Robin could feel the touch of her arm. "For example, how old are you?"

"Seventeen."

"Why, I'm a year older than you, so you shall have to be respectful of your elders!" Actually Dorcas was two years older than Robin, but that bit of information she did not reveal.

For the next hour Robin enjoyed himself greatly. He had no idea how a lovely young woman of some experience could draw out a young man who has had none. Finally he said, "I . . . guess we'd better get back. Not that I want to."

"I suppose so." Dorcas rose, but as she moved across the brick flooring, she lost her balance. Robin reached out quickly and caught her.

"Oh, how clumsy of me!" she exclaimed, holding his arm tightly.

Robin smiled. Little experience or no, even he was not completely ignorant. As the girl lay against him, looking up with her lips half parted, he drew her close and kissed her firmly. The taste of her lips and the warmth of her response sent a riot of emotion through him, and he lost himself in the sweetness of her soft embrace.

Too soon for Robin, Dorcas pulled away. "You learn the ways of the court very quickly, Robin Wakefield! You must think very little of me to treat me so!"

"Oh! I didn't mean—!" He broke off, abashed, convinced that he had insulted the young woman. He stood there unable to meet her eyes, then muttered, "I'm very sorry, Dorcas! I'm not—I don't know anything about—about all this."

Dorcas looked down, struggling against the urge to smile at his stuttering reaction. She steadied her voice as she said, "So you say, but I will be more careful in the future. Some men are not to be trusted."

Robin felt like a chastised schoolboy, but he managed a smile. "Thank you, Dorcas. I meant no harm. It's just that, well, you are so pretty!"

"Why, thank you, Robin." Dorcas smiled demurely, then took his arm as they turned toward the door. "You will be here for some time, will you not?"

"Yes. Will you show me around tomorrow?"

"If the queen says I may. She's very careful of us, you know. But I think it might be done. Provided, of course, you promise to behave."

The party lasted until very late, but finally Elizabeth left with her maids. As Dorcas helped get her ready for bed, the queen said, "I noticed you and young Wakefield had a walk in the garden."

"Why yes, Your Majesty."

"Mind it comes to no more than that," Elizabeth said. "Well, what did you think of him?"

"He's very nice."

"His grandfather is fairly well off. He has a son, Thomas, who will inherit the title, but there's property enough for both. Still, he's only a boy. You may do better."

"He's going to be a sailor. If they capture a Spanish treasure ship, he'll be very wealthy. He told me all about it."

"I hope he does, for the Crown will get its share! Now, don't let me hear of any foolishness between the two of you!"

Dorcas looked at the queen, her eyes wide and innocent. "No, Your Majesty! Of course not."

<hr>

Three months of life at Elizabeth's court had served to educate Robin Wakefield greatly. He had learned several interesting things: The morals of those at court were no better than anywhere else; most of those who proclaimed undying loyalty to the queen did so in hope of getting some office; and even the most ornate meals and ceremonies, regardless of cost, could, with repetition, become infinitely boring.

But one thing happened at court that took him wholly by

surprise: He had fallen in love with Dorcas Freeman. And, in the time-honored ways of young men caught by a first love, he succeeded at making quite a fool of himself.

As for the object of his devotion, she kept him dangling so that at times he was convinced she was playing some sort of game with him. At other times, however, she was so warm and pleasing that he felt he could not live without her. Robin had had no idea that love was such a powerful force. And the fact that Dorcas, a beautiful young woman sought by many older men, might return his affections so flustered him that he could scarce recall his name.

"Love is like a fever, Wakefield," Sir Robert Dudley once said to him, noting the flush that rose in the younger man's face when Dorcas entered the room. "A man gets weak in the knees and rather giddy with both illnesses!"

Elizabeth watched young Wakefield as he learned to comport himself, but said no more to Dorcas. She did not approve of hasty matches and had in mind a courtship of several years. That way she could retain the services of her maid and at the same time take credit for the match when it finally happened. To Myles she said, "Your grandson is quite taken with one of my maids. I expect he's told you. I am sure you will agree with me that he should not marry until he's older."

Robin moped and longed for Dorcas—and it was at this stage that Sir Francis Walsingham entered the picture. Robin was surprised when the secretary of the Council invited him to his quarters, and he went at once. When they were alone, Walsingham offered him wine, then entertained him with anecdotes of the great men and women of the court.

After a particularly humorous tale, Walsingham looked at Robin with interest. "And you, sir, intend to be a sailor. Or so your grandfather tells me."

"Why, yes sir. I want it more than anything!"

"A fine calling." Walsingham spoke of the navy and how John

Hawkins had built it to a fine fighting pitch. "There will be a place for fine young sailors such as yourself, and I would like to help you when that time comes."

Robin was stunned. Sir Francis was the most powerful man in England, with the exception of Lord Burghley of course. It was incredible that such a man would offer to promote him! "Sir, I can only thank you. I hope to serve England well when that time comes."

Walsingham leaned forward, his face utterly serious. "You need not wait until then to serve your country, sir. I have asked you here because there is a need that you might fill now."

"Me, Sir Francis? Why, I can't imagine what I could do. My grandfather is more likely—"

"He is already doing what he can, Mister Wakefield, but he is not young." Walsingham's eyes seemed to bore into Robin. He let the silence run for a moment, then said quietly, "Your father was executed by the Catholic Church, I understand."

Robin felt the anger that always rose in him when his father's death was mentioned. "Yes, sir. He was burned at the stake."

"You loved your father's memory. Love it still?"

"Yes, sir!"

"Then hear me out, young man." The secretary leaned forward, his voice intent. "The fires will be lit again at Smithfield if something is not done. I have proof that William Cardinal Allen has established a new college at Douai in France, the sole purpose of which is to train priests called Jesuits."

"Train them for what, Sir Francis?"

"To invade England, and to destroy the Protestant religion!" Walsingham was a fervent Christian, and most of his fervency was dedicated to keeping England free from the Roman Church. He longed to see Protestant Germany and Scotland unite with England in a league against the Catholic powers.

"But what can *I* do?" Robin asked.

"You can do many things. You are well acquainted with Mary, the so-called Queen of Scots. You can keep her under observation. She will never stop plotting to bring Catholicism back to this land."

"So my father says. But how can I—"

"You can be an agent for the Crown. These Jesuits will infiltrate England. We believe they have already come. If Elizabeth and the Protestant religion are to survive, we *must* rid the country of the Jesuits!"

Robin sat with his back straight and, as Walsingham spoke, he found himself agreeing with what the secretary said. The hatred he'd managed to suppress for the last few years suddenly flooded back—and his grandfather's words and warnings fled.

Even before Walsingham finally said, "Well, Mister Wakefield, will you serve the queen in this matter?" Robin's mind was made up.

"Yes, I will do the best I can, sir!"

"Fine! Fine!" The man's face glowed with pleasure. "You will also serve God, for if we do not win against these men who come to destroy us—there will be no true religion in England! Now, let me give you your instructions. . . ."

Robin left the room an official agent of the Crown, dedicated to crushing the Jesuit movement in England. *At last I will avenge my father's death!* The thought stayed with him all night, but he knew his grandfather and grandmother would never approve. The thought of displeasing them hurt him. . . .

But he set his jaw and made plans to serve the queen.

Thirteen

VISIT FROM THE QUEEN

You have never been on one of the queen's progresses, have you, Robin?"

"No. What are they like?"

Robin and Dorcas were riding in a long caravan led by the queen, who was mounted on a milk-white charger. The entourage had left the palace early, and they were making their way down the winding road that led south. Dorcas was clad in a pearl-gray riding costume, her cheeks tinged with the summer sun—and Robin thought she had never looked more beautiful.

"The queen's progresses are like a traveling banquet," Dorcas replied. "Every summer she wants to show herself to her people and to mingle with them."

"They love her, don't they?" Robin observed as the queen stopped the entire procession to lean down and take a bouquet from a group of ragged children. "And no wonder." He studied the scene, then nodded. "I've not learned much this past year, but I think I know the secret of Queen Elizabeth's success. For her, England is a husband. The Virgin Queen needs no other."

"Nor will she ever have one, I am sure." Dorcas gave Robin a sudden brilliant smile. "Nor will I, I sometimes think."

Robin moved his horse closer to her and took her hand. "You will have me!"

"Shall I? But we should have to live in a cottage where I would sweep the floor and you would milk the cow." She spoke lightly, but there was a serious note in her voice. For months he had begged her to marry him, but she had held off. He was an exciting young man, handsome and amorous enough to suit any young woman. As a matter of fact, one of the other maids of the court, a tall beauty named Estelle Godolphin, had said in disgust, "If you don't want him, Dorcas, give him to me. I wouldn't mind having him!"

Dorcas had smiled sweetly and answered, "When *I* have him, Estelle, there will be a wedding ring on my finger."

Now Robin shot her a suspicious look. "I suppose you think Sir Ralph Hastings would suit better, then? I get sick of the sight of that old man running around after you with his tongue hanging out like a hound's!"

"Old? He's no more than forty-five," Dorcas shot back. She didn't add that the knight was crude and disgusted her. That wouldn't help at all in keeping Robin jealous. But when she saw that he was on the brink of becoming angry, she smiled sweetly and squeezed his hand. "Don't be angry with me, Robin! A girl must be careful in these things. I love you, but we have to live."

"When Tom and I take one of Philip's treasure ships next year, I'll cover you with diamonds and gold!"

"Then you wouldn't have to milk the cow—and I could spend all my time making myself attractive for you." The two of them rode on as the procession started up, and Dorcas smiled, pleased with the exchange. *He's got everything but a fortune—and he may soon have that.*

As they approached Kenilworth, the ornate home of Sir Robert Dudley, Robin said, "I think these progresses are to save the queen money. Sir Francis says she's frightfully stingy. And some of her visits have been known to ruin men who aren't as rich as Dudley or Cecil."

Indeed, the cost of entertaining the queen on progress ran as high as a thousand pounds a day; a laborer lived on seven pence a day. This expense was due to the cost of food, which was enormous. Sir Nicholas Backon, the Lord Keeper of England, was obligated to purchase sixty sheep, as well as thirty-four lambs, twenty-six pigs, eighteen calves, eight oxen, ten kids, and dozens upon dozens of birds: over three hundred chickens, more than two hundred pigeons, twelve dozen ducklings and herons, ten dozen geese, sixteen dozen quail, not to mention huge quantities of partridges, larks, curlews, pheasants, and mallards.

Aside from the colossal expense to the host, the towns through which the procession passed also had to make preparations. Once the route had been decided upon, the timetable worked out, and the queen's changes of mind allowed for—the towns and villages on the route were notified. Officials then set to work removing dunghills, pillories, and stocks; covering the streets over which she was to pass with gravel; and strewing the floors of the houses that she was to enter with rushes and herbs. There were fireworks to buy; Latin orations to rehearse; and choirs, musicians, and country dancers to be given repeated practices. Gowns and dresses had to be washed and pressed, mayoral regalia polished, stages erected, and canvas forts and wooden castles built for mock battles and military pageants. Sometimes walls even had to be pulled down to make streets wide enough for the grand processions to pass through.

Still, for all the work and expense, few complained. And Robin saw the reason why that afternoon. A tiny village had done its best to please the queen, and she had spoken graciously, thanking them for their kindness and hospitality. Looking down at their faces as they knelt to her, she had said, "A more powerful prince you may have someday, but a more loving one never!"

The trip to Kenilworth took three days, and the earl met the queen and her train seven miles from his home. He had a feast for her under a tent so vast that, when dismantled, it required seven carts to carry it away. Later, when Robin moved inside the house, he was stunned by the opulence. Scarlet leather hangings stamped with gilt covered the walls, and a Turkish carpet of light blue that was at least fifty feet long muffled the sound of many feet. Glass was everywhere, adding a brilliant magic. The pantry contained rows of glass dishes for cream, and the great rooms were lit by candles resting in glass candlesticks.

Robin paused to stare at one of the candlesticks, a beautiful piece made of blue glass and decorated with gilt. "This thing must have cost as much as a farm!" he exclaimed to Dorcas, then shook his head, his lips tight. "The queen needs ships, not candlesticks and doodads!"

"Oh, Robin, don't be silly!" Dorcas gave him a pinch on the arm. "Just forget your ship and enjoy all of this."

But he was not destined to spend his time with the rest of the party. Sir Francis Walsingham, who had come to Kenilworth unexpectedly, met Robin after a luxurious dinner. "Perhaps we could have a walk in Sir Robert's gardens, Mister Wakefield," he said. "I want to hear about the *Falcon.*"

Robin agreed, suspecting this was only a feint to get him alone. He had been working steadily for the secretary and had been more successful than either he or the secretary had thought he would be. Robin had developed an ability to win people's trust, thereby gaining valuable information from those who never suspected he was, in truth, a spy for the queen. And he found a certain satisfaction in knowing that, every time he exposed a priest or someone who promoted the Catholic religion, he had struck a blow against those who had murdered his father.

His suspicion regarding Walsingham's motives proved correct. As soon as the two men were in the garden, the secretary said, "I have it on good authority that there is a Jesuit hiding in the vicinity of your home."

"You mean Wakefield?" Robin looked startled. "Why, I've not heard anything like that, Sir Francis."

Walsingham nodded thoughtfully. His long face was sober and he said, "I fear it is true, and I count on you to ferret him out. You've done well, Robin. It was through your efforts that we managed to run at least three of the agents of Rome to earth!"

"I—I sometimes worry about putting them to death. Couldn't they be shipped out of the country?"

"The Jesuits?" Walsingham stared at Robin incredulously. "Why, my boy, you've totally misread the thing! Those men have taken a vow to overturn Protestantism in England, whatever the cost. If we merely pack them up and ship them back to France or Spain, why, they'd be back like vipers among us on the next ship!"

"I suppose that's so, but—"

Walsingham put his hand on the tall young man's shoulder. "I know it's hard, but think of it this way: When you become a sailor, what will you do when you sight a Spanish galleon?"

"Why, capture her!"

"Yes, but what if they resist? Which you know they will. You'll fight them to the death, won't you? Well, that's the way you must think of your work as an agent for the queen. The Jesuits are more deadly to her than any Spanish sailor!"

Robin listened carefully and finally asked a question that had long plagued him. "The queen . . . is she a firm Protestant, Sir Francis?"

Walsingham did not answer at once. He kept his eyes on the path as he and Wakefield walked along between two flowerbeds. The air was sweet with the fragrance of the flowers, and there was a humming in the air as the bees tumbled the blossoms. Finally he said, "She is more concerned with state policy than with doctrine, I must confess. Oh, she attends chapel and reads her Bible, but I do not think she is committed to the New Religion, to Protestantism, so deeply as we would hope. However, she *is* committed to keeping England free from the horrors of Catholicism, and she does consent to my policy of hunting the Jesuits down."

"I will see what I can find out, Sir Francis. If the queen will permit me to leave."

"I think that can be arranged." Walsingham smiled, studying the young man carefully. "You don't like being a courtier, do you, lad?"

"No, sir, I don't! 'Tis nothing but vanity." Robin's eyes flashed as he said, "I can't bear much more of it, Sir Francis! Can't you persuade the queen to let me go to sea?"

"I thought you were in the midst of a courtship with a young lady?"

Robin flushed and shook his head. "I must make my own way in the world. My uncle Thomas will inherit Wakefield, which is as it should be. My grandfather will do something for me, I'm sure, but my heart is with the *Falcon*. Just one treasure ship—that's all I need to be my own man, maybe even buy my own ship and sail with Drake!"

"Drake is leaving England. He's going to circumnavigate the world. Hasn't been done since Magellan did it."

"Maybe he'd take me with him!"

"He'll be gone for at least three years. I don't think your grandfather could spare you. He's getting on, you know. How old is he now?"

"He's seventy."

"A ripe old age, but you might never see him again if you were gone for so long." Walsingham saw the longing on the young man's face. "I'll make a bargain with you, Robin. You find this Jesuit who's hidden in your part of the world. That shouldn't be too hard for you, especially since it's not known there that you've been doing work for me. In return, I'll see what can be done to get you aboard your ship. Agreed?"

Robin's eyes brightened. "Yes, Sir Francis! That's a very fair offer."

"Good! Now, I'll make it right with the queen. You be off right away."

Robin sought Dorcas out at once and told her that he must go see his grandparents. She was displeased, but he was adamant. "I'll have some good news for you soon, my love," he said. The two of them were alone in one of the grape arbors, and he took advantage of the time by taking her in his arms.

She came to him, yielding to his fervent kisses, but then pulled back to say, "I'll wait for you, Robin!"

Ten minutes later he was riding down the road toward Wakefield, and the taste of her lips seemed to linger. *Just one of Philip's treasure ships—and she'll be mine!*

Dorcas's promise to wait cheered him, and he kicked the horse into a fast gallop, his head and heart full of Dorcas and the *Falcon*.

<hr />

The sky was a pastel blue, the pale color broken only by dots of fleecy white clouds, when Robin arrived at Wakefield. Spring had transformed the dead brown grass into an emerald carpet, the rich brilliance of which almost hurt his eyes. The odors of the fecund earth came to him rich and strong. He felt old stirrings rise as memories of all the days he'd spent in this place swept over him, and he exclaimed aloud, "I wouldn't trade a day of this for a year of the court!"

His horse was weary, so Robin allowed him to walk slowly down the road. Men were plowing in the fields, turning the rich black earth over in long furrows, and some of the workers hailed him as he rode by. When he passed through the gate, the sight of the castle was like strong medicine. And when he reached the entrance, he swung down and tossed the reins of his mount to

Bart, the young stable hand. "How are you, Bart?" he called out as he mounted the steps.

"Fine, Master Robin—!"

Robin didn't hear the end of the boy's statement, for he was too anxious to see his grandparents. As he stepped into the large foyer, he saw his grandmother coming to meet him.

"Robin!" she cried out, and he ran forward at once, taking her in his arms. She felt very fragile, and he didn't swing her around as he would once have done. She held him close, and when he drew back, there were tears in her eyes. "I'm glad you've come," she said.

"I'm glad to be here," he said. "It's been a long year for me." He glanced at the stairs and asked, "Is Grandfather in the study?"

"No, he's in bed."

Something in her tone brought Robin up short. He stared at her, noting the lines that had not been there when he'd left. Something was wrong.

"Is Grandfather sick?"

"Yes, he is." Hannah dropped her hands and tried to smile. "We didn't know you were coming. You must be hungry—"

"What's wrong with him?"

Hannah bit her lip and said quietly, "It's a very common ailment, my dear, one that comes to all of us." She hesitated, then said, "Old age, and I'm afraid there's no cure for that."

Robin felt a constriction in his throat. His grandfather had been the one constant in his world. No matter how much everything else might change, he'd always known that his grandfather would remain the same. Now as he saw the grief in his grandmother's eyes, he knew that his world was rocking.

"But he was so well when I left. . . ."

"Yes, he was always blessed with good health. Until last winter, when he went down sick twice. His illnesses ruined his lungs, I think. He seemed to get a little better, but he just hasn't been the same."

"Why didn't you send for me?"

"He wouldn't let me, Robin." Hannah shook her head. "He didn't want to admit he was so bad off that you should cut your visit short. And you know how stubborn he can be!"

"There must be *something* the doctors can do!"

"You've been interested in medicine most of your life. You've learned so much from Kate Moody, my dear, so you must know that there's a time when even the best of doctors and medicines do no good. Oh, we've had the doctor here time and again. The last time he tried to tell me that it was just a matter of time."

"I'll go see Grandfather," Robin said.

"Yes, you need to be with him. Thomas is on a voyage, so he won't be here in time. Alice is expecting any day. She wanted to come, but she'd risk losing the baby if she came over those rough roads."

Robin stared at Hannah, then turned and walked heavily up the stairs. When he reached his grandparent's chamber, he knocked, then opened the door. His first glimpse of his grandfather gave him a shock. When he'd left, Myles Wakefield had been a man old in years but strong in body. Now one glance at the wasted form and the sunken eyes told him instantly that his grandmother had not exaggerated.

Struggling to get his emotions under control, Robin straightened his back and moved to stand beside the still form on the bed. "Grandfather, are you awake?"

Myles's eyes fluttered, then opened slowly. Recognition came and a light fired them. "Robin, my boy!"

Robin blinked quickly, denying the tears stinging at his eyes any exit. "Well now, here I go away for a while and you take the opportunity to get sick. That's a fine way to act!" He pulled a chair close to the bed, then reached over and took the frail hand resting on the covers. He could not help thinking of how strong it had been—and now it was like a loose bag of fragile bones. "You'll have to stop this foolishness and get better, sir," he said in a falsely cheerful voice.

Myles's lips were shrunken, but he managed a smile. "Tell me about the court," he said. "Did you learn how to bow and scrape and flatter?"

"Oh, famously," Robin said. He knew his grandfather wanted no great show of grief, so he began to tell of trivial things. "Yes, I can smirk and grovel with the best of them. . . ."

When Hannah came in half an hour later, Robin was exhausted. He wanted to weep, but knew that would never do. Looking up he said, "Well, Grandmother, I'm here for good. Time I did some honest work for a change." He felt the weak hand close on his and looked down at the beloved face. "I'll have you out of that bed in no time. You'll see!"

"I'm—very glad that you're here, my boy," Myles said faintly. Then his eyes closed and he seemed to sink into unconsciousness. It was so sudden that Robin's heart leaped, and he looked at his grandmother with wild eyes.

"It's all right." She nodded. "He drops off like that quite often. Come along, dear, he'll sleep for a time."

She led him out of the room and into the dining room. A servant brought food, but Robin could only pick at it. "Are you really here for a long stay?" Hannah asked.

"Yes. There's need for me here. I was doing nothing in court."

Hannah nodded, and he saw the relief come into her faded eyes. "I'm glad, Robin. He needs you, and so do I!"

For the next few days Robin stayed very close to the house. His grandfather had good times when he was much like his old self, but Robin couldn't deny that he was slowly losing ground. The doctor came, and when he spoke with Robin, he could only say, "He gets weaker every time I see him. There's only one end to that, you know."

Even so, his grandson's presence seemed to help the old man a great deal. He enjoyed games of chess, and twice Robin took him out for a ride to see the fields. They talked, and Robin soon discovered that though Myles's body was breaking down, his mind was not impaired. And with characteristic keenness, it only took a few days for Myles to draw the one thing from Robin that he'd vowed he would not reveal: his courtship of Dorcas Freeman.

"I'm not surprised," Myles said thoughtfully. "You're young and full of sap. Only natural. Is she a Christian girl?"

"Why, she attends church, Grandfather."

"Putting a girl in church doesn't make her a Christian, any more than putting her in a stable makes her a horse!"

Robin laughed. "What a thing to say!"

Myles began to speak of Hannah, and since it would not be long before he would not be around to counsel his grandson, he spoke freely and with an emotion he'd never shown before. He told the whole story of their courtship, stressing how they'd always been more than husband and wife.

"How can a man and woman be *more* than husband and wife?" Robin wondered.

"They can be *friends*, Robin. Never marry a woman who can't be the best friend in the world to you."

Day followed day, and Robin pondered what his grandfather had said. One day he rode over to see John Spenser on business, and on his way he wrestled with the problem. *I can't get Dorcas out of my mind—but I never thought of her as a friend.* This troubled him, and he arrived at the Spenser house with the question unresolved. He dismounted and tied his horse, then knocked on the door. Martha Spenser opened it and stared at him. "Why—I didn't know you were home," she said.

"I came last week, Mrs. Spenser. Is your husband here?"

"No, he's gone to the mill. Will you come in and wait?"

Robin hesitated, then nodded. "If it's not too long."

Mrs. Spenser stepped back from the door, and when Robin entered, he saw a man sitting beside the window reading. "This is Mr. Davis. He's the tutor for the children. Mr. Davis, this is Mr. Robin Wakefield."

The two men spoke, and Martha Spenser said, "I was fixing some tea. I'll bring it with some cakes."

Robin took a seat and asked, "How are your pupils doing, Mr. Davis?"

Davis, a small, dark man with a full beard nodded. "Oh, very well. Do you know them?"

"I know one of them pretty well."

"Yes, that would be Allison. She talks much of you." Davis spoke for some time about the children, adding that he was new to the county. He had a slight accent that Robin could not identify, and he seemed to be a pleasant enough fellow.

Robin took his tea, but after forty-five minutes with no sign of John Spenser, he rose and said, "I can pass close to the mill on my way home, Mrs. Spenser. I'll see your husband there."

"Allison is with him, Mr. Wakefield," Davis said. "She'll be glad to see you."

"Good, I was hoping to see her. I have a trinket I brought her." Robin nodded. "Happy to have met you, sir."

He left the house and rode to the mill where he found Allison playing outside beside the millrace. When she saw it was him, she jumped up. "Mister Robin!" she cried joyfully and came flying to him.

He bent over to take her hug, smiling at her excitement. She spoke so rapidly he had to hold up his hand to stop the flow of words. "Now, let me see your father, then I've got a surprise for you."

Allison followed him inside, and when he'd finished his busi-

190

ness with her father, the two of them stepped outside. She led him to the bubbling stream, and he reached inside his pocket and pulled out a small package. "I missed your birthday, so this is a belated present."

Allison's eyes grew large as she held the package carefully. Removing the paper, she opened the small box and gasped. "Oh, they're so pretty!" Robin had bought the large pearls from a sailor on the docks and had them made up into a pair of earrings for the girl. "You're too young to wear them now, but when you're a grown-up young lady, they'll look very nice on you."

They walked along the stream, and Allison could hardly keep still. When he asked her about Mr. Davis, she said, "He's my teacher."

"And a good one, I'll wager."

"Oh yes, he's been everywhere. In France even."

A tiny alarm went off in Robin's brain. Carefully, he kept the girl talking about Davis.

"He helps us with our reading and all, and he even says the Mass for us on Sabbath, too."

A Jesuit! Robin was dismayed, for he knew that he had no choice but to turn the man in. Doing such a thing had never bothered him before, but then, he'd never found those he sought among people he knew. This time, it was different.

As he watched Allison's animated face, he knew he was trapped.

"I'll see you soon, Allison," he said, and when the girl nodded trustingly, he felt terrible. *Like Judas, I'll wager,* he thought darkly.

He rode home and for two days was so quiet that finally his grandfather said, "What's the trouble, boy? You're worried about something."

"Oh, it's just a matter of—of business. Something to do with the court, Grandfather." He said no more, but was grateful that he hadn't had to deceive his grandfather. He hadn't told him the whole truth, of course. But he hadn't lied, either.

I've got to be sure this man is more than just a teacher, he thought the next day. *I can't accuse him without some kind of proof.* But he had learned how to find proof, and within a week, an innocent statement from Allison had given him concrete evidence that the man Davis was a priest.

Though it tugged at his conscience to use the child this way, he felt bound by his vow to help the queen. At least, that's what he kept telling himself.

In the end he did what he knew he had to do. With a reluctance that greatly troubled him, he sat at the desk in his room and pulled out a sheet of paper.

One letter to Sir Francis Walsingham, and it was done. But after he posted the letter he wished he had not. He considered trying to stop the letter but knew there was no chance to do so.

News came a week later that the man Davis had been taken by officers of the court. The countryside was filled with talk, and finally Robin rode over to the Spensers. As he approached the house, he felt a self-loathing, and when Martha Spenser opened the door, he saw the hatred in her eyes. Her husband came to stand beside her, and it was even harder for Robin to meet his reproachful gaze.

"I came to say—," but he broke off, for Allison had come around the house.

Seeing him, she came to take his hand with confidence, saying, "Can you come and see the ducks, Mister Robin?"

"I don't see how you can face us!" Martha Spenser's face was twisted with rage. "It was your doing!"

John Spenser's face was haggard. "I'll be facing the court for harboring a priest," he said accusingly. "I've always known you hated Catholics, Wakefield, but I didn't think you'd do this to us!"

"Never come back here again! Do you hear?" Martha raged, reaching out toward her daughter. "Come here, Allison! Don't go near that monster!"

Allison stared at her mother, then began to cry. Robin put his hand on her arm, and when she turned to him, he put his arm around her. "Let me explain—," he began, but there were no words forthcoming. What explanation could he give?

The enraged mother came and snatched her daughter from his arms. As she did so, Robin met the woman's accusing gaze. Her face was hard and cold, but Robin saw fear and pain in her eyes. She clutched her daughter to her protectively. "Allison, never speak to this man again! He's a murderer!"

Before Robin could reply, Allison looked at **him, grief** on her small face, and cried out, "Mister Robin—!" But her words were cut off when her mother swept her inside the house.

John, his face pale, turned and went in as well, slamming the door behind him.

Numbly Robin mounted his horse. Later, he could remember nothing of the ride back to Wakefield. But he knew he would never forget the scene at the Spensers, for it was burned into his memory—as was Allison's agonized cry—"Mister Robin!"

For three days he endured the hell that went on in his heart, saying nothing to his grandparents. Then, one morning, his grandmother came to awaken him before dawn, and he knew the end had come for the one man who meant more to him than anyone. Hastily throwing on his clothes, he went to the dying man's room. The feeble glow of the candles cast an amber light on Myles's face. Robin moved woodenly to stand beside him.

"Robin?"

"Yes, Grandfather, I'm here."

Myles Wakefield's eyes opened and he whispered, "I'm . . . glad you came, Robin. Something to—to tell you . . ."

"Yes, Grandfather?"

Myles tried to lift his hand, but could not. Robin took it and held it tightly, his fingers pressing on the pulsepoint, which beat faintly. Myles moistened his lips and spoke again in a dry whisper. "Got to learn to forgive . . . for your father."

Looking into his grandfather's eyes, hearing the whispered plea, Robin Wakefield suddenly knew what real remorse was. Waves of grief washed over him and he leaned his forehead against his clasped hands. "I know, Grandfather," he whispered brokenly.

"Never hate anyone!" Myles lifted himself up with an unexpected strength. His eyes were clear and he said, "Promise me! You won't hate . . ."

"I—I promise!"

Robin's brief words seemed to satisfy the dying man. He smiled, and Robin felt the pressure of his hand. "I have . . . served Jesus, and now I go to him." His eyes moved to the woman beside him, and he whispered, "Hannah . . . my love."

Robin rose and left the room, for this was a very private thing between these two. His eyes were burning with tears as he stumbled down the hall to stand beside one of the long windows. Grief welled up in him, and he knew that he was losing the best friend he had in the world.

When his grandmother came to stand beside him, he turned and saw that she was smiling through her tears. "He's gone to be with his Lord, Robin. And he was so happy!"

"I—I can't think how it will be without him, Grandmother! I can't believe we've . . . we've lost him!"

She slipped her arms around him, holding him close. "Oh, he's not lost! When something is lost, you don't know where it is." Hannah's eyes were luminous in the glow of dawn. "But we *know* where Myles is. He's with our Lord. And we will see him again one day. The Scriptures promise us that."

The two stood there, the tall young man clinging to the frail woman. And of the two of them, despite her years, Hannah Wakefield was much stronger than this tall grandson of hers.

"Remember your promise to him, my dear," she said quietly.

"I won't forget. God help me to remember!"

The light that filtered through the window fell on the young face of Robin Wakefield—and he knew that the final promise he'd made to his grandfather would be as real as anything in his life.

END OF PART TWO

1 5 8 0
Part
THREE
1 5 8 5

Allison

HOME IS THE SAILOR

Snow filtered through the stiff breeze that ruffled the fur on Robin Wakefield's cap. The icy morsels touched his face like tiny elfin fingers, so cold they seemed to burn his flesh. The sky had been leaden all day, and now an ochre color glowed in the east, foreboding the cold that accompanied winter snow.

Long ragged strips of white covered the frozen fields, and the falling snow seemed to muffle all sounds. Robin glanced down at the huge dog that stayed close to his leg, then halted and leaned over to pat the broad head. "You still don't like snow, do you, Pilot?" He tugged the ears, noting that the muzzle was tinted with silver. "Why, you're getting old, Pilot!"

As if to confute his master's words, the mastiff uttered a deep-throated growl, then suddenly reared up on his hind legs and placed his paws on the man's chest. Almost felled by the weight, Robin laughed and grabbed the beast's front paws.

"Get off me, you monster! Go catch a squirrel or something!" he protested, then shoved the dog off and continued his walk through the solitary woods.

The bare trees raised specterlike arms to the leaden sky as though in a manner of sullen prayer. For the next fifteen minutes Robin proceeded in a leisurely fashion, turning aside to visit favorite spots that brought back memories: the frozen stream where he'd caught a big pike, the ravine where he and Pilot had encountered the bear, the huge yew tree where he and his friends had once built a tree house of sorts in the shelter of the branches.

I've missed all this, but it all seems smaller somehow—

Looking up into the yew, he saw only two or three rotting boards held in place by rusty nails to mark the tree house. In his mind the tree had been enormous and the house had been very high in the air—so high that it had made him dizzy to climb to its heights. Now, however, he saw that the shelter had been no more than twelve feet or so from the ground.

His brow wrinkled as he stared upward. *Funny how things seem different.* But the snow was coming down faster in flakes as large as sovereigns, so he turned and made his way back to the path. Soon he reached the river and stopped at the sight of Kate Moody's cabin.

That seems smaller, too, though I never would have believed it possible, he thought as he approached the house. The three years of his absence had not improved the shack. If anything, the small house was more dilapidated than ever. Three bare poles were braced against one side, obviously to keep the entire structure from falling, and the thatch on the roof was moldy and carelessly patched in spots.

Pausing at the door, Robin lifted his hand and knocked. A keening wind moaned far off in the thick woods that banked the river, and he smiled as he remembered his boyhood fears that the sound was made by some sort of spirit. Then the door opened and Kate Moody stood before him.

"Well, it's himself, back from the sea! And did you bring a bag of gold to Kate Moody?"

Quickly he put out his hands and smiled. "Not this time, Kate. I'll have to go back for that."

"Come in out of the cold, boy." Kate stepped back and noted that he had to duck his head as he entered. "Why, you've grown tall as a tree, Robin Wakefield!" The woman half-pushed the tall young man toward one of the two chairs that flanked the small table. "Well, sit now, and we'll have something hot to warm the insides while you tell me about your travels."

For the next half hour Robin spoke of the voyage he'd made on the Spanish Main with his uncle Thomas, captain of the *Falcon*—dwelling for a time on the hardships of sailors.

"You can't imagine the foul smells of a ship—parts of it, at least, Kate. Sweet, sour, and at the bottom of the hull an odor of dark foul stuff—black sand and black water where garbage and scraps find refuge together with the waste of the crew. All this corruption distilled in sand of the ballast, turning into a liquor darker than ink, horrid as witches' brew, until even the captain on his high poop astern can smell and breathe nothing else!"

"Why don't you clean it, then?" Kate demanded, studying the strong features of the man with interest. *He left a boy and came back a man!* His face had filled out, making clean planes that composed a strong jaw and a broad forehead. His hair was thick, and the faint glow of the lamp brought out the reddish tints she'd always admired.

"Clean it?" Robin grinned suddenly. "Why, bless you, Kate, we did. And a filthy job it was, too! But there was no possible way to keep it clean for long. Even so, there were good smells, too—the thick, sweet odor of pitch and tar, for example. But men are wrong about sailors being filthy, for we washed with salt water, both ourselves and our clothing—and picked it clean of lice and vermin." Robin's full, long lips turned upward into a smile as he added, "We looked to our mates, picking each other's vermin where we couldn't reach or see our own. And in foul weather, the rain and the wind did a scouring job, right down to the slick of the bones on every man."

Kate listened avidly as Robin spoke of life on the *Falcon,* then poured more tea into his mug. As she added a light amber liquid, she smiled slyly. "A bad sailorman like you should have something stronger than tea." She leaned back, then, and sipped her own tea. "Tell me about the ships."

"Ah, the ships!" Robin took a large swallow of the concoction she'd poured, then almost choked. His face turned red and he stared at the woman. "What kind of thing do you call this?" he demanded. "You never offered anything like this before."

"You weren't man enough for it. Now, the ships."

If Robin had been a poet, he would have written sonnets about the tall ships. Still, as he spoke there was a poetic strain in his words.

"High-charged, high-riding," he said softly, his eyes glowing with the images of his well-loved *Falcon*. "Made of solid English oak. From Devon, if possible, though more and more made from the timbers of Ireland, from the Baltic, some from Poland and Muscovy. Each made from a whole tree and the trunks of the trees worked into planks in the shipbuilder's yard, but properly seasoned first.

"It's odd, but a ship like the *Falcon* looks small to the eye, yet the length of her keel measures three times the beam. Divided into forecastle, waist, and aftercastle. Beyond the bow and sharp beak is the bowsprit, a thin mast for a single square spritsail. Forecastle, set back from the beak, is small and low and used for storing cables and tackle. And there are no cabins for the sailors. They sleep wherever and whenever they can—on open deck when weather allows."

"I've seen such ships from the shore," Kate said softly, turning the ungainly cup in her strong hands. "Beautiful, the sails are."

"Yes, I love the sails." Robin nodded. "Slender and delicate to the eye—all draped and webbed, the shrouds and tacklings, stays and braces, ratlines for climbing . . . and when the wind fills the sails, the ship skims over the water like a hawk in flight."

The lamp burned low, casting amber shadows over the faces of the pair. As Robin spoke of the sea, Kate thought of how many times as a boy he had sat in that very chair, his youthful face turned toward her. Now she watched him, pleased and intrigued by the changes she saw. *He was always a handsome boy, but the man he's become will break the hearts of many a woman, I doubt not! With that face and form, he's bound to be a favorite.*

Finally Robin shrugged his shoulders and laughed, "Why, Kate, I've become a chattering bird for talk!" Looking across the table he said offhandedly, "I've missed you, Kate—all our talks and the times we had together."

She astonished him by leaning forward and putting her hand over his. He'd never expected such a show of affection. She smiled and said softly, "I've missed you too, Robin, more than you can know." Then she quickly pulled her hand back and laughed shortly. "Another cup of my 'tea' and we'll both be crying over old times like a pair of fools!"

Robin understood. Though she never complained, he knew that Kate was lonely, cut off from most people by their superstitions and fears. Now reaching into his pocket he pulled out a small package wrapped in brown paper and handed it to her. "I didn't get a bag of gold, Kate, but I brought this from a sailor. I thought you might like it. A Christmas present."

Kate took the small package, stared at him, then removed the paper. She grew absolutely still and remained fixed in her chair for so long that she seemed to have turned into a statue. After a long moment, she touched one of the two large pearls, threaded by fine gold wire, then her eyes came to rest on Robin's face. "You shouldn't be spending your money on an old woman, boy." Her voice was rough with emotion.

Robin shrugged lightly. "Why, I look on it as part payment for all the herb lore you taught me," he said. "Now, let's see how they look."

She removed the cheap earrings she'd worn for as long as

Robin could remember and, with hands not quite steady, put on the pearls. Robin smiled. "Have a look at yourself, Kate," he said. as he rose and picked up the small square of polished metal that lay on a shelf. As she took it and studied herself, his smile broadened. "They look very well."

Kate stared at the pearls, enchanted by their warm, luminous glow—then sniffed. "Probably get me killed," she said curtly. "Lots o' folks get murdered in their beds for less than these." But when she turned to him, he saw that her lips had grown soft and there was a hint of tears in her eyes. "I'll think of you every time I see them, Robin Wakefield. And I thank you."

Suddenly embarrassed, he said lightly, "Well, now you must earn them." A shadow crossed his face as he grew serious. "My grandmother, she's not doing well."

"How old is she now?"

"Seventy-four."

"A ripe old age. She misses your grandfather."

"Yes, she does." He frowned and shook his head. "She grows lonely. My uncle Thomas is little company for her, being gone to sea so much."

"But his wife is there, Lady Martha, and their children. They must be fine companions."

"Well, my uncle's wife isn't too well herself. But their children are a delight to my grandmother." Robin bit his lip, then shook his head. "I—I was shocked to see how frail she was, Kate. So thin!"

"She's lived twice as long as most, Robin," Kate said gently. "She must go soon."

"I don't like to think of that," Robin muttered. "She and my grandfather—I always depended on them. They made my life, I think."

"Does she have sickness now?"

"Yes, a terrible cough—almost a spasm when it comes."

Kate rose and went to the battered cabinet fastened to the wall. Opening the door, she came back with two bottles. "You know this as well as I, my friend," she said placing them on the table. "This one, a simple remedy of horehound and comfrey, is to be taken during the day. The second, at night—but I can promise no cure."

"She can't be harmed by it." He lifted the second bottle. "What's in this one?"

"A diacodium. Don't tell anyone you got them from me, or we'll both be in trouble."

"I doubt that, Kate. I've told Sir Thomas and his wife about you. No harm will come to you while he's lord of Wakefield."

"Harm can come to any of us, boy," Kate responded. She was approaching forty now, and time had laid a hard hand on her. Though her eyes were as bright as ever, she had grown more stooped, and her teeth were bad. A thought lit her eyes, and she said, "It's good that I never had wealth. The rich find it hard to leave this life. The consolations of age don't exist for most. Age takes away the things one prizes—and for most it takes away the savor of life itself."

"How do you mean?"

"Why, the sweet taste of life! When you are young all sensations have savor, all the fruits are good. But when you grow old, they lose their relish. That's why," she said quietly, "I'm glad things were never sweet to me. Now I'll not have to grieve over giving them up. And I'll have the good Lord to take care of me."

Robin hesitated then asked, "Did you never love a man, Kate?"

Her dark eyes fixed on him and the silence ran on for a moment. "Aye, once I did. But he loved another."

"I'm sorry."

She moved her shoulders restlessly and laughed. "Why, no doubt he'd have beat me and driven me to an early grave, boy!"

Then she grew serious. "Now, what about you. What of the young woman at court. Dorcas, if I'm not mistaken?"

Robin grew glum at the question. "She married a rich man while I was gone." The first trip he'd made on his return was to go to find Dorcas. When he learned she was married, he fell into a fit of anger and grief. But the ease with which he recovered convinced him that his love for Dorcas Freeman had been less than serious.

"Ah, I see. Well then, have you seen the Spensers since you came home?" Kate demanded.

Robin blinked, then bit his lips with an involuntary action. "No, I haven't," he mumbled. He was still troubled by the memory of how he'd brought disaster to that family. Over the years he'd gone over what he'd done a thousand times—and never could he justify his actions. Though his hatred for all things Catholic still dwelled in his heart, he could not forget the look on Allison's face as her mother had pulled her away from him, calling him a murderer.

"The girl, your little Allison, is nigh a woman now," Kate said, interrupting his thoughts. "A beauty, but strange."

"Strange? How so?"

"Why, she keeps to herself as much as I do! I've seen her wandering in the woods," Kate added. "Sometimes we stop and talk, but she's got a wall built around herself. She seems . . . frightened."

Robin frowned. "Has the family prospered?"

"Not a bit of it! Some men, why, it seems whatever they touch goes sour. That's the way it is with John Spenser. And now he's sick."

"How sick?"

"He won't live," Kate said bluntly. "Some sickness comes of the flesh, boy. But sometimes it begins in the mind. When it's in the flesh, medicines can sometimes help. But when the sickness is in the mind, a man or a woman will die. It's like the mind is telling the body to give up." Kate's eyes grew sharp and she nodded slightly. "His wife blames you for all of it, Robin. Says you put a curse on her, and that *I* taught you how to do such things."

"How foolish!" Robin snapped angrily. "I'm not to blame that they broke the law!"

"No, but when bitterness gets into a person, they don't rest until they find somebody to charge with the blame."

Robin rose, disturbed. Picking up the bottles Kate had given him for his grandmother, he deposited them in his pocket, then nodded. "It's good to see you again. I'll come back before I go."

"Go? Are you off to sea again?"

"No, to court in London." His lips puckered in a wry expression of distaste. "The queen still thinks to make me some sort of ornament—one of the popinjays that strut their finery there." He suddenly reached out and touched the pearl that dangled from Kate's left earlobe. Self-consciously, he grinned at her. "Sell these if you want something else. I'm not much to picking out gifts for women."

Kate regarded him solemnly, then said quietly, "These will go into the ground with me, boy. Now, come back when you can." She followed him to the door and watched him make his way to the line of trees. He looked very tall as he strode away, the dog by his side, and Kate slowly reached up and touched the pearl in her right ear. Turning, she went inside and picked up the mirror, then studied her reflection.

"Now think of that!" she whispered. "All the way from across the sea he brought them!"

⁂

Robin arrived at Nonsuch Palace barely in time for Christmas festivities. Nonsuch was one of Elizabeth's favorites, an extravagance lavishly decorated in the Renaissance style, built by the queen's father as a hunting palace and guesthouse for foreign visitors. Here Elizabeth loved to hunt, wearing clothes and jewels more suitable for the audience chamber than the hunting field and riding her horse so fast she often tired out her frightened companions.

Though men might have thought it odd for any other woman to hunt as Elizabeth did, they made no comment regarding the queen's actions. Near and far it was well known that, as a girl of fifteen, the queen had cut the throat of a fallen buck—and she made it clear that she would go on, without any apparent squeamishness, to kill "the great and fat stagge with my owen Hand."

The morning after his arrival, Robin learned that Queen Elizabeth, even at the age of forty-seven, was still able to sit a horse with considerable skill. He discovered this when he was rousted out of bed by one of the chamberlains with the word, "Her Majesty commands that you ride with her this morning."

Robin arrived at the stables to find the queen and her retinue mounting their horses.

"Ah, the bold sailor, home from the sea!" Elizabeth cried out upon seeing him. "Come, sir, and tell me of your venture."

"With pleasure, Your Majesty," Robin answered, and he swung into the saddle of a tall chestnut stallion. "Good day to you, sir," he bowed to Robert Dudley.

"Good morning, Mr. Wakefield," Dudley said cheerfully. "I see you haven't lost your seat through your long voyage. Still a fine horseman."

"Oh, it's much easier to stay in the saddle of a fine horse than to cling to the top of a mizzenmast in the midst of a blow," Robin replied. He had controlled his expression, but a shock had run along his nerves at the sight of the pair. In his mind he still thought of Elizabeth and Dudley as they had been when he first saw them. But the earl had grown heavy, and his features had thickened so that he looked more like an old man than Robin would have dreamed possible. The slim courtier that had been the pride of the court was gone.

And Elizabeth, Robin thought, seemed to have aged ten years. *I thought of her as a woman of middle age—but she's old!*

It was apparent that the queen was as fond of finery as ever, for she was arrayed in a snow-white gown edged with gold lace. Robin had heard that she considered white most becoming to her aging face. *Not that she needs to worry,* he thought, looking at her now. *Her skin is as beautiful as ever, and her figure is still slender* In truth, the queen carried herself with a natural grace and seemed to be a part of the gray mare she rode.

She glanced at Robin as they turned their horses' heads and began their ride at a fast pace. "Your uncle, Sir Thomas, did not manage to take a Spanish treasure ship," she called to him reproachfully.

"No, I regret to say we had no chance at one of Philip's prizes," Robin said. "But we will do better the next time, Your Majesty."

"You will go back to sea?" Dudley inquired.

"As soon as my uncle sails, my lord."

But Elizabeth gave him a piercing look. "We would have you at court for a time, Mr. Wakefield."

Robin's heart sank. Nevertheless, he smiled. "What could be better for a young man than to be in the sunlight of the ornament of heaven?" He had memorized this speech along with several others, though he had doubted the queen would believe such tripe. But she *did* believe it, and as she beamed a smile upon him, he recalled his days in court when Raleigh and Dudley and Essex had vied over who could make the most outlandish compliment to the aging queen.

Dudley gave Robin a swift glance, then smiled. "I'm surprised that you have learned to make pretty speeches. Life on a fighting ship doesn't usually produce poetry."

"The subject brings forth the poetry, Sir Robert," Robin answered instantly.

Elizabeth laughed and gave the two men an arch look. "Now, Robin—I mean, *Robert*—you should be content that this young fellow has a quick tongue. He will be a welcome addition to our court."

Later, as they wended homeward, Dudley came to join Robin at the end of the procession. He inquired more closely into the particulars of the voyage of the *Falcon*. He was, as Robin already knew, a man of sharp wit and not a little wisdom. His questions were sharp and pointed, and finally he shook his head almost sadly. "War with Philip is upon us, I fear."

"He will never challenge Drake and Hawkins!"

"I would that you were right, but we know of a huge fleet of fighting galleons being constructed in Spain. Our agents tell us that they are being built at record speed. When there are enough of them, they will come for England."

"The dons will never defeat Sir Francis!"

"You admire Drake? Of course you do, and so do I. But even Drake cannot perform miracles. Philip will never stand still for what we have been doing to him at sea."

The two men spoke of the threat of war, but Robin had no fears. He was young and filled with boundless courage. Sir Robert Dudley, however, was well aware that kingdoms could fall just as abruptly as men—and just as tragically.

The party observed some of the Twelve Days of Christmas at Nonsuch, but moved to London for the remainder of the holidays. The palace was filled, every chamber packed with lords and ladies. There were costumes to be adjusted and accessories to be located. The pastry chefs were frantically baking enough Twelfth Night cakes, each with a bead hidden deep inside, to satisfy the appetites of the entire company.

Robin had no further words with the queen and grew weary

of the ceremony. On the Twelfth Night, he entered the Great Hall, which was bright with the characteristic color of candle torch-light. He had heard that ten thousand pounds of wax had been prepared for the spectacle, but he noted that the upper reaches of the hammerbeam ceiling were lost in shadows. He was aware of the fact that, outside the warmth and light of the hall, winter crouched.

Like the old Norse poet said, Life is a lost sparrow who found his way into a hall like this where he found happiness and peace for a moment or two—but all too soon found himself outside in the cold, dying.

Drawing a breath, he shook off his depression and allowed one of the maids of honor to pull him to the table for the feast. She was a sloe-eyed beauty, and Robin was stirred by her. It had been three years since he had been in the company of women, and he found the look in her dark eyes pleasing.

The feast was superlative. The master cooks presented three separate courses consisting of twenty-five dishes each. There were twenty large Twelfth Night cakes, one for each table. The most elaborate one was placed before the queen on an ivory board. It had towers and turrets and a checkerboard design—an exact replica of the palace itself.

At Robin's table, Lord Huntington cut the cake and passed the fruit-glazed slices around. Robin bit down gingerly on his sec-tion—too many people lost a tooth by biting down on the bead placed inside. He placed no stock in the myth that whoever received the bead would have good fortune for a year, but he enjoyed the fine pastry.

"Oh, I have it here!"

The girl beside him squealed and pressed herself close to Robin. She smiled up at him, and Robin wondered if she was aware of the effect she was having on him. Looking into her eyes, he decided her coquettishness was unintended, for she had the wide-eyed look of innocence. Yet, throughout the evening, she favored him with her gaze and often turned to lean against him as she spoke. Finally, she leaned toward him and whispered in his ear, "How warm it has grown in here, do you not agree?"

He nodded slightly, and she smiled. "I believe I shall go outside and refresh myself." She rose, still smiling. "I would not object to company," she said quietly, so that only he could hear, then turned to leave the room.

Blood thudding in his veins, Robin moved to follow. Before he could do so, an imperious voice cut through the noises of the banquet hall: "Robin, come here!"

He cast an anguished glance at the dark-haired beauty who was moving away, then turned to go to the queen.

Elizabeth had seen the interchange between Wakefield and the young woman and had spoken to break up the intrigue. The young men of her court were there to pay her attention, not anyone else.

When Robin came to sit beside her, she looked around. "Give Mr. Wakefield and me some privacy," she said, then smiled at the looks of annoyance on the faces of the lords who sat close by. But they got up at once and moved away.

"You have made enemies for me, my queen," Robin observed. "To be deprived of your presence is something no man of spirit will brook!"

"No duels!" Elizabeth warned. "Use all the hard words you please, but I can't spare a single man."

Robin was uncomfortable, but tried not to show it as Elizabeth spoke rapidly. He managed to hold his own in the conversation, using compliments freely. As he made yet another remark about the pleasure of the queen's company, he found himself wondering how his grandfather would feel about his words. A pang shot through him, which must have been reflected on his face, for the queen grew sober.

"You look sad, Robin. Is it because you miss your grandfather?"

At his silent acknowledgment, she nodded. "So do I." A sigh came from her lips and she looked haggard for a moment. "I need every man who is loyal, and Myles Wakefield was that!"

"Yes, that and much more. We shall not look upon his like again, Your Majesty."

Elizabeth suddenly placed her pale eyes on Robin, holding his gaze. "You know of his service to me?"

At once Robin knew her meaning. "You refer to Mary of Scots?"

"Yes. It was a duty he never liked, Robin, but never once did he complain." The music floated over the hall, and Elizabeth hummed a tune along with it, then faced him fully. "I have lost a good friend, and that grieves me. But perhaps his grandson may replace that loss. Will you help me, Robin?"

At that moment Robin knew how Elizabeth had managed to rule England. Others who wore the crown had fallen quickly— even those who were powerful and clever—but this woman had outlasted most of them, and Robin now understood that it was because she had a power over men.

He could not imagine that a man would die to possess Elizabeth—she was self-willed, dictatorial, and at times seemed almost cold and lacking in the kind of passion which, if strong enough in a man's view, could make him forget any other failings. Yet she had other qualities that aroused the admiration and emotion of men. Pale and frail, glittering with jewels, adorned in a long, narrow bodice and inordinate skirts that looked fit only for a garden lawn, she excited those men whose ambitions were as great as her own.

Now Robin was the focal point of that power, and Elizabeth whispered again, "Will you help me with Mary? She has a son, you know—one who could have an eye to my crown one day. Already some are speaking of him as James I of England!"

Their eyes met, and Robin saw outrage—and fear—reflected

in the queen's gaze as she asked again, "Will you help me, Robin?"

No command would have been less welcome to Robin! He had accompanied his grandfather many times to visit the deposed queen and had felt terrible each time. Now he protested, "Oh, Your Majesty, I am unfitted for such a thing!"

But Elizabeth knew her power and placed her thin, well-shaped hand over his. "Mary will have my life if she can. She has already tried many times to have me assassinated. I need your help, Robin."

He felt he was being drawn into a web wherein danger lay. He longed to protest—but looking into Elizabeth's face, he could only say, "As Your Majesty wishes."

Elizabeth held his hand. "I know you long for the sea, and you shall go again one day. I promise you!"

Then she turned away, and Robin rose. As he walked away, he was heartsick at what lay before him. When he saw the dark-eyed girl on the arm of another, he felt only a brief remorse.

Now I know why Grandfather hated this task so much! Can there be anything more distasteful than to spy on a woman?

Fifteen

THE SNARE OF THE FOWLER

By heaven, I can't wait around this place forever!"
Sir Francis Walsingham gave Robin a benign smile.
"How many young men in England would give ten years
of their lives to 'wait around this place'?"

Robin rose and paced nervously in front of the secretary's massive
oak desk. He had long ago discovered that the court of Elizabeth held
no charms for him, but the last few weeks had become a torment.
"I'm bored out of my skull, Sir Francis!" he groaned. "Send me on
my mission. Let me go to Mary if it must be."

Walsingham nodded. "Your grandfather was the same," he
mused. Plucking up a turkey quill, he wrote a few words on a
sheet of paper, then was interrupted when his clerk appeared.
"The Council is assembled, Sir Francis."

"Very well, Stafford." Walsingham replaced the quill, then rose
and came to stand beside Robin. "You are about to witness how
statesmanship works, Mr. Wakefield."

"Sir?"

"The queen has had a terrible toothache for days now, and the
nation of England is stopped dead still until something can be
done about it!" Walsingham slapped his hands together in an
angry gesture. "She is now over forty and has no children. Who
will rule this land if she dies? Mary, Queen of Scots, has plotted

against Elizabeth for years. Now she plans to have her son, James, placed on the throne of England. I am sure ot it!"

"I wonder why Elizabeth never married and had children."

"She would not bear a master—that's the whole of it!" Walsingham's long face grew sober. "She will let no one make decisions, so that government goes by default. Scarce a month goes past without some plot against her being discovered. Her own physician, Lopez, was executed at Tyburn for trying to poison her. Yet this—this vain woman will *not* name her successor. So we have no rule, no security, no heir. Yet the people do not realize our peril. Everyone is dazzled by the beautiful picture of their Virgin Queen, married to her country!"

"Elizabeth has held England together in troubled times," Robin protested. "A task many men failed to do."

"Yes, it's so. And I admit the picture *is* beautiful, even to me." Walsingham nodded. "But the moment she dies, that canvas will be slashed from top to bottom, side to side. For the first time the common people—and some of the fools that make up the court!—will look behind the portrait, and they will see that we have no government!"

Robin was startled, for though he knew that Walsingham was the sole man in England who would stand up to the queen, he had never heard him speak so bluntly. "And what does the toothache have to do with the question of the succession?" he asked.

"She promised me that as soon as the toothache was gone, she would name a successor to the throne." He smiled grimly. "She has made such promises for years, Mr. Wakefield, but I must hope that this time she will follow through."

"I hope so." Robin thought for a moment, then said, "I have some small knowledge of herb lore, Sir Francis. Perhaps oil of cloves—"

"Oh, it's past that. The physicians have agreed that the tooth cannot be saved. And we have skillful men who can draw the tooth. It would be a mercy for the queen, but she is afraid. She won't let anyone touch her." The grim look on the secretary's face suddenly turned brighter. He laughed aloud, which startled Robin, who had never heard the man laugh before, then nodded with satisfaction. "As I say, you shall witness how statesmanship is practiced, sir."

"I don't understand, Sir Francis."

"Why, the queen is afraid to have a tooth pulled. She's never had one drawn, and some fear is natural. It came to me that all we have to do is *demonstrate* that the operation is fairly painless. But how can we do that? Can you tell me?"

"No, I cannot."

"Because you are not a statesman, young man! Why, the thing is simple, but it takes a politician such as myself to come up with the practical manner of it." Walsingham smiled broadly, then spread his hand in a deprecating gesture. "We must have the queen witness a tooth being drawn. She will see how painless it is, and *voila!* She will then permit the surgeon to draw her tooth."

Robin rubbed his chin doubtfully. "Well, sir, even I can see one flaw in your plan. Drawing a tooth is not such a simple matter as you make it. I've heard strong men cry out in agony when the tooth proved stubborn."

"Oh, I know that, sir, but the proper subject would never allow his pain to be revealed. He would suffer in silence. No doubt this is deception, but such is politics." He put his dark eyes on Robin thoughtfully. "Now you see where I am going?"

"No, I'm afraid not, sir."

"Why, you have plenty of teeth, do you not? A fine set! I've often admired them. And the queen likes you."

Robin stared at the secretary in alarm. "You mean—*my* tooth?"

"Why, sir, you wouldn't refuse your queen this small favor,

would you? Others give their lives in battle for her. Surely you can part with one tooth?"

Stunned, Robin stared at the man. But only for a few moments. Then he nodded slowly. "If it must be done, Sir Francis, I am willing."

Walsingham nodded, pleased. "Well done, Robin Wakefield! Well done, indeed. Your grandfather would be proud of you." And then he clapped Robin on the shoulder. "But you need not look so glum. I have only been testing you. Part of my profession, I'm afraid. When I see an opportunity to test a man's mettle—or his loyalty—I cannot resist."

Robin was stunned for the second time. Then he shook his head in bewilderment. "I would never make a politician, Sir Francis."

"No, you must serve the queen at sea, my boy. Leave the devious art of politics to old men like me. Now, let us go to the queen. The operation will be performed on a much more impressive man than yourself." When Robin gave him a curious look, Walsingham nodded with satisfaction. "The bishop of London will furnish a demonstration for the queen."

"Does he have a bad tooth?"

"Why, bless you my boy, his teeth are as sound as your own—but he has been a troublesome fellow! So I merely informed him that if he did not give the queen a demonstration of how simple an extraction is, he would find himself out of his position."

Robin's eyes widened. "Can one really get rid of a bishop so easily?"

"Well, it's more difficult now," Walsingham admitted. "Elizabeth's father would simply have had his head lopped off. But there are ways. There always are ways." He turned to leave, saying, "I also informed the bishop that if he flinched or showed one trace of discomfort, he would be ousted. So come along, my boy, you may find this instructive."

Robin did find the operation so. The bishop, a large man with a powerful voice, submitted to the extraction with what appeared to be good grace. When the tooth was pulled, he showed no discomfort whatsoever—though he cast a look of hatred toward Walsingham. The queen watched the operation carefully, then, convinced by the bishop's lack of pain, agreed to have her tooth extracted.

When Robin met Walsingham the next day, he said wryly, "I am impressed by your statesmanship, Sir Francis. Was it successful? Did the queen name a successor?"

"No, but I have hopes. These things move slowly, my boy." He gave Robin a careful look, then said, "Go to Mary, Mister Wakefield. You do not have to find out *if* there is a plot. There is *always* a plot—has been since that woman came to England! Try to discover *who* is involved in this one."

"I'll do my best, sir, though I am not a . . . statesman." When Walsingham smiled at his use of the term, Robin added, "She is far more experienced than I could ever be. She knows you have agents."

"Yes, she does. But she is so greedy for a crown that she will try any man she thinks can help her. I have seen to it that she has heard of your rising importance in the court."

"Importance? Why, sir, that is untrue. I have none!"

"Perhaps you do." Walsingham studied the young man, a quizzical expression on his face. "Handsome young men have a way of rising in this place. Look at Essex, or Hatfield. The older the queen grows, the more she likes to have the young about her. If you were a, shall we say, a 'statesman,' you might go far." Seeing the distaste on Robin's face, he shrugged. "But you are what you are, so I must warn you that Mary will test you. Be on your guard! The snare of the fowler is something well known to Mary. She has drawn many men into her devious web. You would do well not to allow yourself to be one of her victims."

As Robin entered the castle of Tutbury, a wave of memories swept over him and the presence of his grandfather seemed almost palpable. Always before when he entered these gates, Myles Wakefield had been at his side. Now as he dismounted, a sense of loneliness swept over him. The bleak January skies seemed to augment his sorrow, and he longed for warmer, sunnier days— when his grandfather had been with him.

The earl of Shrewsbury came to greet him at the entrance of the great house, so he forced his brooding thoughts away. He thrust away also the distaste he had for his task and cried out cheerfully, "Good morrow, sir. It's been a long time. Perhaps you've forgotten me—"

"Not a bit of it, Mister Wakefield!" the earl responded. He had gained weight and there were wrinkles in his narrow face since last the two had met, but he still was smiling and amiable. "Her Majesty will be overjoyed to see you, sir! She's missed your grandfather and has spoken of you often. Come along now, I'll take you to her."

Robin listened to the earl's constant flow of speech, giving his own brief history of how he'd spent his time over the past three years. He was aware that the earl had practically impoverished himself keeping Mary and her small army of retainers, but he showed no signs of regret. *Probably feels it's an honor to house royalty,* Robin guessed.

The earl led him through the large hall and up the curving staircase that he remembered so well, then knocked on a massive oak door. A voice came faintly.

"Come in."

As the two stepped inside, the earl said, "A treat for you this afternoon, Your Majesty. Look and see who's come to visit you!"

"Why, Mister Wakefield!" Mary had been sitting at one of the tall windows, but now she rose elegantly and came to hold out her hand. "What a marvelous surprise!"

Robin bowed and kissed her hand, then said, "It's been too long, Your Majesty."

"Indeed it has!" Mary ran her eyes over him, then said with obvious pleasure, "What a tall, handsome fellow you've become! Sir—" she turned to the earl "—see that the cook outdoes himself for dinner. We have a most welcome guest!" Then turning to Robin she smiled. "You *are* staying overnight, I insist on it. Or even longer!"

"I will consider it, Your Majesty."

The earl left and Mary introduced Robin to the three young women who had risen as the two men had entered. Robin barely had time to catch their names before Mary dismissed them, saying, "You will all have time to spend with Mister Wakefield later. But he and I are old friends with much to speak of."

As soon as they left the room, Mary moved to the sofa and seated herself. "Come and sit by me, Mister Wakefield. Or may I call you Robin?"

"Of course, Your Majesty." Robin sat down beside her, and when she asked for details of his long voyage, he managed to study her carefully as he related his story.

Mary, he saw, had not seemed to age at all. She was nearly forty, but time sat lightly on her. She was as attractive as he remembered; her blue eyes were as clear as ever, her lips as red and well formed. She wore a dress of dark blue silk, which set her eyes off well, and a necklace of red stones that would have looked garish on most older women but somehow gave a lustrous glow to this woman's skin. The dress was trimmed with cloth-of-gold and was cut low.

With her beauty and figure, she's far more alluring than Elizabeth, he thought suddenly. *She seems so young!*

The two sat there for a long time, talking, and Robin felt himself relax as cakes and wine were brought in. As they ate, Mary said suddenly, "I miss your grandfather very much." She had been sipping wine from a crystal goblet, but put it down and looked at Robin. "I have been a prisoner here for twelve years, and it has been a grim life in many ways. But when I think of the good things I have known here, always he is among my best memories."

"How good of you to say so, Your Majesty," Robin answered. He knew this woman was capable of devious behavior, but somehow he felt that she was speaking sincerely.

"I say no more than is true. He was an honest man, and I valued him more than I can say."

Despite himself Robin felt warmed by Mary's praise of his grandfather—as Mary had been sure he would. If there was one thing the Scotswoman knew, it was how to say and do the right thing to stir appreciation and loyalty in a man. And that was exactly what she hoped to do in this particular young man, for she had decided he could prove quite useful.

By the end of the afternoon, Robin was surprised to find that he had enjoyed his time with Mary. But as he told her he should be leaving, she seemed to grow sad.

"I get very lonely here, Robin," Mary said as she rose. "Won't you consider staying a week? We have horses and hawks. You would be doing me a great favor."

Flattered at her obvious desire to have him near, he thought for a moment, then said, "Why, I must go home for a visit soon, but perhaps a day or two. . . ."

The "day or two" stretched out for several days, and he found Mary Queen of Scots to be a fine companion. She had plenty of retainers, but they were all confined in the small world of Tutbury.

Visitors came and went away, most of them strangers to Robin. But every day and most evenings he spent time with his hostess. During those days he did his best to discover anything that could be of use to Walsingham, but there seemed little danger in what he saw and heard.

Then, on a Wednesday evening after a fine meal alone with Mary, he discovered a side of the queen of Scots that he had never seen. She had asked him to draw a couch up in front of the fire so that they could sit together and talk. The servants were dismissed and Robin, full of supper and perhaps a glass or two too many of wine, now sat beside her speaking of the sea. He knew Mary to be a good listener, so he was not surprised that she kept silent except for an occasional question.

She had him fill the golden goblets with wine yet again, and as Robin leaned back, he was aware of a sense of well-being. The leaping yellow flames threw dancing shadows on the walls, and as he faced Mary, her eyes reflected the amber light. Finally he murmured, "I must go home tomorrow, Your Majesty. I've over-stayed my visit."

Mary moved closer—so close that he was engulfed in the subtle aroma of her perfume. She favored a scent of roses, but intermingled with that was the aroma of the woman herself—a scent that was rich and heady. Alarmed, Robin looked at her. What was she up to?

Her eyes were large and luminous in the half-darkness as she gazed at him. "Don't go, Robin," she whispered, leaning toward him, pressing against his arm. The emerald green dress she wore made her skin seem even more luminescent. Her gaze, her presence, stirred him—and suddenly the voice of caution that had been ringing in his mind was stilled.

The wine combined with the moment, and he did what he had never once dreamed of doing. He put his arms around her, drew her close, and kissed her. Her lips were soft under his, and her arms slid around his neck, drawing him closer.

Forgetful of everything else—who and what she was, his role and "duty"—his arms tightened around her.

Suddenly she drew back, gasping, "No—! I mustn't!"

Robin reached for her, so stirred by her embrace that he could not think clearly. But, placing her hand on his chest, she kept him away. For one moment, he thought she was on the verge of surrender—then she shook her head and placed her hand on his lips. "Please, Robin, we must know each other better before—"

She broke off, but Robin caught the inference and reached for her again, but she pushed him away.

"I—I find you very attractive," Mary said haltingly, then she fell silent, as if thinking of something. "You are younger than I, but there is something in you that I find—almost irresistible."

"Why resist?" Robin demanded.

"Because I am not free to choose," Mary said. "I have a destiny, I know it!" Then she grasped his hands. "Sometimes I have second sight, or something like it. Things come to me, things out of the future." Her grip tightened and her eyes held him. "I feel it now . . . that you and I may be tied together."

Robin, despite the dulling power of the drink, felt a thrill of danger. "Tied how?"

"I know not." She leaned forward, pressed herself against him, then lifted her lips. After he kissed her, she stood and stepped back. "Someday I shall be . . . what I am not now. And I feel somehow that you will be much greater in this country than you are at present. You must go now, but do not forget this moment. I know I shall not."

Robin stared at her, aware of the enigmatic light that gleamed in her blue eyes. "I—I should go home, Your Majesty."

"Let it be Mary when we are alone, but wait a few days before that happens again." She shook her head. "I don't trust myself with you. Go now before I—"

She broke off and turned from him, but Robin went to her, lifted her hand and pressed a kiss to it, then left. He stumbled to his room, undressed, and fell into bed, confused and rattled by the encounter. For hours he tossed and turned, unable to forget the raw passion that had taken him—and that he sensed had taken Mary Queen of Scots.

But after he fell into a fitful sleep, he dreamed of his grand-father—and Myles Wakefield's face was unsmiling and grim.

"So you spent a week with her, eh?" Sir Francis Walsingham had received Robin at once on his return, and he listened to the young man's report with a strange expression in his eyes. Now as Robin finished, he spoke thoughtfully. "And did you—get *very* close to her?"

The man's meaning was clear, and though Robin's skin was still tanned from his long sea voyage, he felt the heat rise and a blush cover his face. For one moment he thought of striking out with angry words at the tall man who stood watching him so speculatively, but he recognized at once that he would lose any contest of wits with Sir Francis.

"No, sir, I did not!" he stated firmly. He tried to hold Walsingham's steady gaze, but found that he could not. "I—that is, she was quite—"

Robin broke off in confusion, hating himself for his actions, which now seemed terribly wrong. He had remained for a full week at Tutbury, and each night Mary had dined with him. And, he now realized, each night she had urged wine on him so that he was lost against her. *I was a fool! She was using me!* he thought. *She was tempting men to do what she wished before I was born, I suppose.*

Seeing the misery in the young man's honest eyes, Walsingham relented. "Well, well, it was to be expected," he said more gently. He stroked his beard and studied Robin's face. "I'm surprised that you were able to hold out against her charms. Not all men have been so strong."

Robin said quietly, "I was a fool, Sir Francis. But I—was flattered by her attentions, I suppose."

"Most men would be, my boy, so give it no more thought." Then he halted and cast speculative eyes upon Robin. "Or perhaps you should. Did she invite you back?"

"Oh yes, sir."

"Then go back. She will try to use you again, of course, but you are wiser now. And you can turn the situation to your advantage. She will promise you great things if you will help her become queen of England." So saying, the secretary's face grew hard and determined. "But that she will never be!"

"Must I go back, sir?" Robin protested faintly, but as the secretary explained how important it was, he nodded with resignation. "I will do my best, sir."

"Good man!" Walsingham beamed at him. "Our queen is not unaware of your labors. She wishes a personal report. Go to her at once."

"Yes, Sir Francis."

Robin took his leave and later that afternoon had an audience with the queen. She was feeling rather low and received him in her chambers. One of the maids was working on her hair, but Elizabeth dismissed her. When the young woman was out of the room, the queen at once commanded, "Tell me about her."

Startled at the abrupt request, Robin began diffidently, but soon ran into trouble. He had planned to ignore the less proper side of his adventure, but Elizabeth was even more astute than Sir Francis. "So, she tried to seduce you," she said staring at him. "And did she succeed?"

"Indeed not, Your Majesty!"

Elizabeth studied Robin's face for so long that he felt the heat rising into it. To his surprise Elizabeth broke into laughter. "By the rood!" she cried, "I haven't seen a man blush in years—nor many maids, for that matter." When she saw that the young man was painfully embarrassed, she at once waved her hand and smiled gently. "Never mind, Robin. It's good to know that some virtue still exists in this dark world."

"I am not proud of myself, Your Majesty. I scarcely resisted her on my own merits—and I fear I did little good to you. Truly, I am too dull to be one of your agents."

"Nonsense! You shall see how valuable you are. Tell me everything, and leave nothing out. You will be surprised what valuable information the simplest of conversations can sometimes contain."

It was not a high hour in Robin's life, but it was one he long remembered. The queen of England hung on his words, and when he was finished, she nodded. "You've done well, Robin. One day you will have more than my thanks. But time is critical. Would you go back to Tutbury . . . for your queen?"

If Mary knew how to stir a man's body, Elizabeth Tudor knew how to touch his soul! Robin, though despising the thought of going back to Mary, nodded. "If you command it, Your Majesty, I will go."

Elizabeth was pleased. She put out her hand, and when he knelt and kissed it, she smiled. "You are very like your grandfather. Very like, indeed."

When Robin left the palace the next morning with instructions from Walsingham, he felt depressed. He had obtained permission to visit his grandmother, however, and that cheered him up.

I'll tell her all about it, he decided. *She'll know how to deal with that woman.* He touched his heels to his horse and all morning he thought about the two women: Elizabeth the queen, and Mary, the woman who would be queen. And he knew if Mary was ever on the throne of England, the fires at Smithfield would be lit again—exactly like those that had burned his father.

ALLISON

S top that dawdling, Allison!" Martha Spenser entered the house, her face reddened with the bite of the sharp winter wind. "You've still not started the meal as I told you."

"I'm—I'm sorry, Mother," Allison answered hastily. She rose quickly from the wooden table, attempting to slip the thin book she'd been reading into the pocket of her skirt.

But her mother's sharp eyes were too quick. Stepping to the girl's side, she grabbed her by the arm, thrust her hand into the pocket, and drew the offending article forth, exclaiming, "Reading again. I might have guessed!" She held the book up, stared at it, then gasped, "Why—this is a Bible!"

"Just a part of one, Mother," Allison said nervously. "Giles Horton let me borrow it."

"Giles Horton hates us!" Turning to the fireplace, she started to throw the book into the blaze, but Allison moved quickly and held her mother's arm. Martha, shocked by the unexpected action, stared at the girl. "So, you see what reading has done for you? Made you rebel against your mother!" Raising her hand, she slapped Allison across the face.

Allison blinked at the stinging blow. Her eyes watered, but it was not the first time her mother had struck her. She was aghast at her own actions, but desperately she pleaded, "Mother, I meant no harm, and neither did Giles. Please, don't burn it. Let me give it back. If you burn it, we'll have to pay for it."

Allison's words caught at her mother, for every penny counted in the Spenser household. Poised to throw the book she hated into the fire, she paused to balance the cost of it with the satisfaction of watching it burn—then thrust it back at the girl. "See you give it back, then. And never bring a Protestant book under this roof again, you understand me?"

"Yes, Mother." She pocketed the book, relieved to have gotten off so lightly. "I'll put the potatoes on to boil—"

"Never mind, I'll do it myself." Martha Spenser's broad face assumed a bitter cast. "I can't count on you for any sort of work." Her thin, complaining tone filled the room. "What with your poor father sick, and money as short as it is, the least you could do is cook what little we have." She stared at Allison's distressed countenance, satisfied that she had made her miserable. An unhappy woman herself, she seemed most content when those around her felt her misery. Not that she was aware of this, for she perceived herself to be a good wife and mother. If someone had spoken the truth to her—that she'd nearly driven her husband into the ground with her sharp tongue and made her home a misery for her children—she would have been furious.

Now she began throwing pots around, refusing to let her daughter help and blaming her with every breath for being lazy and thoughtless. Whipping out a sharp knife, she began slicing the mutton, her voice whining and her face flushed. "It's not like I'm a healthy woman. If I had my health, I wouldn't mind doing all my work and yours as well! Forsooth, it's all I can do to get out of bed with my aching joints, and you know how I cough myself to death at times."

"I'm sorry, Mother. I'll try to do better." Allison slipped beside her mother to help with the meal, painfully aware that her mother was the healthiest person in the house. Short and stout and strong,

Martha Spenser was capable of doing anything, but determinedly nursed fancied ailments and experimented with medicines and cures for them.

Allison glanced at her mother's large strong hands and thought of her father's frail, liver-spotted hands. *He's the sick one, not you, Mother.* The thought passed through her mind, but she would never utter such a thing. "You go lie down and rest, Mother," she said instead. "I'll have the meal ready by the time Father gets home."

"I suppose it might help this headache of mine. But mind you don't get to reading and burn the meat!" She left the kitchen with an injured look.

Grateful for the solitude her mother left behind, Allison moved about the kitchen preparing the meal. A gray light filtered through the high window, throwing a faint gleam on her face, and once she moved to look outside. She loved the out-of-doors and longed to leave the house and follow one of the trails that wended through the forest. But she knew better than to consider such a thing.

A short time later, as she waited for the potatoes to boil until they were bursting in their jackets, she moved to the open door and listened stealthily. Her mother's sonorous snores came to her, and quickly she picked the Bible from the table and opened it.

"This is the Gospel of John," Giles had informed her. *"Mister Tyndale's Bible. See you don't get any marks on it—or my father will have my hide!"*

Giles had often loaned her one of his father's books, but never before a Bible. The thin volume had fascinated—and frightened!—the girl, for she had been taught by the priest that it was dangerous to read the Bible. "Only one trained in the study of the Scripture is fit to interpret the Word of God," Father Dailey had told them many times. He said this freely, but he'd told Allison in private, "Look around you, Allison, at what England has come

to—a land of heresy! And how did this happen? Because Henry
VIII began to read the Bible. Trust the Mother church and the
priests and bishops and the pope, Allison! Do not let yourself fall
into mortal sin by meddling with the Bible!"

And yet . . . for some reason that the girl herself could not
comprehend, she was strongly drawn to the forbidden Book. She
had learned to read almost by osmosis, picking up the skill very
easily and proving to be one of those individuals seemingly born
with a voracious appetite for knowledge. Her father more or less
encouraged her in this area, while her mother made no objection
as long as she did her work. She had access to few books, for none
of her family were scholars, but with Giles—and his father's
library—nearby, that wasn't the problem it might have been.

It had been Giles who had triggered her fascination with the
Bible, for he had boasted of his own knowledge of the Scriptures.
"You Catholics don't know the truth about religion," he'd announced to Allison one day. "We Protestants read the Bible for
ourselves, so we know what God wants from us."

Too mild-mannered to argue, Allison had merely asked for
examples, which Giles could not give her readily for he actually
was not much of a reader. He did, however, pique her curiosity
with a few samples of stories from the Gospel of John. Allison had
heard some of the same stories from priests, but as the days went
by a burning curiosity began to grow in her heart. Finally she
asked Giles for a Bible, and he'd brought her the Gospel of John,
promising not to say a word to anyone about the loan.

The Gospel had become a treasure to Allison, for it brought to
life the personality of Jesus. She had always been a devout girl, but
it was a formal sort of thing. Now, the Jesus in the Gospel had
become a living, sentient being—a real man who once walked
the earth. She pored over the book, fascinated and entranced by
Jesus, by his simplicity and his overflowing love for everyone he
met.

Night after night she stayed awake for hours in her small room in the attic, entranced by the book, reading by the stubs of candles she molded from bits and pieces of discarded ones. By the flickering amber light she shivered in the cold, but was so taken by the Scripture that she scarcely noticed. The woman at the well, the Jew named Nicodemus, the man who was born blind, Mary and Martha, the volatile Simon Peter—all came trooping out to people her small, cold room.

And something else happened, too, aside from the pleasure she received from reading the drama that made up the Bible. She discovered that the book had some sort of power—a power that was lacking in any other book she had read. The words seemed to remain in her mind and heart even when she was not actually reading. She'd always had a good memory, but never had a book *taken* her in such a fashion. As she worked or when she walked in the woods, she found phrases from the small book echoing in her mind.

One passage came to her again and again, one which she could neither understand nor forget. Night after night she read the story in the sixth chapter of John's Gospel, about the feeding of the multitudes. Something about the miracle of feeding thousands of people with five barley loaves and two small fish intrigued her. Not for one moment did she doubt the miracle, for she had believed in the power of God from childhood. She developed a powerful and vivid mental picture of the scene: the multitudes milling around restlessly, the disciples standing close to Jesus under the blazing Judean sky, and most of all, the one who performed the miracle.

Allison had a vivid imagination, and as the scene came back to her again and again, she pictured Jesus in a way that startled her. She'd always thought of him as distant, unreachable. But as she read, an impression came to her mind of the man himself, tired and hungry, sweating under the hot skies . . . but most of all she had a sense of the love that flowed from him.

He really cared about those hungry people, she thought with astonishment. She had heard that God loved people, but this simple act of the Savior's—feeding the hungry people—somehow brought him down out of a vague and far-off heaven to the reality of earth. But it was the words Jesus spoke on the day following the miracles that burned into the mind of the young woman. Over and over again she read them: *"I am the bread of life. He who comes to Me shall never hunger, and he who believes in Me shall never thirst."*

Something about this statement captivated Allison. "How can Jesus be *bread?*" she murmured aloud more than once. "I eat the bread at the table, but how can a *person* be bread?"

For weeks she pondered this verse, at times feeling that the priest was right, that no mere individual could understand such things. But she returned to the chapter many times. Then, one night when her eyes were watering with fatigue, she experienced something that both excited and frightened her.

She put the book under her straw mattress, blew out the candle, and pulled the covers up, preparing to go to sleep. Her hands were stiff with cold, for there was no fire in the room. Lifting her back, she slipped her hands under her body and enjoyed the pleasure of feeling them grow warmer. She had worked hard all day and she was not only sleepy but very tired. As she began to drift off into sleep, she murmured the prayer she had memorized as a child: "Hail, Mary, full of grace—"

But suddenly she halted—aware that she was not alone! Her eyes flew open and she stared wildly about the small room, thinking that one of her brothers or sisters had slipped inside; but the full moon threw silver beams through the one small window, bathing the space with cold light.

There's nobody here, Allison thought, fighting down the stab of alarm that had touched her. *I'm just having a dream. Maybe Mother is up and I heard her.*

But when she closed her eyes and tried to go to sleep, the sensation persisted. It was a sensation unlike anything Allison had ever felt before—an inner certainty that *someone* was in her room. The silence was thick, for it was after midnight and all in the house went to bed shortly after dark to save on candles. A persistent wind whispered outside her window, seeming almost to brush the house with inquiring fingers. But what she felt was not the wind, she knew it.

Then she thought of the priest's warnings about the Bible— and she felt a sudden sharp fear. *Maybe it's the devil! He's come to get me for reading the Bible!*

She had heard much about the devil. In fact, it often seemed to her that Satan was more real to many than was God himself. She had seen more than one old woman executed for trafficking with the devil—a sight that gave her nightmares for years! Witches and curses were common in England, and Allison's limbs trembled as she lay there in the silence of the small room.

She tried to pray, but fear was so strong that she could only whisper her memorized prayer—which did not help at all, for the sense of *someone* close to her in the darkness grew even stronger.

Finally she whispered, "O God! Don't let the devil have me!"

And in that instant, her fear suddenly melted away. The room seemed to grow warmer—but it was as though the warmth came from within her, not from without. She relaxed, not knowing what was happening to her, but sure that it was a good thing.

For a long time she lay very still, watchful, letting the silence run on. Finally thoughts came to her, words that she had read many times:

"Most assuredly, I say to you, he who believes in Me has everlasting life. I am the bread of life. Your fathers ate the manna in the wilderness, and are dead. This is the bread which comes down from heaven, that one

may eat of it and not die. I am the living bread which came down from heaven. If anyone eats of this bread, he will live forever; and the bread that I shall give is My flesh, which I shall give for the life of the world."

It was as though Allison could *hear* the words she had so often read and puzzled over, and once again she asked, "But how can a man be like bread?" Then—as if in answer to her question, the words came:

"Most assuredly, I say to you, unless you eat the flesh of the Son of Man and drink His blood, you have no life in you."

Some of her earlier fear now returned. "What does it mean, Lord?" she whispered. "If someone doesn't have life, why, they're dead! I don't want death!"

"Whoever eats My flesh and drinks My blood has eternal life, and I will raise him up at the last day. For My flesh is food indeed, and My blood is drink indeed. He who eats My flesh and drinks My blood abides in Me, and I in him. As the living Father sent Me, and I live because of the Father, so he who feeds on Me will live because of Me. This is the bread which came down from heaven—not as your fathers ate the manna, and are dead. He who eats this bread will live forever."

And as the words echoed in her spirit, Allison suddenly understood. Her heart gave a leap as she said aloud, "Why, it means that just like I eat bread to nourish my body, I need to take Jesus in to give life to my spirit!"

A great wave of joy washed over the young woman as she pondered this truth, and she prayed a simple prayer, almost involuntarily, "Lord, give me this bread, for I am so hungry for you!"

As she prayed, Allison was filled with a sense of . . . *approval*— that was the only way she could describe it—and she felt certain God had heard her prayer! Lying in her small bed, she began to pray fervently, the words rising from the very depths of her heart. For a long time she simply praised God, and her spirit was flooded with the sense of the presence of Jesus. Not as someone far off, but as a warm presence right in the room with her, approving of her and loving her.

As this sense of love washed over her, Allison began to praise the Lord with a fervency she had never known before. Until now, she had gone through the ceremony of prayer out of obedience. This time, she was speaking to a friend—and more than a friend, to a Savior who had done something wonderful in her heart. She cried in a whisper, "O Lord Jesus, let me ever have more of you. Fill every part of me."

All sense of time left, and Allison had no idea how long she prayed that night. She was conscious that human speech became too weak for the waves of gratitude to God that rose in her, and her prayers became both less—and more—than mere words. She had been a quiet girl all her days, but now a joy had come to her that she had never imagined existed. And, as she prayed, she seemed to be praying with the tongue of an angel! A fountain of love seemed to break forth in her spirit, and she expressed this as she never had before, with worship and adoration of God.

Finally she drifted off to sleep, but her last thought was, *Now I'll never have to be afraid again!*

"I don't know what that girl is thinking of, John." Martha Spenser had been watching Allison out the bedroom window and had spoken to her husband with a touch of bewilderment in her voice.

From where John lay on his bed, he could catch a glimpse of his youngest daughter as she plucked a goose. She was singing softly, and on her face was a look of contentment.

"What's the trouble, Marth—" He broke off as a terrible spasm of coughing seized him. He grabbed his chest, and the bed shook as convulsions wracked his thin body. Martha turned quickly to get a cup of water, and finally the cough subsided enough that he could take a drink. Gasping for breath, he choked out, "Every time that happens I think I'm going to die."

His wife stared at him, aware that he was not the sturdy man he once had been. The sickness had been slow coming, but the past winter had seemed to draw the strength out of him. His eyes were sunk back in his head, and his mouth was a thin line drawn tight by pain. He caught her look and shook his head. "I'm all right now. What's the matter with Allison?"

"Oh, nothing, I suppose." Martha sat down beside him and stared out the window at the girl. "In a way she's doing better than ever. She even does her work without forgetting."

"She's always been an obedient child, more so than any of the others."

"You always defend her." Cocking her head to one side, the woman listened to the song that came faintly through the window, then shook her head. "It's nothing to trouble you, John. But for weeks now she's been going around smiling and singing. Just like she is now. Forsooth!" she snapped, her eyes cloudy with doubt, "I don't know what she's got to sing about. Nor any of us for that matter!"

John Spenser fought down another spasm that he felt would have torn him in two. Silently he lay there, wanting to assure his wife that all would be well, but in truth he was not at all certain it would. His affairs had been bad enough before he became bedfast, but now they were a disaster. He'd looked at the books until his eyes watered, trying to find a way to meet his debts. Now in despair he thought, *We're lost! I can't work and we'll lose this place—if I don't die first!*

"Well, Wife," he said finally, "I'm glad the girl is happy."

Martha stared at him, wanting to speak but not certain if she should. The past months had left her even more worried than usual. Now she set her lips together as if facing an unpleasant chore. "Have you thought about don Alfredo's offer, John?"

Her question at once brought a troubled light into the sick man's eyes. He stirred his thin shoulders, gazed up at the ceiling, then looked across to her. "I don't think the girl would be happy."

Now that the subject was open, Martha pressed harder. She had thought of what to say, had even practiced it when alone. She knew neither bluntness nor harshness would prevail. So she spoke quietly. "It's not what we want, but we must think of the family. Allison must marry. If she marries a poor farmer, she'll be worked hard, have a baby every year, and be an old woman before she's thirty. Do you want that for her?"

"No, of course not, but—"

"I know, you're worried about sending her away to a foreign country—but think what advantages she'd have." Martha spoke persuasively, leaning forward with eagerness. "She'd be the wife of a rich man, and the dowry Señor Corona has offered will pay this place off with a goodly sum left over . . ."

John listened as his wife went on, feeling despair overtake him again. He did not want to bring his beloved Allison pain, to marry her to a man merely because he was wealthy, but he grew more desperate with each passing day.

It might well be that Allison's marriage to a man she did not love was the only way their family would survive.

***

Outside the house, Allison finished plucking the goose. She tied the mouth of the sack stuffed with the fine soft feathers, then took the fowl to the backyard, where she proceeded to dress it. "You'll be a tasty morsel, I don't doubt," she said cheerfully, holding the bird high. "Father will love a juicy bite of you!"

For weeks now, ever since the night she'd called on God, Allison had been living in a different world. She still attended Mass, of course, but that was only one brief time when she could worship. Actually she woke up each morning with a prayer on her lips, went about her work all day singing, and felt such a joy inside that she believed the verse she'd read in the third chapter of the Gospel *must* refer to what had happened to her: "You must be born again."

Many times she whispered to herself, "That must be what's happened to me. I feel like a new person, newly born!"

Now as she hung the goose's limp body on a peg, she took off her apron and washed her face and hands at the pump. Then she put on a light coat and went to the door, calling out, "Mother, I'm going to the mill for the flour. I'll be back soon."

Five minutes later she was on the path that wended around the village. As usual, she took a shortcut that led through the tall trees. Spring had stirred the earth, loosing earthy smells, and overhead the trees were tipped with gold and birds chattered among them like singers in a choir.

Allison was meditating on one of the passages in the Scripture and was so preoccupied that she didn't see the tall figure who had stepped into the path until she was upon him.

"Oh!" she gasped and started to turn aside, and then she recognized the man. Her face turned pale and she stood stock still looking up at him. "Mister Wakefield!" she gasped. "I—I didn't see you."

Robin had been to see Kate Moody and was on his way home. "I'm glad to see you, Allison," he said at once, but then stopped, at a loss for words. Twice since his return he had seen Allison at a distance but had not sought to speak with her. Now, however, he knew he wanted to say something, for the memory of their history troubled him.

"You're looking well." He smiled at her, noting that she had grown taller, as was expected. She was no longer a child, as the slim curves of her figure testified. Her ash-blonde hair hung down her back almost to her waist, and in the April sun it glowed with a fine sheen. Her violet eyes had always been striking, and now he saw that they were large and well shaped, made somewhat mysterious by the heavy dark lashes. Her face was oval-shaped and had none of the childish look he remembered. Her lips were wide and mobile, and there was a classic sweep to her jaw.

Robin shook his head in wonder. "I left you a little girl," he said, admiration in his glance, "and now I return to find a most attractive young woman."

Allison's clear cheeks flushed at his words, but she shook her head. Several young men had told her as much, but she found no reason to believe them or to dwell on what they said. "I—I heard that you'd come back, Mister Wakefield," she said. "Did you have a good voyage?"

"Call me Robin, Allison. And yes, I did have a good voyage." He glanced down the path and asked, "Are you going to the mill?" When she nodded, he said quickly, "Let me walk with you. There's something I want to say to you."

Allison glanced involuntarily toward her house, then shook her head. "I'd best not be seen with you. My mother wouldn't like it."

"I can't fault her for that, since I've brought such grief to her," his eyes and voice entreated her. "But please give me just a few minutes." When she hesitated, he spoke quickly, "It's just that—well, I've felt so badly about what happened. Do you hate me, Allison?"

"Oh, no!"

Her quick protest made him feel better, and he smiled at her. "That's like you, I know, but it is a sweet music to my ears. And I thank you for your forgiveness. It means more to me than you realize. It's been . . . a source of grief to me to have hurt you—and your family, of course. Now, tell me about yourself."

"There's little to tell—" Allison broke off as a sudden impulse to tell Robin about her new walk with God came to her, but she felt too awkward. "My father has been ill, and things have been troublesome. I think he's afraid we will lose our place."

"I'm sorry to hear it. I've heard of his sickness." Robin admired the sheen of her glowing cheeks, then added, "I'd call on him, but that might not be wise. Nevertheless, I'll speak to my uncle, Thomas. I'm sure something can be done to help."

Allison's smile was instant. "Oh, would you, Robin?"

"Of course I will! Now, what about you?" His eyes twinkled. "Must be a line of young fellows at your door, eh?"

"No, sir, not really."

"The more fools they!" Robin quipped. Then he took her arm and said, "Come, let me walk with you. I'm home for a few days, maybe a week. Perhaps you could meet me and we'll go looking for wildflowers like we used to."

"My mother wouldn't like it, Robin."

He regarded her silently for a moment. "Surely there's no harm in picking flowers," he argued. He glanced at her face and saw, or thought he did, that she wanted to see him. "We always had fun, didn't we, Allison?"

Allison nodded, thinking of those days when she had been a child and Robin Wakefield had been the idol of her heart. Now he was a tall, strong man—and from the admiring look in his eyes she could tell he was not unaware of her as a woman. The thought brought a flash of pleasure to her, but she shook her head. "I'm sorry, Robin. I can't go against my mother's wishes."

Robin was aware that pressure would do no good, but he determined to do something for the young woman. "I won't urge you to disobey your mother, Allison. 'Tis a noble thing to honor one's parents."

Allison arrived at home with the sack of flour over her shoulder, and all day she thought of Robin. The next day, she was surprised to see him when she went to the village for her father, and he insisted on walking along the streets with her. She could not very well avoid him—a fact that pleased her, for she had little wish to do so. They walked and talked together, and before parting Robin bought some sweets from a small shop, and the two of them devoured the treats with gusto, licking their fingers and laughing, just as they had in days gone by.

That scene, or one much like it, took place frequently in the next few days. Somehow when Allison left her house and went to tend the animals or walked to the village or the mill, Robin was usually there. She grew more and more eager to see him, but never agreed to meet him as he often urged.

It was on a Thursday afternoon, when she returned from taking the cow to a better pasture, that her mother met her at the door. "Allison, come with me!" She turned and led the girl to the large bedroom. Motioning for her to enter, she said, "Here she is, John."

Allison felt a touch of apprehension, for her father's face was pale and his lips were thin. "Yes, Father?" she asked at once.

John Spenser gave an agonized glance at his wife, but found no comfort in her stern features. With a sigh, he said, "Allison, we've got something to tell you, and I hope it will make you happy." When the girl didn't speak, he cleared his throat. "You're going to be married, Allison."

If her father had said that she was going to sprout wings and fly, Allison couldn't have been more astonished. "Married, Father?"

"Yes. I know you're a little young, but many young women are married at the age of sixteen, and it will be a fine match for you."

The room seemed to grow dim, but Allison managed to ask, "Who—who is it that I'm to marry?"

Martha Spenser spoke briskly, before her husband could reply, "He is the son of don Alfredo Corona, and his name is Jaime."

"But . . . who is he? I don't know any families by that name."

"Why, he is the son of a Spanish nobleman. You'll live in Spain, of course," Martha said at once. Seeing the distress on the girl's face, she said sharply, "It's time you were married. Do you think we don't know you've been sneaking around with that villain, Robin Wakefield!" Anger flared in her eyes and she shook her head. "You'll not disgrace us by consorting with such a man!"

Allison's father said urgently, "I don't think evil of you, Child, but Wakefield has surely been spoiled by the court. You don't know their free and easy ways." His lips twisted suddenly and he whispered, "I . . . won't always be around to take care of you. This way, you'll have a good home. Don Alfredo is getting on in years, but he's a distant cousin of ours. He's a wealthy man, and his son will inherit his estate."

"I trust you'll be thankful to your father for making such good arrangements for you," Martha said. "Not many girls have such a chance as this!"

"I—I do thank you . . . both of you," Allison forced the words past her lips. She was as unhappy and frightened as she'd ever been. To leave her home . . . to leave England and go to a strange country where she didn't even speak the language!

With a nod, her mother turned to leave the room. "I'll fix supper while you talk to your father about the marriage."

As soon as she was gone, John reached out and took the girl's trembling hand. "I'm . . . sorry, Allison," he whispered, his misery plain in his eyes. "It's the best I can do. At least you'll have a place of your own."

Allison blinked back the tears and forced a smile. "I'll be very happy, I'm sure. But I'll hate to leave you, and—" She broke off. "And the rest of the family," she finished lamely.

Spenser knew death was near, but he could not speak of this to his daughter. He patted her hand and said in a strained voice, "It's best, Daughter . . . for all of us."

That night when Allison lay in bed, she prayed, but somehow

the heavens were brass. The presence of God was not there—or so it seemed to the frightened young woman.

"Is this of you, Lord?" she whispered brokenly.

But there was only silence and darkness as the long dark night of the soul came upon Allison Spenser.

HOLY WEDLOCK

News of the coming marriage of John Spenser's daughter to a fabulously wealthy Spanish don ran through the village like wildfire. When it was announced that the bride-to-be would leave for Spain in less than two weeks, the tongues wagged furiously.

But Allison was unaware of the fodder her circumstances were providing for the most vicious of the town gossips. She lived as if in a dream—and not a pleasant one. She allowed her mother to take charge of all the arrangements, and her lack of interest only made Martha angry.

"It's your wedding, girl!" the older woman said sharply when Allison showed no enthusiasm over the preliminaries. "You'd think it was a wake you were going to instead of your wedding!"

Sometimes I wish it were a wake! My own funeral.

The desperate thought flashed into Allison's mind, but she forced it away and did her best to take more interest in what was happening to her. Her nights were long, and for hours she would pray, seeking to recover the lost sense of God's presence. *Have I sinned so greatly that God has cast me off?* The thought brought waves of black grief over her, and she wept in the darkness, wondering how she had so sinned that God had slammed the door to heaven in her face.

Days came and fled so quickly that Allison could feel the irrevocable passage of time—almost she thought she could sense the rolling of the earth itself, each revolution bringing her closer to the time when she would see her home and family no more.

Only once did she see Robin for a few brief moments. Before she had a chance to tell him what had happened to her, he told her that he had to go to London on business. When it was a few days before her departure and he still hadn't returned, she was certain that she would never see him again. She could not deny that this grieved her, for despite the difficulties that had separated them, her heart had held to its feelings for him.

But she did see him again—three days before she sailed for Spain. She had spent as much time with her father as possible, for they both knew—though neither spoke openly of it—that these were probably their last days together. Mrs. Spenser left on an errand with Allison's two married sisters, Mary and Deborah. Her brothers were old enough to entertain themselves, so when she grew restless, Allison left the house and went for a walk. She drank in the sights about her, wanting to store memories of this village deep in her mind. But so many people stopped her to talk about her leaving that she soon grew overwhelmed, so she left the street and meandered down one of the paths that led to the small river that curled in serpentine fashion around the flat land.

For an hour she soaked in the familiar scenes that she'd beheld almost every day of her life. Sadness swept over her. *Will I ever see this field again?* she wondered disconsolately. Preoccupied with such thoughts, she at first didn't hear her name being called. When she did hear it, she turned to see Robin emerge from the line of trees that followed the stream.

When he drew close, she saw his face was tense. He came to stand in front of her and said abruptly, "I've just heard about your marriage." He was wearing a buff pair of breeches and a forest-green doublet. A pure white shirt set off the bronze tint of his face, and she noted yet again the strength and grace about him that she had always admired.

Her wide eyes met his. "I—didn't think I'd get to say good-bye to you—" Her voice broke as she said this, and she looked away.

He studied her face and was quick to recognize that the peace that usually marked it was gone. She looked drawn and was slightly pale, and he knew at once how it was with her. "Do you have to do this, Allison?"

She nodded wearily. "Yes, my parents have already made the arrangements." Trying to smile, she added, "It will be a good marriage. My husband-to-be has great wealth."

"But you don't love him," Robin returned swiftly. "You've never even seen him."

"No, but that's not necessary. You know that these things are common. Many young women have their husbands selected for them by their parents." She knew she was merely echoing her mother's sentiments, but she didn't know what else to say.

"You make it sound like you're buying a dress! This is much more than that," Robin insisted. Allison looked small and defenseless, and he felt a pang of loss. "You're so young!"

Allison lifted her chin in a sudden, defiant gesture. "I am *not* a child. I am a woman, Robin Wakefield!" She looked up into his face, but when their eyes met, try as she might, she could not keep her lower lip from beginning to tremble. She bit it swiftly to cover her weakness, but she could not conceal the tears that suddenly filled her eyes. Blindly she turned and would have run away, but he seized her arm and turned her back to him.

"Let me go!" she raged helplessly.

"Allison, wait!" Ignoring her attempts to free herself, Robin pulled her close. She was trembling like a bird, and he whispered, "Remember, when you were just a little girl and we saw a bear. How frightened you were?"

Allison buried her face against his chest, inhaling the scent of him, trying to draw in a portion of his strength. Images of the adventure he mentioned flitted through her mind, and she could see again the small black bear they had met while roaming the woods. "Yes . . . I remember."

"I held you just like this until you weren't afraid anymore."

Safe in the circle of his arms, she lifted her face. Tears ran down her rounded cheeks and tragedy shaded her fine eyes. "I was a child, Robin. You can't make the fear go like that anymore."

Robin stared down at her, stunned—though not by her words. He suddenly was acutely aware that this was not a child he held, but a woman. Her slim figure pressed against him, and suddenly he felt a strong desire stirring deep within him—a desire to shelter and protect her, not as a child but as one who was precious to him in a way that he was only beginning to understand. As he looked at her he felt a fierce determination to somehow place himself between her and anything, or anyone, that might threaten her. His arms tightened around her unconsciously.

Allison felt the change in his hold, saw a darkening in his eyes, and was alarmed. "Let me go!"

But Robin, filled with compassion—and with something else that he couldn't quite name—was looking down at her as though mesmerized. She had tilted her head back and her lips were parted, and before he knew what he was doing, he lowered his head and let his lips gently touch hers. At first she stiffened, then her lips softened and responded—and he found himself pressing her closer, savoring the scent and touch of her.

As though acting of their own volition, Allison's hands went around his neck and she drew even closer. This was the first time she had ever been kissed, but she felt no fear, no hesitation. It was as though she had at last come to a place she long dreamed of, a place where she belonged. This was what she wanted, this was the man for whom she longed . . . not some unknown Spanish lord—

The thought of her future husband was like a spray of cold water. With a choked cry, Allison abruptly drew back.

"Allison, I—"

But Robin never completed his words, for she whirled and ran away. He called to her, but she never looked back. When she disappeared around the curve in the path, he turned heavily toward Wakefield.

What sort of man are you? he raged at himself. *Taking advantage of her like that?*

But even the guilt that swept over him could not alter one fact: Something had changed deep within his heart. Allison was no longer just his dear little friend. She was a vital and necessary part of him . . . one that he would never be able to claim, for she belonged to another man. A sudden sharp sense of loss cut through him, leaving an emptiness in his heart. When he got home, he said nothing to his grandmother about the meeting, but the taste of Allison's lips and the memory of her embrace would not leave him.

As for Allison, she found a quiet spot deep in the woods and threw herself to the ground, loosing the hot tears she had been restraining. She wept for the first time since being told that she was to be married. Slumping down on the cold ground, she buried her face in her hands and sobbed. How long she sat there weeping she never knew. Finally she grew quieter, but the sadness that had come to her seemed, if anything, even keener and more poignant than before her meeting with Robin.

He thinks of you as a child, she scolded herself, but the memory of his kiss swept over her, and she knew that was no longer true. He had held her like a woman—but even that was a tragedy. She had been lonely for most of her life, and her best memories were of the times she and Robin shared. Now, thinking of how she had felt when he'd held her close, her cheeks glowed with an unexpected warmth. She touched one of them, pondering for a moment, then shook her head. Getting slowly to her feet, she wiped her eyes with her handkerchief, then said firmly, "I must put him behind me, along with all else here in this place."

Turning back toward the village, she prayed, but as before, felt nothing. The future was a dark street filled with uncertainties, and fear seemed her only companion. "I'll believe in you, Lord," she whispered almost fiercely, "even if I *never* feel anything again! You are real, and what I have felt in my heart was real! And I will honor you, even in this marriage that so frightens me."

She set her jaw firmly and moved along down the path, devoid of hope—but determined to be true to her God and to her marriage.

All the family had said good-bye to Allison on the morning of her departure—and to her surprise her mother's eyes were wet with tears as she embraced her.

Martha's arms closed tightly around the girl, and when she stepped back, she had to clear her throat before she could speak. "This—may have seemed hard to you, Allison, but I want more for you than being a farmer's wife."

"I know, Mother." Allison embraced her again, then after bidding good-bye to her brothers, said, "Let me say one more word to Father." Turning, she moved quickly into the bedroom and went to stoop over and put her arms around the frail form of the sick man.

He surprised her by the fierceness of his hug, the depth of his emotions channeling strength into his emaciated arms. "Daughter, you have been my good girl always!"

"Good-bye, dearest father. Pray for me!"

Allison tore herself away and left the house. It had been decided that none of her family would go to see her off, so she bent and kissed Perkins and Daniel, then her mother, before moving to the carriage. A short swarthy man helped her inside, then got in beside her and said, "All right, go now!"

The horses stepped out smartly, and when they had gone a hundred yards, Allison looked out the window. Her mother was crying and the two boys were staring after her with drooping shoulders. She could not see her father, of course, but she knew he was grieved to lose her.

Her companion, seeing her struggle to hold back the tears, said nothing for some time. Finally, when she'd gained control of herself, he said quietly, "Señor Jaime was sorry that he could not come for you personally, señorita, but it was impossible, I assure you."

Allison nodded to the middle-aged man who had come to escort her to Spain. "I understand, Señor Manti. And I thank you for your trouble."

Manti smiled uneasily at her, but nodded firmly. "He will be delighted to find such a beautiful bride. And the family as well, they are most anxious to receive you."

Manti spoke of the fine home and the estate that would be her home for a time, then subsided into a moody silence. He was, in fact, a saturnine man, but had been courteous enough to Allison's family. He had served the Corona family for many years. Allison might have wished for a more talkative escort, for though Manti spoke of the estate freely, he was strangely reticent about the man she was going to marry.

Finally they reached the dock, and Allison got into a small boat and was rowed across the harbor. She was lifted by two sailors, who placed her on deck, whereupon Manti escorted her down to a paneled cabin.

"I trust you will be comfortable here, señorita. My cabin is across from this one." He hesitated, then added carefully, "Sailors are rather rough. If you want to go on deck, please let me escort you."

"Thank you, Señor Manti. Could we go up and watch the ship leave the harbor?"

"Certainly!"

The two of them returned to the deck, and Allison watched from the aftercastle as the mariners sang at the capstan and the anchor was weighed. Manti explained everything, adding proudly, "I am a sailor myself, señorita. Señor Corona has two fine ships, and I have served as an officer on both of them."

Slowly the ship was towed out of the harbor and the sails were unfurled. Allison watched as the sailors scrambled like monkeys out over the yards, and then the huge stretches of canvas bellied outward and upward. For the first time Allison felt a ship come alive under her feet—the bow dipping and the first hiss of white bubbles and foam going along the side.

A small crowd had gathered on the wharf, but their farewell calls to the passengers who lined the rail only deepened her sadness. She was leaving England and might never return.

But she was determined not to give in to homesickness. Discovering quickly that she had a natural liking for the sea, she delighted in the days that followed. A long quarter swell built up, and for four days and nights the ship raced along, slipping backward down each wave as it overtook her, wallowing heavily as the next one came up, and making a dazzling white wake that trailed astern like a huge, ragged scar across the aquamarine ocean.

In the evenings there was usually singing on deck to the accompaniment of a lute, though it sounded like sorrowful music to Allison's ears. She often went to her cabin and lay for hours, listening to the plaintive sound of the lute, seeking to find God.

Señor Manti came to stand beside her one evening as she looked down at the sparkling wake of the ship. "We will be in Cádiz soon," he said. "Two days perhaps." When she didn't respond, he studied her profile, which was etched against the dark clouds that seemed to race along with the ship. He had kept an impersonal attitude all during the voyage, but now something about the girl's face seemed to move him to an uncharacteristic concern. "You are sad, Señorita Spenser?"

"Oh, I suppose I am." She gave him a wan smile. "I've never been more than five miles from the house where I was born, Señor Manti."

Manti looked troubled, as though he wanted to say something. But he merely looked out at the sea broodingly. After a moment his face relaxed and he said, "You must give the thing time, señorita. Marriage is a big step—but to leave your native country and marry into another race, why, that will take great patience."

"God must help me. I fear I am not fitted for such difficult things."

Her simple words seemed to strike a chord in the Spaniard, and he nodded his agreement. He started to speak, halted—then seemed to reach some sort of decision. When he spoke it was in a very careful tone and there was a guarded expression in his dark eyes. "Señorita, you must be patient . . . with your husband."

His words startled her and she cast a half-fearful look at him. "Is he such a hard man, señor?"

"Ah, that is not for me to say. But others say he is." Manti struggled with his thoughts, but couldn't seem to find the words he wanted. He threw up his hands in a Latin gesture. "All men are hard, or would seem so to such a tender young lady such as yourself. Señor Jaime is, well, he is accustomed to having his own way. His parents admit that they indulged him too much when he was younger. And that has made him . . . difficult."

Allison thought of what Manti was saying. He seemed to be trying to warn her—but why? "I will be an obedient and faithful wife to him, señor." She looked into his face, then frowned. "Is there something else? Something I should guard against? I only ask because I want to please him."

Manti hesitated, seemingly balanced on some sort of difficulty. Finally he said, "You must be patient, as I said. Don Jaime is . . . different."

Allison was mystified by Manti's hints, but he seemed to have said all he was going to say on the subject. When she was alone, she pondered long over the conversation, growing more and more apprehensive. *If I only knew what to do—how to act!* Her mother had given her some practical hints on the physical aspects of marriage, but that facet of what lay before her was shrouded with a reluctant fear. She had no experience in such things, and the bits she had heard from older girls seemed to be useless.

God, please help me! she prayed fervently. *Help me to be a good wife to my husband.*

Two days later, just after dawn, the *Princess* sailed into the Bay of Cádiz and lowered anchor. When Allison stepped out on deck, she saw the crew working furiously, the bo's'n directing a mammoth cleaning and scrubbing operation. New banners were being bent onto halyards ready for hoisting, and every piece of brass in sight was being polished.

"Why are they cleaning the ship so well?" Allison asked.

"Ah, don Jaime will meet us, señorita," Manti said. He had expected to be given charge of a spoiled, overdressed woman who would spend the entire voyage in her cot with her maidservant running about in attendance. It had been a complete, and very pleasant, surprise to find in Allison an odd mixture of childish enthusiasm and womanly grace.

"Is he so important?" Allison asked.

"Yes, he is."

"Señor Manti, why didn't don Jaime come for me himself?"

Manti stared at her, but only shook his head, saying, "He is a busy man, señorita."

A few hours later Allison saw a white boat approaching the

Princess. "That is Señor Jaime," Manti said, nodding at the boat. "He is in the prow."

Allison fixed her eyes on the man she was to marry, and when he finally stepped on board, her first reaction was disappointment. Don Jaime Corona was short and somewhat overweight. He had a round face, a chin that was hidden by a short beard, and a pair of smallish eyes that fixed on her as soon as he stepped on deck.

"Señor Corona," Manti said at once, "may I present the young lady who is to be your wife, Señorita Allison Spenser."

Don Jaime responded in Spanish, then frowned at the look of confusion on the young woman's face. "Can it be that you do not speak Spanish? Only the barbarous English?"

"I—I'm afraid so, señor," Allison said quickly. "But I want to learn your beautiful language."

"Ah well, we will have a tutor for you." Don Jaime was wearing a bright crimson doublet with hose of pure white. The fluffy breeches were pleated in the Spanish fashion, and his legs looked like fat sausages. Gold rings adorned his fingers, and a huge diamond sparkled as it caught the sun. He moved forward and took her hand, kissed it, then cocked his head to one side, staring at her as if she were a horse he had purchased sight unseen.

He looks as though he's not sure he got a good bargain, Allison thought, but she dared not speak.

Finally Corona shrugged. "We must be off," he said, then he whirled and stepped back to the rail. He glanced back at Allison, a sudden smirk on his round face. "Well, come along, señorita. The sooner we get home the sooner you can learn from my mother what pleases me!" He laughed, a high-pitched sound, then clambered down the ladder.

Manti and two sailors helped Allison down, then Manti nodded. "It has been a pleasant voyage, señorita."

Allison felt a pang of fear. "Aren't you coming?"

"Coming? Of course he's coming!" don Jaime snorted. "You

257

English women may run free, but our Spanish ladies would never appear alone with a man, even if he were her future husband. Come along, Manti. My parents are anxious to see the brood mare who's going to produce a litter of sons for the honor of the name of Corona!"

As he said this, he reached over and put his arm around Allison and gave her a kiss. His lips were wet and his breath smelled like the black olives that had been served with every meal on the ship. She tried to conceal her feeling of repugnance, but don Jaime saw it.

He hooted in laughter and shouted, "Look! She doesn't like her husband's kisses!" He winked lewdly at the sailors, who were sending the craft through the waters, and then leered back at Allison. "But there are ways to make a woman enjoy her husband's attentions, aren't there, men?"

Allison dropped her eyes, her cheeks red with shame. When she looked up, she saw that Señor Manti's eyes were fixed on her, filled with compassion. She suddenly remembered his words and tried to smile at him. *I must be patient,* she told herself. *It will be all right. God will be with me!*

When the carriage stopped, don Jaime leaped out and then watched as a servant helped Allison to the ground. "Come now, my parents are anxious to meet you."

Allison took in the imposing arched entrance, then passed through heavy double doors. She was aware of flowering creepers and a statue of the Blessed Virgin over another heavy doorway. They entered a courtyard, and faces appeared at windows then quickly withdrew.

A door opened and a voice said, "Welcome to your new home, señorita." The speaker was an elderly man of sixty, tall and thin with a full head of silvery hair. "I am Alfredo Corona, and this is my wife, doña María."

"How do you like her?" don Jaime broke in. "Is she worth what you paid for her?"

"Don Jaime! You will shame her!" Doña María was a short fat woman with black hair threaded with silver. She came forward to give Allison a kiss on the cheek, saying, "Come inside. You must be worn out from your trip."

When they were inside the house, don Alfredo smiled at his wife stiffly. "Take the señorita to her room, doña María." Then he glanced at Allison. "Take a little rest, señorita, before dinner."

"Get all the rest you can," don Jaime said with a grin. "You won't get much after we're married!"

Doña María led Allison through a heavy door that led into a wide tiled hallway. On each side were tiled rooms. Everywhere there were tiles, all of them blue. In the hall one of the walls was given over entirely to a tiled picture of Christ displaying "His Sacred Heart"; another depicted the Blessed Virgin being carried upward to heaven by a host of angels; a third was of St. Anthony holding a lily and looking tenderly down at the beholder.

Then doña María opened a door and stepped back. "This will be your room, señorita. I hope you will find it comfortable. I will assign a servant to be your maid."

"Thank you, doña María," Allison said. She was weary with the journey and emotionally drained. Turning to the short woman she said, "I want to be a good wife to your son. Please teach me how!"

Her words surprised the woman. And seemed to trouble her. She paused for a long moment, then said, "Come, sit down for a moment, child." Drawing the girl down, she looked full into Allison's face, studying her carefully. Her own face, Allison saw, was marked with strain and lines of care. And there was a hopelessness in doña María that puzzled the girl.

"You're a pure girl, aren't you, Allison?"

Allison blushed and nodded.

"I have prayed for God to send a wife to our son. He is the last of our blood. We grow old, his father and I, and we long to see grandchildren."

Something about the way the woman spoke brought fear to Allison. She had seen something strange in Señor Manti's eyes. A similar look had lurked on don Alfredo Corona's face as well.

Suddenly she had to know. "Why has don Jaime never married, señora?"

The question seemed to strike the older woman hard. She dropped her eyes and, reaching over, took Allison's hands. "You must pray much, my dear! Do you believe in God? That he answers prayer?"

"Oh yes!"

Her answer brought a nod, but doña María's lips suddenly quivered. "I—I had planned to talk to you—but not so soon."

"Talk to me, señora?"

"Yes, about . . . about my son's . . . problem."

A nameless fear, cold and deep, seeped into Allison's heart. She whispered, "What *is* it, señora? Is it that he loves women and will not be faithful?"

Doña María shook her head and tears gathered in her eyes then rolled down her cheeks. "No! It's not other women—would to God that *were* the trouble! His father and I could bear that, for many men have that weakness." She hesitated, then said so mutedly that Allison could barely hear her words: "That—at least—is a weakness of the flesh!"

Allison could not bear the suspense. "Please, señora, you are frightening me! What *is* he—the man I've come to marry?"

Doña María looked fully in Allison's eyes. Taking a deep sobbing breath, she expelled it, then dropped her eyes.

"He—our son—he is not . . . normal. In his mind."

Allison frowned. "I don't understand."

Doña María shook her head, and her eyes were filled with pain.

"He seems well enough. Indeed, there are certain things that he does with such ease that it is difficult to believe there is anything wrong. He has an ability to conduct business well, to make decisions that are sound . . . for a while, at least. But then—then the madness comes." She paused, then looked at Allison. "You asked me why Jaime has never married. The truth is that he was engaged once. To a lovely young woman, Rosalita de Cartagena. She was the daughter of our closest friends." Tears filled the woman's eyes, and her voice fell to an anguished whisper. "We had always hoped our children would marry and join our families, so you can imagine our great joy when it seemed that was to come to pass."

Allison nodded, but said nothing.

"Rosalita was a gentle child. We hoped she would be successful in bringing peace to our son, that her warmth and kindness would win him over. But with each day, as the wedding drew closer, he grew more and more restless. More . . . troubled. Even his business involvements became too much for him to handle. And there were many . . . incidences."

"*Incidences,* señora?"

Doña María would not meet Allison's eyes. She stared at the wall and spoke in a flat tone. "He would wander about in the hallways, talking first in whispers and then screaming." She closed her eyes, as though she would close out the memories. "He said crazy things, accused Rosalita of being unfaithful, of stealing and lying, of so many things." Her eyes opened and her gaze flew to Allison's face, and the woman's torment was so intense Allison had to fight the urge to weep. "We thought it was because of the increasing pressures upon him, of all the attention. Our two families had been part of the nobility for generations. When such families join in marriage, it is only natural that the people are interested, that everyone talks of the event. But Jaime could not bear that his privacy was being 'invaded.' He was never able to bear scrutiny, not even as a small child. And so his rages grew worse . . . much worse. Until he began to accuse Rosalita of plotting to kill him.

"Of course, Rosalita denied any wrongdoing. We all knew she would never so shame her family, or ours. Jaime would have none of it. He refused to marry her, screamed any time she came near him, demanded she leave our home and never return. His father and I tried to talk with him, to calm him, but we were ineffective. Finally, Rosalita went to talk with him one last time. She was sure she could calm his troubled spirit, and we thought he would listen to her. She was such a gentle, beautiful girl. . . ."

Her voice trailed off, and Allison realized there were tears running down doña María's face. Silent, agonized tears. She reached out to grasp the older woman's hand and hold it comfortingly between her own.

"Please, if this is too difficult—"

Doña María cut her off. "No! You must hear this. It will not change anything, but you must know what has happened. And I want you to hear it from me, not one of the servants or the townspeople." She drew a calming breath, then continued, her expression resolute. "I do not know what transpired that evening. No one does. Because we never saw Rosalita again."

Allison sat back, stunned. "Surely, señora, you are not suggesting—," she began, but could not complete the horrible question.

Jaime's mother only nodded. "Truly, we do not know what happened. Jaime swore he never saw Rosalita, that she never came to talk with him, but there was blood on his clothing—" She broke off, her voice choked with tears. "I could not believe it, that my son would commit such a heinous crime! That he could destroy anyone so filled with goodness and beauty! The men searched for Rosalita for days, everyone from our houses, from the town. Everyone—but Jaime. He only sat in his room, muttering to himself and . . ."

"And?"

"And laughing." Doña María drew a ragged breath and looked at Allison. "Word spread quickly that our son was a murderer. There was no proof, no—no body . . . so he could not be punished. But all became convinced of his guilt. And so we were left without any recourse. If Jaime was to marry, if we were to have grandchildren, if we were to keep our family name from dying," she squeezed Allison's hands, "we had to find a bride from a faraway place, a place where no one had ever heard of Jaime—or Rosalita." Allison sat in horrified silence, feeling the room spin around her as doña María continued. "A place where no one knew that our poor, dear son . . . is a murderer."

Eighteen

So Well She
Endured Her
Going Forth

I 'm sick of it all, Thomas! Just let me go back to sea!"

Thomas Wakefield leaned back in his chair, casting a thoughtful look at Robin. As though the younger man had not spoken, he held a brass instrument up, saying, "You need to practice your navigation, Robin. Take this astrolabe and work with it."

Robin stared at the instrument glumly. The astrolabe was used along with cross-staves to measure the altitude of the sun and the stars. "I can use it as well as any man, but what good does that do when the queen won't let me go to sea?"

"She feels you're more important here. And Sir Francis agrees with her." Thomas stared through the small ring for a moment, then put the instrument down. "Don't be discouraged. We'll both be at sea very soon." When Robin's eyes lit up, he held up his hand. "But neither of us can leave with Mother so ill, can we?"

Robin's face fell, but he said at once, "No, of course not."

"You got a letter from the Spenser girl?"

"How did you know that?"

"Bribed a servant of course," Thomas confessed cheerfully. "How is she? Taking her father's death pretty hard, I suppose?"

"Yes, she is. That's why she wrote to me the first time. Asked me to try and help her family." With a grimace he faced his uncle, adding, "I tried, but Martha Spenser hates me for turning in her priest. Can't say I blame her much."

"You were obeying orders from the queen. But what about the girl? She ought to be happy in Spain. It's hardly dangerous to be a Catholic there. And her husband is rich, or so rumor has it."

A puzzled frown creased Robin's face. "I can't make it out, Thomas. She writes cheerfully enough—about everything but her husband. From what I get out of her letters, she's become very fond of her in-laws. She's got everything she needs—lives in a mansion called the Casa Loma just outside Cádiz—but somehow I have the feeling something's wrong."

"You two were pretty close when she was a child," Thomas said thoughtfully. He cast a critical look at the younger man, then remarked innocently, "Allison Spenser grew up to be a fine-looking woman. Don't suppose you noticed that—"

"I noticed."

Thomas lifted his eyebrows at the curtness of Robin's tone, but held his silence. He knew his nephew was unhappy, but there was little he could do. The queen often kept young men of the court close when all they longed for was action, and he was sorry for them.

Glad I'm not one of her favorites, he thought, then put that aside and began to go over the charts of the Spanish Main with Robin.

❦

"Sir, . . . your grandmother. She's very bad!"

Robin had been awakened from a sound sleep by Matthew, the steward. Even before the man spoke the words, he knew what was happening. "I'll be right there, Matthew. Has the doctor been called?"

"Sir Thomas sent Jeremiah to fetch him."

Ten minutes later Robin entered the large bedroom and found Thomas kneeling beside the sick woman. "She's been asking for

you, Robin," he said. Casting a warning look at his nephew, he
shook his head.

Robin read the gesture and moved at once to the other side of
the bed. Hannah Wakefield lay so still that his heart skipped a beat,
then her eyelids fluttered and slowly opened.

"Robin—?"

"I'm here, Grandmother."

She lifted her hand, and he took it at once. It seemed frail, and
he could see the blue veins tracing their courses just under the
pale white skin. "Can I get you anything, Grandmother?" he
whispered.

"No." It was, both men saw, an effort for her to speak. She had
been failing for weeks, and now they knew the end had come.

Holding to the fragile hand, Robin thought of how round and
strong and firm it had been when he was a boy. How many times
this same hand had dressed his wounds, combed his hair, administered a firm slap when necessary!

And now she was going. Slipping out, like a ship weighs anchor
and slowly moves away from shore to be swallowed up in the
misty reaches of a shadowy ocean.

"Robin, I've been thinking of your father . . . and your
mother."

"Yes, Grandmother?"

"They loved you so much! Dear William! More than anything
he wanted . . . to raise a son!"

Slowly she turned her head and fixed her eyes on his. "He
wanted a strong son to carry on for him. How proud he would
have been to see you!"

"I—wish I could have known him."

"You will, Robin. You will!" She smiled sweetly. "Christians
never . . . say good-bye, do they?"

"No, Grandmother."

"Robin . . . I must leave you. But promise me . . ."

Hannah's voice faltered, and she seemed to have slipped into sleep for a moment. Robin waited quietly, fighting the tears that threatened to overcome him. At last she opened her eyes again, and he felt her squeeze his hand with unexpected force.

"Do not forget love, my boy!"

Robin blinked with surprise. "What do you mean?"

"Life is for loving, not hating. That's . . . what the dear Savior said."

Robin nodded slowly. "You mean—the Catholics?"

"Don't hate anyone, Robin. It's a deadly thing!" She looked up at him and studied his face. There was a calmness about her now, and finally she smiled. "Myles and I prayed for you every day. Since he . . . left . . . I have prayed alone."

Robin Wakefield's throat grew thick with emotion as he knelt there beside the woman he loved best of all human beings. He knew without a doubt that she was leaving him and there was nothing he could do to hold her back. A sharp grief swept over him, seeming to pierce his whole spirit, and he whispered, "I love you, Grandmother!"

She saw the tears on his cheeks and lifted her hand to wipe them away. "Why, you . . . mustn't cry, my dear!" A look of wonder came to her, and she nodded. "It's time to go home . . . and I'll tell Myles and William what a fine man . . . you've become."

She fell silent then, and Robin buried his face against the bedding, letting the tears flow freely. Her shallow breathing was the only sound in the room for some time. At last he rose and stood with his back to the wall as others came to bid Hannah Wakefield farewell. The room was dark except for one yellow bar of sunlight that slanted down from the high window. It bathed Hannah's worn face with amber light, easing the lines that the years had etched in her fine features.

Finally all her good-byes were said. Just after dawn she opened her eyes, took a deep breath, and said clearly, "It is time. I go to him who loves me!"

And then she was gone.

Thomas put his hand gently on her head and murmured, "She was the finest in life. And how well she endured her going forth!"

Robin felt suddenly that the sun had gone out of his world. All his dreams and hopes seemed bitter and tasteless. *The strongest tie I had in my life—and now she's gone!*

He bore the days that followed, but the funeral meant little to him. He could not think of Hannah except as she had been when she was well and strong. Even when he stood beside the grave and saw the casket lowered, he could not accept it.

A few days later Thomas came to him and said, "I sail next week, Robin. Come with me."

"What about the queen?"

"She won't be on the ship."

"She'll be here when we get back, though."

Thomas studied the younger man; his pain had been evident over the last few days. It had been hard for Thomas, too, for he had lost his mother—but he still had his own family, while Robin had no one. He put his hand on his nephew's strong shoulder. "If we bring back a treasure ship, the queen will be in a forgiving mood."

"If we don't?"

"Why, you can pay her pretty compliments until you're back in favor—that's what Raleigh and Essex do!"

Robin took a deep breath. "I'll do it!" And the very thought of being at sea—of being done with spying on Mary of Scots and free from the intrigues of Elizabeth's court—was like a tonic! Energy surged through Robin, and he grinned for the first time in weeks. "We'll win a prize this time, Thomas!" he exclaimed. "I know it!"

As he spoke, the picture of a vivid scene ran through his mind.

He saw himself presenting a king's ransom to the queen. Letting his thoughts run wild, he saw himself kneeling on board the *Falcon,* and he could almost feel the light touch of a sword on his shoulder as Elizabeth's voice rang out, "Arise, Sir Robin Wakefield!"

Nineteen

CAPTURED!

WHEN the *Falcon* sailed out of Plymouth Harbor a fortnight after Hannah Wakefield's funeral, both the captain and his second officer were glad to see the coast fade into the hazy distance. Robin had been given the post of second lieutenant, having proved to Thomas's satisfaction that he could navigate the ship.

With a brisk northwester on the starboard beam, the *Falcon* made a fast passage diagonally across the Sleeve, past Ushant, and out into the Atlantic.

Thomas laid out his plan for Robin as they stood on the quarterdeck their first morning at sea. "What we will do, Lieutenant," he said cheerfully, "is head south for the West Indies, where we'll hope to swoop down on Philip's slave and treasure ships. Rob him of those and his wars and territorial ambitions will come to a quick enough halt!"

Robin was occupied with scanning the deck, but all the men were working well. "We'll be treated as pirates if we're captured," he remarked. Then a smile broadened his lips. "We'll be in good company, though, with Hawkins, Drake, and Frobisher."

"England's enemies always find vile names for her finest sons. Have you heard what the Spanish call Drake? 'The Master Thief'!"

"They call him worse than that, sir," Robin said with a nod. He studied the trackless ocean that rolled in great swells, lifting the *Falcon* then letting her glide down into the smooth troughs. "We'll get a prize this time—I know it. And we'll strike a blow against popery, too!"

Thomas watched the younger man's face for a moment, then spoke thoughtfully. "Robin, don't forget what Mother told you. And what Father always used to say. They both were troubled by this hatred you have for Spain."

Robin's face grew hard. "Spain murdered my parents!"

Thomas shook his head, his eyes troubled. "Do you remember the last voyage we took, when we went ashore and took that town?"

"Yes, of course I remember."

"And do you remember how you stood by the gun and cut the defenders to pieces?" The young man nodded reluctantly. "Don't you imagine some of those men had children? And would it surprise you that they look upon you as the murderer of their father?"

Robin glanced up, startled. "Why—that was *war!*"

"And it was war that killed your father," Thomas insisted. "It's just a different kind of war, Nephew. Many have died for their faithfulness to God. You heard your grandfather speak many times of how William Tyndale died. Why, he even spoke of him as God's soldier! Tyndale was burned for the same reason as your father."

He put his hand on the young man's shoulder, then withdrew it quickly. It would not do for any in the crew to see him showing affection or favoritism to the boy. He met Robin's frustrated gaze with equanimity. "You must learn to fight, Robin, we both know that. But you must also learn to forgive your enemies."

Robin held his uncle's gaze, then turned to stare out at the ocean. "I'll—think of it, sir," he said, then added more to himself than to Thomas, "Indeed, I already think of it a great deal."

CAPTURED!

The *Falcon* moved along under cloudless skies, and morale on the ship was excellent. Members of the crew, all of whom would have a share in any prize taken, were confident that they'd come home rich. Every day at dawn and dusk Robin was up in the aftercastle sighting the stars with his cross-staff. Every day, hope of intercepting a prize grew higher. From time to time, Lieutenant Boswell, the gunnery officer, would drill the gun crew. The roar of the weapons and black clouds of smoke that issued from their muzzles gave everyone a feeling of heightened confidence and power.

As dawn came up on the fifteenth day out of Plymouth there came a cry of "Sail-ho!" from the foretop, and a buzz went quickly around the *Falcon* that the vessel sighted was Spanish.

Robin, his blue eyes sparkling with excitement, exclaimed, "She's a fighting galleon, sir! Look at her guns!"

Captain Wakefield paced up and down the deck slapping his hands together with excitement. "We'll take her, Lieutenant!"

The bo's'n's call trilled and Boswell's coarse voice bellowed down the hatches: "For'd part for'd, after part aft! Guns' crews stand to your guns, ship-boys to the magazine!" Within seconds the early morning quiet was transformed into a flurry of activity. The gunners were shouting "And heave! . . . And heave!" as the falconets were taken from their sea stowages and trundled into position. The men and powder boys scurried about with kegs of powder, some of the lads bowed down with the weight of several round shot.

"Ease bowlines! Ease yard braces! Bear away!" the captain shouted as he took up his position next to the steersman on the whipstaff to con the ship into a windward position for the attack.

The gap between the two ships narrowed rapidly as the *Falcon* bore down. Before they came within gun range, the Spanish ship started firing. "Go down and direct the port guns, Lieutenant!"

the captain ordered. "We'll come about and give her a double broadside."

"Aye, sir!"

Robin raced down the ladder and ordered the guns run out. "Men, we're going to engage that ship! Take your time and obey orders and all will be well." He moved to stand beside one of the guns, his heart pumping wildly, then looked around at the men. One member of the crew was a boy of no more than fifteen—Will Blevins. "Now, Blevins, we'll give the dons a lesson, eh? Come now, let's see to the slow match." He caught the glance of one of the older men, Pike Cothen, and winked. "A fair prize, Cothen. We'll see gold before long!"

"Aye, sir, that us will!"

Topside, the captain was waiting until the last moment to set his sail, for if he timed it right, the Spanish ship would come under his guns for one moment before she could bring her own guns to bear.

"Stand ready to go about!" he shouted.

The mizzen yard was squeaking and the helmsman cried out, "Ready, sir!"

"Put the helm down!"

At the order, the men went into action, and the ship began to swing into the wind. The bo's'n screamed at the men at the braces as the sails boomed and swelled overhead. The ship continued to swing, and then the captain shouted, "Off tacks and sheets!"

This was the moment that counted. If the ship did not answer, she would lie helpless in the water, unable to do anything but endure the broadside of the galleon.

Suddenly the bo's'n cried out in alarm. Startled, Thomas took his eyes off the enemy. Turning quickly, he saw the tangle of flapping sails and jerking shrouds—and knew with a sickening fear that the maneuver had been unsuccessful.

"She'll blow us out of the water!" the helmsman, a small muscular man named Grimes, whispered.

"Lieutenant Sikeston, get marksmen into the shrouds! Shoot the sail handlers!" The lieutenant rushed to do his captain's bidding, grateful that his position was not one that could result in death for making such an error!

Below deck Robin felt the ship fall back and knew what to expect. His eyes met those of the old sailor, Cothen, and he forced a smile. "For what we are about to receive, may we be duly grateful!" Cothen smiled faintly at the old joke, and then Robin lifted his voice. "Men, we'll have to let them have the first shot, but our turn will come!"

Suddenly the hull shuddered beneath his feet and splintering woodwork flew in every direction. The air quivered and shook as the crash of guns and the nerve-jarring scream of cannon balls whipped through the smoke.

The scream of passing shot mingled with closer, more un-earthly sounds as flying splinters ripped into the gunners. Soon the deck was scarlet, painted with the blood of dying men. Midshipman Jones, who was in charge of gun number seven, fell to the deck, clawing at it as though he could burrow into it and hide.

Robin ran to him, pulled him to his feet and slapped him hard across the face. "Get to your guns, you coward!"

At that moment, many of the gunners panicked. Most of them had never seen action, and blind fear caused them to stampede. They made for the ladder, not thinking that there was no safety above. Their single-minded thought was to escape the hell of smoke and shot that filled the gundeck.

Drawing his sword, Robin leaped to stand at the foot of the ladder. His face was pale with rage, and his blade was a flash of silver in the smoke-filled air. "Back to those guns!" he screamed, and drove the men back, so that with the help of the more experienced gunners the tide turned.

Back and forth Robin moved, shouting and pushing the men into position. "Load!" he screamed. "Look, the captain's got us moving! All we have to do is let her have a bellyful, lads! Fire! Fire! Bring your guns to bear!"

The *Falcon* shuddered as her guns exploded. Up on deck, Thomas cried out, "That's it! We hurt her that time! We'll bring her about and give her another taste of shot!"

The battle raged for hours, and the galleon gave a good account of herself. Fully one quarter of the *Falcon's* crew lay dead or wounded before Captain Wakefield shouted, "Look! She's struck the white flag!"

Thomas turned to one of the hands. "Have Lieutenant Wakefield report to the deck." Within minutes, Robin stood before him, his face black with powder stains. Thomas smiled triumphantly. "Lieutenant, I want you to take a prize crew. The admiral wants a Spanish ship brought to England."

"To study her guns and how she sails," Robin agreed with a nod. "Can't we man her, and we'll sail back together?"

"No. We must keep to our own duty and find what other treasures are awaiting us. You take ten men and we'll go aboard to get all ready for you to sail. But be sure you keep the Spanish officers and crew locked up tight during the voyage. If they get loose, they'll butcher you and take the ship back."

The exchange took some time. Many of the Spanish sailors and officers were dead, others so badly wounded they would not survive. Thomas went aboard and saw to making the ship into a sort of floating prison. When all was ready, he stood on the deck of the *Santa Luisa,* as she was called, and extended his hand to his nephew. "Yours is the more dangerous job, Robin. God go with you!"

"Aye, and thank you, Uncle. I'll be a captain for a little while, won't I?"

His words were prophetic, for on the second day as they made for England, the foretopman shouted, "Three sails to starboard!"

Robin stared at the specks that had appeared, and when the lookout cried, "Spanish galleons!" his heart sank.

"Shall we run for it, sir?" Eli Framden asked, his face pale.

"No hope," Robin said slowly. "We'll have to surrender."

Framden swallowed hard. "It'll be a Spanish prison for us, or the galleys—if they don't hang us. I reckon I'd rather die than be in one of them galleys pulling an oar for them devils!"

Robin had heard the horror tales of all that captured English sailors endured in Spanish galleys. They ate swill and were lashed mercilessly by the galleymaster. Chained to their wooden seats, they sat in their own filth until they died.

"God help us all," Robin whispered as the sails grew larger. He thought of his dream of returning to England in a blaze of glory—then said, "Run up the white flag, Mr. Framden. We're in God's hands now."

"No, sir!" came the bitter reply. "We're in the hands o' devils!"

<hr/>

The underground dungeon at Cádiz was solitary and dark. Three adjoining cells stood at the end of a long low tunnel. In one of those cells, Robin Wakefield stood staring out of a barred window through which he saw a courtyard and another passage running crosswise at a higher level. The cell next to his was occupied by a Spanish sailor who had been caught robbing one of the king's treasure chests. His name was Juan Hernandez, and he spoke English fairly well.

The other members of Robin's prize crew had been taken away. The captain of the Spanish ship somehow became convinced that they could get a ransom for Robin since he was an officer, and so they had brought him to the port and clapped him in the dungeon.

The cell was as silent as a tomb for the most part. Almost the only sounds were occasional footfalls ringing on the hard stone of the upper passage and the prison bell audible in the high distance.

At first Robin was relieved at his escape from the galleys, and he himself had hope of being ransomed and set free. Surely Thomas would help, or even Sir Francis or the queen herself. But the days passed until he decided he had been forgotten; it seemed, in the way of all bureaucracies, that Robin Wakefield had been buried alive. Whoever was dealing with such things had put him far down at the end of a long list.

The guards told him nothing, and his only diversion was learning Spanish. Hernandez was a dull fellow, bored out of reason, and was willing to spend long hours going over Spanish words and drilling Robin in conversation.

The food was bad, a monotonous diet consisting of fish soup and hard bread with the occasional addition of a mess of over-cooked vegetables dumped on the tin plate that was shoved under the door twice a day.

Robin marked off the days with his wooden spoon, scratching the wall over his bunk. After six months he gave up on any hope of being set free. He knew that it was August of 1585, but the date meant nothing to him. As time went by the burden of loneliness became a danger to his mind—which he feared he was losing.

He asked for pen and paper, and this was refused. He asked for a book—any book—or something to make or do. Nothing came. When he asked if he would ever be ransomed, he was told that the commandant had no instructions. One of the guards grinned one day, saying, "I think they're saving you for an *auto-da-fé*." A wicked gleam came into his eyes at the thought of the Spanish

Inquisition's method of executing heretics. "I hope to be there when they burn you, *inglés!*"

Sometimes he banged on the door like a maniac, demanding to be released. To this, Hernandez stated, "You might as well give up, Wakefield. Both of us will rot in here until they throw us into the lime pit."

Robin shook his head. "No, we'll get out." He forced himself to make conversation. His Spanish was becoming very good, for he had a quick ear, a fine memory, and all the time there was to practice. "Tell me, Juan, did you ever hear of a place called Casa Loma?"

"Casa Loma, the home of Alfredo Corona?"

"Yes. You know it then?"

"Certainly. He is a very wealthy man. How do you know of him?"

"A—friend of mine lives there."

"He is at a good place then! Corona is a good man!"

"Is Casa Loma close to this place?"

"Oh yes, not far." Robin insisted on details, and Hernandez complied by giving explicit details of the location of the Corona estate. A wicked humor tinged his voice as he asked, "Do you plan to visit the gentleman? I'm sure he'd be glad to welcome you, an English pirate!"

Robin turned the jibe away, and several times after that he evoked what information he could from Hernandez about the Corona family. Over and over he went through the directions for finding the place, though he despaired of it ever coming to anything. Still, it gave him a feeling of calm to know that Allison was only a few miles from where he lay buried in a fetid dungeon.

That week he worked two rusty nails loose from his bunk, and a sense of hope returned. At once he began scratching at the base of one of the bars in his cell window—and he was astonished to discover that he was so weak he could not work for more than thirty minutes. The poor diet had robbed him of strength, and his hands were so weak that he had difficulty holding the nail. When he could hold it, he could only work a short time before his hands cramped, sending spasms of pain that turned his fingers to claws.

At first he paced the floor for hours, but as his strength ebbed, he lay on his bunk staring at the ceiling. His mind wandered as a fever came upon him, and he often wondered if all this had come in payment for his long hatred of the Catholics. He wondered if this was a judgment against him that would end in death—and fear coursed through him that he would then have to face God!

He thought endlessly about Myles and Hannah, how they'd warned him—pleaded with him—to turn from such hatred. At times he seemed to hear their voices and see their faces. Once he wept when his fever was high, crying out to God for mercy, but none seemed to come.

He scratched his leg, causing a tiny wound, but due to his poor condition it stubbornly refused to heal. Instead, it became infected to the point that putting his weight on it was agony. *Let it kill me,* he thought stubbornly. *Death would be better than this!*

The food grew worse—which he had not thought possible. The fish was rancid, the bread full of weevils, the water was foul. He gagged it down, the instinct for life stronger than his desire to die and escape. And, as often as he was able, he kept working at the mortar that held the bar.

Some days he would laboriously push the nail against the adamant concrete for only five or ten minutes before his hands cramped. On a good day he might last thirty minutes.

One day the guards came and took Juan Hernandez away to be executed. Robin called out, "God be with you, Juan," but he received no answer. The horror of death was on the man, and he left his cell wordlessly. Robin stood on his bunk and watched the execution, which took place in the courtyard just outside of his cell. It was not as he had pictured it, however. He had imagined a firing squad with the victim standing against a wall.

As he watched through feverish eyes, he saw two soldiers who had to support the small form of the prisoner as far as a scraggly tree, where they let him collapse. An officer appeared, walked over to the struggling Hernandez, and pulled his pistol. Carelessly, he put the muzzle to the man's head and pulled the trigger. Robin saw the emaciated body leap convulsively, then flop limply to the stone paving. The lieutenant gestured and the soldiers came to drag the body off, each taking a heel. The gruesome sight of the dead man being dragged away was too much for Robin, and he staggered away from the window to retch violently in the corner of the room.

Dear God, I can't stand this! he thought desperately. *Either let me go free or let me die. But don't make me stay here any longer.*

The end came so suddenly that it was like a dream. Robin had awakened in the middle of the night, suffocating with the sultry heat of late summer. Listlessly he pulled the nail out of the hiding place, stood on the bunk, and began to scratch at the concrete. He did so with a total lack of hope; it was merely a reflex action, something to do.

The nail was blunt and slid in the groove he had spent so many hours creating—and as it made a faint scratching sound, Robin thought suddenly of Allison.

The image of her face the last time he'd seen her came to him. In the heat and filth of the cell, the memory of her freshness swept over him, and it was almost as though he could feel again the soft gentleness of her young lips. It was not the first time he'd thought of their kiss—but strangely enough as he stood there trembling with fatigue, the memory was sharper, more poignant than ever.

So engrossed was he in his memories that he didn't realize he was working longer than usual. But he came abruptly out of his somnambulistic state when the nail seemed to disappear!

Blinking with astonishment, he peered down and, in the darkness illuminated only by a full moon, saw that he had punched through the cement! With trembling fingers he retrieved the nail and began to dig at the cavity. He had evidently hit a hollow spot, a weakness in the concrete itself, for the cement crumbled at a mere touch of the nail! Almost sobbing, he punched and scraped at the base of the bar and was weak with relief when he discovered that the cavity was as deep as the bar itself. For an hour he kept at it, his fingers bleeding and cramped, until he finally freed the bottom of the bar.

"Got to find something to pry with!" he croaked hoarsely. His choices were few, for the cot was the only furniture in the cell. Throwing the straw ticking to the floor, he began to pull at the rough boards and succeeded in separating the rails from the legs. This gave him four short legs and two long staves. He knew that the top of the bar was firmly set—no cavity there!—but his time at sea had taught him that a man can do a great deal with a lever if he has a fulcrum.

Carefully he used the short pieces to build a framework that would serve as a base for his longer piece. They would not stay in place and fell to the cell floor with such a racket that he stopped dead still, his heart pounding, as he waited for a guard to come and investigate. Time ran on and he broke into a cold sweat. No one came, and he turned back to his task.

He worked steadily, his head swarming with ideas as he tried in a hundred ways to use his "equipment" to get a good bite on the bar. *This is the last chance—when they find my bed broken up, they'll look around and see what I've done to the window. Got to get out tonight!*

But try as he might, nothing worked. Finally his arms grew dead with effort and he slumped to the floor, his face in his hands. *Can't do it! I can't do it!*

For a long time he sat there, weeping with frustration. The

silvery moonlight bathed the cell with a ghostly light, and the silence lay over the dungeon like a heavy blanket. Slowly he began to regain control and stop weeping. He had not wept for years except at the deaths of his grandparents, and somehow the tears had opened some sort of door in his spirit. At least he thought of it that way as he sat there in the hot darkness.

Finally he grew still, not only in body but in mind, and in that stillness, he seemed to hear something. At first he thought it was just a faint echo of some of the guards on the next floor . . . then he grew rigid as he realized it was a voice he had heard often during his life, a voice that had not been heard on this earth for years . . . the voice of his grandfather, Myles Wakefield!

At first Robin thought he was going mad—or that he was already mad. Then he remembered that this had happened to him before. His grandfather had read aloud from the Bible every night, and years of listening to the Scripture had caused the words to lodge somewhere deep in the boy's subconscious. From time to time Robin would remember those times, and often could almost hear the sound of that mellow voice reading the old stories of faith.

And now, far from the soil of England that contained the dust of Myles Wakefield, his grandson seemed to hear the words:

And all things, whatever you ask in prayer, believing, you will receive.

As the words seemed to hang in the air like echoes of an old sweet song heard long ago, Robin began to go over all the promises that Myles and Hannah had shown him in the Bible. Finally he took a deep breath and whispered, "Lord, I'm not a man who can ask in faith, for I've been a sinful man. But I stand on the faith of my grandfather and my grandmother. *They* believed in you, and as best I can, I claim the promise I've just heard. I ask a lot: let me get that bar out and then get me back to England somehow!"

There was no sound in the dark cell, save that of his own

breathing and the cry of a night bird that floated over the forest flanking the prison. Nor was there any voice to tell him that he'd been heard—not a single indication that anything was different.

But Robin got to his feet and studied the pieces of wood. Slowly a solution came, elusive at first, but falling into place. "It'll work . . . but how can I hold the fulcrum in place?" he asked.

Use your shirt to make a tie—

Robin blinked, then instantly slipped out of his ragged shirt. Ripping it into strips, he managed to weave the fragments into a rope of sorts and soon had tied the pieces of wood in place. Picking up one of the rails, he studied it, then shook his head. *Not strong enough*. He picked up the other, tied them together, then inserted them so that the ends fit behind the loosened bar. The doubled lever was now in place, six feet long—but would it stand the strain? Would the fulcrum hold?

At that moment Robin knew his first flash of blind faith. Somehow he *knew* that the bar would give, and without further hesitation, he bent his back and threw his weight against the lever. At first nothing happened, but when he drew back and fiercely shoved again at the lever—he heard a grating sound, and then it moved!

Shoving with all his might, he felt the lever move a few more inches—and then the lever snapped. He fell to the floor, but leaped up at once and peered at the window. It was higher than his head, but he saw that the bar was standing out almost at a forty-five degree angle!

"Thank you, God!" he gasped. With the bed demolished, there was only one thing to stand on. He grabbed the smelly bucket that served for sanitation, emptied it, then turned it upside down. When he stood on it, he saw that the space between the bars was wide enough to admit his starved body.

Reaching upward, he grasped the two accompanying bars on each side of the bent one and pulled himself upward. As weak as he was, he fell back once, but determination blended with desperation and he managed to throw his arm over the lower part of the window. Loosing his grip on the other bar, he soon had both arms over the window. Wiggling madly, he pulled his body through.

He didn't even pause. He got his body through the opening and fell at once to the hard surface of the pavement in the passageway. The fall drove the wind out of him, but gasping for breath he rose and staggered toward the door. The guards mostly gambled or slept at night, but there was always a chance he might be seen.

As he made his way along, he knew his chances were small. He was in a foreign country, wherein every man was his enemy. He was starving and sick, and the patrols would be searching every ditch by noon the next day.

But as Robin Wakefield reached the line of trees that marked the end of Cádiz and the beginning of open country, he had one thought: *Allison! I've got to find Allison!*

He stumbled into the bush, his mind dulled and his body aching with the effort. Still he was free for the moment, and he knew that God had done it!

Twenty

A PLACE OF SAFETY

One August morning, Allison appeared late for breakfast. Taking in the young woman's wan face, doña María asked, "Aren't you feeling well, my dear?"

At once Allison understood the suppressed hope that threaded her mother-in-law's tone. The one overwhelming desire of her heart was to have a grandson to carry on the Corona line, and a case of morning sickness would be a good sign, both to doña María and to don Alfredo. The older woman had spoken freely of this desire ever since Allison's arrival, and even her husband longed for it so desperately that he had once spoken to her quite frankly.

"My son is—not what a man should be," he had told her as they had talked quietly in solitude one afternoon. The admission had pained him, and he had apologized, adding, "I was wrong not to inform you of his ways. But we cannot let our family die because of his illness—"

He had broken off, and his grief was so profound that Allison had put her hand on his saying, "God is able to do all things. We will pray for his touch and wisdom."

Now as Allison sat down at the table with doña María, she destroyed the woman's hopes by saying, "I am not unwell, but I was restless last night." The eager expression in the older woman's eyes died, and Allison was seized by the impulse to tell the truth—that there was no chance whatsoever of her bearing a child, for her husband would not come near her!

But the pain and grief in doña María's face brought a compassion to her heart, and she said nothing. As she ate the fruit that was placed before her, she thought suddenly of her wedding night. That experience had been one of the most painful aspects of her life in Cádiz, and though she had managed to bury most of it in some deep recess of her spirit, she now felt a flash of shame and anger as it came back.

She had prepared herself for bed, wearing a beautiful white silk gown. The wedding preparations, then the ceremony itself—and the interminable reception afterward—had exhausted her. Her innocence and apprehensions had drawn her nerves like a fine wire, and when don Jaime had come into the bedroom, she was filled with fear.

"Ah, my virginal bride!" he had shouted, so loudly that Allison knew the servants could hear him. "You *are* a virgin, aren't you?"

"Yes, don Jaime," she had answered simply.

"I didn't think any were left in England, that barbaric, licentious race! Except for Elizabeth, the Virgin Queen of course." He had stripped off his shirt, cursing drunkenly, and the sight of his pudgy body, which was pale and unhealthy, reminded her of the slugs that infested the garden.

He had stalked around the room, shouting and cursing, taking long drinks from the bottle of wine that had been placed on the table. From time to time he had reeled to bend over the frightened girl who lay watching him. He had ripped her gown and then grabbed a handful of her abundant hair. Jerking her head he had cursed the English, then cursed her and his parents.

"You all want me gone, don't you?" he screamed. "I know it every time I look at you, Rosalita."

Cold fingers of horror had run up Allison's skin, for it became more and more evident that don Jaime wasn't even seeing her, but another woman entirely.

"I got rid of you once, you remember? I can do it again. And everyone will search for you and search for you, and the old women will cry . . . but they'll never find you. Never, never, never . . ."

His words had trailed off into that chilling laughter that Allison was coming to know all too well. She'd wanted to jump off the bed and bolt through the door to safety, but there was nowhere for her to go. And so she had sat, curled up on the bed, as her husband drank and raved for hours.

Never had Allison imagined such a terrible thing happening to her, but she was too paralyzed with fear to even protest. Finally it had ended. Corona's eyes had glazed over with hatred, and he had grabbed her hair and dragged her out of the bed. "You think I need a woman like you? No! I despise the sight of you! Sleep on the floor—or better still, go to the bay and drown yourself!"

With that he had collapsed in a drunken, unconscious heap on the bed, and she had crept away to sleep in the adjoining dressing room.

As this cruel memory flashed through Allison's mind, she was conscious of one blessed relief: *At least he's never shamed me like that again!* He had shared the bedroom with her for a week, but had drunk himself into a stupor each night, saying, "Sleep on the floor, English witch!"

Allison had been grateful to do so, and the next week, Jaime had told his parents, "My bride is very nervous. She sleeps poorly. We will give her a room of her own, where I will pay her a husbandly visit until it is no longer necessary."

For the last five years, Allison had been left alone for the most part. Her husband had resumed his old way of life—which was to make long circuitous business trips with only his most trusted companions—men paid to watch over him and keep him from hurting himself or anyone else. His business ventures prospered, which gave him reason to come home but rarely, and those visits were blessedly short.

Looking across the table at doña María, Allison felt a keen pity. *She must have so little hope left—her son was her life, and now he is a monster!* Though she was sure she would never be able to give the two older people the grandchildren they so desperately wanted, she determined to be a good daughter-in-law to them in whatever way she could. Now she smiled at her mother-in-law. "Why don't you and I go into town for a little shopping today?"

"Why, we must go to the *auto-da-fé,* Allison," doña María responded. "Did you forget?"

"N-no, but I'd rather not go."

"Not go! But you *must* go, my dear!" Doña María's round face was suddenly troubled. "You know that the Inquisition is . . . watchful of who attends, and—"

"And since I am English, they'll be even more so?"

"Exactly! Now I know you're a good Catholic girl, but one must not give the Fathers any occasion to—to suspect."

Allison said no more, for she was well aware that even the most devout members of the church were terrified of being accused of heresy. She put on her most somber dress, and that afternoon when she arrived with don Alfredo and doña María at the Plaza Mayor, two or three thousand people were already there, as well as hundreds crowding the balconies of the four-story houses. At one side of the square was the king's balcony, and opposite on a raised dais two cages in which a small group of prisoners was housed. The wooden stands were packed, but special seats had been reserved for the nobility, and as Allison took one of them, she thought wryly, *I would rather not have a front-row seat for this—better to be as far away as possible!*

A tall, lean priest came by and was introduced to her as Father Securo, the head of the Inquisition. She nodded and spoke faintly to him, but saw that his glittering eyes were fixed on her in an almost predatory manner. A flicker of fear ran through her. *Just as well I came,* she thought with a shiver.

Half an hour later King Philip and his retinue began to take their seats, and as soon as they were settled, the procession began. This consisted of perhaps a hundred charcoal men carrying muskets and pikes, and two or three hundred Dominican monks with banners, led by a man on a white horse carrying the standard of the Holy Office, red with a silver sword in a crown of laurel. Then there were halberdiers and three men bearing a crucifix wrapped in black crepe. The crucifix and the standard were fixed on the altar, and prayers began.

Allison hated it all—the avid eyes of the spectators, the solid ranks of glittering soldiery, the massed squares of monks. It was a part of her faith that she could never accept—and she could fully understand why, in England, the Inquisition was the chief symbol of the hated papacy.

After another parade the Grand Inquisitor began to preach. The sun burned on Allison's head and the heat became stifling. Some of the spectators took out rolls of bread and began to eat them, along with garlic and leeks. Stall holders had set up trestles at the foot of the stands, and they did a good trade selling cups of cordial and bowls of broth. A monk in the strange hood of a Capuchin was collecting gifts for the poor.

Finally the Grand Inquisitor finished, and the king rose to reply. Although his voice was dry and thin, there was a quiet passion in it. Several times he roused his listeners to murmurs of approval, and once there was a grumbling roar when he mentioned reconversion by fire and sword. As he finished, a procession of monks made a circuit of the amphitheater bearing statues and effigies of saints and a dozen coffins with flames painted round them. These, don Alfredo informed Allison, contained the bones of heretics who had recently died in prison.

Now the prisoners were brought forward one by one and their crimes were read. One of the four women and five of the thirteen men were condemned to death. The others went to the galleys, to imprisonment, or to be scourged.

Mass was celebrated in the growing shadows. Litter and dirt were everywhere, and bags of wine were passed around—which Allison only tasted. Her appetite was gone and she dreaded that which was to come.

Finally the prisoners were bound to stakes in the middle of the square. Faggots and charcoal were piled around them by black-coated burners and priests of the Holy Office. Now the flag with the white cross flapped in the breeze, and one of the prisoners cried aloud in a strange language.

"He's gone off his head," don Alfredo said. "Terrible to go meet God like that!"

A man was trying to get his little boy of eight through to see more clearly, and then the charcoal men were passing cords round the necks of the four prisoners who had recanted—thus showing them the mercy of being strangled before the fires were lit. One was shouting, another was reciting the Lord's Prayer in Latin. One of the officials signaled to a man who raised a long brass trumpet and blew a shrill blast. The crowd grew silent, and the cursing and praying of the prisoners ended in a strangled coughing as the executioners hauled back on the cords. Soon they were dead. The people sighed; a monk's high voice intoned a prayer.

Allison was nauseated, but there was worse to come. The men bearing torches lit the faggots of the remaining victims, and flames licked round their feet. One of them, a man dressed in tattered black clothing, began to scream in a high-pitched voice, like a horse Allison had heard being clumsily slaughtered. The other made no sound, but as the flames licked up, blisters rose and burst quickly on his skin like bubbles in a boiling pot. As they burst, the rich red blood poured from them and from his nose.

Overcome by the gruesome scene, Allison turned her head quickly and threw up. Doña María cast a look at the Grand Inquisitor, saw his hawkish eyes take in the English girl's reaction, and reached to draw the girl upright as they left the box.

"It's a terrible thing for a young woman to have to watch," don Alfredo muttered, holding Allison's arm. "But heretics must be rooted out or the truth will perish."

Allison was too drained to speak, but everything in her revolted against what she had seen. *This isn't the love of Jesus!* was the cry of protest that she bit back as the couple led her out of the arena.

⁂

For weeks after the *auto-da-fé* Allison slept poorly. She would drop off into a fitful sleep, but would come out of it with a start as vivid images of the horrible deaths seemed to fill her mind. Some nights she would sit up until dawn, afraid to sleep, and at those times she read from the worn Gospel of John that Giles had given back to her just before she left for Spain. She knew it by heart, but somehow handling the familiar book gave her a sense of the past—those days when she was safe at home with family.

One afternoon a priest, Father Cortez, came to visit. He drank tea with don Alfredo and doña María, then asked to meet the beautiful bride of don Jaime.

"He's the special agent for the Grand Inquisitor," doña María whispered when she came to get Allison. "Be very careful how you speak. The Inquisition can be very hard on foreigners!"

But the priest was genial, nodding his approval when the Coronas heaped praise on their daughter-in-law. Finally he said, "Perhaps, señora, you would show me your garden? I love flowers, you know."

"Of course, Father."

For half an hour the two roamed through the extensive garden of the estate, and Father Cortez was indeed a connoisseur of flowers. Finally he asked, "Are these like your English flowers, señora? I've never been to England."

"Oh no, not at all, Father." Allison's cheeks warmed as she spoke freely of the English gardens and wildflowers, and when she paused, Father Cortez asked, "Do you miss your home?"

"Yes, very much." It would be useless to lie to this man, Allison knew instinctively. As a member of the Inquisition he would be an expert in reading people. "I think I miss the flowers most of all, though these are very beautiful," she added quickly.

Cortez had a round, bland face, but behind a pair of mild brown eyes lay a razor-keen mind. The Grand Inquisitor had sent him to probe this English girl, adding, *"She seems meek enough, but go to her soul, Cortez—you know how heresy is rank among English Catholics!"*

Now the small priest said delicately, "And your marriage—you are happy with your husband?"

Allison dropped her eyes for a moment, then lifted them. "No, Father," she replied simply.

Her straightforward answer found approval with Cortez. He knew, of course, of the aberration of the son of the Corona family, and he had spoken with the parish priest about the matter before coming to see Allison. He had been told that the old people had become desperate and sent for an English girl—hoping that don Jaime would at least produce a son. *"But I have heard the young woman's confession,"* he had added. *"Don Jaime has not changed and I fear the young woman is trapped."*

Cortez said gently, "Marriage is hard at best, Allison. With you—it is more difficult than for most."

Quickly Allison looked into his eyes. *He knows!* she thought, then whispered, "I . . . would like to be a good wife, but . . ."

As the young woman faltered, Father Cortez said quickly, "I understand. We will pray for your husband. Be a good daughter to Señor Corona and his good wife. Be faithful to the church. I have a good report on you from Father Gonzales. We will see. . . ."

When Cortez gave his report to the Grand Inquisitor, he shrugged. "The son of don Alfredo is a man who is sick of mind and spirit. We have long known of that. The young woman? She is a simple child, but a good Catholic. I will check on her from time to time if you desire, but I see nothing good coming from the marriage. A tragedy for the Coronas, a good man and a good woman! When they die, the aberrant son will go to ruin quickly enough, I suppose."

"Be wary, José! These English are clever!" Anger reddened the Grand Inquisitor's face. "The head of their secret service trapped three Jesuits last month and executed them after torture! One of them was so broken by the rack he could not lift his hand when he was tried! And they have the effrontery to charge *us* with cruelty!"

"Someday it will be different." Cortez nodded. "When we invade England and put a good Catholic on the throne, then we shall see who is executed."

"Ah, you favor Mary, Queen of Scots?"

"Certainly!"

"Well, she *is* in the line, and she is a devoted daughter of the church." Leaning forward, he lowered his voice, adding, "Have you heard any more of the plot to, ah, *remove* Elizabeth?"

"I know a little. Our agents tell us that it will not be difficult. Elizabeth scorns to protect herself, they say. We will find a time, never fear!"

"The Inquisition will be busy when Mary rules!" The tall man's eyes seemed to burn, but he smiled, adding, "I can think of no priest more fitted to serve as chief of the Inquisition in England than you, Father Cortez!"

"It will be as God wills, Father!"

Allison often walked along the path that led to the river. The servants of the great house used this same path to take their clothes to a secluded spot shaded by a clump of trees, where they did laundry and sometimes bathed.

The sun was falling in the west one September evening when she reached the river. She looked out at the water, noting how the yellow globe seem to touch the liquid surface, transforming the brown water into a golden stream. Sitting down on one of the rocks that bordered the small river, Allison pulled her feet up and hugged her knees, a habit she'd had since she was a small child.

From far away the tinkle of bells came to her—sheep bells, she knew, faint and melodious. Then in counterpoint, the church bell tolled the Angelus, a mellow sound that floated on the still air.

Allison treasured the quietness and sat for a long time, watching the small fish rise and take the flies that touched the surface. Each time one rose for a fly, the action sent a perfect ripple over the water that spread until it reached the banks at her feet. Picking up a stone, she tossed it in and watched the ripples—perfect, simple, clean. She began to toss more stones and noticed that while one stone made a simple pattern, two of them would send ripples that touched and broke apart. And when she threw a handful of them, the patterns grew so complex that the simple circle could not be seen at all.

That's what I would like life to be—simple! But it's not. Oh, that I were back home, milking the cow, cooking for my family. That was so simple! But life is like the water when you throw in a handful of stones—everything's so confused.

Abruptly she came out of her reverie when sounds came from behind her. Leaping to her feet, Allison whirled to see a gaunt man emerge from the woods. He was ragged, his eyes were hollows, and his feet were bare; she could see the bloody tracks he made as he advanced.

"If you need food, go to the kitchen," she said quickly, fighting a flash of fear. He looked weak, but there was a desperate expression on his face. Quickly she moved to leave, but then he spoke to her.

"Allison——!"

The voice was cracked and thin, but something about it caught at her. She stopped and peered at him. "Who are you?" she whispered. "How do you know my name?"

The beggar swayed as he stood there, seemingly about to fall. "You don't recognize me . . . ," he whispered. "Of course—how could you?" And then he took a step forward, but weakness seemed to overcome him. He put his hand out, but slowly fell forward, striking the ground with a dull thud.

Allison was tempted to run away, but something about the finality of the man's collapse prevented that. Cautiously she moved toward the still form, and when he didn't move, she asked nervously, "Are you all right?"

But the man lay still. *Maybe he's dead!* The thought alarmed her, and she advanced to where he lay, then suddenly knelt down. Fearfully she put her hand on his shoulder, shook it, then when he didn't respond, she rolled him over. The last rays of the sun caught the haggard, bearded face, and she saw that he was unconscious. Quickly she rose and went to the river, wet her handkerchief, then returned to the unconscious man. Awkwardly she pulled him to a sitting position, ignoring the terrible smell, and bathed his face.

Slowly the eyes opened, and she saw that they were blue. *How long has it been since I've seen someone with blue eyes?* she wondered vaguely. These were not Spanish eyes! "Who are you?" she whispered. "How do you know me?"

He tried to speak, then licked his lips painfully. "Allison . . . it's me . . . Robin!"

Her head jerked backward, and a sense of unreality descended on her—as if the whole scene were a dream. Staring into the wan face, she saw that it *was* Robin Wakefield!

"What—how did you get here?" she whispered. She was supporting him with one arm and was aware that the strong man she had known had been reduced to little more than a skeleton.

"Captured months ago . . . escaped from prison yesterday . . ."

Thoughts flew through the young woman's mind, but one thing was clear. "You'll be found," she exclaimed. "Was it the prison in Cádiz?" When he nodded, she said, "They'll search the whole countryside!"

"Couldn't . . . think of anywhere else to go . . . "

Allison knew at once that if he were found he would die. Her mind raced and she said, "There's an old abandoned shack downriver. Nobody goes there. I'm not even sure anyone else knows it's there. Can you walk at all, Robin?"

"Try—!" he gasped. His mind was reeling, for he was burning with fever, and the long hours of hiding in the woods had exhausted him. He came to his feet but would have fallen if she had not caught him.

"Put your arm over my shoulder," she urged. "Lean on me."

She took his weight and could not help but remember how she'd ridden on his powerful shoulders when she'd been a child. Carefully she moved down the river, slowly so that he would not fall. He was gasping for breath by the time they got to the old shack, and when they were inside, he collapsed on a dusty, dilapidated old cot beside the single window.

"I'll go get you something to eat, then we'll have to get your fever down," she said. She turned to go, but his voice caught at her, calling her name. "Yes, what is it?"

His eyes were sunken into their sockets and his lips were

cracked. Lifting a thin hand, he protested, "Can't risk . . . them finding you with me . . . helping me. Mustn't come . . . back!"

Allison came to him at once and knelt beside the broken down cot. She took his thin, clammy hand and held it with both of hers.

"Robin, I will not leave you here. You are my friend, and you have brought me something wonderful today." Her voice was choked with unshed tears, and he looked at her questioningly. "When I saw your face, when I knew it was you, I felt . . . the presence of God come over me." Her eyes shone with a gladness that was dazzling. "I cannot explain why, Robin, but I felt God's presence, and I knew what he wanted me to do!"

Her heart felt as though it would overflow with joy, for she hadn't felt the Lord in this way since she left England. But now, in the darkness of the fetid room, with a dying man on her hands, and the risk hanging over her of being burned alive if she were caught—even with this, she was suddenly exalted. She had been sickened by the executions at the *auto-da-fé*, and now she had been given a chance to *give* life!

Leaning down she brushed his damp hair back from his forehead. "God brought me to Spain, Robin. I've always known it, but I never knew why. Now I know. It was to save you. And that is what I will do, with God's help!"

Robin Wakefield stared up at her smooth face, suddenly flooded by a host of sweet memories. He could not speak, but swallowed convulsively, then whispered, "Yes—God has saved me!"

Allison felt the pressure of his hand and returned the squeeze. "Now, I must leave. But I'll be back with food."

And then she was gone.

But the darkness of the shack was not like the blackness of his dungeon. Robin had been truly alone in that place, but now he knew that someone was with him. Someone other than the young woman who had just left.

"God is here!" he exclaimed—and then added with a faint smile, "And Allison . . . she's here, too!"

END OF PART THREE

Part

FOUR

Armada!

Twenty-one

LADY OF SPAIN

A mild April sun threw warm bars of yellow light across the tiled floor as Allison entered the room. She went at once to a heavy oak bookcase, pulled several leather-bound volumes down, and placed them on the table. Quickly she reached behind the remaining books and extracted a slender notebook bound in blue leather. Casting a nervous look toward the door, she sat down at the carved mahogany desk, picked up a quill, found her place in the book, and began to write.

> April 5, 1586
> Jaime left yesterday for Madrid. He came to my bedroom last night and taunted me, calling me Rosalita again and threatening to 'help me go to a place where no one will ever find me.' He does it to unnerve me, and he succeeded. He screamed at me and threw books at me—but soon tired of that sport and left to go to the cantina. Thank God he leaves me alone most of the time!

She dipped the pen into the ink, nibbled at the end of it thoughtfully, then resumed writing:

> When Robin appeared six months ago, my greatest fear was

303

that the prison authorities would find him, but they seemed not to care. One patrol came by and inquired of the Coronas three days after I put him in the shack, but I had not told anyone of his coming, so the patrol went away and never came back.

That seems so long ago! Only a few months, but looking back on it, I think if he hadn't come—well, I don't want to think on it. It was a challenge for me, getting him well, keeping him hidden until he was able to take care of himself. How sick he was for a week. I had to feed him and wash him like a baby!

Then he wanted to leave as soon as he could totter around. I was so frustrated I had to scold him. It took some convincing, but he finally realized it was impossible for him to leave. Especially when I told him I could end up in trouble if they caught him close to Casa Loma. Father Securo still seems far too interested in me, and such a discovery would only heighten his interest and rouse his suspicion! Besides, I had a perfect plan. At first Robin said it wouldn't work, but he finally agreed to try it. I don't know what he was so worried about. He looked ragged enough to have come to the door begging for work. And everyone in the house knows how I long to help those who are less fortunate. So convincing them that I had found a man to work in the garden and the vineyards was quite simple. So that is done, and Robin is safely established at Casa Loma. Now the task is to see about getting him out of Spain.

Though I must admit I will hate to see him go. Oh, how I shall miss him!

Allison paused to dip her pen in the ink, but instead of writing more, she rose and walked to the window. Downstairs she saw Robin sitting in the shade of the big fig tree, talking and laughing with Anita. A frown crossed her brow, but then she thought, *She's a very pretty girl—it's only natural for him to enjoy being with her.* Nevertheless, she made a mental note to tell him to be very careful—one word could give him away.

She stood there, watching him. He was wearing a pair of cut-off cotton trousers and had cut the sleeves from a white shirt. A wide-brimmed straw hat was pushed back on his head, and he wore a pair of leather-thonged sandals. *He doesn't look much like the plucked chicken he resembled when I found him by the river!* She found herself admiring his strong, bronzed arms, corded with muscle, and the lean contours of his face. His auburn hair was long and slightly curly, and his blue-gray eyes were bright and clear.

Allison kept her eyes on the pair for a while, then turned and moved back to the table. She sat there for a few moments, remembering how difficult it had been when she'd first brought Robin to Casa Loma. People were curious about any stranger. Together they had concocted the story that he was Norwegian, had been a sailor, but had grown sick and was left onshore by his captain. It was a weak enough tale, and if any true Norwegian had happened by, the game would have been up. But she had said, "I doubt if there's a Norwegian within a thousand miles of here, Robin—and with your fair skin and blue eyes, they'll know you're an Englishman if we don't have a story."

He had smiled at her, she remembered, saying, "When I used to take you hunting, perched on my shoulder, for bird's eggs, I never thought you'd turn out to be such a plotter!" Then she remembered his eyes had grown very serious, and he'd said, "I owe you my life, Allison."

Her cheeks flushed suddenly as she remembered he'd taken her hand and kissed it. But she had no time to think more on that, for a knock at the door startled her. Leaping up, she replaced the diary, jammed the heavy volumes over it, then ran to the door and opened it.

Doña María stood there. "Are you ready, Allison?"

"Oh yes. I just came to get my list of supplies."

"You'd better wear that wide-brimmed hat of yours. The sun is very warm and you burn so easily."

"Yes, I will." Allison moved to the wall and pulled a white straw hat from a peg, then moved to the mirror to adjust it.

The older woman watched as Allison tucked strands of ash-blonde hair under the hat, and her gaze held affection and admiration. When Allison had first come, doña María had been afraid that the strain would be too much for the young girl. Neither she nor her husband had dreamed such a sweet girl would come to them, but during the long months, they had both come to love her as a daughter. Now doña María admired the clear, pale skin, so unlike that of Spanish women. And the dark eyes—violet, no less! There was something almost mysterious about those eyes.

The older woman studied her daughter-in-law's slender figure and felt a pang of disappointment. Still slim as ever, though fully curved and beautifully formed. *Jaime is not being a husband to her,* was her thought, but she had never pressed Allison for details of her marital life. She didn't want to lose at least a ray of hope.

"How long will we be gone?"

"Oh, I'm not going," doña María said. "I didn't get a chance to tell you, but one of my oldest friends is coming this afternoon. You'll have to do the shopping alone." She frowned, adding, "Perhaps you should wait until tomorrow?"

"No, of course not. You enjoy your visit." She moved toward the door, adding casually, "I'll take Roberto along to carry the heavy things."

"Yes, that would be good." She moved to Allison and kissed the girl's glowing cheek. "You're looking so well," she murmured. "For the last few months you've been much happier than when you first came. I'm very glad. It's been a hard thing for you, I fear. But now you are happy again."

"Oh, I suppose that's because it's spring," Allison said quickly. "I'll be sure and pick out some nice cloth for your new dress. You can't entertain the marquis of Santa Cruz in anything less than the finest, can you now?"

Allison left the house and called out sharply, "Roberto, bring the carriage! You two have been loafing all morning!"

Robin leaped to his feet, yanked his straw hat off, and said respectfully, "*Sí, señora! At once!*" He moved quickly toward the stable and was back shortly with a black carriage drawn by a fine team of matched white mares. Leaping to the ground, he took her hand. "I am sorry to have kept you waiting, señora." He squeezed her hand slightly, and she could see the trace of a smile touch his broad lips.

"Very well, see that you do better next time!" Allison spoke shortly to him, keeping her tone even firmer than doña María had taught her to do with the servants, and allowing a shade of sharpness to come into her words.

Anita stood watching as the carriage moved down the road, sending a spiral of fine beige dust into the air. A tall, gangling young man with a pair of laughing black eyes came to stand beside her. "You lost your lover, Anita. Maybe I'll do instead."

"Don't be a fool, Manolito!" the girl snapped.

"Am I a fool because I say the Norwegian is your lover, or because I want to take his place?"

Anita laughed suddenly, for she was fond of Manolito. "Both! But I will let you take me to the fiesta at the village this afternoon and buy me anything I want." She kept up a repartee with the young man, but her eyes followed the carriage. "He's a strange one, Manolito. And don Jaime's wife—she seems to despise him. Why is that?"

"Women cannot be explained—but they can be loved and

adored!" She giggled and slapped his hands, then the two of them moved away toward the path that led to the river.

As soon as the buggy had pulled away from Casa Loma, Robin turned to look at Allison. "You were especially harsh this morning, Señora Corona," he said with a smile. "But I forgive you."

She sent him an arch look. "I should hope so, since it was your idea that I treat you that way to avoid any suspicion!"

"Ah, but how was I to know you would take to the task with such earnestness?"

She colored slightly and turned away, while he laughed. "You look very well today, Señora Corona. I've grown quite fond of that hat."

Allison tilted her head higher and appeared to be fascinated with the traffic that flowed along the dusty highway leading to Cádiz. As on every Saturday the narrow width was crowded with horsemen in wide-brimmed sombreros, carriages, and buggies of every description. And, of course, there was a line of peasants headed for the market with their wares on their own backs or on the backs of diminutive donkeys with enormous ears.

Robin threaded the carriage expertly through the maze, sitting idly on the seat. He had developed some of the Latin gift for being relaxed during his stay and now swayed loosely with the motions of the buggy. He noted that Allison was determined to remain silent for some reason. A sudden thought crossed his mind, making him frown. *I've hurt her feelings somehow! What could it have been?*

In the last few months he had come to realize how little he understood this girl—or woman, rather. Knowing her as a child had given him certain insights, and yet that fact had also brought him confusion, for despite himself the images that came to him of Allison when he was alone were always dual. One instant he would see her smooth cheeks, full womanly lips and form—and then a memory of a little girl with her hair flying as she raced across a meadow with all the awkward grace of a young colt would appear.

For long weeks after his coming to work at Casa Loma she had spoken to him only in the presence of others—and spoken sharply, too. It had been very difficult, those first weeks. He'd lived on the fine line of desperation, expecting to be found out at any moment. He'd developed no friendships to speak of, choosing instead to keep to himself. At first he'd been closely watched, but he'd done his work and faded into the background of the busy estate very well.

Now, as they approached the city of Cádiz, he gave Allison a covert glance. She was still sitting very straight, and her eyes were fixed on the outlines of the buildings ahead. Abruptly she turned and caught him staring. "Why are you looking at me like that?" she demanded.

Robin shrugged. "I've offended you and I don't know how." He shoved his hat back so that it hung from the leather thong, then ran his hand through his hair. When he spoke again there was a touch of loneliness in his voice. "You're the only friend I've got in this place. I don't like feeling distant from you."

At this Allison turned to him and put her hand on his bare arm. "Oh, Robin, it was nothing!" She bit her lip and shook her head. "I guess I'm just being a silly woman! Don't pay any attention to me."

"You're not a silly woman." Robin had wanted for a long time to express how he felt, but had never really had the opportunity. Now he took a deep breath and said, "I—I guess you think I'm the world's biggest ingrate. I've let you risk everything—even your life—and I've never had a chance to thank you."

Allison dropped her eyes. "I'm glad I was able to help," she said quietly. Then she looked up, and he thought again how lovely her eyes were. "If I helped you, Robin, you helped me, too."

"I don't see that."

"Do you remember what I said the night you came to me?"

"Yes. You said that God brought me to you." He let that thought have its way with him, and his eyes grew sober. "I never told you about how I got out of prison, did I?"

"No, you never did."

Robin related the story, and Allison listened, her eyes fixed on his profile. He spoke slowly, telling how he would never have gotten out if it had not been for finding a way to use the pieces of wood that provided the answer. He ended by saying, "I gave up, you know. After I'd tried everything I knew, I just wanted to quit. And then—I prayed."

"And God answered your prayer?"

"Yes! It was like nothing I'd ever felt, Allison!" As he relived the moment he reached out unconsciously and held her forearm. He squeezed it so hard that it hurt her, but she didn't say anything for fear of stopping the words flowing from him. "It just came to me—and I knew it must be God!"

"And the way you found me," Allison added. "If that particular man who knew our house had not been in the cell with you, why, you'd never have found Casa Loma!"

Robin suddenly realized that he was squeezing her arm, and he released her hastily. "I'm sorry. I—didn't mean to do that."

"It's all right."

The two of them talked quietly of the way he'd been delivered, and she asked suddenly, "Robin, do you still hate those who killed your parents?"

Startled, he turned to stare at her. "Odd you should ask that, Allison. Since I've been here, surrounded by Catholics, things have seemed . . . different." He struggled to frame his thoughts and finally shook his head. "Perhaps I'm older now, more under-standing. When I was a child I struck out at whatever was connected to my parent's deaths. And you know how it is in England—everything that goes wrong is the pope's fault!"

The right front wheel of the carriage dropped into a pothole, and the violent dipping of the frame threw Allison against Robin. He reacted instinctively by throwing his arm around her to steady her. "Careful!" The rear wheel struck bottom, and he held her tightly. He could smell her faint perfume, and the pressure of her body against him sent a strong current along his nerves.

Allison felt it as well, but noted that a young rider dressed in black and silver was passing and had seen the incident. "Let me go, Robin," she whispered. Drawing back she said, "We must be careful."

"You're right," he agreed, and they said nothing until they were almost at the city gates. Then he said abruptly, "I must tell you, if I feel differently about things—about Catholics—it's all due to you."

"To me?"

"Why yes. I've always been fond of you, but seeing you here, your risking your life for me—" He shrugged his shoulders slightly, then said, "I'm coming to understand that it was a *system* that killed my father. A bad system, I think—but one can't hate a system. That's why I fastened my hatred on people. But it's brought me no happiness or satisfaction. My grandparents tried to tell me how dangerous such an obsession was, but I couldn't throw it off. But now I've seen you, Allison."

"Why, Robin—"

They were within a few yards of the gate, and he turned to say, "You're the loveliest and gentlest woman I've ever known. You've taught me to look farther than just a label—because you know God, Allison—and he's in you. And that's what I want, no matter what sort of name is put to it!"

He said no more, for they were now inside the city and many eyes were on them. Nor did they have opportunity to speak on the way home, for a cousin of doña María's asked to ride back to

Casa Loma for a visit. All the way back to the estate the lady talked, and "Roberto" drove silently, slumped and indolent.

⁂

Ramoñ Varga was a young man who was quick to seize opportunity when it presented itself. He was a worthless sort, the youngest son of an impoverished family that had lost their fortune. He existed by being an entertaining companion, and one of those who was willing to provide him with dinners and wine was don Jaime Corona.

Varga encountered don Jaime one evening while at the cantina, and while the two were fairly well on the way to being drunk, Varga jibed, "Better stay home, Corona. You might find yourself missing a wife!"

Jaime stared at the other man. "What does *that* mean?" he demanded. He listened as Varga related how he'd been riding on the road from town where he'd seen a servant hugging Señora Allison Corona.

At first, Jaime was amused. "You're lying, Ramoñ," he charged. "Pshaw! She's too pure to have anything to do with a man—especially a peasant."

"No woman's that pure, Jaime." Varga shrugged. "And who *is* that fellow, anyway? He's handsome enough to get into the heart of a lonesome young wife. And into the moneybags of her husband. You'd better watch yourself, or you may wind up with a knife in the back while your fair wife shares her inheritance with a new man."

Varga got nothing but a cursing from Jaime—that and a fine meal and enough wine to get drunk on. The two parted, and Corona went to bed, but when he awoke the next morning, he found that Ramoñ Varga's insinuations would not leave his mind.

"She is not clever enough to hatch such a plot," he assured himself irritably. But somehow, he couldn't quite make himself believe that. Soon he was not only considering Varga's words, but convinced they were true. "She does not relish being married to me. She's looked at me with contempt. But she's no better than I, and if she thinks to slit my throat, she will have to be much more clever than this!"

His anger grew, and he rode toward Casa Loma determined to expose Allison's deceit. Throwing himself off his horse, he stomped into the house, his face set with anger. When he didn't find Allison in her room, he sought his parents. "Why, they are gone for a visit with your uncle, don Jaime," the steward said.

"And my wife?"

"I believe she's in the vineyard, sir."

Don Jaime whirled and made his way out of the house. When he came to the edge of the extensive vineyards, he halted, for he saw Allison wearing a white headdress and a light blue dress working with the vines. This was not unusual, for she loved the vineyard.

But there, not five feet away from her, was the pale-faced Norwegian! Don Jaime's lips curved upward in a cruel smile. "We shall see . . ." He retraced his steps and reentered the house. Quickly he went to his room, opened a drawer, and picked up a fine pistol. He always kept it loaded—one could never tell when an enemy might creep into one's room—but checked it carefully all the same. "We shall see, we shall see . . . ," he chanted in a singsong voice. Satisfied that the gun was ready, he left the house again and went into the vineyards.

Allison had no warning, for she was studying the vines, trimming excess growth. Suddenly don Jaime's voice rang out, "So, I find you here with your lover!"

Startled, Allison whirled around, and her face grew pale as she saw the pistol pointed at her. "Don Jaime!"

"Shut your mouth," Jaime said brutally. "I'll tend to you after I take care of this—this stud horse!" He gestured angrily toward

Robin, but kept his eyes on Allison. Suddenly his face crumpled, like a child whose heart was broken.

"You were supposed to love me!" he whined. "You're my wife! But you will not accomplish your plans."

"Don Jaime," Allison said, trying to keep her voice calm. "You are upset. Let me call one of the servants—"

"Shut up! Shut up!" he screamed, waving the gun at her. Then he stood there, weaving back and forth, and chanting, "We shall see, we shall see, who lives the longest, you two or me!"

Allison felt a chill of horror race through her. He was totally mad. The tiny spark of reason that had been in his eyes was gone, and don Jaime Corona was beyond any reasoning.

Robin had been filling a basket with cuttings when Allison's husband came in, but now he stood stock still, watching carefully what was happening. He saw madness—and murder—in Corona's eyes, and his mind worked rapidly. He knew enough of Spanish customs to realize that one of the aristocracy could shoot a servant suspected of having an affair with his wife. There would be no defense, and, if he survived, the best he could hope for was another Spanish prison.

"Stand still, scum!" Jaime's dull gaze focused on Robin, and his eyes narrowed. "Shall I kill you?" he asked almost conversationally. "No, I don't believe I shall. I think I would much rather see you ripped by the whip. I will teach you what it means to dally with the wife of a Corona!"

"Jaime, it's not true!" Allison came to touch her husband's arm, but he struck out at her, catching her across the mouth with his outstretched palm.

Even as Corona turned to hit Allison, Robin was moving. He knew he would have no second chance, so he threw himself forward, striking out with his fist. He caught don Jaime on the jaw, and the smaller man was driven back to the ground by the

314

force of the blow and knocked unconscious. Robin snatched the gun from the ground, and Allison ran to his side.

"You'll have to get away, you can no longer stay here safely!" She thought quickly. "Come, I'll get you money and clothes." Robin hesitated, but she shook her head. "I know a way that we both will be safe. Come on!"

Robin ran with her to the house, and she said, "Wait here." She disappeared, and when she returned she carried a bulky bundle in her arms. "Here are clothes. They belong to don Alfredo. I was taking them to give to the poor." She removed a small leather pouch and shoved it at him. "There's gold in there, Robin. You'll need it to get away."

"Allison, they'll know you helped me!"

"No, they won't. They may suspect it, but they won't know it. If you stay here, he'll have you killed."

"I can't leave you—!"

She cut him off. "If you stay, we both will die! There's a little village named Cayo on the coast. Go to Cádiz—it's about five miles from there. You can be there tomorrow. Ships come there, small ones from everywhere. There's a good harbor there. Get on board one going any place, then make your way to England!"

Confused by the catastrophe, Robin shook his head. "I won't go, Allison!"

Her eyes were enormous as she watched him. She had not known until this moment, when she must lose him, how much he had filled her life. "You must live, Robin," she whispered. "God saved you from death for a purpose. You must find that purpose if you—if *we*—are to honor him! And I could not bear it if you were killed!"

Suddenly Robin put his arms out and drew her to him. He saw the startled look on her face, but knew what he wanted. "Come with me, Allison! I need you!"

Tears suddenly filled her eyes, and for one moment she leaned against him. He held her closely, whispering with his lips against her hair, "Come with me . . . I love you!"

Allison's heart filled with emotion—and then felt as though it shattered. She drew away from his embrace, and her back straightened. Her lips grew firm and she shook her head. "No, Robin. I—have a husband!"

"He's no husband to you, Allison!"

"In the sight of God, he is." Pain shot through her, but she knew what she had to do. She took his arm and pushed him toward the gate, exclaiming, "Go now, Robin. We have no time, you *must* leave—and God will keep you!" Abruptly she whirled and ran toward the house, leaving him standing there.

He had no choice. He picked up the bundle, stuffed the gold into his pocket, then turned and ran toward the woods. He knew the country well enough to avoid the villages, and though he saw a few farmers in the distance, by nightfall he came to the coast. He made his way along the coast. Darkness fell early, and he found a tavern with a room on the outskirts of town.

Early the next morning, he went to the harbor and engaged an elderly man in conversation, asking about the ships. The man, whose white hair formed a crown over his weather-beaten face, knew every vessel there. He named them off—and one he mentioned caught Robin's ear.

"She's sailing today? For where?"

"Back to France. Taking a cargo of sheep. They loaded this morning. The mate, he told me the captain wanted to leave early."

Robin left the old man, and when he got to the French ship, he found the captain willing to take a passenger—for a price.

Two hours later the coast of Spain was a ragged line on the horizon. Robin went to the bow and leaned on the rail.

Somewhere ahead lay England! The breeze ruffled his hair and he drank in the salt air. But despite his exultation at being free and the hope of seeing home, he could not keep from turning to look again at the fading line on the horizon.

"Allison . . . ," he whispered, his heart suddenly heavy. Then he turned his face toward England.

I'll see you again, my dear—somehow! he vowed, and he knew he would never rest until it was so.

Twenty-two

DEATH OF A QUEEN

R obin used the last of the small store of gold that Allison had given him to buy a seat on the coach passing through Wakefield. He had spent the rest of his finances on food and for his fare on a ship that sailed from France to Dover. Ashore at last, he now longed to see his home.

When he stepped down from the coach, he turned and made his way on foot to the castle. He was met by Hunter, a huge mastiff whose grandsire had been the faithful Pilot. At first, Hunter came toward Robin as he approached the house, his huge head down and growling deep in his throat.

"Hunter!" Robin exclaimed, and at the sound of his voice, the huge animal came forward at once, frantically leaping up and nearly upsetting the man. "I hope everyone is as glad to see me as you are, boy!" Robin laughed, for the dog was a virtual copy of his beloved Pilot. The sight of the great dog brought joy to his heart. He knew now that he was home, that his time of separation from those he loved was over—and he quickly moved to the door and entered without knocking.

Anna, the ancient maid who'd served his grandmother for many years, came into the foyer holding a tray of dishes. Taking one look at him, she uttered a small cry and dropped the tray. "Anna, it's me!" Robin saw the old woman's face turn pale as dust and leaped to her side to put his arm around her. She was trembling and would have fallen if he had not held her. "Are you all right?"

"Master Robin! You're alive!"

"Why, of course I am. Did you think I'd died?"

Anna began to weep and picked at his sleeve with thin fingers. "Aye, that we did! No word all these months, and Master Thomas trying all he knew to get word of you—" The tears ran down her wrinkled face, but her old eyes were bright. "You must go to your uncle! He's in the master's study."

"The master" was, to Anna's mind, Myles Wakefield. No matter who was the current holder of the title, she lived in the past, much more thoughtful of the days when her beloved master and mistress ruled than of present days.

"I'll go to him at once." He looked down at her, saying, "It's good to see you, Anna," then released her and almost ran down the hall and knocked on the sturdy oak door. When his uncle's voice said "Come in," he opened the door and entered.

Thomas Wakefield was sitting at his desk, which was littered with maps and books. At the sight of Robin, he froze as though stunned, then leaped to his feet. His lips were trembling so much that Robin could only read his name as it was formed. Lurching around the desk, Thomas threw his arms around Robin and held him fast. Robin was crushed by the embrace, and he held just as fast to his uncle. When the big man drew back, there were tears in his fine eyes. "My boy! We thought you were lost!"

"I've been in a Spanish prison, Uncle," Robin said. He was shaken by the encounter, for he had longed every day of his captivity for the sight of his dear uncle. "I sent you one letter— but it must have miscarried."

"It never came," Thomas said. He bit his lips, then pulled himself together. "You shouldn't give an old man such a fright, Robin!" Then he said, "Come, we'll have to tell Martha."

"Where are Mary and Robert?" Robin asked eagerly. "Not a day's gone by that I didn't think of them." He caught the look of anguish that swept over his uncle's face and knew that something was wrong.

"We—lost Rob, my boy."

Robert had been the pride of his father's life, and Robin saw that the grief was like a raw wound for his uncle. And it was like a sword in his own heart, for Robin had loved the bright youngster deeply. "How did it happen?"

"The plague. We almost lost Mary as well, but she finally recovered." Thomas's shoulders sagged, and his eyes were stricken. "Well, God must give us comfort. Come along, we will find Martha—and then we'll tell Mary."

The news of his cousin's death palled Robin's joy at his homecoming. Thomas tried to be cheerful—and he was indeed filled with gratitude to have his nephew back. The two men spent much time together, hunting and simply tramping through the fields. Somehow the loss of Robert drew them closer together than they'd ever been, and once Thomas said, "I have no son, Robin. You will wear the title after me."

"No fear of that," Robin said quickly. "You'll become an admiral and outlive me fifty years."

Thomas didn't comment, but changed the subject. "You must go to the queen at once. She grieved over you, Robin." The two of them stopped on the crest of a hill, and Thomas let his eyes move over the valley below. "She's afraid of death, you know. Not for herself, I think, but for what it can take from her. She clings to people, and when death steals them away, she dies a little with them, it seems."

"Is she well?"

"Yes, but these are hard times." Thomas looked at him, shaking his head. "There was yet another plot against her life."

"What happened?"

"Sir Francis Walsingham discovered that Mary had been in communication with the enemy, making plans to have Elizabeth assassinated. Walsingham devised an elaborate scheme to get solid evidence against Mary."

"I can't believe she'd do such a thing! Even though she wants to be queen, she'd not stoop to murder!"

"Yes, it's been proven that she would do just that—which Walsingham has insisted for years. Oh, the evidence is conclusive, I'm afraid. So strong that even Elizabeth couldn't ignore it."

Robin thought of the beautiful woman who'd stirred him so, and he shook his head slightly. "What will happen now?"

"I think that even Elizabeth will have to consider execution. It's what the entire Council has been urging for years, but the queen would never hear of it."

"I hope it doesn't come to that, Uncle."

Thomas gave his nephew a thoughtful examination. "You know Mary very well, don't you? Since you were a boy, really. What's she like? One hears such stories it's hard to know how to imagine her."

Robin hesitated, then said, "She's a strange woman. Terribly ambitious, of course. Once a woman's worn a crown—or a man, for that matter—there will always be something in them that longed for that power again."

"Very likely." Thomas shook his head. "Let's get back. I wrote a letter to the queen telling her of your safe return. You'll be sent for soon."

"When do you go to sea?" Robin asked at once. "I must go with you." He saw his uncle's interested look and knew he was wondering at Robin's intensity. But Robin felt his reasons were too personal to share. It was enough that he knew for himself that he had to go to sea to forget the one woman he would always love—but could not have.

"The queen may have other ideas." He grinned. "She usually

does. But I'd love to see you aboard the *Falcon,* Robin! Let's hope for that, in any case. Come now, let's be going."

The summons for Robin to attend the queen came the next day—in the form of a letter from Sir Francis Walsingham. Robin left the next morning, giving his cousin Mary a hug and tossing her into the air. "I'll bring you a pretty from London, sweetheart. You take care of your mother and father while I'm gone."

"I will, Cousin Robin," Mary exclaimed. She clung to him eagerly, and Robin thought of the days when Allison had been no older. He kissed her, then turned to his aunt. "Martha, you've taken good care of me. I hope you're feeling better soon." His uncle's wife, who had been afflicted with the plague that had taken her son, smiled wanly, saying, "Come back when you can, my dear. Mary misses you."

The two men walked outside, and when Robin swung into the saddle, Thomas looked up fondly. "Use all the charm you have to get the queen to let you make the voyage with me. Drake is planning something big, and he's invited me to join him with the *Falcon.* I'd like us to be together."

"I'll do my best. You know how I long for the sea."

Robin rode out of the gates and made a quick journey to London. He reported to Sir Francis Walsingham, who was delighted to see him. Robin was rather astonished at the warmth of the secretary's greeting, for he'd always thought the man rather withdrawn. There was, however, no mistaking the genuine welcome in the secretary's voice and expression. "Well, my boy, this is a happy day for me—and for the queen!" He shook Robin's hand, pumping it up and down, and drew him into his study. For the next two hours he listened avidly as Robin traced the history of the past months.

"That you are alive and here is a miracle from God, my dear

Robin!" he exclaimed, nodding his head. "No other explanation!"

"I believe you're right, sir," Robin answered. "And I thank him
for it." He related how he'd gotten close to God through the
experience, and Walsingham was highly pleased.

"Fine! Fine! Nothing like coming to the end of the tether to
make a man realize how close God is to him, is there?"

Finally Walsingham asked, "Did you hear anything about the
Armada while you were in Spain?"

"Why yes, a great deal. Everyone's talking about it, sir. Even the
peasants in the fields."

"So I understand. Did you hear anything specific? We have our
agents there, of course, but you were in a peculiar position. People
would have spoken freely in front of you."

Robin thought for a moment, then nodded. "There was a man
who came once to visit the Corona family. His name was don
Alvero. He was a nobleman of some sort——"

His interest kindled, Walsingham broke in. "Yes, indeed, he's the
marquis of Santa Cruz. Did you see him?"

"Only from a distance, sir. I was only a field servant—but one
of the house servants, a young lady, served at the table. She's a
clever girl, and as you might imagine, when she told me of the
conversation that went on, I listened closely."

"What did the girl say?"

"She said that the marquis was going to lead the Armada. Oh,
she was excited about it, sir, and very proud." Robin took a sip
of the wine that the secretary had provided, his mind going back
to his conversation with Anita. "She said that don Alfredo asked
the marquis how much chance there was for success. The marquis
told him that he'd have a fleet of two hundred ships, and that the
duke of Parma would lead a land army against England at the
same time the Armada struck."

"That report agrees with what my agents tell me. Did you see any of the ships?"

"There were always ships in the harbor of Cádiz, Sir Francis. . . ." Robin spoke for some time about what he'd been able to observe, then finally asked, "Can we endure such a force?"

"That's in God's hands," Walsingham said with a shrug. Then he smiled. "But God uses men, and as long as England has men like Hawkins and Drake and Howard—and like Robin Wakefield, I might add!—we can hope for victory!"

"Will the queen let me go with my uncle?"

Walsingham became elusive. "We will see what she says." He got up, saying, "Come now, my boy. She's most anxious to see you."

Robin followed the secretary to the large public room of the palace, and, seeing the large crowd made up of poor people, Walsingham said, "She's touching for the King's Evil," he whispered as the two drew closer. "We'll wait until she's finished."

Robin had always been fascinated by the disease and the cures. He'd heard of monarchs "touching" those afflicted with scrofula, but had never seen such a practice before. The disease was a rather frightening malady and from the time of Edward the Confessor was thought in England to be curable by the sovereign's touch. Robin had spoken of this to Kate Moody, and her answer had been, "Much disease goes deeper than the skin, boy! Sometimes it's in the mind. And when it's there, no herb can touch it. But I've seen strange things along this line. Because it's in the mind, as soon as the mind believes the disease is gone, why, the disease has to go!"

The queen was seated on a straight chair, and her attendants were keeping the crowd back. They allowed one supplicant at a time to approach Elizabeth, who put her hands on the person's head and seemed to pray.

Robin saw no "miracle" but was impressed with the compassion on Elizabeth's face. Walsingham whispered, "How often I've seen her exquisite hands touch the sores and ulcers with nothing but compassion on her face. Once in a single day she touched over a hundred victims!"

"Are they actually healed?"

"Ah, that's up to God!"

The two waited patiently. After the last of the sick had been touched, Elizabeth lifted her head and said in a rather sad voice, "Would that I could give you all help and succor. God . . . God is the best and greatest physician. You must pray to him!"

Then to Robin's surprise, she bowed her head and prayed. "Thou hast set me on high, O Lord. My flesh is frail and weak. If I at any time forget thee, touch my heart, O Lord, that I may again remember thee!"

"Sometimes I think," Walsingham said fervently, "that these are the queen's finest moments! Come along, Robin. We'll go to her chambers."

The two had to wait for nearly an hour, for the matron in charge of the maids of honor informed them that the queen required time to compose herself. The two waited in a small room, speaking quietly of the invasion Philip was planning.

"Drake wants to hit the Spanish where they live," the secretary said. "He feels that if he could take an Armada of our own, he could destroy Philip's fleet before they could attack."

Robin's imagination leaped at the idea. "Why, of course! That's what he wants with my uncle and his ship! Please, Sir Francis, you *must* persuade the queen to let me go on the *Falcon!*"

But he could wring no promise from Walsingham, and somehow he felt that some plan concerning himself had already been formed in the tall man's mind. Finally the matron came to say, "Her Majesty will receive you now."

The two men found the queen, not in her chamber, but in the extensive rose garden just outside. She was wearing one of her magnificent dresses, white and crimson satin sewn all over with pearls and tiny diamonds.

Robin knelt as she approached, kissed the hand she held out—noticing that it was firm and strong as always. "Robin! Thank God you've come back to me!" Robin rose at her bidding, and Elizabeth studied his face. "Like Myles Wakefield restored!" she exclaimed. Then she nodded. "You may go, Sir Francis!"

Sir Francis Walsingham, probably the second most powerful man in all of England, was accustomed to such treatment—as were all members of Elizabeth's council. He bowed. "Come to me when you are finished, Mister Wakefield."

"Come now, tell me of your capture," Elizabeth said, motioning to a bench. Robin repeated the story, and when he was finished, the queen said at once, "And the young woman, she's English, you say?"

"Yes, Your Majesty. I've known her since she was a child."

Elizabeth watched his face closely, her keen eyes seeming to take in every nuance of his expression. Of all the details of Robin's capture, she seemed most interested in this facet of the story. For half an hour she questioned him, then finally smiled. "She's not a little girl any longer, this Allison of yours, is she?"

Robin hardly knew how to answer. "No, Your Majesty. She's one of the loveliest young women in the world."

"And married to a Spanish don?"

"Y-yes, my queen."

Elizabeth studied his face, her smallish eyes thoughtful. Then she rose and seemed to put the matter aside. "Come and see my roses," she commanded. Soon Robin was admiring the tidy beds of roses blooming with such heavy loads of flowers on their stems that it seemed the branches might break for color, weight, and profusion. The south and west exposures of the walls were one mass of climbing roses, so that each brick had twenty blooms spread out upon it.

"You see these?" Elizabeth called his attention to the climbing roses by holding one in her white hand. "I started these years ago. I call them 'Savior's Blood.' Do you see the color?"

Robin stared at the blossom, then asked, "Can you obtain any color of rose, Your Majesty?"

"In time, perhaps."

He had a thought, and he touched the vine. "Would it be possible to produce a rose without a thorn?"

Elizabeth blinked with surprise. "The thorns seem to be a part of the flower, Robin. Some green, some sharper than others—but for every stem there must needs be thorns, I think."

"But if you tried?"

Elizabeth suddenly looked old. Her face was covered with white powder and, unlike her smooth hands, bore many wrinkles. She was, he knew, fifty-five years old, but as the sunlight illuminated her face, she looked ancient.

"A rose without thorns—" The words came as a whisper, and she stared blankly at the blossom in her hand. Then she lifted her eyes and shook her head, saying, "Life has its thorns. You're learning that, I sense. I have Philip and the Armada for my thorns, and you . . . you have the loss of the young woman in Spain." She smiled at his startled look. "You are very young, Robin, and have not learned to hide your feelings. You do love her, don't you?"

"Yes, Your Majesty, but it's hopeless. She will stay with her husband and be true to her marriage vows, though it's a bitter thing for her."

"Ah, she has her thorns, too, you see?" She turned the flower over in her hands and studied it. "How delicate—as fragile as our lives!"

It seemed to Robin that a strange mood settled over the queen, and he studied her as she began to speak softly, her eyes cloudy with memory.

"I remember my father as a young man, his days filled with

bone-shattering exercise—hunting, wrestling, riding. How he danced, too, vigorously and continuously, leaping and bounding with the abandon of a young stag!" Elizabeth touched her withered cheek with the fresh young rose, then went on. "I tell you, the ground shook under Henry VIII. He looked like a divinity, so huge and strong, wearing shimmering satins and thick, glowing brocades, his fingers gleaming with jeweled rings, his person aglow with gold!"

Then she crushed the delicate flower and let it fall to the ground. "And he has been dead for many years—and what did it all mean?"

"Your Majesty," Robin said at once, "you are feeling downcast today, but no one knows better than yourself that life *does* have meaning. Look at your own reign, how you have held this country together singlehandedly! We will both die, of course, but Englishmen will speak of Elizabeth as long as there is an England!"

The queen stared at him, and then color came to her cheeks. She put her hand out and let it rest on his arm. "You're so like your grandfather! Many times he would give me a cheering word when I felt lonely or sad. Now you, too, have blessed your sovereign, Robin Wakefield!"

"That is more reward than a man dare desire, Your Majesty!" He saw that she was weary, and soon she smiled and dismissed him, saying, "I will find you a companion. One who will do something to cause you to forget your young woman in Spain."

"That is impossible, even for the queen!"

"We shall see." She hesitated, then said, "You long for the sea, do you not?"

"More than anything, my queen!"

Elizabeth grew sober and cast a careful look at the young man. "You can serve me best in another way, Robin. And this is the test of a good soldier—to serve in a way he himself would not choose."

"How can I serve Your Majesty?"

She hesitated, then said almost painfully, "When Mary is executed, Philip will strike. There are many men who will serve bravely with the navy—but there is one thing that you can do that they cannot."

"Name it, Your Majesty!"

"Sir Francis mentioned it. He has contacts in Spain, and he wants to send an agent to be a part of the Armada!"

Robin stood absolutely still. "Why, that's not possible!"

"Sir Francis insists that it is," Elizabeth said intently. "Think what that would mean to our admiral and to his commanders! To get information from someone in the very center of the enemy's fleet!" She saw his downcast look and smiled gently. "Can you do this for your queen, Robin?"

Robin did not hesitate. "Yes, Your Majesty!"

Elizabeth kept her eyes on him. "So like your grandfather. I shall not forget this, Robin Wakefield. Go to Sir Francis now, but we will talk more."

Life turns on small things—so Robin Wakefield discovered. One conversation with a queen, and his entire life was wrenched from his ambitions and thrown into an intrigue that he hated. The court of any monarch of England seethed with intrigue. The coils of conspiracy and disloyalty wrapped themselves snakelike around almost every courtier, be he powerful or vulnerable, ultimately making him sacrifice everything—even his reputation and his life.

From the moment Sir Francis enlisted Robin, all ease was over for that young man. For months he studied with the secretary's clerks—learning all that could be learned from the agents. He spent hours practicing his Spanish. One good aspect emerged: He spent hours with the captains of the war vessels. He even spoke with Admiral Howard, who was deep into every aspect of the Armada.

And then, in February of 1587, he was called upon for special duty. "I want you to come with me," Walsingham said at the end of one of their meetings. The secretary's eyes were hard as he added, "I want you to witness the execution."

Robin had known that Mary was to die, but he shrank from the idea of being a witness. "Sir, must I?"

"You have a weakness for that woman!" Walsingham, who certainly had none, said. "She is the greatest enemy England has, and I want you to come to grips with what she is. You can't take with you any regrets about her when you go to Spain."

Robin nodded. "I will obey your orders, Sir Francis."

The next morning he went with Walsingham to the great hall of Fotheringay Castle. He stood rigidly as Mary, accompanied by six of her attendants, appeared at the appointed hour clad in black satin. A heaviness fell on Robin as he watched her walk with stately movements to the cloth-covered scaffold, which had been erected near the fireplace.

Mary of the Scots looked over the crowd, and her gaze came to rest on Robin. She made no sign, but he was certain that she recognized him.

The solemn formalities were smoothly completed, but the zealous dean of Peterborough attempted to force upon the queen a last minute conversion. With splendid dignity she brushed aside his loud exhortation. "Mr. Dean," she replied in ringing tones, "I am a Catholic and must die a Catholic."

Mary had arrayed herself superbly for the final scene of her life. As she disrobed for the headsman's axe, her garments of black satin were removed by the weeping handmaids, revealing a bodice and petticoat of crimson velvet. One of her ladies handed her a pair of crimson sleeves, which she put on. There was a deathly hush throughout the hall as she knelt . . . and at once the deed was done. The headsman reached down and lifted high the head of Mary Queen of Scots.

"Now that is over." Sir Francis took a deep breath as he and Robin left the hall. He stopped abruptly, directed his gaze on the young man, and said, "You have hated Catholics all your life. This should have made you happy."

Robin lifted his head and spoke in an even voice. "No, sir, it did not."

Sir Francis's eyes narrowed. "I perceive you have weakened in your feelings. Do you feel capable of serving as the queen's agent?"

Robin nodded stiffly. "Yes, I will serve my country and my queen. What I will not do is rejoice over the death of a tragic and pitiful woman!"

Strangely enough, Walsingham seemed to approve of this speech. "Yes, we must not lose our compassion." He nodded, then he said suddenly, "You leave for Spain tomorrow, if you are ready."

Robin inclined his head, his lips tight. "I will do my best."

"That, sir," Walsingham said grimly, "is all that any of us can do—and what we *must* do if England is to be saved!"

The next day Robin left England, bound in a roundabout journey for Spain. And even as his thoughts had been of Allison as he'd left Spain, so now they leaped ahead to the image of her eyes and her smile as the ship rose and fell, cleaving the green water, bearing him closer to his mission—and his destiny.

Twenty-three

A STRANGE SORT OF ENGLISHMAN

And so you still insist that you know nothing of the man called Roberto? That he was nothing to you?"

The voice of the Grand Inquisitor shook with pious fury. It was the fourth day of the inquisition of the Englishwoman, Allison Corona, and she had known little respite. Father Cortez and other agents of the Inquisition had questioned her for hours, and now her eyes were hollow from lack of sleep as she said quietly, "There was nothing between us, Father. He was a servant who did his work."

"But it was *you* who asked that he be hired!"

"He had some experience in gardening, and we needed more help. I hired several men for work like that."

"But you did know he was an Englishman?"

"He said he was Norwegian."

The Grand Inquisitor ground his teeth with rage. He and the others had tried every way they could devise to entrap the young woman, but she sat there with that infernal calmness on her face, never showing fear or anger. In all the inquisitions they had done, none of them had ever experienced anything similar to this. Father Cortez finally said in private, "I believe she's telling the truth. No guilty woman could keep this up for so long without giving herself away!"

But the Grand Inquisitor was not convinced. His hatred of the English would not let him rest. "Your husband has sworn that he saw you and the Englishman making love." When the young woman said nothing, he shouted, "Well? It's true isn't it?"

"No, it is not."

The simplicity of her answers only seemed to anger the Grand Inquisitor. "Will you make the sign of the cross before us, before the Savior, his Holy Mother, and all the saints that you are innocent, that you did not make love to this man and that you played no part in his escape?"

Allison drew herself up and spoke with complete control. "With God as my judge, Father, I swear before you that my conscience is clear."

The Inquisitor took out a large silk handkerchief and pressed it against his forehead. His dark eyes moved sideways over his assistants, but he saw nothing in their faces. *They have been charmed by her pretty face,* he thought angrily, *but she will not have me so easily!*

"Allison Corona, taking into consideration the faithfulness and loyalty of the Corona family, I have decided on a course of great leniency. There is no doubt in my own mind that you have been deeply immersed in the slough of mortal sin, and to save your soul, much penance is necessary."

"As you will, Father," Allison said quietly. Despite himself, the Inquisitor could not stop the thought that she looked as innocent as the Blessed Virgin herself! But his mind was made up, so he spoke harshly.

"It is my decision that you will be placed in seclusion, under the charge of Father Cortez. You will be belted and shaved and are to wear only a single shift of coarse cloth so that you will be reminded of your deceits and misdeeds. You are to eat only the food of servants. When Father Cortez feels that you have regained your state of grace, your case will be reviewed. If a good report is *not* forthcoming, you may have one last opportunity to offer up your vile body in a true act of faith. Now may God grant you the will through penance to save your mortal flesh from the temporal fire and your immortal soul from the eternal fires of hell. In the name of the Father, and of the Son, and of the Holy Ghost. Amen."

The execution of Mary Queen of Scots brought outrage to the continent. The shock waves radiated first to Paris, where the court went into full mourning, then to the palace where King Philip administered his empire, then to Rome, where priests reviled Elizabeth, the murderous "Whore of Babylon"; and the cry went up, "Arise, Lord, and vindicate thy cause."

The demands for an invasion of England rose to a hysterical pitch, and when King Philip finally bowed to the pressure and gave orders for the Enterprise of England, as the invasion was called, to be launched, a great sigh of relief went up in Spain, and every able-bodied man of spirit considered it his pious duty to offer his services.

Cádiz, like every other city in Spain, was in a ferment of excitement. The streets were full of gallants, ships were arriving every week, and the talk in all the inns and lodging houses was of the Enterprise of England. When the ship *Fortune* arrived from Rome, the sail was struck and salutes were exchanged with the guard ship and the harbor battery, the long sweeps dipped in unison, and the great ship slid in past the Punta Candelaria and came to anchor among the other ships of the great fleet.

Within minutes the oars were stored and a flotilla of tenders and barges was taking off stores and ferrying the officers and passengers ashore.

Among the people being ferried was Robin Wakefield.

He was dressed in cloak, buff jerkin, velvet venetians, and

buckled shoes. Stepping ashore at the landing stage below the city battery, he was met by an ensign on the staff of General Savaldo.

Though it was still early the city was bustling with activity. Morning sun was streaming down between the adobe buildings, and the narrow alleys were full of street traders, donkey carts, washerwomen, and slaves. In the marketplace, hundreds of chained blacks were being herded, groaning and wailing, into enclosures for the auction to be held that day. The young ensign stroked his bushy mustache and smiled at Robin. "You like our city?"

"It is very beautiful," Robin answered in flawless Spanish.

"We are very busy these days." The ensign nodded. "We will conquer the English soon." He led Robin into the city, and they reached the cathedral square. Inland a veil of mist lay like gossamer on the Andalusian hills, and to the south the long white beaches glittered in the morning sun. When the cathedral bell clanged as they passed, Robin dropped to his knees, making the sign of the cross. The ensign looked on, somewhat abashed at such piety, then cleared his throat and said, "We will go now."

Robin was guided to a large whitewashed building and then to an office on the second floor. A short, muscular man with white hair was sitting behind a table littered with papers. The ensign said, "Sir, this gentleman is Mister Robert Hawkins. Señor Hawkins, you stand before General Miguel Savaldo."

The general stared at Robin, then sneered. "Another knight in shining armor, I suppose." He took the paper Robin handed him, and his eyebrows went up when he saw the papal seal. Robin smiled slightly. Apparently the small fortune Walsingham had paid for that seal was now justified! The general handed the letter back and stared for a moment at the tall young man. "So you are to be billeted here."

"Yes, General. I have been sent to assist the Holy Enterprise in any way I can."

"And what can you do?"

"I have served as an aide to a distant relative, Admiral Hawkins. That might be of some value to your admiral, I feel."

Savaldo's eyebrows ascended again. "Ah? And how did that happen?"

"My father was a ship owner, sir. I learned the trade of a sailor and became an excellent navigator. Admiral Hawkins is always anxious to find men with this ability."

"I daresay he is." The man regarded him with cold eyes. "And how does an Englishman come to speak Spanish so well?"

Robin had a ready answer, for he and his mentors in England had anticipated the question. "I learned it in a Spanish prison." The eyebrows moved upward and he added, "I was on board a small craft that was captured off the coast."

"And you escaped, I suppose?"

"No, my father paid a large ransom for my freedom. It is not, General Savaldo, an easy way to learn a language."

Savaldo suddenly laughed and slapped his hard palm down on the table, sending papers flying. "I learned my English in an English prison, Mr. Hawkins, so I know what you say is true!" Somehow the fact that they both had been in prison seemed to loosen the general. "Come, I will introduce you to the admiral, the marquis of Santa Cruz."

An hour later the two men stood on the shore and viewed the fleet. "What a truly magnificent sight!" Robin exclaimed, then blinked with surprise at Salvado's contemptuous snort. He glanced at the older man. "Do you have doubts that the Enterprise will succeed?"

"I believe it *can* succeed, certainly. But our task would be a great deal easier if the king would listen more to the marquis and less to the duke of Parma." Doubt filled the man's dark eyes, and he muttered, "It's all very well to call this Armada 'invincible,' but to my mind a fleet is invincible only when it has proven to be so in battle."

"Do you have so little faith in the power of our Lady and all the saints, General? Our cause is a holy one and blessed by Christ's vicar on earth."

But the stocky general shook his head, saying, "Come, we will go aboard the admiral's flagship." He commandeered a small boat, and while they were moving across the sparkling green water, he began to speak again. "The Armada has little organization and is short of provisions. And it's a mistake to split the invasion between Parma and the marquis. We asked for 150 ships and got 90! Well, we'll do our best, of course, but I wouldn't be surprised if we had to wait another year."

The admiral was gone, they discovered, but the general persuaded his second in command to accept Hawkins as an adviser on English pilotage and naval tactics. It was a fantastic stroke of good fortune to become a member of the officers' mess, and that night in the privacy of his cabin Robin wrote his first report in code. Though a garbled mess to untrained eyes, he knew Walsingham's agents would get the message.

Great ships lying at Cádiz. Preparations hindered by lack of funds. Planned departure end of July, but shortage of stores may cause further delay. Six galleys defend the harbor. Few ships are manned or gunned for war. Few of the city's cannon bear on the harbor. Squadron of galleons could wreak much damage.

The next morning he met his contact agent in the marketplace, and the message was on its way back to Walsingham and Admiral Howard. It seemed a small thing, but Robin had done all he could for his queen.

Casa Loma was set on a hill, and on the night of April 19, 1587, all eyes were drawn to the hundreds of candles and lamps servants lit as night fell. Even the lowest of servants sensed that something important was taking place—and it was Carlos, the butler, who expressed the thing.

"It's because the wife of don Jaime has returned." He nodded wisely at Delores, his wife and the cook. "And she's still the same. The Inquisition made a mistake about her. She was innocent of any wrongdoing."

"Shut your mouth, fool!" Delores looked around nervously, then hissed, "You know what happens to those who criticize the Inquisition!"

But Carlos was a stubborn man and muttered defiantly, "We know what her husband is. He has no honor!" He moved around the kitchen sniffing the food that simmered in iron pots and skillets. "This had better be good. You know who the guest of honor is."

"Some sailor, I hear."

Carlos gave her a withering look. " '*Some sailor,*' " he mimicked. "It's the marquis of Santa Cruz, the admiral who will lead the Invincible Armada!"

Indeed it was a signal event. Ever since Allison had been taken to do penance under the tender mercies of the Inquisition there had been no banquets or celebrations at Casa Loma. Neither don Alfredo nor doña María had wanted company. But now that Allison had returned, they felt it wise to show their welcome to her with a dinner.

"And what better way than by having the famous marquis as our guest," don Alfredo had said.

Jaime had promised to attend—and even as the guests were gathering, he had come to Allison's room. She had not seen him since her return, but one look and she knew he had not changed. He came to pace behind her as she sat at her dressing table. "Well, the naughty wife is back in her husband's arms, eh?" When he saw that she wouldn't turn to look at him, he grabbed her shoulders and forced her to face him. "You should be dead. Why aren't you dead? I thought I took care of you long ago. . . ." His voice trailed off, and the dazed look in his eyes let Allison know that he was talking to Rosalita again, not to her. Suddenly his gaze focused on her face, and he stepped back as though she were a viper he had suddenly discovered hiding under the covers. "If the Inquisition had anyone but that fool Securo at its head, you'd have been burned at the stake!" he snarled.

"I'm sorry you feel that way, Jaime," Allison said calmly. The long weeks she'd been away had been a time of loneliness and prayer for her. She had not minded the poor food and the lack of conveniences; her dark night of the soul was over. She once again knew the presence of her Lord. The sense of Jesus had been so real to her that the days had passed unnoticed. When Father Cortez had come to tell her that he was sending her home, she had been rather dismayed, concerned that the peace she had come to love would be broken by don Jaime.

Now she stood and faced him, noting that he had gained weight and his eyes were red-rimmed from drink. "Please, Jaime, I am not your enemy," she said with quiet sincerity. "Can't we try to be kind to one another?"

Jaime stared at her, blinking in confusion. She wondered if he had expected anger from her, but she felt none of that. Only the desire to live peacefully and to help her husband, if she could.

"Why don't you go back to England?" he asked suddenly.

"I'm your wife. Only death can change that."

He stared at her, then said sharply, "Come, we'll go down together. I'd like to please the marquis." As they left her bedroom and moved toward the stairs, he added, "I want something from

340

him." He caught her look of surprise and laughed that self-pleased, chilling laugh. "I'm going to be an ambassador, dear wife. An ambassador in France. That's what I want, to live in France with people who will treat me well."

Allison frowned, unable to understand her husband's reasoning. But she had long ago learned that what made sense to don Jaime seldom made sense to anyone else. So she only looked at him with curiosity. "How can the marquis help you, Jaime? Doesn't the king choose ambassadors?"

"Yes, but the king is listening to the marquis right now. Be nice to the old man, tell him how brilliant your husband is—and how you'd like to go to France." He actually seemed serious, as though he truly understood—and wanted—what he was saying. "If we could get away, things might be different." He looked around nervously, as though expecting to find someone following them or listening to them. He stopped and turned to face her, dropping his voice to a low whisper. "I'd get you your own apartment, Rosalita. You could have your own life—and I could have mine. We would never have to meet, and I would not have to make you go away. . . ."

His voice trailed off as he looked at her, confusion again filling his eyes. He tilted his head to one side as he stared at her. "I thought you were gone. . . ?" Then he shrugged and grasped her arm, urging her toward the dining room.

They entered the room and Jaime led her to the head table, where they greeted his parents. "The marquis and his staff have just arrived," don Alfredo told them. "We'll get the latest on the Armada from him."

Allison sat down, and in a few moments the marquis and his staff of three entered. Allison had met him before at the Corona house, but she noted how he'd aged since their last meeting. Then she heard him introducing his staff. The names meant nothing to her. She nodded at the first two soldiers in fine uniforms—and then her mind seemed to stop, for the third man was Robin Wakefield!

He looked nothing like Roberto, the servant. He stood tall and strong, and a neat beard covered the lower part of his face. Still, she wondered that no one had challenged him. He bowed over her hand and kissed it, as had the other officers, but said nothing. His eyes, however, spoke volumes. For one moment their glances locked, and she felt the force of his love sweep over her.

The guests were seated and the food was brought in, but sumptuous as the fare was, everyone at the table was more interested in the marquis than in eating. Finally he smiled and said, "You are all wondering about the Great Enterprise. Well, I may as well tell you about it. That is the only way you will enjoy your meal. Or perhaps I will let my staff inform you." His eyes ran over the men he'd brought, and he said suddenly, "We have a most interesting officer with us, an Englishman, Ensign Robert Hawkins."

Don Jaime exclaimed, "An Englishman? Your queen is a trollop and a murderess!"

Without blinking an eye, Robin said calmly, "I am not of her party, sir. I have come as a servant of the Holy Father, to help with the Great Enterprise and win England back for Spain."

"We have examined Ensign Hawkins's credentials closely, you may be sure, don Jaime," the marquis remarked. "He is loyal."

"I would like to hear what Ensign Hawkins has to say," don Alfredo said quietly. "I favor the old fashioned way to battle: grapple with the enemy and board him."

"Right!" one of the lieutenants rapped out. "Our ships can row rings around the English! You don't deny that, do you, Hawkins?"

Carefully Robin said, "I agree that if the English keep their distance they will be able to do little damage against the strong timbers of our ships, but their hulls are as strong as ours. Therefore, I believe that we must engage them as closely as we may." This was the sort of misdirection that Robin and Walsingham had agreed must be fed to the Spanish command, and Robin argued it well.

The marquis was pleased with the young Englishman, and he spoke freely of the difficulties of getting supplies. He paused after a time and said, "I have come to make a request of the house of Corona."

Eagerly don Alfredo nodded. "It is granted, sir! We will do anything to assist you!"

The marquis inclined his head in thanks. "I take you at your word, don Alfredo." He smiled slightly and said, "I ask you to lend your name to the Enterprise, and I ask for a token of your willingness to aid the cause." He looked straight at don Jaime. "It would be my wish that the son of don Alfredo de Corona would serve under me."

Allison shot a look at her husband and saw that he had gone pale as paste at the marquis' words. "Sir!" he stammered, "I am not a soldier, nor a sailor, either!"

"No, but you are a Corona," the marquis said evenly. "And the nation is looking to the nobility to join in this venture. We will . . . find a place for you."

Don Jaime was trapped, and he knew it. One look at his father's stern face, and he well understood to refuse would bring dishonor on his father's house—and that would mean being disinherited. His father's sense of loyalty and honor was tremendous. He could not argue against that and win.

Swallowing hard, he looked back to the marquis. "Certainly, sir, it is a great honor." But his whining tone belied the words.

The marquis seemed not to notice. "Splendid! Report for duty aboard my flagship tomorrow." The marquis well knew how worthless young Corona would be as a fighting man, but he also knew that once don Alfredo's son was actively engaged in the venture, he would support the cause with his purse. And he was certain they could find a place for Corona that would keep him under strict surveillance and out of the way. "Now, let us enjoy our dinner," he said, turning to his food.

The company ate well, all except don Jaime. He merely picked at his food, and after the meal he excused himself, saying in a thin voice, "I must prepare for tomorrow. I'm going to sea."

Coffee and cakes were served, and the guests wandered about, most of them clustering around the marquis. Robin was standing next to Allison and bowed in a courtly gesture.

"Señora Corona, the marquis has told me of your splendid collections of paintings. Would I be permitted to see them?"

"Of course!" Don Alfredo beamed and nodded toward Allison. "Show the gentleman to the gallery, my dear."

"Yes, sir."

Allison's heart was beating fast, but she said nothing until the two of them were alone in the long gallery. She closed the doors as they entered, then, certain they were away from anyone who could overhear them, she turned to look at him with wide eyes. "Robin, you must be insane!"

He ignored her words, but reached out and took her hands. "You're more lovely than ever," he whispered. "I've thought about you every day since I left."

"You mustn't!" she protested, but could not free her hands from his grasp. "Why did you come back?"

"I'm an agent of the English government, Allison. I've sworn to do all I can to prevent the Armada from conquering my country."

Allison was breathing rapidly, shaken by his very presence. He was so handsome in his uniform, and the memory of the time they had been together while she cared for him when he was sick and raging with fever washed over her. "Please be careful!" she said. "If anything happened to you—!"

He reached out to take her hand and drew it to his lips, pressing a kiss into her palm. It was all he dared do, he knew. As much as he longed to hold her, to feel his lips on hers, she was a married woman. He had ignored that fact only once, and out of respect for her and for the sanctity of the vows she had made, he would never do so again. But that did not stop his heart from loving her more than he had ever dreamed possible. And he knew that he would never marry another, even if a time never came when they could be together.

His blue-gray eyes were dark with his feelings as he met and held her gaze. "We Wakefield men love only one woman, and out of all the women on earth, you are the one for me, Allison. I'll love you as long as there's breath in my body." She started to speak, but his look stopped her. "I know that nothing can come of my love, not as long as you are married to don Jaime. Though my heart cries out for me to take you away from this torturous life you endure, I will honor your decision to remain. And I will entrust you to God's care. Now you must do the same with me, believing that God is with me and that nothing beyond his care will happen to me."

Wordlessly, she nodded, stirred deeply by his words and by the expression in his eyes. The urge to tell him how she felt welled up within her. "Robin——," she said, but whatever she was going to say was cut off when a sudden shout and then a babble of voices came from the main section of the house.

"Something's happened," Robin said, and they hurried back to the dining room, where the group had gathered around an officer who was dusty from a quick ride on the road.

"What is it?" Robin asked one of his fellow officers.

"Drake! Drake is raiding Cádiz!"

Without another word, the marquis raced from the room. Robin followed, joining him in the carriage with the other members of the staff. As they traveled, they spoke in clipped voices.

"What does this mean, sir?" one of the men asked the marquis. His only response was a stony silence.

At last the carriage stopped, and they piled out—only to stand in stunned silence as they gazed at the scene before them. The harbor was ablaze with burning ships!

The marquis stood looking at the sight, his face filled with a cold fury. When he spoke, his voice shook with the rage running through him. "Gentlemen, this means that the Great Enterprise will be delayed for a year! That man Drake!" he spat out the Englishman's name as though it were something vile and obscene. "He's done this to us!"

Cries of anger and rage went around the group, and Robin joined in the outcry. But he saw a ship in the distance, pounding the Spanish galleons—and recognized it as the *Falcon!*

Give it to them, Thomas, he cried in his spirit. *I'd love to be beside you throwing iron at Philip's Armada!* He longed to shout and wave and cheer—instead he stayed there until midnight, when the English fleet finally caught the breeze and, following Drake's lantern, the ships slipped out one by one.

The daring of one man had set King Philip of Spain, the most powerful monarch on the face of the earth, back on his heels! The Armada would have to be rebuilt—and Robin prayed that the time it would take to do so would give England the time to build ships and ready themselves to meet the Spanish fleet when it finally came.

Twenty-four

THE ARMADA SAILS

Almost a year later, Robin walked in the orchards at Casa Loma, studying the bare branches of the fig trees. Beside him don Jaime Corona paced, complaining bitterly of the impossibility of the task Robin had brought from the admiral. The fleet had been assembled at Lisbon, and Robin made the journey to Cádiz at least once a week.

"I tell you, Hawkins, it's impossible!" His round face was wan with the strain of the task the marquis had assigned to him—keeping all the paperwork for the Great Enterprise. It was Robin who had tactfully suggested this to the marquis, for he had become a liaison between the commanders of the fleet and Jaime Corona. It had given him a reason to come to Casa Loma often, and during the past months he had become a welcome guest there. It gave him some sort of grim satisfaction to be treated so after having been a serf laboring in the fields.

Now he watched don Jaime pace the floor. "I cannot produce the official *relación* as a man would produce a penny from his pocket!" don Jaime groaned. The *relación* was the complete inventory of all supplies and equipment for 130 ships and thousands of men who would be on them. The younger Corona had thrown himself into the task, hoping to convince the marquis that he was efficient, determined to have a post in France. But the job had

347

turned into a nightmare! His efforts to bring even a semblance of order to this vast chaotic collection of ships and men had only resulted in a sense of despair, in strain, and even in illness.

If it had been any other man in such a position, Robin might have felt some pity. As it was, he simply watched the agitated man with detachment. "The marquis says it must be done, sir. The king himself has ordered that the Armada must sail on February the fifteenth, even if only forty ships sail. He orders that you print the *relación* at least one week before that date."

Corona threw up his pudgy hands in a hopeless gesture. "How can I print the list if the list is not complete? You must speak to him, Señor Hawkins! He listens to you!"

If Corona had even guessed at how pleased the tall Englishman had been at the chaos that had marred the invasion plans, he would have been shocked. But Robin let none of his exultation show as he replied with apparent sympathy, "I understand your problems, don Jaime, but the marquis is firm on this. Why don't you make out the entire *relación,* every item, but leave the numbers out where they are not available? Then you can begin and print each list as it becomes complete."

Don Jaime's face lit up, and he clapped his tall companion on the shoulder, exclaiming, "Excellent! Why didn't I think of that?"

"It requires the mind of a clerk, sir," Robin replied modestly. "Really the nobility should not be required to dabble in such mundane matters."

"Why, I believe you're right, Hawkins! My normal business ventures are much more complex. Now, come into the house and we'll have some wine. I'll give you what is done so far on the list for the marquis."

The two entered the house, where they were met by doña María. "Ah," she said with a gracious smile, "I was just coming to find you and invite you to join us for tea."

"Go with her, Hawkins," Jaime said. "I'll go get those papers."

Robin followed doña María into the large living room, where don Alfredo and Allison were already seated. "Come and join us," the old man said, smiling warmly. "Did you and my son complete your business?"

"Don Jaime is collecting some papers for me to take to the marquis," Robin said. "How are you today, sir? And you, señora?"

Over the past months, Allison had learned to keep a calm expression whenever Robin came to the house. While they had not been alone together more than half a dozen times since the night Drake had singed the beard of the king of Spain by raiding Cádiz, they saw each other several times a week in the presence of others. She nodded and spoke pleasantly, then sat quietly as the two men discussed the Armada.

Finally a servant came to say, "Don Alfredo, a messenger for you. He insists on a private audience."

Corona got to his feet. "Excuse me, Señor Hawkins," and left the room. His wife rose and followed him, saying, "I must see to the servants. Entertain our guest, Allison."

Robin suddenly smiled and said, "Yes, entertain your guest, Allison."

"Shall I read to you, Señor Hawkins? I have some excellent sermons that would do your soul much good."

"No, I'd rather go outside with you and hunt for bird's eggs."

She dropped her eyes, a small smile playing at her lips. "An activity I greatly enjoyed as a child, sir. Did you do so as well?" she murmured in a low voice.

"Of course."

"I think of those times almost every day," she said, and her face fell into repose. Watching her, Robin admired the clean sweep of her jaw and the fine texture of her skin. "I recall once finding a nest of baby larks." She slanted a look at him. "I was out exploring with a very dear friend."

"I'll wager it was in April," he said at once, doing his best not to give in to the smile that tugged at him. "Their parents probably were killed by a hawk. And I can imagine you taking the fledglings to your house and keeping them alive by feeding them worms dug out of the garden."

"Indeed," she said, her eyes twinkling. "Though it surprises me that you should know me so well." She rose and went to the window to stare out.

He came at once to stand beside her. When she turned to him, he felt as though her violet eyes filled his world. There was a gentleness and goodness in Allison that seemed to touch everyone she came close to. His grandmother had been like that, and he often thought of Hannah when he looked at the young woman.

"Let me guess," he said with a grin. "I daresay you even *named* your three birds!"

She stared at him in surprise. "Even if I did, no one would remember such a thing!"

"I'll wager you I can guess those names, señora. If I can't, I'll bring you a bottle of scent from town."

"And what will I pay if I lose?"

Suddenly all teasing was gone from his eyes, and his answer was low and solemn. "If I had my way, Allison, your fine and wonderful self."

At once she turned and stared out the window, for she didn't want him to see the desire in her eyes. *I must stop this at once!* she thought, struggling to catch her breath. When she spoke, her voice was barely above a whisper, though she couldn't have said whether it was from caution or the effect Robin was having on her. "You must not speak of such things, Robin. I have told you before. And if you continue to do so, I—I must refuse to see you."

"I will only think them, then," he said. "A man can think as he likes, even you must admit that—" He broke off, turning at a sound at the doorway. Raising his voice, he spoke as though in the middle of a discussion: "And so we must see to the guns before we leave——"

Don Alfredo stood in the doorway, his face pale. "I have the most terrible news!"

"What is it, sir?"

"I have just received word . . . that don Alvaro de Bazan, marquis of Santa Cruz . . . is dead!"

Shock ran along Robin's nerves and he gasped, "But—I saw him only two days ago!"

"His heart." Don Alfredo nodded, sadness in his fine old eyes. "He always hoped to die in battle, but he went in his sleep." Shaking his head he asked plaintively, "What will happen to the Enterprise of England now that he is gone?"

Doña María came to place her arm around him. "God will send us a man," she whispered.

For a fortnight, all Spain mourned the passing of the man who had won so many glorious victories and whose confident promise to win back England for Spain had spurred King Philip into authorizing the assembly of the mightiest Armada the world had ever seen.

In Madrid, bells tolled all day, and Masses for the repose of the marquis's soul were said in every chapel and at every altar, while the admirals, generals, and staff officers whispered nervously to each other in the halls and corridors. Preparations for the Enterprise—for which the late marquis had worked himself to death—came to a complete halt for a week.

But plans were far too advanced for the Armada to be dispersed, and King Philip, who had delayed so long, was now afire with enthusiasm to press ahead. The fated year of 1588 had come at last, and all Europe waited with bated breath for the cataclysm that seemed to lie ahead.

The official word on the successor for the marquis came a week after his funeral, and Philip's choice was don Alonso Pérez de Guzmán el Bueno, the duke of Medina Sidonia. Robin waited anxiously for the duke's appearance, knowing that the British commanders would need an appraisal of their new adversary.

But the man who arrived in Cádiz was not at all the sort of person Robin had expected. Instead of being a buff military type, the duke of Medina Sidonia looked exactly what he was: a self-effacing, elderly country gentleman who was unused to war and all too conscious of his inadequacy to carry the great burden of responsibility the king had practically forced him to shoulder.

He also had a runny nose, and it was soon evident that the new captain general of the Spanish Armada always caught cold when he went in a boat!

"The duke," Robin put in a report to Walsingham, "takes a far different approach to the Enterprise than his predecessor. Santa Cruz imposed his will upon his subordinates, but Medina Sidonia readily admits his inexperience in naval tactics. He is not the warrior that the marquis was, thus will be less daring."

Still, while the duke was no warrior, he was an excellent administrator. Under his hand chaos became order. As spring approached, the books were balanced, the soldiers were paid, and new additions to the fleet were brought in, swelling the total number to 150.

Robin noted that many of the ships were unfit for battle, some of them rotten below the waterline. He put this information into a report, adding, "Stores arriving by wagon train are off-loaded into the first barge available and dumped into the first ship willing to take them. Mountains of biscuit go moldy in the warehouse. Some ships have more than their full complement of cannon but no round shot, while others are loaded to the gunwales with ball of too great a caliber for their light guns. Some of the warships are being converted to freighters to carry the huge mountains of food, powder, and shot required for the army abroad."

He passed the report to his confederate as quickly as possible, but learned that there had been no hurry. It had already been more than a year since the queen of England had had her cousin beheaded, and all Catholic Christendom had been pressuring Philip to avenge her death. The sailing date had been fixed for the end of April, and the atmosphere of expectation in Lisbon became almost tangible.

Every day long lines formed at confessionals in the churches and monasteries. The duke of Medina Sidonia had ordered that every man who sailed with the Armada must do so in a state of grace, having confessed his sins and received the Holy Sacrament. No women were to be permitted aboard any ship, no blasphemous or foul language was to be allowed, and immoral conduct of any sort was to be punished severely by the ninescore priests and friars who would be with the fleet.

April went by, then May arrived with the worst weather in living memory. Day after day, gales and storms lashed in from the Atlantic, and day after day—for another twenty days—the departure of the Invincible Armada was postponed.

Finally, inevitably, the day arrived. Don Alfredo had come with his family to Lisbon to see don Jaime off, and the night before the departure, Robin joined them for the farewell supper. Don Jaime was pale and drank much, and his parents were exhausted with the activities.

"They shouldn't have come," Robin murmured to Allison after the meal. The two of them were sitting on the balcony looking down on the forest of masts that filled the harbor. "They're too old for all this."

"They think it might be the last time they'll see their son," Allison answered. Casting her glance down over the streets that were packed with jostling crowds, she added rather sadly, "Many of those who leave will never come back. Their women are holding on to them until the last minute. That's what don Alfredo and doña María are doing."

"How can they love him?" Robin mused. "He's torn their hearts to shreds for years—and even now they love him."

"Love doesn't change."

Robin stared at her with astonishment. "You don't believe that!"

"Yes, I do." She smiled at his expression. "God's love never changes, does it? He knew what we were before he sent Jesus to die for our sins. And as terrible as men and women have been, he loves us still."

"Oh well, that's *God.*" Robin shrugged. "But human beings aren't like that."

"Some of them are." She had a thought and smiled at him. "You've told me so much about your grandparents. Why, you told me once that they loved each other more when they were old than they did when they were young!"

"Why, that's so." He closed his eyes, thinking of the pair that had been so dear to him, and then opened them. "I give you that, Allison. Their love never changed—except to grow greater, perhaps."

They sat there quietly, listening to the voices that floated up to them from the street below. A minstrel wandered by, his song plaintive and sad. Inside the house the family sat talking quietly, and finally a thought came to Robin. "I ran across a poem I liked a few years ago when I was in court."

"You didn't write it?"

"Oh, no! Chap named Shakespeare wrote it—an actor, I believe. The queen was fond of his plays. I went with her and her party to see one of them at a theater called the Globe. Didn't understand much of it myself, but the queen was delighted."

"Do you have a copy of the poem?"

"Up here." Robin grinned as he tapped his temple. "I liked it so much I started saying lines of it, and I found out one day I'd memorized the whole thing!"

"I'd like to hear it, Robin."

"Would you? Well, it goes like this:

"Let me not to the marriage of true minds
Admit impediments. Love is not love
Which alters when it alteration finds,
Or bends with the remover to remove:
Oh, no! it is an ever fixed mark,
That looks on tempests and is never shaken;
It is the star to every wandering bark,
Whose worth's unknown, although his height be taken.
Love's not Time's fool, though rosy lips and cheeks
Within his bending sickle's compass come;
Love alters not with his brief hours and weeks,
But bears it out even to the edge of doom:
If this be error and upon me proved,
I never writ, nor no man ever loved."

Allison had listened to him, her lips parted and her eyes fixed on his face. When he finished, she cried, "Why, that's what I believe! 'Love is not love which alters when it alteration finds.' We don't stop loving people when they change."

"Many people do," Robin said, sadness in his tone. Then he looked at her and said huskily, "That's why I loved my grandparents. I knew no matter what I did or what I became, they'd always love me. And that's how I know I love you."

"Robin—!" she protested, but he held up his hand.

"Just let me say this, and I will say no more. You were right about this voyage. Many of us won't survive. So I want you to know that what I feel for you is different from what I have felt for other women." He touched her smooth hand, trying to find the words to say what was in his heart. Finally he looked into her eyes. "The poet said that he'd love his sweetheart even though rosy lips and cheeks will fade with time. I saw that in my grandfather—he loved my grandmother when she was no longer young and beautiful."

"Robin, we can never—"

"I know, you have a husband. I can't help that. But I want you to know Allison, when you're an old woman with gray hair and a wrinkled face, I believe I will still love you as I do this moment."

She turned her face away, and she could not hold back the tears. When she turned to him, she whispered, "And I'll always love you that way, Robin. I always have, even when I was a little girl."

He wanted to take her in his arms—but that was impossible. They sat there thinking of the future, and finally when he got up and said his farewells, he bent over her hand, kissed it, then nodded. "I covet your prayers, Señora Corona."

The two of them went to join the Coronas, and Robin kissed doña María's hand in farewell, too. As he left the room, doña María began to weep, leaning on her husband. "I can't bear it, Alfredo!"

Don Alfredo kept his face stiff as he said woodenly, "It must be, my dear. And we will pray that God will be merciful to our good soldiers and sailors."

The next morning Allison stood on the beach where women stood weeping and screaming out their prayers, gathering their skirts to move along the shoreline, trying to keep pace with their menfolk's ships as long as possible.

Hour after hour the fleet continued to sail out in single file through the narrow entrance. First the great Portuguese galleons, next the Biscayan squadron, after them the Guipúzcoans and Castilians, and behind them the Andalusians—the great flagship *Nuestra Señora del Rosario,* on which Robin stood at the rail.

As the great ship moved away, Robin lifted a brass telescope that belonged to one of the officers. He swept the coast, studying the faces of the crowd—and then he saw Allison.

Steadying the glass, he studied her beloved face, and love for her filled his heart once again. He kept her in sight as long as he could. When the ship heeled over and cut its way through the channel, he slowly closed the telescope and handed it to the lieutenant.

Don Jaime came to stand beside him, his face a sickly pallor. "I wish this were over," he moaned. "I hate the sea!"

"You'll get over the sickness soon, don Jaime," Robin said, his thoughts on Allison. Then he turned and said quietly, "Some of us will not survive. A man should be right with God when he sails into battle."

But don Jaime only stared at him blankly. "I confessed and took the Holy Sacrament." He shrugged. "What else can a man do?"

Robin shook his head. "There's more to knowing God than that, don Jaime." He thought it strange that he should be concerned with this man. He should loathe don Jaime—he was a Catholic, a man who was careless with those who loved him, and the main source of Allison's pain—as well as the barrier to his happiness, for he and Allison could never marry as long as don Jaime lived.

Still, there was something pitiful about the small man, and Robin tried once more to help him understand. "When a man faces death, he has to look at what his life had been. Sometimes God puts us in dangerous places to try and show us what we've been, and the things we need to surrender to him for his guidance and help."

Don Jaime's mouth drew into a puckered line. "I don't need to change anything," he muttered.

"We all have areas that we withhold from God," Robin said firmly. "And we all need to surrender ourselves to God's mercy. I think that's what Jesus meant when he said 'Ye must be born again.'"

"Jesus said that?" A frown came to don Jaime's face. "What does it mean—and how do you know he said it?"

"Oh, I think our priest mentioned it. I think it means that when a man truly meets the Lord, he changes inside."

"'Born again?' Impossible!"

"Not with God, don Jaime."

A longing came into the face of the smaller man. He said finally, "I've wondered . . . about myself, about what is . . . wrong with me. But I won't change. I don't think I can." He looked very small and sick as he stood there, and finally whispered, "It's too late, anyway," then turned and left the deck.

Robin leaned on the rail thinking of the despicable things the man had done, but hatred was not in him. He realized this with a pleasant start and, looking out at the ships that were making for England, whispered, "Grandfather, Grandmother, thank you! Your prayers for me have come true, and at last you can be proud of me! I no longer hate!"

The prow of the ship suddenly lifted, and a sense of joy ran through Robin as he realized that the bitterness that had fettered his spirit for years had vanished. It was, he thought as he stood on the tilting deck, like walking out of a dark dungeon into a world of sunshine and bright skies!

Twenty-five

THE WINDS OF GOD

Lord Admiral Howard was engaged in a game of bowls with his greatest captains—Sir John Hawkins, Sir Martin Frobisher, and Sir Francis Drake—when the four men looked up to see Captain Thomas Fleming running toward them. Fleming halted in front of the admiral and gasped, "Sir! The Spanish fleet has been sighted! They are hove-to off the Lizard!"

If Fleming expected the four great captains to drop their game and run to the fleet, he was disappointed. Admiral Howard smiled gently, saying, "Thank you, Captain Fleming, we will be with you as soon as we finish our game."

And so as the Invincible Armada came to subdue England, the four men who were charged with the responsibility of repulsing the great fleet calmly finished their game.

But that night the forest of masts in the Cattewater and Sutton Pool vanished as completely as if it had dissolved in the mist that covered the gray ocean surrounding Plymouth. These ships, the very heart and pride of England, left the harbor, and by midday of July 30 moved toward destiny.

When the sun was no more than four fingers above the horizon, a cry came from a lookout in the maintop of the *Ark Royal,* Howard's flagship:

"Armada! Armada in sight!"

At dawn the duke of Medina Sidonia came to the deck of his flagship, the *San Martin*. He had no naval training, but one look over the rail caused him to exclaim, "Don Diego, the English fleet—it's to windward?"

Don Diego looked pained. "I'm afraid so, Admiral."

"But—I don't understand. Didn't we agree last night that our single most important aim was to prevent them from gaining that advantage?"

"Sir, the trouble is, some of our heavy ships can't sail as close to the wind as our galleons, and we couldn't risk leaving them unprotected. But they have only a small advantage. They can't attack without approaching us, and when they do so, we shall crush them at close quarters where our superiority is overwhelming."

"Very well, but let us assume our formation, don Diego."

Diego gave the order, and soon the ships began taking a strange formation, which had been designed three months earlier. From the air, the line of ships resembled the horns of a bull, with the six squadrons spread out in a long line. The best fighting galleons were on the forward-probing tips of the line, and the unwieldy hulks carrying the arms, mules, and soldiers for the invasion lay between them.

The first engagement started two hours later. The *Ark Royal* moved in, her long-range culverins thundering. The Spanish admiral attempted to force the English to close quarters, but at once it was evident that the Spanish ships could not hope to match the speed and maneuverability of Howard's fleet.

The duke of Medina Sidonia was beside himself at the failure, but don Diego said, "Sir, we must lure them into close quarters as I have said all along."

"And how do you propose to do that?" the duke snapped.

"Howard would be a fool to let us get close to him. All he has to do is stand off and pound us with those long-range cannon. And all we can do is take the shot he throws at us!"

Despite his lack of training, the duke saw the thing clearer than his officers. All of them were so indoctrinated with the old tradition they could not understand that the new breed of ships designed by Sir John Hawkins made the old style of naval warfare obsolete. In the past, all navies had huge, ungainly ships and the only way to fight was to draw ship-to-ship and send boarding parties. Thus, the battle became, in effect, a land battle fought by sailors. But the duke saw that the amazing speed and turning power of the low-built English ships made such tactics impossible.

When the sun went down, the two fleets prepared for the next day's battle. And at dawn of the second of August, Drake took the *Nuestra Señora del Rosario* for a prize, while the *San Salvador*— stinking of burning corpses—was abandoned by the Spanish and towed into Weymouth by Thomas Fleming's pinnace.

Though several of the Spanish Armada's ships lay in ruins, not a single English ship had been destroyed! As the sun went down, the duke of Medina Sidonia thought, *We are lost! Unless God comes to our aid, we will never leave these waters alive.*

For don Jaime it was like being plunged into the fires of hell. He crouched beside a bulkhead, eyes closed, trembling from head to foot. The English culverins were belching out flame and smoke, round shot was buzzing overhead, and great plumes of water were leaping up close to the ship.

Terror suddenly overcame him, and he leaped to his feet and ran to the poop deck, where he stood shaking like a straw in the wind and whispering, "Holy Mary! Holy Mary!"

The deck heaved and shook as the *San Martin* fired a ten-gun broadside. Don Jaime staggered back, clutching at the rail to steady himself. A heavy harquebus, balanced on a tripod, went off with an ear-splitting crack at his side. Captain Diego was screaming at the helmsman to bear away, and a major was bellowing orders at his soldiers. In the waist a massive spar with a vicious looking grappling hook was being hoisted and swung outboard, and the soldiers were screaming abuse at their opponents to come alongside and fight honorably.

But the English ship clearly had no intention of coming any closer. She discharged a second broadside and loosed a couple of rounds from her stern ports before pulling quickly away and making room for the next galleon in line. Don Jaime saw the captain of this ship clearly. The man was standing nonchalantly on her quarterdeck with a feather in his hat and a sword at his side. He lifted his sword and gave a command, and the demiculverins discharged.

The rain of shot and shell was a return to hell for don Jaime Corona. The noise of muskets and harquebuses followed the roar of the larger pieces. A pall of smoke enveloped the ship and the air became acrid and foul. Men were screaming in pain and terror, and some were crawling along the bloody deck like cut worms.

Suddenly don Jaime could stand it no more. He ducked his head and made for the ladder.

Robin, who had been transferred to the *San Martin* to aid in the battle strategy, held his position on the poop deck. From his vantage point, Robin saw don Jaime—and felt pity. *He's no use up here—he may as well go hide where he'll be safer.*

But don Jaime did not find the dark place he was seeking. When he was almost to the ladder, a shell exploded on the deck of the *San Martin,* not ten feet away from the luckless man. The force of the fragments drove him through the air, and he disappeared down the very hatchway he'd been seeking.

"Don Jaime!" Robin called. He left the poop deck in a leap

and crossed to the hatchway. Inside he found the crumpled body of the small man curled in a ball, clutching his stomach. Robin tried to pull his hands away, but when he saw the bleeding mass, he replaced the hands regretfully.

"Please! Don't let me die!" Don Jaime's mouth was drawn up into a bow, and blood suddenly ran down from his lips.

"I can't help you, Jaime," Robin said quietly.

His words caught at the dying man. Terror came to his eyes, and he began to weep. He begged piteously for help, calling for his parents and for Rosalita and Allison. Robin put his arm around the man's shoulders and said, "Ask God to forgive your sins, Jaime. Do it now!"

"But there's no priest—!"

"God will hear you," Robin said. He saw that the man was losing blood so rapidly that his face was draining white. "Jesus loves you, he won't turn you away."

Don Jaime stared at him with wild eyes. Robin wondered if the man really understood what was happening to him, so he was surprised when don Jaime looked at him, eyes filled with regret. "I—I am too great a sinner! I have taken an innocent life . . . my little Rosalita . . ."

"No, Jesus died to save sinners. And he will accept you, too, if you but confess your sins to him and ask his forgiveness."

"I don't . . . know how to pray. . . ."

"Just talk to God, the way you would talk to me. He will hear you!"

Don Jaime's eyes flickered, and his chest heaved. But he whispered, *"Dios mio . . . how I have . . . sinned. O Cristo, save me!"*

Even as the dying man prayed, his mouth filled with blood, choking him and spilling on his shirt. He gagged, and Robin found his heart full of compassion—and prayer—for the man he thought he'd hated, *O God—hear his prayer—save him!*

Even as he prayed, don Jaime's body grew still and a dull glaze came over his eyes. He whispered, *"Jesús—!"* and then his form went limp and still.

Robin laid him down and rose to his feet. Looking down on the shattered body, he felt a rush of regret. "I did the best I could for him, Allison." Then he turned and made his way back to the poop deck and fixed his eyes on the English ships swooping down on the Invincible Armada, throwing shot into the helpless galleons—then lightly turning and flying away over the sparkling waters.

❦

Robin never forgot the time that followed don Jaime's death. Day after day the Armada moved along the English coast, harried by the ships of the Sea Hawks. Each time one of the crew of the *San Martin* was cut down into a bloody bundle, Robin felt a surge of compassion. These were the enemies of England—but he knew them as men with hopes and dreams—and families.

He obtained permission to embalm don Jaime's body in a barrel of wine, purposing to return the body to his parents. If he lived, of course. And that was no certainty, for before long, the whole sea power of England came against the Armada—and the Spanish duke made a fatal mistake. When darkness fell, the English sent eight fire ships directly into the formation of the Armada. These ships were filled with explosives and, as a series of explosions rocked the air, the duke panicked. He gave orders for the cables to be cut, and the Armada made for the open sea. Collisions without number followed, and chaos reigned in the flaming darkness.

By dawn the "Invincible" Armada had been transformed from a fleet into a rabble dispersed over a wide area, each ship acting for herself.

The English fleet got underway at first light, picking off stragglers. The Spanish fought valiantly, not for Spain or Christendom, but for their lives! They fought for the hope of seeing loved ones again. They fought for shady courtyards, blue-tiled arches, the scent of herbs, the promise of kisses. They fought for the laughter of children and the love of wives.

The winds shrieked and whistled in the stays. The ships heeled sharply over, whipping back the white sheets over decks that ran with blood.

Finally the reality dawned: The Invincible Armada was no more than a scattered fleet of wrecks, their hulls holed and leaking, their generals and camp-masters, nobles and hidalgos, gray-faced and hollow-eyed with physical exhaustion and the stark knowledge of defeat.

As the two fleets battled off the coast, the queen came to Tilbury to review the army. Dressed in a steel corselet and a helmet with a white plume, she addressed them with the stirring words:

"My loving people, let tyrants fear. I have always so behaved myself that, under God, I have placed my chiefest strength and safeguard in the loyal hearts and goodwill of my subjects; and therefore I am come to you, as you see, resolved, in the midst and heat of battle, to live or die amongst you all, to lay down for my God, and for my kingdom, and for my people, my honor and my blood, even in the dust. I know I have the body of a weak and feeble woman, but I have the heart and stomach of a king, and of a king of England, too, and think foul scorn of Parma or Spain or any prince of Europe who should dare to invade the borders of my realm; to which, rather than any dishonour shall grow by me, I myself will take up arms, I myself will be your general, judge, and rewarder of everyone of our virtues in the field."

The shattered Armada continued north, the weather grew colder, and every day more men died. The ships were dying, too. Every morning when muster was taken of the fleet, some were simply not there. When the Armada reached northern Ireland, the storms struck. Off that barren, windswept coast, dozens of ships and hundreds of men were destroyed by the shrieking winds—winds that the English named "The Wind of God."

Indeed, it seemed to the duke and his officers that God was against them. By October when the Armada reached Spain, only 65 ships remained of the 130 that had sailed so proudly a few months earlier.

The English had not lost a single ship, and scarcely a hundred men. For thirty years the shadow of Spanish power had loomed over England. Now the defeat of the Armada seemed miraculous. A medal struck to commemorate the victory bore the inscription: *Afflavit Deus et dissipantur*—"God blew and they were scattered."

Elizabeth and her seamen knew how true this was. The Armada had indeed been bruised in battle, but it was demoralized and set on the run by the weather.

England was transported with relief and pride. Sometime later, Shakespeare wrote these words, which caught the spirit of the victory, in a play called *King John*:

> Come the three corners of the world in arms,
> And we shall shock them. Nought shall make us rue
> If England to itself do rest but true.

Twenty-six

THE MASTER OF WAKEFIELD

The defeat of the Armada sent shock waves all over the Western world. The bells of England rang joyously in celebration—while the bells of Spain tolled sonorously for the dead.

Almost every noble Spanish house suffered loss, and one grieving father put it, "We are like Egypt when the angel of death passed over, slaying the sons of the royal houses!"

The news of the defeat came to the house of Alfredo Corona in the form of a message from the duke himself: "Our Armada has suffered a defeat, but I call upon you, don Alfredo, to stand with your nation in a dark hour. There will be other Armadas, and England will yet be ours."

"He doesn't say anything about don Jaime," doña María said with relief when her husband read the message to her. "He would have said something if anything had happened to our son." She could not know that the duke was so swamped with the myriad details of getting the survivors back to Spain that he had no time to send sympathy to individuals. He had, in fact, agreed at once to Robin's request to take the body of Jaime Corona to his home.

The fleet reached Spain, and the battered ships deposited the bleary-eyed crews on the shore. As Robin saw to having the cask containing the body of Corona taken ashore, he looked around, noting the sad faces and the women in black. *Not at all like our glorious departure,* he thought grimly. He saw to the loading of the cask in a wagon, climbed into the seat, and gave instructions to the driver. As he passed through the streets, the weeping women brought a pang of grief to him. He gazed about with compassion, then shifted his gaze to avoid the sight of the grief of the families.

The undertaker informed him that proper treatment for the body would take a week—but he caved in when Robin gave him three gold pieces, saying gruffly, "I'll be here to pick the body up in the morning."

He left the dank, evil-smelling building and walked for hours along the coast. The cold October wind cut him to the bone, but he was hardened to that and paid no heed. As he moved along the shoreline the gulls screamed overhead, making white slashes against the gray horizon that rimmed all. Some of the bleak atmosphere of the place seemed to stain his spirit. The future was as blank as the sky itself, and he slowed his pace trying to imagine what lay ahead of him.

For months he had thought that the future would be clear for him if only don Jaime were dead. Without the obstacle of Allison's unbalanced husband, Robin had believed he would be able to claim the woman he loved for his own. But now that those dreams had become reality, things were far less clear than he had imagined. As he pondered Allison's reaction to her husband's death, Robin was fairly sure of one thing: she would feel obligated to remain for her in-laws. Her affection for the Coronas had been clear to him during the time he'd spent at Casa Loma, and Allison was not one to abandon them in their grief. She would not feel free to leave—and he could not ask it of her.

The only choice left to her would be to stay as long as don Alfredo and doña María lived. And that could be years.

I can't go back and be an ornament in Elizabeth's court—I won't do that! He had never liked that life, and memories of the emptiness of it disgusted him. Picking up a stone, he threw it almost angrily into the sea, then stared moodily at the tiny splash it made as it was swallowed up by the sullen waves.

For two hours he moved slowly along the rock-strewn coast, burdened by his thoughts. The deaths of so many men—some of them his friends, Catholic or not—lay on his mind. *If I'd been an officer on the* Falcon—*that would have been different,* was his gloomy thought. He had never reconciled himself to his task, and his hatred for his role as a spy grew even stronger.

Finally he gritted his teeth and made a vow: "I'll go to sea in the *Falcon*. Or if Uncle Thomas won't have me, I'll go to sea with Drake!" He thought of Wakefield, but Thomas was master there, and though his uncle had great affection for him, he knew there could only be one lord of a manor.

When the skies were almost black, he returned to town and took a room in an inn. He slept poorly, and the next morning rose with a heaviness on his spirit. *I'll take don Jaime home,* he thought. *Then I'll go back to England.*

<hr />

"The *San Martin* has surely docked by this time," don Alfredo said at the breakfast table. "I can't understand why don Jaime hasn't come to us."

Allison buttered a piece of fresh bread and put it on a plate. Placing it in front of don Alfredo, she said, "There would be much work to do, wouldn't there?"

The older man pressed his lips together, and Allison noted how hollow his eyes had become. The defeat of the Armada had shaken him terribly. He had agonized over it, praying and desperately seeking to discover why God had let such a terrible calamity befall his nation. Now he just shook his head and pushed the plate to one side, then rose and walked rapidly from the room.

Allison gave him a compassionate look, then said, "He's very troubled, doña María. I've never seen him like this."

Doña María bit her lower lip nervously. "Nor have I, my dear. He's not a young man—and he put such hope in the Armada."

"We must pray that God will give him peace." Allison rose and the two women moved out of the dining room into the sewing room. They sat down and began to work on their needlework, speaking softly from time to time. Allison stole a look at the older woman and was concerned at the lines of strain that scored her round face. *It's been too much for both of them.*

They sat there working quietly for over an hour, speaking rarely, and finally a diminutive maid named Delores came to say, "Doña María, a gentleman is here asking for don Alfredo, but I cannot find him."

"Who is it, Delores? Do you know him?"

"Yes, it is the tall gentleman who was on the staff of the marquis—Señor Hawkins."

Allison's busy hands stopped abruptly, and doña María exclaimed, "Why, he must have a message from don Jaime!" Leaping to her feet she said excitedly, "Allison, come!"

The two women hurried down the corridor to a large room just off the foyer. Allison faltered when she saw Robin, and she stood back as doña María went to him at once, hands outstretched. "Señor Hawkins!" the older woman cried and clasped his hands as she stared up into his face. "I rejoice to see you safely returned."

Robin looked into the woman's face, then glanced at Allison. "I—came as soon as I could. But there was much—"

"Señor Hawkins!" Don Alfredo entered through the door, his face alight with welcome. "How wonderful that you have come!"

Taking the old man's proffered thin hand, Robin nodded and forced himself to say, "Thank you, sir. It has been . . . a hard time."

"Of course! Of course!" Don Alfredo's eyes were fixed on

Robin's face as if seeking some sort of assurance. "Defeat is bitter—but it is not forever. Spain will fight again!"

"Certainly, don Alfredo," Robin agreed. He had tried desperately to think of some way to break the news to the family, but no words could change what lay in the ornate casket outside in the wagon.

A thick silence came over the room, and doña María said in a faltering voice, "Don Jaime—he is still at the ship? He could not be spared at the moment?" Fear was in her eyes, and her lips trembled as the tall man hesitated.

It was don Alfredo who spoke the words his wife dared not frame. "Is he injured, señor? Our son?"

Robin wished he were anyplace in the world but in the room with these two old people. Their eyes pleaded with him to deny what their hearts told them was true. But he could not keep silent, and in a voice that was not steady, he said, "I—I am grieved to tell you—that your son died in action off the coast of England—"

Doña María gave a piercing cry and fell against her husband's chest. Don Alfredo's back stiffened as if he had taken a bullet, and he put his arms around his wife in a gesture of comfort. His face was pale and stretched with pain as he stared at Robin.

Allison gave a small gasp, and Robin's eyes flew to her face. She seemed dazed as she turned and walked to stare out of the window. Somehow she had never expected such a thing! In her secret heart, she had struggled with fear that Robin might die—but never once had she thought that her husband would perish.

I should have prayed for him more—! The anguished thought brought a sharp pang of grief that lodged in her like a stone. *I was not kind to him—I never showed my concern—only my fear of him. Now I can never do anything to change that!*

The quietness of the room was stirred by the sobs of the

grieving mother, and finally don Alfredo asked hoarsely, "How did he die?"

Robin had settled this in his mind. The tale of Jaime's coward-ice need not be told. There was no point in bringing more pain to this father and mother. "He died in action, doing his duty. You should be proud of him, you and his mother." He hesitated, then added, "At the last, he seemed aware of all he had done, of the sins he had committed. I held him in my arms, and he called on the Lord Jesus to forgive him for all his sins."

"Thank God!"

Allison turned and ran to put her arms around the Coronas. Tears ran down her cheeks but there was a light of joy in her eyes. "God has been merciful! He has reached through the madness that held your son captive for so long and touched his heart. And he has set him free now, for eternity." Stepping back, she dashed the tears from her eyes and stood straight and tall before them. "I grieve that he is dead, but I rejoice that he was reconciled with our God!"

Don Alfredo stared at her. "Do you truly believe that, Allison? Can God reach a man—as troubled as our son?"

"We have only to think of many our Lord touched and healed—and of the dying thief—to answer that, don Alfredo!"

Her words brought a glimmer of hope into the old man's eyes. He nodded slowly, then whispered, "You are right—our son has long been unhappy. But I believe God will be merciful in his judgments and Jaime will soon be in paradise with the thief that the Lord Jesus saved!"

Robin felt a great wave of relief, and for the next hour he sat with the three, giving details of the battle. He made the most of every facet of the story that dealt with don Jaime, and since in his own heart he was convinced that the man had indeed found forgiveness in the last moments of life, he managed to give comfort to the parents.

Finally he rose and said, "I have brought him home. May I stay for the funeral?"

The grieved parents stood and pressed him to remain, and for the next two days, they seemed to cling to him. Allison kept to herself, but came once to ask, "You have told the truth about Jaime?"

"Yes, he called on God, and I believe God heard him."

Allison's face had been tense, but now she smiled. "I am glad you were with him, Robin. I know you must have been a comfort to him."

"I trust that I was—but I shall always believe that it was your influence that made him reach out."

She shook her head sadly. "I don't think that can be so."

Robin nodded slowly. "He spoke of you more than once, Allison. He seemed genuinely puzzled by what you are. He once told me that he didn't understand why you didn't hate him."

"What did you say?"

"Why, I told him that you had such a love for God—for the Lord Jesus Christ—that you got your love from him."

Allison's eyes brimmed with tears, and she whispered, "Thank you, Robin, for the comfort you have brought the Coronas—and me."

The funeral of don Jaime Corona was well attended. The church was filled with those who came to pay their last respects. The parents knew—as did Robin and Allison—that many came to show their love for the family rather than for more personal reasons. But it did the grieving parents good to receive such an expression of support.

And then the funeral was over. Robin stayed overnight, but the next morning he said, "I must go back to England."

"No, stay a little while longer. Please!" Doña María seemed to need him, and don Alfredo told him privately, "It would be a comfort to my wife if you would stay, for at least a few more days."

"Certainly, sir. I will do what I can to help you both."

For the next three days Robin moved through the house, taking his meals with the family. He rode over the fields on a fine horse, remembering how he'd labored as a serf—but those memories seemed vague to him.

One Tuesday evening he was sitting in the living area drinking tea with don Alfredo and received a shock when the old man said suddenly, "My wife and I will be having a new life, Señor Hawkins." He sipped the tea and sat there silently. In the time he'd spent with the old man, Robin had noted that he often made startling statements, then paused to gather his thoughts, so he made no effort to rush him. After a few moments, don Alfredo continued. "Since I have no son—nor ever shall have—I have asked my nephew to come to Casa Loma."

"Your nephew? What will he do here, don Alfredo?"

Again the long hesitation. "I grow old—and neither my wife nor I are well. My only brother died last year, and our nephew is his only son. He is a fine boy, señor! We are all very proud of him. He begged to go with the Armada, but his father forbade him."

"How old is he?" Robin inquired.

"He is seventeen."

"He will be a great comfort to you, sir, and to doña María."

Don Alfredo studied the Englishman, then said in a subdued fashion, "He is—what I should have liked my son to be." Then after another long pause, he added, "He will be the master of Casa Loma, señor. I have made him my heir."

"I see. That seems very wise, sir." A thought came to Robin, and he asked, "And what of Señora Allison?"

"Oh, she will have a home here as long as we live!"

I fear that won't be too long, Robin thought. But he said only, "I

374

am glad to hear that there will be a Corona to carry on the family honor."

"Thank you, señor, for your compassion, for all that you have done."

Robin fell into deep thought after this, and for two days watched Allison closely. She spent much time with doña María, seemingly determined to do all she could for the woman.

Robin surprised her late on Wednesday afternoon by saying, "Allison—could we take a walk?"

"Why—it's rather cold for a walk "

"Please, come."

Allison hesitated, then nodded when she saw the urgency on his face. "I'll have to get my coat—"

Soon the two of them were walking along the path that led to the river. The cold air turned their cheeks red, and they spoke little until they reached the river. He turned and stared down the bank, then asked, "Is the shack still there? Where you hid me?"

"No, some boys burned it down."

"I'd like to have seen it again," he murmured. "I've dreamed about that place so many times!" He stood quietly, his mind going back to that time, then said, "You took care of me. I would have died if you hadn't been there to help."

"It all seems so long ago," Allison murmured. Her lips curved upward in a slight smile. "You were a terrible sight when you came. I was afraid of you."

Robin turned to face her. "I don't believe it," he said, looking down into her face. "I don't believe you've ever been afraid of anything." He studied the curve of her cheek, admired the fine bone structure and the clean lines of her brow. There was a quietness in her that he greatly admired.

"Why are you looking at me like that?"

He reached out and ran his finger down her cheek, marveling at the satiny smoothness of her skin. "I was thinking of the little girl I used to know." He placed his hands on her shoulders, and when she looked up with her wide eyes, he mused, "Whatever happened to her?" When she didn't answer, he said, "She grew up into a beautiful woman."

"Robin . . ." Allison tried to pull away, but he held her fast. She ceased to struggle and then said, "I have a favor to ask."

"Anything!"

"Take me with you when you go back to England."

Shock filled Robin's face, and he uttered a slight cry of surprise. "Why, Allison, that's why I brought you here—to beg you to go back with me!"

The two of them stood very still. She had prayed for guidance about what to do with her life, and early this very morning, she had been given an answer. "I have nothing here, Robin," she said slowly. "Don Alfredo and doña María have urged me to stay, but I can't."

"No, it would not be a good life for you," Robin said quickly. And then he took a deep breath and stepped closer to her. "But you will return to England as my wife, Allison."

Her eyes widened and she said, "Robin!" but his lips came down on hers, forestalling whatever she had intended to say.

At first Allison stiffened, then she relaxed against him with a small sigh. Her arms slid around his neck, and she returned his kiss with an ardor that surprised them both. Her lips were soft and tender under his, and when he lifted his head, he said simply, "I love you, Allison. That has never changed. And I will not go home without you by my side."

Reaching up to caress his cheek, Allison said in a tremulous voice, "I love you, too, Robin. I think I fell in love with you when I was ten years old."

He kissed her again, holding her close, and then whispered, "Well, I'm a poor man. No big estate like this one. We'll probably live in a little cottage, and you'll have to milk the cow."

"I don't care, as long as I have you, dear Robin. I'd be happy in any house!"

They walked along the riverbank, holding hands and speaking of the things of which lovers speak. She said once, "I—must tell you this, Robin—" A deep blush touched her fair skin, but she held her head high as she said, "I will come to you a virgin."

Robin stared at her, understanding that this was all she would ever say about her marriage to don Jaime. He nodded. "We must be married as soon as we get back to England." Then a thought came to him, and he laughed ruefully. "I have barely enough money to pay our passages. When we step off the ship in England—we'll be absolutely penniless!"

"God will provide!" Allison smiled, then took his hand. "We will have to be careful about telling the Coronas why I am leaving. But soon we will be back in England, and we can tell anyone we wish that we are in love."

Robin grinned broadly. "I will contain my desire to shout it to the world. But only until we reach England!"

When the freighter *Resolution* docked at Southhampton, Robin and Allison stepped ashore. Allison looked up at him, and tears brimmed her fine eyes. "I can't believe I'm back in England!"

"And penniless," Robin added with a smile. "We'll go to Wakefield. My uncle will be happy to take me in."

"Even with a wife?"

"Especially with a wife like you! You know, I think Thomas has known for a long time that I was in love with you."

"We'll have to go see my mother before we marry, Robin."

"Of course, but first to Wakefield."

"Robin! Robin Wakefield!"

A strong voice caught him, and Robin turned to see Sir Francis Walsingham striding toward him. The secretary's eyes were bright with welcome, and he threw his arm around Robin's shoulder. "Why, my boy? Why didn't you tell me you were coming?"

Robin explained haltingly, introducing Allison, then said, "What are you doing here, Sir Francis?"

"I came down to meet with Sir Francis Drake." He hesitated, then asked with a peculiar look in his dark eyes, "Have you been talking with anyone—about the battle?"

"Why no, sir!"

"Then—" Sir Francis was not a man who was often forced to search for words, but Robin saw some sort of hesitancy in him.

"Is there trouble, Sir Francis?" He thought instantly of his mission and demanded, "Have I done something wrong?"

"Oh no—no, my dear fellow!" Walsingham protested, holding up a hand. "Quite the contrary! Your mission was highly success-ful, so much so that the queen has commanded your presence. But—"

Robin stared at Walsingham. Even as he stood there a thought came to him, and he asked, "What is it, Sir Francis? I can see it's bad news."

"It *is* bad news, my boy, and I'm sorry to have to be the one to tell you." Walsingham suddenly put his hand on Robin's shoulder and said gently, "It's your uncle, Thomas—" Taking a deep breath, he added, "He was killed at his post the last day of the battle."

The world seemed to reel, and Robin felt Allison's hand touch his arm. "Oh, Robin!" she gasped. "I'm so sorry!"

Walsingham stood there, watching the grief that rose to cloud young Wakefield's eyes. Then he said, "You were very close, weren't you?"

"Very close, sir!"

"He was a good and fine man—loyal and courageous. Very like his father."

Robin blinked suddenly and said, "I must get home. Martha

must be distraught—and poor Mary! Her father was her whole world!"

"Yes, go at once," Walsingham urged. He hesitated, then added, "You must be very tired, but there is no time to rest. You have much to do."

"Sir?"

"Why, you are the master of Wakefield now!"

Robin stared at Walsingham, saying, "Did Thomas request that?"

"Yes, he did. He took good care that his wife was provided for, but you are the closest male heir." Walsingham nodded and a faint smile touched his lips. "So from now on I must address you as Lord Robin Wakefield."

The secretary spoke briefly, making Robin agree to come and see him as soon as was convenient. Then he shook Robin's hand, bowed to Allison, and left the dock, boarding a tall ship.

Robin said quietly, "We must go to Wakefield, Allison. Martha is not in good health."

"Perhaps I shouldn't go—?"

He took her hand and kissed it. "I can't do this alone. Please come and help me. I know Mary needs a friend, and you would be so good for her."

"All right, Robin, if you say so."

The two stood there, and he suddenly put his arm around her. She protested, but he hugged her tighter.

"Do you know what we'll be after we're married?"

"Why, Mr. and Mrs. Wakefield!"

He kissed her soundly on the lips, causing a deckhand passing by to laugh approvingly.

"No, we won't be that!" Robin said.

"What then?"

"We'll be Lord Robin and Lady Allison!" He pulled his hat off and faced the north where he seemed to see the fields and the castle. "The lord and the mistress of Wakefield, just like Grandfather and Grandmother . . . and like Uncle Thomas." He smiled at her tenderly. "We have a fine heritage, Allison. The best of the best have gone before us as the masters and mistresses of Wakefield. Now you and I can honor their memories with our lives. God has blessed our family in many ways . . . and now he has blessed me with you." He took her hand and pulled her along the dock.

"Come on, Lady Allison, let us see what the future—and God—hold for us."

And she moved with him, her hand in his as they walked together toward the waiting coach.

High overhead a peregrine falcon watched them move, then uttered a sharp, piercing cry and split the air with powerful strokes of strong wings, carried along by the sweeping winds of God.

THE END

In addition to this series . . .

THE WAKEFIELD DYNASTY
#1 The Sword of Truth   0-8423-6228-2
#2 The Winds of God   0-8423-7953-3

. . . look for more captivating historical fiction from Gilbert Morris!

THE APPOMATTOX SAGA
Intriguing, realistic stories capture the emotional and spiritual strife of the tragic Civil War era.
#1 A Covenant of Love   0-8423-5497-2
#2 Gate of His Enemies   0-8423-1069-X
#3 Where Honor Dwells   0-8423-6799-3
#4 Land of the Shadow   0-8423-5742-4
#5 Out of the Whirlwind   0-8423-1658-2
#6 The Shadow of His Wings *(New! Fall 1994)*   0-8423-5987-7

RENO WESTERN SAGA
A Civil War drifter faces the challenges of the frontier, searching for a deeper sense of meaning in his life.
#1 Reno   0-8423-1058-4
#2 Rimrock   0-8423-1059-2
#3 Ride the Wild River   0-8423-5795-5
#4 Boomtown   0-8423-7789-1

Just for kids

THE OZARK ADVENTURES   *(New! Fall 1994)*
Barney Buck and his brothers learn about spiritual values and faith in God through outrageous capers in the back hills of the Ozarks.
#1 The Bucks of Goober Holler   0-8423-4392-X
#2 The Rustlers of Panther Gap   0-8423-4393-8
#3 The Phantom of the Circus   0-8423-5097-7